A Deal
with the Devil

David Norton

DEDICATION

Dedicated to the four people dearest to me. Karen, Jodi, Jessica and Wade. Four people that changed my life for the better. I will be forever thankful for them.

ACKNOWLEDGMENTS

A special thanks to my wife, Karen for reading and correcting over and over and over. You're a star.

Thanks to Karen (again), Jodi, Jessica and Wade for reading this when it was pretty rough and giving me the incentive to continue. You four are the best.

Thanks to Jamilah Kolocotronis and Naazneen Manjoo for correcting and guiding me on issues of the Islamic faith. While I took most of your valuable feedback into account, I might have used a little "artistic license" to keep the story interesting.

Thanks to John Carr (http://www.carrtracks.com) for the helpful information you provided.

Thanks to Allan Sneedon, Chantal Kippen, Jothie Punchu, Lindie Schoeman, Lesley Douglas, Jeff Fisher and Gary Steffens for the errors you pointed out and for some really great feedback.

Lastly, where would any writer be without his editor. Thanks Ginny Porter for a thorough job and for your suggestions and feedback.

WEDNESDAY, 1ST

"What the hell have you brought me into?"

"Roger I swear to you, this country was at peace yesterday. I'd never have brought you out if I thought this would happen."

A stray bullet whined overhead. Both men ducked but too late to have done any good.

Periodic cracks of rifle fire accompanied by occasional bursts of automatic weapons echoed between the buildings. It appeared as if some force had opened fire on a small group of soldiers from the opposite end of the street. The street had emptied at the first gunshot and only the two Americans were left crouching between two sheets of wood at the edge of the street. The boards would never stop a bullet, but nobody was aiming at them.

Roger Macadam and Mike Parker had met while studying at university and had been buddies ever since. They had been the top two in their class at NYU and both qualified as chemical engineers. Soon after graduation they were head-hunted by Alan Foggarty for his company which specialized in selling equipment to the oil industry.

They had started at the Houston based company about twenty years ago and had spent the years since perfecting their individual talents. Mike, the salesman, was stockier than Roger and more outgoing. At forty-three, he had a full head of hair, slightly greying at the temples and was the better-looking of the two. Roger on the other hand had finished at the top of his class by a considerable margin. His thin features and thinner hair made him look older than Mike, even though he was six months younger.

In business the two were good at what they did. They would both fully research the prospective client, the client's business and their technical processes. Mike would visit and woo prospective clients into buying their massively expensive oil processing equipment, then Roger would cost, design and install the equipment. Alan had mentioned too often that Mike would sweet-talk the clients into bed so that Roger could screw them. Since the beginning of their careers, Roger had been more technical than Mike but Mike had the edge in the boardroom. They were a formidable team.

The meeting at the Oman Oil Company had not gone well. Mike had landed in Muscat earlier in the week and spent the time softening up the OOC executives. Roger had landed this morning thinking they were about to sign, only to find they had done a one hundred and eighty degree turnabout. The two had left the meeting more than a little disappointed. They were due back in the boardroom at OOC the following day, but they both knew the momentum had been lost.

"Do you think today can get any worse?" Mike had asked seconds before the gunfire had started.

The engineers had landed themselves in a similar position in Kuwait a few years earlier.

"It's time we found a less interesting job," said Roger. Mike turned to Roger and smiled, remembering he had said those exact words in Kuwait.

The gunfire had subsided to the odd crack as both sides dug in at opposite ends of the street. Each group was waiting for the other's move. The rebels would be aware the government troops would have backup on the way, so this could never be a long standoff. The two Americans knew they could do nothing but sit it out.

"I want to take a look!"

"Rog, what on earth for? Lay low and wait. Nobody even knows we're here."

Roger noticed a puff of dust in the street as the rifle cracked and then another. The shots were being aimed at an excavation hole in the road. Roger raised himself up as much as he dared. Straining his eyes into the brightness beyond their wooden refuge, he could see what looked like hands clasped around the back of a grey-haired head. An old man was struggling to lie as flat as possible. The shooters knew he was there, but they couldn't see him behind a pile of sand lying adjacent to the excavation.

"Those bastards!" Roger reacted without thinking. He shuffled backward out of his hiding place.

"Rog! What are you doing?"

He squeezed out into the street, his eyes taking a second to adjust to the brightness. He wasn't even aware of the distressed shouts from his long-time friend. Keeping low and tight against the wall, he made his way to a large gap between two buildings where he had seen building and excavation going on. A bulldozer with a large front blade and caterpillar tracks was parked in the open space. Although he had never driven such a thing before, he quickly orientated himself to the controls.

He glanced around as the engine roared into life and the monster edged forward as he tested the controls but stopped again when he looked down in despair at the naked engine.

"Damn!" he muttered to himself. Roger knew that one well-placed shell could stop this engine and leave him high and dry between the two feuding forces. He had seen that the bullets being aimed at the old man were only coming from one end of the street. He hoped the shooters at the other end would have no interest in him, as he planned to be in their view by ducking onto the running board on the left-hand side of the dozer.

In the meantime he scanned the building site for something to protect the engine. Running and grabbing from the building materials around him, Roger dragged and attached a few steel plates, a steel grid and a wooden pallet to the right-hand side of the dozer, with wire and a piece of nylon rope. Scrambling onto the beast, he felt ready. Getting the feel for the levers, Roger aimed the vehicle to the right of the excavation to attempt to cut off the view of the old man from the rebels.

Windows rattled as the beast shuddered forward. When he pulled onto the street, Roger slipped off the seat and onto the guard over the rattling steel track. Settling next to the engine, he ripped off the sleeve from his white shirt and attached it to a small piece of wood. In movies he had seen people waving a white flag to demonstrate peaceful intentions. He hoped the shooters had seen the same movies.

As he'd guessed, the moment the vehicle entered the street, rounds started to rain down on it. The few intermittent cracks of a short while ago became a thunderous roar as rifle shells tore into the vehicle on the right-hand side. Roger felt vulnerable and covered his head while lying with his back to the onslaught and waving a pathetic white flag. It seemed to do the trick and pretty soon Roger was trundling across the road, heading for the hole where the old man was hiding.

His aim was not as good as he'd hoped. As the bulldozer approached the hole, Roger realized it was going to be closer than he'd thought.

"Hey! Look here!" he shouted, but to no avail. His voice was drowned by the noise of the engine and rifle fire. Besides, even if the old man had heard, it was unlikely he would lift his head. Roger wriggled to try to reach the steering levers, but soon realized the shots were too fast and furious to attempt steering the vehicle. He tried shouting again.

"Hey! Old man! I need you to look here. ... Damn!" He realized he was going to have to jump. Roger waited until he thought the time was right, then with all the grace and elegance of a

3

middle-aged engineer, he leaped from the side of the bulldozer and sprinted forward, diving head-first into the shallow hole. The fact that the old man survived it would amaze Roger for years to come. He convulsed and shook from the shock of Roger landing on him, but was only given a split second to regain his composure as the corner of the scoop moved over the edge of the hole. Roger grabbed the man under his armpits and pulled with all his strength and they rolled out onto the road next to the moving vehicle.

"Come! Quick! On your feet!" Roger barked at the old man. He realized the back of the moving vehicle was approaching and with that came open season for the shooters. The old man was still dazed. Roger reacted by lifting him the way he would cradle a sleeping ten-year-old. He was not as small and frail as he'd looked and Roger's legs staggered as he walked.

The slow pace of their movement gave the old man the moment he needed to regain his composure.

"Put me down. I can walk!" he shouted above the noise of the bulldozer.

Roger was as thankful as if the old man had saved *his* life. He grunted as he lowered the old man's feet.

The two walked on in silence next to the thunderous noise of the large vehicle as it approached the opposite side of the street. The dozer was headed for the entrance of a large commercial bank and Roger became aware of the possibility of people being caught inside.

"Move to the front!" he shouted.

The old man looked back at Roger.

"Move forward!" Roger yelled gesturing to the man at which he picked up his pace a little.

Roger ran at the side of the bulldozer and threw himself onto the runner above the moving tracks. Keeping himself low, he reached for the lever at the left of the seat, pushing it back and turning the beast to its left. The old man, realizing what was happening, positioned himself at the front of the vehicle in order to be in front of it as it came around, keeping the steel between him and the shooting which had all but stopped by now. The rebels had started moving out as the government reinforcements were approaching.

As soon as Roger felt the vehicle was in position, he raised himself up as much as he dared and showed his upper torso to the rebels. Fully expecting to feel the thud of a bullet hitting him in the chest, he reached and switched off the engine. The monster shuddered to a halt and a deafening silence rang out between the buildings. Roger rolled off the machine, landing flat on his stomach on the hard road. Winded and sore, he tried to stand up but couldn't get his legs moving. From out of nowhere, hands were picking him up and he was carried away to the edge of the street. The old guy had already gone.

As the soldiers lowered Roger to his feet, his legs collapsed under him and he dropped in an ungainly heap onto the road. For a brief moment, he wished a bullet had at least grazed him so that he could have shown blood loss for this dramatic collapse, but in a short while he didn't care. He was just happy to be sitting.

The troops were smiling and a few of them approached him, shaking his hand.

Mike arrived and knelt down next to Roger. "What the hell were you thinking, Rambo?" came the expected sarcastic comment laced with a fair degree of pride. "I thought you had gone insane. Bud! That was pretty impressive. Weren't you scared?"

"Then? No! Now I am! Look at me shaking." He held out a trembling hand. "I wasn't thinking. It was stupid!"

"Nah! All's well and all that ... let me help you back to the hotel. There's one old guy smiling now and a whole platoon that must be pissing themselves when they think of you carrying him. That looked pretty funny dude! I have to admit."

"The old guy was heavier than he looked. Here! Help me up."

Mike helped Roger to his feet and the two walked back to their hotel a short distance away. They laughed and joked about the events of the last hour. The disastrous meeting at OOC was a distant memory.

THURSDAY, 2ND

The next morning, Roger awoke to a knocking on his hotel room door. Focusing his confused mind, which was still in that no-man's-land between asleep and awake, he managed to grunt out a muffled "I'm coming …" from a throat, still husky with sleep.

He staggered like a drunk to open the door. The large Arab filling the doorway appeared to be unamused by the appearance of the American.

"Yes sir! Can I help you?" Roger said, battling with his early morning smile.

The Arab wasn't about to make light conversation either. "The gentleman you helped in the street yesterday has invited you to join him this afternoon at his residence. Be ready at three outside. You will be picked up."

Without waiting for a confirmation, he turned and walked down the passage. At that moment Mike poked his nose out from his room next door.

"What time is it? What did the big guy want?"

"Six fifteen and he invited me to the old guy's house."

Mike disappeared into his room without another word.

-- o --- o0o --- o --

After a quick shower and clean-up the Americans headed downstairs. At the table Mike asked the question. "Did you let Anne know what a hero you are?"

In college, Roger had been the class geek and what his wife, Anne, had seen in him, he still didn't know. From day one he knew the only way to keep this woman was to work hard at making sure she was the happiest woman alive. He always felt she was way out of his league so he attended to her, not only on those three special days in the year, but like his life depended on it. Anne had been Roger's main focus for twenty years. Mike on the other hand had never married, but had a long string of short relationships.

"I chatted to Anne and Katie last night." Katie was Roger's eighteen-year-old daughter. He and Anne had never had more kids. Not so much a conscious decision, as Katie making the family feel complete. "If I start telling her about being shot at, she'll start to worry." Anne hated it when Roger came to the Middle East. She never held back her view that sooner or later something bad would happen.

6

After they had eaten, Mike and Roger tidied up a few loose ends for the final 'feedback-and-follow-up' session at the Oman Oil Company. It seemed a waste of time as the executives had shown disinterest and an unwillingness to pay the price, but in the interests of greed and profit maximization, the obligatory last ditch effort to encourage them sign over a few million had to take place. They were due to see the operations team this time. This whole visit had been done in the wrong order.

The OOC offices were a short distance away from the hotel so the two set off walking. Knowing they were being turned down, they didn't bother with laptops and other paraphernalia. They chatted as they walked, mostly about the pending journey home and how they were going to explain this outcome to Alan after Mike had reported how well things were going earlier in the week.

They entered the grand and over-done entrance to the OOC offices and approached the receptionist dressed in the usual abaya, the loose black cloak with the white hijab scarf covering her head. This was common dress for Omani women. On occasion you would see a veil which would partially cover the face. It was unusual to see an Omani woman in a burkha or with the face covering niqab.

The receptionist appeared happy to see them. A contrast from the last time they had approached her when she had greeted them politely and presented them to the executives in a professional manner. This time there was a broad smile and an almost flustered look about the girl.

"I think she likes you, dude," Mike said as the girl near sprinted away to announce the Americans' arrival, something she could have done in the usual way over the phone.

"Omani girls don't do non-Muslim guys," replied Roger "but she does seem happier this time."

Even more unusual was the way the executive director and not the operations manager emerged from the door, almost at a run with a broad smile on his face. He walked straight up to Roger, greeting him profusely and shaking his hand. Now as a rule, you can expect profuse greetings in Oman, but this one was way over the top with a bobbing of the head almost as if he was bowing to Roger.

"Mr Macadam. Please. Come in. Come in!" he said in the usual excellent Omani English. "You too Mr Parker, come in!"

More than a little taken aback, the two Americans edged forward with caution.

7

As they entered the boardroom, all seven of the seated staff members leaped out of their chairs as one causing both Americans to take a step backward. The five male executives all lined up and greeted the two with unusually vigorous handshakes. The two female executives held back, but expressed their pleasure with broad smiles, not dissimilar to the one displayed by the receptionist. First Roger was given the attention and then it was Mike's turn. Afterwards, the two were ushered toward the two seats available to them.

The scene was hard to believe. Yesterday this same group of people had been talking amongst themselves while Mike had been presenting to them. Roger's implementation plan had been stopped half way through, at which point he was told not to bother continuing as they were not going to spend that much money. There was no sign of the operations team at all.

Now, a little under twenty-four hours later they were greeted like old friends. What followed was even more bizarre. The executive, introduced as Mahmood, sat down at the opposite end of the table. He placed his elbows on the table and touched his fingertips together. He looked thoughtful. "We would like you to commission three of your UniGo units. One at each of our fields and then a gas processing unit for our plant at Salalah."

The two Americans looked on with blank expressions waiting for the executive to say something comprehensible. In the last four years, they had sold three processors and this was 'good times'. There was no way the executives had ordered four units.

After a long silence, Mike began talking but with the verbal dexterity of a five-year-old. "Err! Mmm! I mean, how … ? That is…. Why? What changed your minds?" His sales trainer would have been proud.

Mahmood continued. His smile was getting broader as the meeting progressed. "Does it matter what the reason? Go now and have the documents drawn up. We'll meet here at the same time tomorrow."

Now it was Roger's turn to try to change their minds. "I … I mean, we didn't bring the paperwork with us." Then with a puzzled expression, "Are you sure you want four units? That's a lot of money. We gave you the quotes, right?"

Mahmood was nearly laughing. "Mr Macadam, I know you don't have the paperwork. That is why I suggested you go away and have it drawn up."

Mike was not going to yield to their desires. "Four? Three oil units and one gas? Are you sure?"

"Mr Parker. I assure you that is exactly what we want. Now go and draw up the agreement."

Roger was not finished trying to wreck this deal. "We are heading home tomorrow morning."

"Then you will have to change your flight plan. I am convinced your commission will make it worthwhile."

"Of course ... of course it will ... I mean we will!" The Americans were starting to ease their way out of their mental block and it began dawning on them that they had closed a big deal. Smiles broke on their faces. Smiles which were soon as broad as the executives'. They stood and worked their way around the room shaking the eager out-stretched hands, careful not to offer their hands to the women, but acknowledging their gratitude with a smile and a half nod of the head.

As Mike and Roger were leaving, Mahmood called to them. "Mr Macadam. Please ensure you reschedule your flight for Saturday as I would like you to be here in case any questions arise. Better yet, have our receptionist handle it. We have contacts in Emirates Air. We don't want you getting back in the middle of next week."

Still somewhat shell shocked, Roger answered. "Of course. Thank you. Thank you very much."

"Good! Then we'll see you tomorrow with the documents. Goodbye Mr Macadam, Mr Parker."

-- o --- oOo --- o --

Outside the boardroom, Roger passed on the message to the receptionist who took down the note, smiled and led them out the main entrance.

After walking for a few blocks Roger turned to Mike. "Better than expected?"

"What the hell happened in there?" Mike was still looking puzzled. "I pride myself in my ability to read people. Those executives were not going to buy and even with your 'are you sure you want four?' speech, they still changed their minds."

Roger laughed. "Hell! We tried everything in our power to stop them spending their money. What is wrong with us?"

Mike thought for a second "I don't know but if this deal goes through I'm going to take a holiday in the Greek Islands and spend a week tanning naked on the beach with a little Greek goddess."

"Ok! Let's go do the paperwork." Roger was still in disbelief. "…and earn our commission."

They picked up their pace and walked with a renewed zeal. When the two reached the hotel they headed straight into lunch. They were directed to a table and after cursory scan of the à la carte menu and telling the waiter of their desires, Mike and Roger sat back in silence contemplating the strange goings on at OOC. Even though they both knew the executives had spelled out in plain English what they wanted, neither of them believed it.

-- o --- oOo --- o --

Mike and Roger spent the afternoon in their rooms putting the final touches to their project and preparing the documents for signing. Tomorrow was Friday and they should have been going home. Under the circumstances, Roger was sure Anne and Katie would not be too unhappy. He wanted to call them, but two in the afternoon in Muscat meant five in the morning in Houston. Not a clever idea! He'd wait until later.

By three o'clock Roger had finished his paperwork, cleaned up and was waiting out front for the old man to pick him up. He'd contemplated not going downstairs, but opted to go because he couldn't be sure how far the old guy would have to travel. On the stroke of three, a stately S-Class Mercedes Pullman pulled up front. Roger moved aside but hung around to see who the dignitary was. Statesmen and women from all over the world stayed in these hotels from time to time, as well as the rich and famous, holidaying or filming in Muscat. The front of the hotel was regularly adorned with the finest automotive pearls.

A large Arab climbed out of the driver's seat and from the opposite side of the vehicle, scanned the people, scattered around the entrance of the hotel. Finally, he looked at Roger, then beckoned to the American. Still unable to equate an S-Class with the old man, Roger did the whole 'who me?' thing, looking around in case the Arab was signaling somebody behind him. There was nobody. He moved toward the Arab, slowly at first but soon recognized him as the Arab that had woken him in the morning.

He still wore his traditional dishdasha, the long, white, collarless gown with the muzzar, folded into a turban on his head. Roger noticed the curved sheath of the obligatory khanjar in his belt. He hadn't noticed it this morning, but then he had only just woken up. Roger secretly coveted the curved decorative dagger which Omani men use on formal occasions.

The Arab beckoned again as if he wanted Roger to run. His countenance was one you should never take lightly and Roger picked up his pace a little.

"Masa'a AlKair," said Roger.

"Good afternoon, Mr Macadam," he replied with professional courtesy but seemed suitably impressed by Roger, regardless of the bad pronunciation, using the greeting at the right time of the day.

By this stage the Arab had reached Roger's side of the vehicle and opened the rear door for him. He climbed into the spacious and luxurious interior. The driver shut his door, walked around the back of the vehicle and climbed into the driver's seat. The car glided as he eased off into the traffic.

The driver headed eastward from the hotel toward Muttrah on the main dual carriageway. After a few miles, they approached what Roger knew to be the old city wall, beyond which lay the old part of town known as 'old Muscat'. After going through the Al Kabir gate, the driver drove on a few hundred yards allowing him to see the fort overlooking the Muscat Harbor. The Pullman stopped in front of a pair of impressive gates which were opened by a guard and the driver proceeded to enter.

As they pulled into the large, elaborate property, Roger realized this was not simply a big house. The ornate exterior of the building was spectacular. The main structure was made up of large funnel shaped columns in gold and a blue, exactly matching the deep blue of the sky and sea. The columns touched at the top, leaving tall, intricate, arch-shaped walls inbetween, with what looked like dark rattan panels. The wide front doors were wooden with golden inlays.

The driver, looking in his rear view mirror spotted Roger's awe-struck expression. "Welcome to Al Alam Palace!"

On each side of the high structure, the building spread out in opposite directions, lower than the central structure but each equally impressive. Decorative and meticulously tended gardens lined the entrance area.

"Wow! Can I take a photo?" Roger asked, holding up his cell phone to take a picture.

"Of course! Many photos are taken of the palace every day."

"Who lives here?"

"His Majesty, Sultan Qaboos Bin Sa'id of Oman," the driver replied with a degree of pride in his voice.

"Wow! This is a beautiful building." Roger was talking to himself. "Why have you brought me here?" The driver turned his head and a big, toothy grin cracked across his face. Roger became uneasy. It was the smile you would expect from a cannibal if you asked him what's for supper.

The driver pulled up to the front entrance and Roger started to open his door. "Don't get out!" the Arab said. Roger looked around thinking there might be guard dogs. The driver made his way around to Roger's door. He opened it and his passenger exited feeling a little vulnerable.

The main door opened and a smaller man wearing the same outfit as the driver walked out to greet him. "Al salaam a'alaykum, Mr Macadam, please come in."

Roger was led into a huge entrance area which was as impressive as the outside of the building with intricate, ornamental detail in typical Omani style, but with the stamp of excessive wealth.

"Please follow me," the smaller Arab said.

He led the American into a large lounge area with impressive, old-styled furniture.

"His Majesty will be with you momentarily," said the young man in immaculate English. He turned and started to move toward the door.

"Excuse me!" Roger called him back. "Are you serious, the Sultan?"

"Yes, the Sultan," he replied in a matter of fact manner.

"I've never met a Sultan. What do I do?"

"Ha!" said the butler. "Anything he asks of course, he is the Sultan after all." The butler had the same 'wolf watching an approaching lamb' smile on his face.

"I mean do I bow? Do I shake his hand?"

"Relax Mr Macadam. You are the Sultan's guest. Be yourself." The butler turned and walked out.

"What if he doesn't like 'myself'," thought Roger, suddenly alone.

Up to this point it hadn't occurred to Roger that the 'old guy' had managed to track him down, let alone do so in such a short space of time. It hadn't occurred to him that he hadn't spoken to the old guy after the incident yet only hours later, there was his representative in his doorway using his name. Thoughts started spinning around his head. Unanswered questions which he hadn't even thought of rushed into his mind at a dizzying pace. The thoughts were cut short by a voice behind him.

"Mr Macadam!"

Roger spun round. Facing him was the 'old guy', now looking proud and powerful. Dressed in a brilliant white dishdasha with a splendid khanjar in his belt. He wore sandals and on his head, a regal-looking turban. Although this was the face of the person he'd carried in the street, this looked like a different man, taller and far more stately.

Roger moved cautiously toward the Sultan holding out his hand and attempting a clumsy, on-the-move half bow. "Salam Alaikum, Your Majesty." Roger was about as nervous as a geeky junior asking the homecoming queen on a date.

"Walaikum assalaam. Please, be seated and relax. Can I offer you something to drink?"

The words 'triple scotch in a big glass with no ice' ran through his mind but his mouth translated, "No thanks. I'm fine!" He knew of the Islamic rules regarding alcohol.

A stern look came over the Sultan's face. "Let's cut to the chase Mr Macadam. Yesterday you shouted an order at me on the street. It was heard by my guards and I don't appreciate public humiliation."

Disbelief clouded Roger's mind. His throat and mouth went dry. His hands started to tremble. He had been to Oman a couple of times and never experienced problems, but all the scare stories he'd heard before his first trip began shooting through his thoughts. 'They cut off people's hands.' 'Torture and stoning …' and lots more.

The Sultan was waiting for a reply but Roger couldn't speak.

The Sultan threw back his head laughing "Ha! Ha! Ha! Mr Macadam, you are going to be way too easy." He managed to control himself somewhat and then laughed again when he saw the 'about to hurl' look on Roger's face. "I apologize Mr Macadam. You don't appreciate my sense of humor."

"I do," he said starting to relax. "You took me by surprise. I'll try to appear less gullible from now on."

The young butler walked in carrying a tray with an ornate teapot and two cups. He placed them on the table.

"You have met my eunuch Hussein, Mr Macadam?"

"Eunuch?"

"Yes he keeps a close eye on the ladies in my harem. He keeps them honest."

"Harem?"

"Tell me Mr Macadam, is this your 'less gullible' look?" The Sultan broke down into another fit of laughter. This time Roger managed something between an embarrassed grin and a chuckle. He was going to have to be on his toes, but he was starting to relax. "I believe you could manage tea now Mr Macadam?"

"I think I might need tea now. Thank you."

"Mr Macadam. On a more serious note, I want to thank you for what you did yesterday." The Sultan spoke while pouring the tea and passing it to his guest. He continued. "As you know I didn't see much of the rescue, but my sources say you were quite a hero."

Roger shook his head, "I don't think so."

"It was not a pleasant experience. Are you not intrigued as to how a sultan ended up in a hole in the road?"

"I have to admit I haven't thought about it. Until now, I didn't even know it was a sultan in the hole."

The Sultan smiled. "I'm ashamed to say that I froze."

"I don't believe those conditions warrant shame Your Majesty."

"Thank you for your kindness but I not only froze, I also fought off the soldiers trying to protect me. One of my men thought I would be less of a target by throwing me in the hole. I'm sure he would have stayed too but as you saw, it was a one sultan hole."

"We all act differently in stressful conditions Your Majesty."

"Thankfully for me you acted the way you did. What you did was brave."

"I don't think it was anything most people wouldn't have done," Roger replied, never able to take a compliment well. "I reacted without thought which is not always clever."

"Modesty is a good trait, but the street was crowded with my people and I had a small regiment of my special guards watching over me. Still only one man came to my rescue. I owe you my life."

Still refusing to accept the thanks, Roger replied. "Maybe it's because they knew who you were…" He stumbled on his words. "Didn't sound so great did it? What I meant was, had I known you were the Sultan, maybe I too might have thought before doing something stupid. Your guards might have mistaken me for another attacker."

"This is true. Again, lucky for me you are who you are." Then after a pause, "I want to reward you with something valuable to me."

"That is genuinely not necessary."

"Believe me Mr Macadam, if I believed you thought you should be rewarded, I wouldn't be giving you what I have in mind. This gift is only for somebody brave enough to do what you did with no thoughts of the consequences and then modest and humble enough not to expect a reward. I owe you my life which I cannot give you. I must give you the next-most valuable item to me. It's only fair."

"Then I thank you Your Majesty."

"We will have a little get-together tomorrow evening in your honor, at which the members of my personal guard will be hanged. I'd like you to attend."

"Hanged?"

"I'm too good for you Mr Macadam." The Sultan laughed again. "Such a straight face and you walk into it every time.

"Joking aside," he continued. "I will have my driver take you back to your hotel now. He will pick you up again tomorrow at three. Please invite Mr Parker also."

"Thank you again Your Majesty." Roger turned as the Sultan gestured toward the door but then turned back. "Umm! Could I ask a small favor Your Majesty?"

"You saved my life. Name it and it will be done Mr Macadam."

"My friend ..." Roger thought about how to say it. "Err! He won't be expecting your sense of humor... "

The Sultan lifted his hand. "Say no more Mr Macadam." He laughed at the thought.

"It's been an honor Mr Macadam. It's not often I am able to share time with a man who saved my life. I am deeply in your debt."

"Thank you again for you kindness Your Majesty. I will be here tomorrow."

The Sultan signalled his butler to take Roger out and back to the waiting luxury Mercedes.

Back at the hotel, Roger knocked on Mike's door before going into his room. "Back already dude? Must've been a hell of a meal?" Mike asked. "I expected you back much later…What? …. WHAT? Why the stupid grin?"

"Guess who the old guy was."

"How would I know?"

"Yesterday I saved the life of none other than the Sultan of Oman."

"Bullshit! Are you for real? The Sultan?"

"Sultan Qaboos Bin Sa'id."

"I don't believe it." Mike thought for a moment. "No wonder those OOC executives were bending over backwards for us."

"What do you mean?" Roger didn't see the connection.

"The Oman Oil Company is owned by the Oman government. No wonder they were smiling. You saved the life of their boss." He laughed. "This is big dude! You could use this. At the meeting on Friday, we should throw in a few more suggestions about what else they can use."

"He's invited us to a little get together tomorrow."

"Us? Me too? This is awesome."

"Quite a nice guy." Roger wasn't going to say more. He was already laughing inside.

"What's the time now?" Roger asked even though he was looking at his watch. "Quarter after five…that's," counting on his fingers, "eight fifteen. Anne is awake now. I'm going to give her a ring." Roger left and headed into his room.

The phone rang. Roger had called the reception and they called him back with the connected call.

"Hi Love! How's things?"

"Hey Rog! We're doing ok! Missing you though."

"I'm missing you too." He wanted to get the small talk over. "I have bad news. I'm afraid we're only getting out of here on Saturday."

"No Roger! You were supposed to be leaving tomorrow." She was angry and Roger could hear it. He needed to move quickly and give her the good news.

"It's not all bad though. The client is signing up for three oil units and a gas unit."

Anne had no idea what it meant so Roger continued. "You remember our last commission payment?" Of course she did, but she was still mad about Saturday. "Multiply it by four and add about two year's target bonuses."

All was forgiven in an instant "What? By four? That's a lot. Are you sure?"

"Yup! We're going to have a serious bank balance for a while. The client has asked me to hang around until Saturday in case they have any questions. We'll be handing them the sales documents tomorrow morning so they'll need more time to go over them."

"I understand." It's amazing how the correct motivation can clarify an unclear situation, provide a basis for forgiveness and bring out the kitten in a tiger. Would she have understood if the airport had been destroyed and they had had to walk through the desert to Dubai to catch a plane?

"There's something else," he said, not knowing how to start but wanting to tell her. "You remember yesterday when I called?"

"Yes." She was starting to have doubts again from the uncertainty in his voice.

"Well! I saved an old guy in the street yesterday. It turns out this old guy was the Sultan of Oman. Can you believe it?"

"What do you mean?"

"I saved the life of the Sultan. He's like the king. He's having a party for me tomorrow night at his palace. Oh! I forgot. I took a picture of the palace. I'll send it to you. You can see where your husband will be partying with the rich and famous of Oman."

"What kind of party?"

"I don't know. I've never been to an Omani party before. I'll tell you all about it when I get home. The client is arranging our flights so I don't know when yet but as soon as I do, you will too. Anyway, I'd better go. It was good to hear your voice again."

They said the usual goodbyes and hung up. Roger thought it had gone well. There was no hard feeling about leaving on Saturday. He felt a definite warmth about the situation. He had withheld the part about the possibility of a valuable reward from the Sultan so he could give her more next call. Life was good in the world of the wife manipulator.

-- o --- oOo --- o --

He returned to Mike's room a little later and they headed on down for supper. They decided to indulge in a celebratory glass of wine. Drinks were only available in the hotels in Oman and even then, only in the internationally owned hotels. Locally owned hotels were not allowed to sell liquor. As a rule, the two Americans tended to not drink while on assignment in the Middle East, given their surroundings, but tonight they were going to celebrate – a little, they still had to complete their documents before morning.

The two guys ate their supper while chatting about how to best structure the implementation of the systems at OOC. As much as they would never admit it, the two engineers were nerds at heart and loved their trade. They could chat for hours on things like the separation of solids from liquids using ultrasonic separation methods. Alan had known this at their first interview and used it to his best advantage. Placing the two together for days on end at a remote location ensured him of the best possible solution for the client. That's why he paid such a great commission and bonus structure.

Tonight they chatted and sank a bottle of red wine. By the end of supper the project had been planned and optimized and theoretically implemented. They had already done their homework before leaving the US so they knew the layout of the plants, the difficulties in implementation and the possible problems with phasing the project in. Of course they had not planned on a four-way implementation, but it was only a matter of resources. They loved what they did.

Relatively late by their standards, the two left the table and headed to their respective rooms to finish the documentation. After a couple of hours, Roger leaned back in his chair to focus his eyes on something other than his laptop. There was a quiet tap on his door.

It wasn't Mike's heavy knock so Roger stood and opened the door. A young Chinese girl, twenty or so years old, was standing at the door. She looked out of place dressed in tight fitting western clothes.

She was stunning. Her tight jeans fitted her tiny frame like body paint with a looser t-shirt cut extremely low. Her long, straight, black hair hung long down her chest and framed her face like a painting. The oriental eyes and porcelain skin completed the picture. The girl knew who he was. "Hello Mr Macadam, I have been sent for you," she said in well spoken English, with a hint of a Chinese accent.

Assuming she had been sent by the hotel, Roger stood back as she pushed past him. She was confident. "Every now and then and only on special request, the Hyatt will add a special service for its special clients."

"I don't need anything." Roger was slow when interpreting the messages from women, but he was beginning to understand. As always happened, when a beautiful woman pushed him outside of his comfort zone, he became nervous and found it difficult to look at the girl.

Seeing Roger's apparent nervousness, the Chinese girl assumed he had known why she was there. "My name is Mae Ling and tonight I am yours for the whole night."

"Why did you come here?" he asked, already knowing the answer.

She smiled a stunning smile as she answered, "I was sent to give you pleasure."

"Why? Who sent you?"

"The hotel manager. But not him. Someone else made the request."

"I thought the law here didn't allow for prosti... working girls."

"It's ok Mr Macadam. I don't mind. I am working to take money back to China." She sat on the edge of his bed. "Since Oman became a tourist attraction, the authorities knew they would have to close their eyes to Western desires to attract the tourists. Girls come here from China, India, the Philippines, Russia, even Europe. There are even a few local girls but I never met any yet. I can take you to a club right now where you will find maybe one hundred and twenty girls for only fifty guys."

"I'm not going anywhere. Look! You need to go. You can't stay here."

The smile left here face as she stood. "If I go, maybe I won't get paid. Maybe I can stay here. I'll sleep on the floor."

"Definitely not. Sit here and I'll go and see if Felix is still here." Roger walked out of the room shutting the door behind him without looking back.

Felix was the night manager for this week and Roger found him shutting up the bar and about to turn in for the evening. When working night shift, the managers stayed in the hotel overnight.

"Since when did the Hyatt become a whorehouse?" Roger was a little upset at the situation.

"Mr Macadam. We only answer to the demands of our clients. This service is select. We do not rent rooms by the hour if that's what you mean."

"You had a young girl come up to my room and offer her services to me. How does that differ from renting rooms by the hour?"

"Only in perception Mr Macadam. I assure you I would not do such a thing unless it was requested."

"But I didn't request anything."

"No! In your case it was somewhat different. Somebody else requested on your behalf."

"Who?"

"I'm afraid I'm not at liberty to tell you. The client wanted to remain anonymous."

"I don't think my company will be sending anybody back here."

"I am sorry to hear that. I understand your feelings Mr Macadam, but please understand it would have been the same in any hotel. We all go out of our way to keep our customers happy no matter how repugnant the task. The customer is always right."

The possibility of losing out on the once a year visit from the Americans didn't appear to alarm the manager too much and in reality wouldn't impact too much on the Hyatt's bottom line. It was clear the sponsoring client had much more muscle than Roger's company.

Roger lowered his tone a little, realizing the 'tough' approach would yield nothing. "You do understand we have signed a deal with OOC. That means we will have a couple of visits this year."

"I do sir," the night manager replied. Shocked at his answer, Roger guessed at what might be going on. Either OOC or the Sultan was the sex sponsoring client. Roger was more than a little shocked.

"Ok! There is no point to my getting angry. You are clearly the middle man in this. I'll tell you what." Roger was speaking like he was reasoning with a five-year-old. "I will let this slide and not mention it to my company on a couple of conditions."

"Anything I can do Mr Macadam."

"The girl…"

"Mae Ling?"

"Yes! Mae Ling. I will not be taking advantage of this generous service. I hope this won't affect her payment."

"Of course not sir! We would never cheat our…suppliers."

"Nor will it affect the generous tip being given to her by the hotel over and above her payment from your client for a job well done."

"I wouldn't have it any other way, sir."

"Good!" Roger was starting to enjoy himself. "Good! Then we are in agreement. Have the driver pull up to the front entrance to take her home. I'll fetch her from my room."

Roger returned to his room and was a little disturbed to find her lying stretched out on his bed. "I have arranged a driver to take you home. Felix said you will be paid in the morning as usual."

She grinned, said goodbye and left his room, looking back briefly and waving as she rounded the corner of the passage.

Roger waited for her to go then closed the door and went back to the desk to re-check his documents.

FRIDAY, 3RD

In the morning, Roger was once again awakened by the sound of a knocking on his door.

"What are you not telling me?" Mike burst in looking bright- eyed and bushy-tailed the moment the door was opened.

Roger had no idea what he was on about, nor why he was up this early and looking as fresh as a daisy. "What are you talking about?" Roger asked in a flat and uninterested manner.

"I went online to check our bookings. I didn't have the references so I used our passport numbers to locate the reservation. There are now three reservations, not two and I might add, in the names of Mr M. Parker, Mr R. Macadam and Mrs A. Macadam. What do you have to say for yourself now?" Mike showed his absolute pleasure at the situation. He knew something Roger didn't.

"I don't understand. Do you think they are flying Anne out here? How would they know about Anne?"

"The same way they found you. This guy must have an entire intelligence department at his service."

Roger remembered how the driver had located them early on the day after the incident. It was quick work. He guessed it must be possible to locate his wife through his details. It excited Roger to think of her on her way to him.

"Do you think she could be on her way right now?" Roger exclaimed, suddenly enthusiastic.

"Dunno dude! I do know the three of us will be flying first class. Not business class, first class."

"What? Alan will go mad. He won't pay for first class."

"Not by choice he won't." Mike tapped the side of his nose. "Not a word." He nodded his head smugly in full agreement with an unspoken thought flashing through his mind. "So anyway! The three of us are sitting in first class. This will be our best flight ever. Twenty- five and a half hours of free drinks and little hot white towels - stopping over in Dubai and New York. Yeah!" Mike punched the air. "Maybe I'll find a first class babe and join the mile high club somewhere over the Atlantic." Roger just shook his head.

-- o --- oOo --- o --

Later at the OOC offices, the staff gave the guys the same heartfelt hero's welcome. This time Roger and Mike were aware of their newfound status and therefore not as surprised.

Having dealt with Middle-Eastern businessmen on more than one occasion, it was the first time they had witnessed a quick document signing. For the first time money was no object. The two Americans gave a brief overview of their findings and the implementation schedule. Roger gave a short rundown of potential problems in the implementation and Mike discussed how they would slot seamlessly into their annual turnaround project while the plants were shutdown. Only two executives attended this meeting and they were smiling as if they hadn't heard a word.

They couldn't sign the documents fast enough. They whipped through the pages, signing in all the spots Mike pointed to. Roger and Mike looked at each other, still disbelieving. They shrugged, shook their heads and left feeling empty but with undertones of joy, as if they'd heard six of the seven lottery numbers and were in so far, but missed the last number. It felt like it hadn't happened yet, but might soon.

"Oh! Mr Macadam." Here it came! Nothing was this easy. They've changed their minds. They want the entire project in by the end of next week. "We will be taking care of your flight home tomorrow. You will be leaving on the 5:00am flight from Seeb International and flying to Dubai. You will be flying from there directly to New York and then on Continental Air to Houston."

"It's extremely generous of you."

"No problem Mr Macadam. It is our pleasure."

They walked out in silence, waiting for the "Hold on!" from the executives. It never came.

-- o --- oOo --- o --

Roger sat alone through lunch and spent a couple of hours alone, by the pool. Mike had gone back to his room and didn't even show his face.

He enjoyed the peace and quiet and eventually, with only half an hour to go before the Sultan's driver would appear, Roger thought he had better chase Mike. He walked upstairs and knocked on Mike's door.

He came to the door with a sheet wrapped round his body.

"Mike. We need to get going. The driver will be here at three. Yesterday he was dead on time."

"Ok! I'll meet you downstairs."

Roger dressed and headed down to wait for Mike in the hotel foyer. He couldn't help wondering whether Mike had maybe succumbed to temptation to climb into bed again - he was almost amazed to see Mike stumbling down the steps a few minutes before three.

"I was beginning to think you were back in bed again."

"I almost was!"

The two headed outside to wait for the driver. They didn't wait long. The S-Class Pullman pulled up in front of the hotel at exactly three. The large Arab driver walked round behind the long vehicle and opened the rear doors. The two engineers climbed in. Pretty soon they were headed toward old Muscat.

-- o --- oOo --- o --

Mike was awestruck as they pulled up to the front of the palace. The contrasting gold and blue pillars made for an eye-catching scene, set against the backdrop of Muscat harbor.

"We need to do more sightseeing when we come back. This is amazing."

The driver looked over his shoulder and said "Welcome to Al Alam Palace." It was the same tone and sound he'd used yesterday. Roger couldn't help wondering how many times he had said it.

Like clockwork, Hussein, the 'eunuch', opened the door as the two approached and welcomed them to the palace. This time, he led the visitors down a few passages to a room toward the back of the palace. He stood aside and allowed the visitors to enter first. Inside, the small room was as ornate and decorative as the rest of the palace. Hanging on hooks were two dishdashas, one the normal white color, the other black.

Hussein pointed toward the outfits. "His Majesty has requested you wear our traditional outfits. It's not compulsory, but he is the Sultan." Hussein was a diplomat. "Mr Macadam, yours is the black one as is the black bisht since you occupy a special place here today. I will be outside. Please call if you experience difficulty with the attire. I will be in shortly to help you with the turban." Hussein left the room.

Roger examined the black bisht. It was a black cloak to wear over his dishdasha, but the edges were embroidered in an intricate pattern with gold thread. The workmanship was exceptional and the quality outstanding.

"Dude, this is heavy stuff. Do you know how to put this dress on?"

"Let's have a look." Roger lifted the black outfit off the hook. "This looks easy but what do you wear underneath?"

The two Americans removed their clothes and dressed in their dishdashas. They also had a few pairs of local sandals to choose from. These they managed to work out but it was as far as they could go. The belt, khanjar and turban, they needed help with.

"Hussein!" Roger called out, opening the door.

"Yes sir!"

Roger said nothing but simply held up the articles. Hussein laughed and helped them to finish getting dressed. After they had dressed, both Americans decided they looked pretty cool and took a few photos of each other with their mobiles.

Roger drew his khanjar from the sheath and admired the short angled, decorative blade. He rubbed his thumb along the sharp edge. It wasn't sharp at all. Disappointed, he replaced the knife back into its sheath. "Right! Let's go."

Hussein led them out of the small change room through a few more passages and out through the back doors of the palace. Outside was a large crowd of people, all men and all dressed in traditional gear. The scene was like something out of Arabian Nights. The back of the palace opened out onto a large, flat, grassed area about half the size of a football field. A white marquee dominated this area off to the right hand side.

Beyond the grass lay the Muscat harbor which looked as ornate as the palace in the afternoon sun. The sea and sky formed a frame of turquoise blue matching the blue columns of the palace and the distant beaches echoed the gold of the remaining columns. On each side, the palace was flanked by old forts on cliffs above the water. In former times, these forts would have protected the town of Muscat. Off to the side of the palace dazzling white buildings of all different shapes and sizes were perched on the hill overlooking the harbor.

The background view was breathtaking and the foreground scene even more so. One hundred or so men of varying ages were dancing around, brandishing short bladed daggers about their heads. Others had ancient rifles slung over their shoulders. Several were singing while others were dancing. Musicians were dotted around playing traditional instruments. Everybody looked happy and seemed to be having a good time.

Suddenly, almost as one, a large group of the younger men took off and ran around the marquee and back to the front again.

Women in the marquee made their presence felt with occasional bouts of ululating. More dancing and singing, then off they ran again, doing laps around the marquee spurred on by the voices of the women inside the tent. The Americans were stopped in their tracks, in awe of the sight before them. Never had they witnessed a scene with such color and mystique.

When the Sultan saw Roger and Mike exit the building he stood up from where he was seated. He withdrew his khanjar and shouted out a short Arabic phrase. The whole crowd turned and looked at the two Americans. They all waved their khanjars in the air and shouted. He turned and walked towards them. "My friends, my friends. Please come over and join the festivities."

"Al salaam a'alaykum Your Majesty" Roger bowed his head forward and stretched out his hand in greeting. The Sultan shook his hand. Turning to Mike, Roger added, "My colleague and long-time friend Mike Parker."

The Sultan stiffened and the smile was swept from his face. "Ah!" he spoke slowly and with emphasis. "The cowardly infidel. The gutless dog that left me to die in the road. The one that stood back while his 'so-called' friend risked his life in his moment of bravery?" The Sultan paused and then shouted. "Guards. Take him away!"

The color drained from Mike's face. His entire body weakened and his knees wobbled. He half reached out for support from his companion while he scanned the faces of all the Arabs staring straight at him, each one either holding a blade or a rifle.

It was enough! The Sultan threw back his head and laughed hard. The crowds too started laughing and shouting. Mike turned to his friend in bewilderment to find him doubled up laughing. This had gone even better than Roger had expected. One or two more seconds and the pee would have been running down Mike's leg. It was perfect.

"I love being Sultan." He managed to gasp these words out between bouts of laughter. Mike breathed a sigh of relief and started to relax, looking at the faces around him in disbelief. He turned to Roger and punched him hard in the arm, much to the merriment of the ring of faces around him.

"Mr Parker. Please join the gentlemen over there for a Pepsi. I would like to have a private word with Mr Macadam." Mike, by now had realize the joke had been at his expense and was also joining in the laughter. Although still a little unsure, he started to walk toward the runners. They circled around him, helping him to remove his dagger. Pretty soon, Mike too, was waving his khanjar around his head and sprinting around the marquee with the other Arabs. Except for the lack of facial hair, he blended in perfectly.

The Sultan led Roger into a library furnished with floor-to-ceiling bookshelves. There were thousands of books.

"Please, have a seat Mr Macadam." He pointed to a large velvet couch.

"Please, call me Roger your Majesty. My father was Mr Macadam."

"Of course, on condition you call me by my name, Qabus ibn Sa'id ibn Taymur Al Bu Sa'idi."

"Huh!" Roger had missed the whole thing.

The Sultan laughed again. "You may call me Qaboos for short."

"Roger!" He became all business. "I mentioned to you yesterday it was my intention to present a gift to you for saving my life."

"I did say it was not necessary."

He waved his hand in the air, dismissing the comment. "I'm afraid a decision from you is needed." He pulled from his clothes a small scrunched up cloth. Carefully unraveling it in the palm of his hand, he revealed a large diamond ring. Roger knew nothing about diamonds but he knew the ring he'd bought for Anne. The one-quarter carat ring which he had given her at their engagement was minute by comparison with this rock. He estimated this diamond to be about five carats. It was closer to fifteen. This was bling which people would never believe to be real. The sparkle as the surfaces of the diamond caught the light from the spot lights, was astounding. The gem seemed to possess an internal glow. Even with the little knowledge he had, Roger could see this was a costly item.

He was unable to avert his gaze from the stone. "It's not necessary."

"This is yours." He reached out and gave the rock to Roger. He was shocked by the weight of the ring. "However, I am hoping you will be happy to give it away."

He looked up at the Sultan, not understanding. "I am giving you the choice. You are entitled to accept this ring and I will be happy with your decision. I am confident your wife would appreciate this gift. However, if you are willing to give this away I will present you with a gift of far greater value."

Roger was puzzled. He started to hand the ring back to the Sultan who threw both hands into the air. "No Mr …. Roger. This is now yours. I do not want it back, ever."

He knew the Sultan would have told him what the other gift was had he wanted to. "Can I ask you a simple question?" he asked the Sultan, then without waiting for an answer. "Which gift do you want me to take?" Roger thought this was a fair question. He did not understand why the Sultan was asking him to choose. He thought maybe the second gift was too great a value and the Sultan was having second thoughts.

"Ah! You want me to answer for you. Do you take the money, or the box? No hesitation. I want you to give the ring away." He looked at the puzzled expression on Roger's face. "My sister's daughter has paid for this party and she, I suppose, is the owner of the other gift. If you give her this ring, she will hand over the second gift to you. This ring has been in the family for centuries. She has wanted this ring for years."

"Ok! One more question. Which gift would your sister's daughter want me to choose?"

"Well done Roger! Covering all your bases! Again! No hesitation. She wants you to give her the ring."

"Then I accept the second gift." Again he attempted to hand the ring back.

"No, Roger. This is yours now. I have already given it to you. Once you have given this gift to my sister's daughter we will continue with the party. You will receive your gift tomorrow. I will deliver your gift to you at the airport myself, prior to your departure. Is that ok with you?"

"Sounds perfect." He was dying to phone Anne. Where was Anne? He had thought she would be here. Maybe it was an admin error at the airport. Maybe she would still pitch up. He rolled up the ring into the cloth and clutched it in his hand, not knowing whether there were pockets in his outfit and not wanting to start scratching to find out.

"Good! Come with me." He started to lead the way back outside and Roger followed. "You will sit with me. I will send for Ablaa, my sister's daughter. Her name means 'perfectly formed'. You will soon see she's not. Anyway, when she comes out of the tent, you have to give her the ring and say these words *I give you this*

28

mahr in exchange for the gift you give me. Mahr is a gift for the family by the way."

Roger repeated it as if memorizing. "I give you this mahr in exchange for the gift you give me. Ok! I have it!"

Back outside, the dancing and singing was still going on. Mike was laughing and joking with a small bunch of the older Arabs. He was sprawled on one of the plastic chairs. The sweat patch, on the front of his dishdasha showed why he was now sitting with the older men.

Roger followed the Sultan to his seat which was more like a throne when compared to everybody else's plastic chairs. He signalled for Roger to sit next to him on the only other throne-like chair. He caught the attention of his trusted servant, Hussein and with a wave of his hand Hussein scuttled off in the general direction of the women's marquee. He was obviously expectant of what might transpire after the meeting. Hussein spoke to one of the women through the tent.

The flap of the tent opened and three women came out. Two were wearing non-typical, black scarves with their abayas. The third was dressed in a white burkha, which was something not often seen. The woman in white remained at the door, while the other two made their way toward the Sultan. Women in Oman are generally slightly built. The younger of the two women enjoyed her food. She would not have been obese back home, but she seemed to stand out here in Oman. Her round face was smiling. She looked to be about the same age as Roger. As they approached, the Sultan introduced them.

"Roger! This ugly old woman is my big sister." The old woman smiled, clearly accustomed to the Sultan's humor. "And this is her daughter, Ablaa."

"I am pleased to meet you," Roger said. He nodded his head to acknowledge the women. Addressing the younger woman directly, Roger got straight to the point. He held out the rumpled cloth at the woman and said "I give you this mahr in exchange for the gift you give me."

The woman smiled and muttered something in Arabic. She then turned and headed back to the tent. The old woman followed. As they entered the tent, a chorus of ululating emanated from within and a shout of joy rose up from the men outside. The younger men took off for another lap around the tent.

An official-looking man stood up in front of the tent and started addressing the crowd in Arabic. The process looked official but relaxed with the talker addressing both the crowd of men, now seated on the plastic chairs in front of the tent and occasionally turning to the tent and addressing those inside. A few times the talker would wait for a response from various members of the crowd. The whole process looked lighthearted and seemed to pass quickly. Then he turned to Roger and rattled off something in Arabic to him. The Sultan leaned over. "He's asking you if you are happy to take the responsibility for such a beautiful gift."

"I don't know what it is but yes, I assume so."

"Then tell the man."

"Yes I am," Roger called out to the talker. The man continued addressing the crowd. When he eventually stood down, it was followed by a huge whoop of joy from the men and unconstrained ululating from within the tent.

"Now! Let us have something cool to drink and bring out the food." The Sultan waved to Hussein again sending him scurrying to arrange the banquet. Staff began running out with trays and trolleys laden with food. Ten or so girls led trolleys and trays into the tent, while several young men darted in and out amongst the guests, laying food on the various tables dotted around.

The Sultan was in his usual high spirits, laughing and talking to those around him. "Do you like classical music Roger?"

"I'm not an avid listener, but I have enjoyed several pieces! If you ever tell Mike I told you that, I will deny it." The Sultan laughed.

"It's not something to be ashamed of. I have a passion for music. When I became sultan, one of the things I set about doing was creating a full orchestra in Oman. I think it was the first in the Middle-East. Today my orchestra does regular trips around the world playing at the foremost venues and is now mainly made up of Omanis. It is my pride and my joy. I am known as the Sultan of Swing."

Roger laughed. "I'd like to hear them sometime."

"Good! They will be playing while we eat."

The whole scene seemed surreal. Roger felt drunk, although he hadn't touched a drop of alcohol. The musicians streamed in to his left and were seated on stools which had been placed there previously. He hadn't noticed them before. The conductor counted them in and they started playing. Throughout the rest of the evening, the orchestra played various classical and contemporary pieces. They were placed far enough from the guests to be background music, but close enough to hear every note. Again Roger's thoughts drifted to Anne. He was sure by tomorrow he would not have been able to describe this scene properly. He leaned over to the Sultan. "Would you excuse me while I get my phone? I would love to take photos of this to show my wife."

"No need," the Sultan replied. "look!" He pointed at a videographer filming the proceedings, then another and another. "The videographer will work through the night and I will bring a copy to you at the airport in the morning. You can sit and re-live it with your wife at your leisure."

Roger expressed his gratitude and continued snacking on the food as it was brought to him. The Sultan spent much time describing and ensuring the American sampled all the traditional Omani dishes. The dishes seemed simple, being centered around a staple of rice and either meat or fish, but the infusions of marinade and spices made the tastes as spectacular as the rest of the scene. There was yellow maqbous rice, tinged with saffron, Shuwa which was meat which the Sultan said was cooked in an underground oven for a whole day and there was mashuai, lemon roasted kingfish. The range of tastes was astounding, with the meal being accompanied by various breads, buttermilk and yogurt drinks in various tastes and all followed by dates and sweetmeats or halwa.

Throughout the meal, attendants kept filling up the cups with the strong, bitter kahwa, the Omani coffee. On its own, Roger doubted he would have enjoyed the flavor of the coffee, but with the sweetness of the various accompanying dishes it was superb. Mike too made a whole bunch of new friends and ate way too much, but as the evening wore on into night, he approached the honorary guest. "Dude! We have to be at the airport by about four tomorrow. Do you think, maybe, we should kick down?"

"I suppose we should." Roger turned to the Sultan. "Your Majesty. We have had a great evening, but we have an early start in the morning and a long flight tomorrow."

"Of course! I'll have the driver take you back to your hotel." The Sultan waved to Hussein who sprang into action again. He led the two Americans back to the room where their clothes hung far more neatly than the way they had left them. The two removed their Omani outfits and dressed in their own clothes. A mist seemed to have lifted from the two, as if they had stepped out of a movie and back into the real world. Tired and having over-eaten, the two Americans were almost disappointed to go back to reality.

"I have to be honest, I wasn't looking forward to this alcohol-free party and when I saw the chicks were in the tent I wanted to go home, but I enjoyed it." Mike was going over the evening in his mind.

"Me too! The food was incredible."

The two were given a hero's sendoff from the palace by the Sultan and the other guests. They chatted until they disembarked from the car at the hotel. They said goodbye to the driver and headed upstairs to their rooms.

Roger checked his watch. "It's lunch time at home. I'm going to phone Anne."

Inside his room, Roger called Anne. He was missing her more than ever. Probably from the expectation that she might have turned up. He spoke to Anne for a good thirty minutes relating the evening to her and telling her about the food. Eventually he said goodnight, had a quick shower and climbed into bed.

SATURDAY, 4TH

Roger awoke early to the sound of the phone ringing beside his bed. He fumbled in the darkness until he located the handset.

"Your morning call Mr Macadam."

"Thank you." He replaced the handset.

He switched on the light. Squinting through the slits that were once his eyes, he managed to see the numbers on the clock. "It's three in the morning. I'm sure I asked for three-thirty."

Roger had another shower as the nights are hot in Oman. Afterwards he packed his belongings into his case, pulled on his jeans, t-shirt and sneakers and was soon ready to go. The 'going home' excitement started to set in. He heard Mike's door click and knew he was on his way too.

After a last check to see if he had forgotten anything, Roger closed his door behind him and headed down to the foyer. The hotel bus had already been arranged and was waiting outside the door. The two of them loaded their luggage into the back seats of the bus and climbed in. The driver greeted them quietly. He didn't seem happy to be driving around at this time.

Seeb International was not as big, nor as busy as other airports, nonetheless it was an international airport and even at this early hour, several people were hanging around. Business people with laptops and cell phones were seated alongside holidaymakers.

While Mike sat in the lounge, Roger headed over to the Emirates Air office with his passport, to pick up the tickets. As he arrived at the window, there was a tap on his shoulder. He turned. "Hussein! How are you?"

"I'm very well Mr Macadam. Thank you." The goodbyes of seven hours ago seemed distant. "The Sultan is on his way here. He will likely be here in the next five minutes. I need to tell you something."

"Sure. What is it?"

"I don't have time to explain fully, but I will before you board the plane. When His Majesty gives you your gift, accept it graciously and politely. On no account must you question it."

"What do you mean?"

"I promise I will explain. Remember, don't question. Smile and accept."

"Is this another one of the Sultan's jokes?" Roger asked. He looked around to try to spot the Sultan having a laugh.

"No! No joke. He cannot see me here. Do you understand? Accept, don't question."

"Ok!" Roger had questions, but Hussein had already turned and slipped away. Roger was perplexed and a little troubled by Hussein's actions. He turned to find he had lost his position in the line. He stepped back a little and aligned himself with the person in front. Pretty soon there was another tap on his shoulder.

"Mr Macadam, or should I say, Roger. Good morning, how are you this morning?"

"Good morning, Your Majesty," Roger said looking round at the entourage. The three women were there, the two he'd met were wearing the more common black abaya and white hijab scarf. The third woman held back. He assumed this to be the woman in white from last night, only now she was dressed in black. Numerous other individuals were hanging around in their little groups. The public had backed off, visibly stunned at the presence of their Sultan in the public terminal. The only sounds emanating from the terminal were from people that hadn't yet noticed his presence.

"I am here to present you with your gift at last." He was smiling. "The anticipation must be killing you."

"Your hospitality was gift enough, your Majesty." The Sultan laughed a little too hard for the moment.

"Firstly, let me present you with your DVD from last night." He turned and was handed the package by one of the entourage. He handed it to Roger who thanked him accordingly.

"Now Roger, I told you this gift was one of the most valuable in the Sultanate and I meant it. I can see the anticipation in your eyes, but first I want to tell you that the girl who came to your room last night was a test. You passed spectacularly." Roger looked puzzled but the Sultan pushed on. "So! I'm not going to keep you in suspense any longer. Roger Macadam, I present to you the Rose of Oman, your wife Atifah Macadam."

Roger's eyes widened and he became numb with shock. Mrs A. Macadam, his wife! The reserved seat on the plane was for his wife Atifah, not Anne. His mind flitted back to his disappointment at not seeing Anne at the function. He had discarded the ticket for A. Macadam as an error. Why had he not thought about it? Why had he not simply accepted the ring? Roger's mind was racing. This wasn't one of the Sultan's jokes. The periphery of his vision started to blur. All he could see was the Sultan's mouth moving, congratulating him on choosing the better of the two gifts. He had chosen a wonderful gift. He had chosen a gift that would add value to his life. He had selected from the delectable fruits of Oman. He had chosen a gift that would last him well into his old age. Roger heard none of it. He was sure the Sultan knew he had a wife. How could he be so presumptuous? How could this be his wife? He hadn't married her had he?

He took a deep breath and in the distance behind the small crowd a movement caught his eye. A quick glance and he could see Hussein waving his arms reminding him of his earlier conversation. His very being screamed out at him, telling him to shout out "I already have a wife. No! I cannot accept your gift. No! I'm going home to my wife." He felt sick with apprehension. He looked around the small group of Arabs all looking on expectantly, all waiting for him to speak. Which one was Atifah? Only the three women were in the group. One was way too old. The ring! He had given the ring to the middle-aged woman. Was this an act of marriage? He looked at the round, smiling face. How could this be? Hussein in the background was becoming frantic, urging Roger to make a move. The smallest of the three women dressed in her black burkha stepped forward. Roger was shaken by the sudden movement. He looked into her eyes. The beautiful big green eyes were hesitant with fear and hurt. He knew the fear in her eyes, was a reflection of the fear in his. The hurt a result of his panic.

Roger pulled himself together as best he could. His mind was shouting 'You are married! Run!' he resisted the urge. Slowly he withdrew his gaze from the captivating eyes staring deeply into his.

He turned to the Sultan who still had a smile on his face. "Those are the most beautiful eyes I have ever seen," were the words Roger blurted out. The Sultan pounced on Roger's flailing hand. He threw his arm around Roger's shoulder. "Welcome to the family Roger. You are now a member of the Sa'id dynasty." Roger shook the hand of the Sultan and thanked him. He smiled trying to look as confident as he could. He held out his hand to his new bride who hesitantly took it. A quick glance back over the shoulders of his send-off party revealed Hussein giving Roger the thumbs up before disappearing.

One of the entourage had already collected the tickets and handed them to Roger. The Sultan was looking proud and happy. He was garrulously wishing the newly-weds a long and prosperous life together, but his words blurred together into a constant stream of un-decipherable noise. He might as well have been talking in Arabic.

After a round of teary goodbyes, smiles and well-wishes, the entourage turned and headed out. Roger was left standing, tickets in one hand and his new wife in the other. He had no idea what to do. "Come! Let's find Mike." Roger started to walk. Atifah followed slipping her hand out of his. Roger didn't object. He was not comfortable holding this woman's hand. He led her back to where Mike was seated, laughing at an image on a television close by.

Roger turned to Atifah as they approached and said "Atifah, this is Mike. Mike, this is Atifah. She will be flying with us." Nods and at least one smile meant the introductions were over. Mike appeared completely unmoved by the presence of the woman. "Please sit." Roger pointed to an open seat. "I'll be back in a sec!"

"Rog!" Mike called, but Roger had already gone. Roger headed in the direction of where he had last seen Hussein. He was nowhere to be found. He looked around the corner where Hussein had disappeared. Nothing! He turned to head back and bumped into Hussein standing right behind him. "How'd you do that?" Roger was startled. "I've just looked there."

Hussein dismissed the question. "Mr Macadam. I am so sorry. I wanted to warn you last night, but there was no chance. There was always somebody with you."

"It's done! What's the story?"

"We don't have much time so listen carefully. Last night you were married to the Sultan's sister's granddaughter. She is a wonderful and well-loved girl and although it may not feel like it to you right now, this is a prestigious gift to you. Thank you for heeding my warning and accepting her."

"Why did he do this? He knows I am a married man."

"Yes I know! After the attempt on his life, he wanted to ensure she would not become a target."

"But I'm married!"

"I understand, but Islamic law allows for up to four wives. To the Sultan, you only had one, so no problem."

"No problem? You haven't met my wife. Tell me. How do I escape this?"

"The process is simple, especially the way it is practised today, however, thought should go into the action. Shariah law allows you, as a husband, to simply tell her three times you divorce her and the marriage is over. In Islam the marriage is a strong covenant, but it is not a sacrament. You can reverse it." Hussein was looking solemn.

Roger saw a glimmer of hope. "It's that simple? I can go over to her right now and tell her that I divorce her and go home?"

"As far as the marriage is concerned, yes that simple…"

Roger turned. He was going to end this charade right now. "Wait! Mr Macadam. When is anything in life so simple?"

"But you said…"

"I know what I said. I was telling you the truth. Let me finish. Although Sultan Qaboos has made great strides in developing the law in Oman, Shariah law is still the basis of family law. The royal family and many Omani's practise Ibadhism." Hussein paused as if waiting for a reaction from Roger. None came. "Ibadhism is a branch of Islam like Sunni or Shia. Mainly the branches are the same, but one of the subtle differences is that Ibadhi women are not permitted to marry non-Muslim men."

"Then why did she go through with it?"

"She didn't know you weren't Muslim."

"What happens when she finds out?"

"I think she has already guessed. I'm afraid you weren't convincing at looking like you knew you were getting married and that's a problem. You see, now she has broken the law. In her own mind she is as good as a fornicator."

"But I haven't…"

"I know it. You know it and she knows it, but nobody else knows. It is not always good for Islamic women on issues of family law. She can never land in this country as a woman divorced of a non-Muslim man. The law allows for stoning her to death. I'm sure the Sultan would grant her clemency under the circumstances, but she could sit for years in jail. You must look after her. You are the only family she has. Besides, even if you divorce her, few divorcees ever remarry. Do you believe she deserves that?"

"I don't even know her. She doesn't know me. How could this have happened?"

He continued, "Many marriages in Oman are arranged. Couples may not even see each other until their wedding day. She didn't need to know you. She probably never expected to see her husband before the marriage. The Sultan showed great affection for you in this matter as he has made you a member of an elite and old family. One that stretches back centuries. You will always be treated with great respect in Oman while you are married to Atifah. By rejecting her you will both be unwelcome here for different reasons."

"This is ridiculous." Resignation was in Roger's voice. "So there's no way out?"

"Maybe, but I haven't thought of it yet. I beg you to look after her. She is a special person. I will continue to search the law for you."

"Does she speak English?"

"A little. I have to go." Hussein looked around nervously. "I am going to be missed at the palace. Goodbye Mr Macadam." He paused, then stared dramatically into Roger's eyes. "Take care of her. Take care of her or I will hunt you down and kill you… like a dog!" His head tipped to one side, as he thought to himself briefly, then shrugging he said, "Why is it so funny when the Sultan says things like that but not when I do?" Focusing again on Roger he said, "Mr Macadam. Take this phone." He handed Roger a new and elaborate cell phone. "It is a hotline to the Sultan. I wanted to give it to you last night. It will be paid for by the Sultanate and you will be able to call from almost anywhere in the world. If you need anything, anything at all, you call him and he will deliver. Also, Atifah will be able to call her family from it, so she will at least feel close to them."

-- o --- o0o --- o --

Roger turned and walked back to Mike and his new wife. When he reached them, rather than sit, he suggested they go through customs. Reaching the desk, their immediate reaction was to join the queue, but as soon as they stopped four attendants rushed up to them taking their baggage trolleys from them and guiding them through the gate in double-quick time. Their passports were stamped and they were ushered through. They were cleared through passport control and customs before a single person had left the queue. Every official in the airport was wearing their best smile for the three.

Mike spoke first. "We have about thirty minutes before we need to board. Want to get something to eat?" Roger agreed it was time for breakfast, but Atifah kept quiet and followed. Roger glanced at her. pitying for the poor woman. The situation was bad for him, but he couldn't help feeling it was worse for her. Her eyes were darting around with insecurity etched into the greenness. She looked at Roger and he once again saw a deep fear in her eyes. They were screaming for help and he didn't know what to do.

The group located a small American-style steakhouse offering Western breakfasts and followed a young waiter inside. They were seated in the corner. Another waiter handed the group a menu each. Atifah placed the menu on the table. Roger looked at her. "You want to eat?" he said, demonstrating the action with his hands. Her eyes closed and the burkha hood shook gently back and forth. He tried again. "Do you want to drink something?" Again he imitated somebody drinking and again she said no. This was going to be a long day.

"Mike. I'm going to take a leak."

"So? ... Oh! Ok! I'm coming."

Roger turned to the girl and spoke in slow deliberate speech. "We will be back shortly."

The two men left the table and headed for the restrooms. Once inside Roger let it all out. "Mike, I am in big shit! Big, big shit!"

"What are you talking about Dude?" he answered, sensing the panic in his partner's voice. Roger needed to unload, but the words didn't come.

"That little party that we had last night, that little get-together, that shindig that we enjoyed so much..."

"Dude! Nobody says shindig anymore."

Roger looked numbly at his friend.

"Out with it Dude."

"It was my wedding."

Mike took a moment to digest what he had heard and it all started to fall into place. "Mrs A. Mac..."

"...Adam! Bingo! What the hell am I going to do?"

"Geez! Why are you taking her? Fuck it dude! Leave her here."

"It's a long story. Hell! I don't even know the story. The bottomline is if she comes back to Oman she will be stoned to death. Is it fair to land this on me, or her for that matter?"

"I would love to be there when you tell Anne."

Roger deflated. "Oh shit! I haven't even thought of how I'm going to tell Anne. What the hell is she going to think? 'Hi Annie, meet my new wife'."

"Who the hell is she and why did she want to marry you?"

"She is the Sultan's sister's granddaughter and the marriage was arranged. She didn't want to marry me. Who the hell would want to marry me? If she had any choice at all it was probably out of obedience to the Sultan. I'm in deep."

"I … am … big!" Mike spoke slowly.

Roger was confused "What?"

"I am big. What's the opposite of 'I am big'?"

"You are small?"

"No! Not the opposite, I mean say it backwards."

"I am big? Big am I… big am I? …Oh! My God! Bigamy! I'm a bigamist. I don't think bigamy is legal back home is it?"

"Of course it's not. It's what we all strive for, but it's not legal. You'll be every man's icon. Sadly, you'll be in jail."

"This gets worse and worse." Panic gripped Roger's chest and he started to hyperventilate. He needed to sit down and stumbled into one of the open stalls and sat holding his head in his hands.

"Come on Dude. Pull yourself together. They're not going to know when you land so you'll have time to speak to your lawyer. You need to think about how you are going to break this news to Anne. At least some good comes out of this."

"What?" Roger needed some good news.

"Anne won't be crapping on me for keeping you here until today. I'm off the hook."

"That's the best good news you can find for me?"

"Come on Rog. You have twenty-five hours to decide how you will tell Anne. Let's go and meet the old ball and chain."

Roger was happy to have been able to tell somebody. They strolled back to find Atifah conversing with one of the waiters. When the two approached, she stopped talking and the waiter moved off.

The steakhouse made a tasty local breakfast of macon and a hash brown with the usual trimmings, which they ate quickly before heading for the boarding gate. Prior to boarding, Roger sent a text message to Anne to let her know he was boarding and said he would call her when he landed at about this time tomorrow. He had left his car at the airport and so would see Anne at home an hour or so after they landed in Houston. For the first time in his married life, Roger was not looking forward to going home.

-- o --- o0o --- o --

Arriving at the boarding gate, a small party of airport attendants greeted them and led them through a 'No Entry' door where they boarded a vehicle which took them to the Airbus. They were seated before the gates had been opened. They took their seats in the front of the plane to the welcoming smiles of the flight attendants. Mike leaned over to Roger, "Bud! All is forgiven. This has been the best boarding I have ever had. You have my permission to marry her." Roger scowled.

The flight attendants didn't leave them alone all the way to Dubai. From past experience both of the guys knew Dubai would be different. Roger had seen the Dubai authorities reduce people to tears in the way they threw their hand luggage out, discarding personal items at will.

When they landed it was not at the main terminal and through the window the bus could be seen pulling up beside the airplane. The three descended the steps first, where an airport attendant met them and ushered them into a black limo. They were taken to the large, ultra-modern terminal building and ushered straight into the first class lounge where they were served coffee. At boarding time they were called personally by an attendant and were once again escorted to the boarding gate. No questions, no searching. The passports were stamped and they were on their way onto a much larger Emirates Boeing 777 attached to the terminal by a sloping, retractable umbilical cord.

Once inside, the opulence of the first class was apparent. Mike was in his lounging chair for three seconds before he started to play with the buttons. Throughout the entire journey thus far, Atifah hadn't said a word. Roger took a moment from his worrying to laugh inwardly as he thought he had a wife he would walk past in the street. He didn't know what she looked like, sounded like, how old she was. Nothing! She was a total stranger to him, yet she was married to him. He started to worry again as he thought of introducing her to Anne. He looked at Atifah and found her looking at him. She turned away quickly. A flight attendant walked past them on a busy journey to somewhere. Roger called to her. "Hi, you do speak Arabic?" Stupid question as she was almost certainly a native of the Emirates.

"Yes Mr Macadam." That was a bit of a shock. She knew him by name. "Can I help you?"

"Yes. Would you please tell my wife here ..." Ouch it hurt a little to say those words! "that everything will be ok! And she mustn't be scared."

Not at all puzzled by the request the attendant relayed the message to the seated girl. She turned to Roger and in a slow deliberate speech said, "Thank you."

It wasn't much, but at least he had heard her speak. She turned to the flight attendant and spoke in Arabic.

"Mr Macadam, your wife said she will try not to be scared and that Qaboos was right about you."

"Good," he said to Atifah trying to sound comforting, then turning to the attendant, "I hope it was something nice he was right about." The attendant smiled and moved to the plane door as the other passengers started to board.

The airplane was full, at least to the point where Roger was unable to see any empty seats from his location. In first class there seemed to be ample room. As soon as they were in the air, Mike pushed his seat back into a flat bed and crashed. He would sleep for a good few hours. Atifah had remained seated, but the drone of the plane had been too much for her. She had fallen asleep with her neck twisted to the side. Roger looked at this little, lost person and felt guilty about the position he had landed her in. He asked the attendant for a pillow. He gently lifted her head and slid the pillow underneath. She didn't stir. Roger gazed out of the window at the light, sandy landscape thousands of meters below. The stark blue-grey rocky ridges contrasted against smooth stretches of windblown sand looking as though they were a few hundred feet below, not a few thousand.

The whole time he was peering out of the window, he didn't see a thing. His mind was going through the hundreds of possible ways which he was going to explain this to Anne and Katie. He turned and looked at the sleeping form in the black shiny outfit. It felt like she had been around forever, but it was only a few short hours. Through the hole in the hood her eyes were closed and relaxed. This was the first time he had seen her relaxed since they had met. Roger kept on thinking about the ways he might have avoided this. Why hadn't he seen it coming? Had he missed any signs he should have seen? Roger pulled his thoughts back into breaking this disaster to Anne. There was no good way to say it. "Hi Honey! I'm home. Meet my new wife, Atifah..." or maybe, "Anybody not called Mrs Macadam, come and give me a kiss. That's you Katie." He was doomed.

-- o --- oOo --- o --

Roger half woke still seated in his chair. He was slumped to his left conscious of Atifah's steady breathing close to him. He jolted awake. She stirred and shifted in her seat placing her head back on the pillow he had given her. Hopelessness flooded back into his being. Once again, he started thinking about how this situation must look from her standpoint. Although he hadn't seen her, he guessed her age to be less than thirty and possibly less than twenty-five, judging from the sound of her voice. She was flying away from her family on a one-way ticket to a land she didn't know. She was accompanying an 'old' man, to whom she was married, but didn't know and couldn't even converse with. As disastrous as his situation seemed, he couldn't help feeling her position was far worse. The future must seem a little fragmented to her at this point.

Lunch time found the three of them awake. Mike was laughing loudly at the small screen in front of him. A strained silence from the other two contrasted the scene. All around people sat and chatted, a few played cards, still others had the ubiquitous airline headphones on and either watched the small dropdown screens or had their eyes closed, probably listening to music.

A couple of rows behind them, a youngish woman was seated in typically bright Omani traditional dress with lots of bright and expensive jewellery. Roger guessed she might be the wife of a wealthy Omani businessman. He had seen her on the flight from Muscat. She appeared to be flying alone.

Roger stood up and strolled over to her. She greeted him by name, which was more than a little disconcerting.

"Hello Mr Macadam."

"Hello!" He paused, "I'm sorry, have we met?" His mind was sifting through the people he had met over the last couple of days.

"No! I'm sorry! I knew you from the television."

"The television?"

"Yes, they have played your rescue of the Sultan several times on Al Jazeera TV. You are quite a celebrity in Oman."

"I didn't even realize. So I was on TV?"

Roger lost his focus for a second, basking in his own glory. "You wanted something from me, Mr Macadam?"

"Yes." He came back to his senses. "Yes, I have a favor to ask of you."

"Whatever I can do to help." She looked on expectantly.

"I am traveling with an Omani national …"

"I had noticed." She glanced over at the area where Roger was seated.

"The truth is we don't have too much to say to each other. Since you appear to be traveling alone, I was wondering whether you would like to swap seats with me. At least the two of you can have a conversation."

"It would be an honor Mr Macadam. I thought what you did was very brave."

"Quite honestly," he said to her, his face going a little vacant for a second as his mind raced over the events of the last few days. "I thought what I did was a little stupid."

"What is your friend's name?" The brightly clothed woman asked, changing the subject when she saw the solemn look in Roger's eyes.

"Atifah," Roger said, snapping out of his trance.

"Atifah? The Atifah? The Rose of Oman?"

"The same," he replied not realizing the possible implications of what he was saying.

"It's no wonder she is veiled. You should be very careful who you tell these things," the woman said.

"What do you mean?"

"Atifah is known to be protected by the Sultan to the extreme." She seemed to know his wife better than he did. "He is very fond of her. He must have much trust in you, as she is a sought after prize. Only the richest men in Oman have a chance of getting close to her." Roger lost focus a little as she started talking, but she continued. "The Sultan was always worried about somebody kidnapping her as a child. I would never have thought she would have her name on a plane reservation alone."

If only she knew, Roger thought.

"Alright-y then!" Roger was still a little shell-shocked. "When you speak to her, please ensure she knows it's not me wanting to sit elsewhere."

"Of course!" The elegantly dressed woman stood and headed over to Atifah. The two seemed to hit it off straight away and following what seemed like a formal greeting, they started talking in a relaxed and friendly manner with plenty of laughing and giggling. With Mike still engrossed in his comedy and Atifah contentedly chatting, Roger was happy to sit back and listen to music.

With the exception of a couple of interactions over lunch and supper, the balance of the journey to New York was reasonably quiet for Roger. The large Indian businessman, now seated next to him, had slept the majority of the day and snored a little. Luckily, Roger had been watching a movie. He increased the volume to cancel the noise.

At around nine in the evening on Roger's watch, which was still set on Muscat time, the captain announced the beginning of the descent into JF Kennedy. The time in New York was one in the afternoon.

After a pleasant first class flight, including a seven course meal, the thought of landing in the US as a bigamist and a felon caused a pain to grip his chest. Roger found himself short of breath. Even the Indian looked at Roger and waved to the attendant, thinking Roger was about to have a heart attack.

Roger waved to the flight attendant. "It's no problem. I don't fly well." Roger started to pull himself together a bit. This behavior was causing varying levels of anxiety around him.

Roger leaned back in the chair and closed his eyes. He opened them a few minutes later to find the colorful woman staring into his face. "Oh! Hello Mr Macadam. I thought you may be sleeping."

"No! I had my eyes closed. Not sleeping"

"You have a very lovely wife." She spoke as if she had known all along they were married. "I thought you might want to take your seat again."

"Oh!" Roger said. "Thank you."

Closing his eyes and getting perspective helped slow the heartbeat down a little.

-- o --- oOo --- o --

At JFK, the three travelers were no longer shown the courtesy and respect which they had enjoyed in the Middle East. They walked off the plane directly into the terminal. Since they were taking a new airline to Houston, they were taken through customs. The customs officials took one look at Atifah and decided to go all out, stopping short of a body cavity search. The pleasures of entering the US with a Muslim included a hand scan and pat-down for each of the team and an extensive search of their hand luggage.

At passport control Atifah was required to lift her veil, which she did without any protest. Both Mike and Roger found themselves leaning forward to take a peek at the elusive face of this woman, but were not successful. Roger felt a little hurt that an airport employee had seen more of his 'wife' than he had.

Satisfied with what he saw, the passport control worker stamped the passport after asking the usual questions like: Where will you be staying? How long will you be staying? Do you have a boyfriend? Do you like to go out at night and which building in Houston have you earmarked for destruction? He was polite and courteous, but had the usual air of 'suck my dick!' we have come to expect from the US airport staff since 09/11.

Atifah, not having a clue what he was talking about, turned to Roger. Roger stepped forward, not having heard the question. "Is there a problem with my wife's passport, officer?" He hadn't wanted to say it, but he visualized hours of low grade waiting rooms and cross questioning from doughnut eating passport and immigration inspectors. He thought that as a US citizen, he would have more clout.

"Your wife?" The passport officer raised his eyebrows showing his thoughts. 'This is no more your wife than Brittney Spears is mine.'

"Correct!" Roger hesitated, "Is there a problem?"

"No! Everything appears to be in order. Mrs Atifah Macadam." He didn't look convinced.

They must have pulled out all the stops at the Omani passport department. Roger hadn't thought about it until now. She had been booked on as A. Macadam. These tickets were booked on Friday and her passport was ready early on Saturday morning. Not bad going for a passport department. The Sultan must have had a lot of faith in his plan to have arranged this in one day.

The inspector called to Roger who had regained his composure. "Mr Macadam! Can I ask what you will be doing while you are in America?" He didn't look happy.

"No problem!" Roger was becoming a little annoyed again, but way more worried than annoyed. He kept his cool. The pain gripped his chest again and he could hear the breath going out of his lungs like a leaky old tire. The sweat was running down his side in small torrents and he knew it would soon be showing on his shirt. "I'm not visiting America. You may have noticed from my American passport I will be going home to my ... home." Oops!

Close! He almost told the official he was going home to his wife. Roger's knees weakened. This could not go on much longer. He could hear himself shouting out "OK! OK! I'm a bigamist. Arrest me! Take me away!" Instead he looked into the eyes of the official. The passport guy didn't look like he had noticed the near slip. "I live in Houston. We will be boarding the Continental link home in a short while."

The official looked deep into Roger's eyes, searching for a hesitation. Roger was sure he suspected something, but he looked back into the officials eyes. Semi-satisfied and a little hesitantly, he handed back the passports. Roger and Atifah started moving along with Mike. He had gone through in quick time, but had come back to rescue Roger. "Oh! Mrs Macadam!" Roger's heart stood still and his feet froze to the immigration department's vinyl floor tiles. Slowly he turned. He was relieved to find Atifah had already turned and faced the gaze of the official. He was holding up a pen. "Is this yours?" he asked.

Atifah leaned forward, examining the object "No!" She uttered the sweetest word Roger had ever heard. Small and simple, but gave the official the answer he was looking for. Relieved, Roger led Atifah out of the official-looking passport zone and into the bustling airport. American soil!

With the exception of a few mild anxiety attacks, the rest of the journey was uneventful. Roger had called Anne briefly in New York to let her know he had landed safely and pretty soon the three were back in the air again for the short trip to Houston.

By the time the luggage had been located and the three had exited the terminal, the Houston sky was already dark. Roger once again called Anne. This time he knew she was around the corner and he missed her so much. His mind was in complete conflict. He longed to see her, but he didn't want to go home. He asked Anne to arrange the guest bed as he was bringing home a visitor. A visitor?

Turning out into the street, they started the near ten mile trip to the office. Roger and Mike had left the office using Roger's car. Mike therefore had to be taken back to the office to pick up his vehicle. Atifah sat in silence, looking around at the unfolding scenery. It should have been the two of them sitting quietly as usual, discussing the trip. Instead, the silence and anxiety was giving Roger a pain in the back of his head.

After dropping off Mike, Roger headed down Main Street and started the longest nine miles of his life. The two of them sat in silence as he navigated the road. Whether he was driving slowly, or whether the journey simply seemed long, he wasn't sure, but it seemed an eternity before he pulled into his Bellaire driveway. Stopping the car, he switched off the engine, took a deep breath and stepped out the car. There was no turning back and no way out. This was the moment he had been dreading since he had met Atifah at the airport.

Roger had become accustomed to the black-clad figure walking beside him. In a strange way he hadn't once felt uncomfortable at the silence between them. It was as if the veil had protected the need to be personally acquainted with the woman.

Roger lifted the bags from the trunk as the door opened and Anne and Katie burst out. They both ran across the small lawn to meet Roger. Both were almost stopped in their tracks at the sight of a veiled Muslim woman in their yard. Neither was able to hide their shock at seeing the small figure draped in silky black with a beautiful pair of frightened eyes being the only visible part.

"Hello you two!" Roger snapped them out of their daze.

"Daddy!" Katie still called him Daddy. She had gone through phases of referring to Roger as Dad, Pa and even Roger for a while, but these days it was back to Daddy and he was happy with that. She was slim and somewhat taller than Anne. Roger had always thought she might be a model one day, but she'd never shown the slightest interest in modeling. She threw her arms around Roger as though he had been away for months.

Katie excelled at school and would be starting at Rice University in the fall studying, of all things, computer science. Roger hadn't seen it coming. She was intelligent and hardworking enough. He was proud of her achievements.

Anne was still a little wary of the newcomer and gave a half-hearted "Hello," in Atifah's direction, then approached Roger, giving him a peck on the cheek. This visitor, Anne had not expected.

"Let's go inside and I'll do the introductions." This was not going to be fun.

Inside, Roger dumped his and Atifah's bags in the entrance hall and led the way into the lounge. "Have a seat everybody." He could see from the cake on the table and the champagne glasses that he was about to destroy a perfectly good home-coming celebration.

He began. "There is no easy way to say this. Believe me, I have thought of all of them, so I'm merely going to say it. Understand that there is a story to follow." He looked at Atifah who was still standing. "Sit," he said, pointing to an open chair. Talking to Atifah he said, "This is my daughter, Katie." He reached for a photo in a frame on the table. A family photo of the three of them about fifteen years earlier. He pointed at the young child and then at Katie.

Katie led the way. "Hello!" she said, getting up from her chair and holding out her hand.

Atifah shook her hand and replied, in hesitant English, "Hello Katie. My name is Atifah."

Now came the difficult and hurtful part of the introduction. "Atifah! This is my wife Anne. Anne! This is Atifah. She is also my wife."

Anne started well, but Roger's words kicked in about mid-sentence. "Hello Atifah! Nice to … What did you say?"

Atifah uttered a lonely "Hello", but Anne hadn't heard. Katie's jaw dropped and she sat with a disbelieving look on her face.

"Roger!" Anne was frighteningly calm. "I think I would like to talk to you in the bedroom." She stood and strode out of the lounge in one fluid motion without looking back. She knew Roger would follow.

"Please tell me this is a joke. Not a good one, but at least a bad joke."

"It's not."

"You waltz into our house and introduce … her … as your wife."

"Believe me honey, I …"

"Don't honey me. How do you think it made me feel to hear you introduce her as your wife?"

"Do you think it was easy to say it to you? I have agonized for the last twenty-four hours on how to tell you."

"And the best you could come up with was … blurting it out?"

"Tell me! How would you like to have heard it? Should I have told you on the phone, or texted you? If I had told you the story first and then ended with 'We're married!' Would it have been less shocking?"

She thought about it and he was right. "Ok! What's the story?"

Roger was taken aback. She had calmed to about three on the Richter scale. "Let's go to the lounge so Katie can hear the story. She must have questions too."

They walked through to the lounge and Anne sat back down in the same seat as before, but sitting taller and somewhat menacing, she turned toward Atifah looking her straight in the eyes. "Hello Atifah." Anne had a smile on her face, but it wasn't hiding much.

Atifah returned the greeting respectfully, but knew danger was around. Katie was still seated in the same position with what looked to be a tear in her eye. No words had been spoken in this lounge since the two of them left.

"Ok!" he began. "I am going to explain the last few days to you. I don't want to sound like a lecturer, but if you have questions at any point please stop me. You too Katie, ok? ... " No answer from either. "Ok?" Two grunts meant he could continue.

"On Wednesday I was caught in the crossfire of a military skirmish in Muscat."

"Why didn't you tell me?" Anne liked to be kept in the loop.

"I would never worry you with this over the phone. It was all over quickly and I was ok!" He paused as if waiting for a question. None came.

"Anyway, I rescued an old man in the street and it turns out he was the Sultan of Oman. He was grateful to be rescued and apparently it was on TV over there a few times but I didn't see it. To show his gratitude he invited me and Mike to his palace for a function. I told you about the party. It was supposed to be in my honor. I told you about this on the phone."

"Yes but you didn't tell me about the gunfire." This wouldn't die.

Roger continued, "It appears this whole function was my wedding, but I didn't know about it."

"How could you not know you were getting married?" Anne was visualizing a church service.

"It wasn't a wedding ceremony as we know it. I have it on DVD, you can watch it later and you can decide for yourself if I should have known."

Katie cut in, "Didn't he know you were married? The Sultan I mean."

"Yes honey! He did know. There is still a lot I don't know, but I will find out."

"Isn't it illegal to have two wives?" she continued.

"Yes again! I'm not sure about the details - I will have to seek legal advice."

"Couldn't you have said no?" she was on a roll now.

"I was coming to that. As I said I didn't know it had happened. I only found out the following morning at the airport in Muscat. The Sultan pitched up and presented me with my gift. The reason I couldn't say no is I was warned by the Sultan's butler that in Oman women are not allowed to marry non-Muslim men. He said he wasn't sure, but there was a possibility she could be stoned to death for doing it." There was silence in the lounge. "So you see. I couldn't leave her there."

It was Anne's turn. "Why did she agree to this?"

"She probably didn't. Apparently marriages are organized by the families and often the couple only meet on the wedding day."

"Ok! So how do you end it?"

"Again, I was told it's easy to divorce her. The problem lies in the results of a divorce. If I divorce her immigration will send her back to Oman in an instant and then she will face jail or death. She is as innocent as I am in this. I don't think it would be fair to her. I need to find out more first."

The two girls were deep in thought.

Anne looked at the figure sitting alone outside of the conversation in silence. "Does she speak much?"

"Until she greeted Katie, I think I have heard three words and two of those were 'no'. Remember, as strange as this is to us, this girl has been forced to leave her country, her family and everything she knows. God knows what is going through her head at the moment. She must be terrified."

"How old is she?"

"I have no idea. You've seen what I've seen."

"You don't even know what she looks like?"

"No! Not a clue."

Anne stood slowly and walked to Atifah. Relieving the tension, Anne held out her hand to the girl. "Hello Atifah. It's nice to meet you."

Atifah visibly relaxed. Her shoulders dropped sufficiently to say thank goodness. "Hello Mrs Macadam." Anne noted the relaxation and felt sorry for the girl. She had been tense and seemed to be picking up on parts of the conversation if not all of it.

"Do you understand English?"

"Little bit." She held up her hand showing a small gap between her index finger and her thumb.

"Let me take you to your room. Rog! Bring her bags up." Anne led her up the stairs to the guest room with Roger and Katie in tow.

"Here is your bed," Anne stated the obvious. She opened the empty closet. "You can hang your clothes here."

Not knowing what else to do, but wanting Atifah to feel welcome, Anne gave the girl a hug and said "Welcome."

"Thank you," Atifah spoke again.

"Come you two." Anne was in control. "Let's let Atifah settle in."

Turning to Atifah she said, "Do you want to eat or drink?" Anne gave the relevant charades signals and Atifah understood.

"Water ... Please." she answered and started to open her bags as the others left the room.

Roger grabbed his bags and took them back upstairs to his bedroom. He was busy unpacking when Anne walked in with a blank look on her face. "You have no idea what Atifah looks like?" she asked.

"No idea at all. I would walk past her in the street."

"You are quite sure?"

"What's going on Anne?" She looked serious.

"I took in her water. She was getting changed."

"You've seen her?" Roger was a little too excited for his own good. Realizing his excitement had been noticed, he toned down a little. "Then you've seen more than me."

"Oh yes! I've seen her."

"Well?"

"She's stunning." Anne's mind was racing through what she had seen. All of a sudden the helpless girl was a gorgeous husband stealing siren. She controlled her thoughts and realized there was no reason to panic. "I walked in on her in her underwear. She seemed embarrassed." She flopped back on the bed. "She could be a Victoria's Secret model. I think she was wearing Victoria's Secret." She sat up and pinched Roger's stomach. "You SOB she's beautiful. You knew about this didn't you?" She was playing around now.

"Beautiful is she?" Roger was taking it all in. She had been called the Rose of Oman, but he had linked it to her status, not her physical beauty. In fact, he was starting to see her with a permanent veil. He hadn't thought about her face or her body beneath those loose fitting clothes. He felt a little disgusted for not paying more attention.

"She is! Wow! She really is!" Anne was shaking her head, very confused about her feelings.

"I assure you I have no idea what she looks like." He was smiling at the blank look on Anne's face. "Do I sense a little worry or anxiety? Are you feeling like you have a little competition? So! How old is she?"

"I don't know, twenty-one, twenty-two..."

"No problem then. She's way too young for me."

"Too young? You're married to her. Who'd have thought you would be married to a young Selma Hayek?"

Roger stretched his arms right around his wife in a tight embrace. "No I'm not!"

"You are too you bigamist." She pulled away playfully.

"Ah! The B-word." Roger sat back on the bed, shaken by the reminder of what the future could hold. Anne saw the reaction and realized this had taken its toll on Roger far more than he had shown.

"I'm sure it will be ok!" she reassured him.

"Of course it will. I'm sure I can't be guilty of something I had no control over." He was trying to sound sure and believed he did a good job. "It's been a long, long day." He meant it literally. He had been woken up at three in the morning, by the wakeup service at the hotel. He had traveled for a full twenty-four hours, including the trip from the airport and it was nine-thirty. A long day indeed.

"Ok! Mr Macadam. It's bedtime. Leave your bag until morning. I want you to explain to me how you bravely fought off the rebel forces single-handedly." She pushed him backward onto the bed and hauled herself over to sit astride him. She leaned forward and kissed his mouth.

"Mmm! That's why I love to come home." Roger slid his hands up her sides and around her back. He pulled her toward him feeling the exquisite pressure of her body on his. "You know I would never do anything to lose this don't you?"

"I do."

"You know I ..."

"Shut up Roger."

SUNDAY, 5TH

Roger half woke when he felt somebody climbing into the bed next to him. He shifted over. Instead of moving over into empty space, Roger slid over into someone else. Still half dazed and probably still reminiscent of the days when Katie would run and climb into the bed, Roger, in his state of semi-consciousness, acknowledged he was sandwiched between two people.

Anne turned toward Roger, placing her warm hand on his chest. He turned his head toward her contentedly. The woman to his left placed her hand on his stomach. Roger's eyes opened wide. Anne started to move her hand down slowly across his chest heading for his stomach, all the while Atifah was rubbing and scratching, gently, with her fingernails heading slowly downward. Roger tried to whisper for the Arab girl to stop, but his voice hissed in a hoarse, dry wheeze. Roger looked down and in the dim light of the night he could see the silhouette of Atifah as she sat up, reaching over to gently kiss his stomach, her kiss missing Anne's fingers by inches. Both of the women were going down, down …

Roger grunted as he sat up startled, excited and sweating. Atifah was gone and Anne was well over on her side of the bed. He'd been dreaming. Angry, excited and relieved, Roger sat on the bed, breathing heavily.

"What's wrong Rog?" Anne sat up. "Are you ok?"

Roger was sweating. He was disgusted with himself for not being able to stop it. He wasn't even sure if he had wanted to stop it.

"Roger?"

"I'm ok! A nightmare … I think." He couldn't tell her. He could always tell her before. "The plane was going down." He lied for the first time in years. Maybe he would tell her in the morning. Maybe not!

Roger lay back down and turned. He lay thinking for a long time before falling back to sleep.

He woke again as somebody ran their hand over his stomach. He sat bolt upright, startled. "Whoa tiger! We're a bit jumpy this morning aren't we?"

"Sorry honey! I … wasn't expecting …"

"You don't usually expect it, but I've never seen you react like that."

"You're right! I don't know what it was about. I guess I'm a little highly strung at the moment."

"You poor baby! Lay down, I'll try to relax you."

It worked! Pretty soon Roger was relaxed, contented and smiling. Anne lay next to him also relaxed, contented and smiling. "That was ... pretty good." she whispered in his ear. "Pretty damn good!" Anne as a rule would not comment on sex. Not because she didn't enjoy sex with her husband, but because she wouldn't normally say anything. "That was ... what got into you?"

"I don't know!" Roger said, but he did. His dream had left him strung-out and excited. "I think I was more highly strung than I thought."

"Like a bomb ready to explode?" she added.

Roger rolled onto her and kissed her hard on the mouth. "You're the best. Do you want breakfast?"

"Ok! I'll have a small bowl of cereal. I thought we could take Atifah and show her the city this morning and we can stop somewhere for an early lunch."

"No problem. You're being pretty cool with this ... considering."

"With what? I was shocked at first, but you did the right thing. You always do. She must understand the situation though." She hesitated. "I don't understand how you didn't know you were getting married."

"I can show you," Roger said. "I'll get the DVD."

He ran downstairs and retrieved the DVD from his laptop case. As he was charging back up the stairs, Atifah stepped out of her room and the two met on the landing. She stopped Roger in his tracks. She was the most beautiful woman Roger had ever laid eyes on by miles. Her long streaked black hair hung to her elbows and shone in the morning sunlight. Her perfectly symmetrical features broke into a smile as she saw the look on Roger's face. His dream hadn't even come close. "Good morning," she said, concentrating on her words.

"Good morning." Roger couldn't shift his gaze. "Did you sleep well?"

"I slept nice," she answered, showing a radiant Colgate smile.

"You're awake early." Roger didn't want her to move. Her perfect skin glowed golden in the morning sun. Her black outfit had hidden her so well, Roger had failed to see her as a person. In her long pink pajamas she was well covered, but there was nothing that could dim such beauty. Roger was captivated. Rose of Oman was not a fitting name.

She spoke softly, "Each day I pray before the sun …" she indicated the sun rising.

"Roger." Anne broke the spell. "Bring Atifah in. Let her watch. And wake up Katie. She'll want to watch too."

Roger pointed. "Go in there to Anne." She wasn't sure what he meant. "Come!" He waved and led the way. She entered the main bedroom, looking around and taking it all in. Anne was again struck by this woman's stunning features. She was amazing.

Anne beckoned from the bed. "Come! Sit!" Roger placed the DVD into the player and threw the remote onto the bed near Anne.

"I'll go wake up Katie," said Roger as he left the room. He re-appeared seconds later with Katie rubbing her eyes.

"This had better be good," she mumbled and then. "Wow!" when she saw Atifah.

"You can start! I'll go whip up coffee and breakfast." Roger left the room with Anne beckoning to Atifah to sit. The three women started arranging themselves and getting comfortable on the bed.

From the kitchen he could hear the DVD playing. He could hear the sounds of the cheering as the men ran around the tent. The memories flooded back into his mind, distant memories of things which happened only a few hours ago.

Roger finished the coffee, piled bowls and cereal on a tray and carried it upstairs. As he approached the room he heard the girls laughing. "Pops! You were quite something in your dress there."

"Where are all the women?" Anne asked Atifah. She turned to look at Anne not having caught the question. Anne pointed to the screen. "Where are you?" she said slowly.

"Ah! Inside!" She pointed to the tent. As she said it a resounding ululation emanated from the tent and she smiled as if to say "There! You see!"

After a while, they watched as the three women came out of the tent. The two in black, headed over to the Sultan and Roger seated side by side on their thrones. Seeing herself and her family on the screen, Atifah fell quiet and tears welled up in her eyes. She didn't cry but her eyes became watery. Anne saw it.

"That's you," Anne said pointing to the girl standing by the tent.

"Yes! … And mother and grandmother," she said pointing to the other two women.

"Father?" Anne asked.

"He's dead."

"Oh! I'm sorry," Anne said, thinking she might have opened the flood gates.

"Long time ago," Atifah said. "Three!" she exclaimed, holding up three fingers. Anne guessed she meant when she was three.

"What did you give the woman?" At last a question directed at Roger, but not the question he wanted.

"It was a ring," he said, not wanting to elaborate.

"Why did you give her a ring?" From her tone, Roger guessed a tiny shred of doubt may have entered Anne's thoughts.

"The Sultan told me I could either keep the ring, or I could give it to his sister's child, in exchange for something far more valuable."

"Why didn't you take the ring?"

"Because he said she had wanted it for a long time and was prepared to exchange a more valuable item for it."

"You mean …"

"Yes! Atifah was the gift of higher value." He wanted to say he cursed the day he gave away the ring, but he couldn't. She appeared to be not following the conversation, but he wouldn't take the chance.

"How old are you?" Anne asked.

"Twenty-four!" she answered.

"Too young to marry," Anne said tilting her head to one side as if to say "you poor girl".

"No! Too old," Atifah answered.

Anne laughed. "Too old? You are young and beautiful. Why did you marry this old man?" She had meant it as a joke, but she sensed things became serious.

"Qaboos told me … very nice man. Very brave man. Very good man."

"He is a good man," she said smiling at Roger. "But he's so old," Anne emphasized the 'old', laughing. The Arab girl's face cracked into a grin.

"You also a good woman! Qaboos say you hate me."

It was Anne's turn to have her eyes water up. She wondered what must have been going through this girl's mind the whole time. She had probably known about this marriage before Roger. She reached over pulling the girl to her in a tight hug. "I don't hate you," she said.

They watched the rest of the DVD. At the end Anne turned to Roger and winked. "You were right." She was satisfied.

"Katie! Why don't you show Atifah around? She hasn't seen the house yet and I need to have a chat with your father." Katie agreed and beckoned to Atifah to follow. The two young women left the bedroom.

"So what now?" Anne asked. "She's probably going to be with us for a while."

"I think so. I need to get legal advice on the whole bigamy thing. Maybe the marriage won't be recognized in this country, in which case it won't be a problem from our perspective." Roger was deep in thought. "I'm not sure how that will leave her status with immigration. We can't have her deported back to Oman. Not if she is in trouble with the law over there."

"Of course not. It wouldn't be right."

"I was given a phone by the Sultan to call him anytime. I was told if I needed anything I can call. I think I am in need of information. I'm not going to worry about it today, but tomorrow I'll look for answers."

Anne agreed and said, "I was thinking. If she's going to be here for a while, maybe we could start her at school in the fall with Katie. At least it will keep her busy and it will be like an exchange student. I'm sure Katie will learn from her. Do you think she's wealthy?"

"She's from a ridiculously rich family. She lives in a palace. She's probably already educated. She's like a princess."

"A princess?"

"Yeah! The Sultan is like the king. I heard he didn't have kids, so I suppose it means she is somebody special." He thought of the Omani woman on the plane. "I know he singled her out for special protection. I told a woman on the plane who she was and she warned me against telling anybody else."

"The Rose of Oman? I'm yet to see a rose as beautiful. She is perfect. You don't think somebody will try to kidnap her do you?"

Roger was thoughtful. "I think only a few people know what she looks like. Even the woman on the plane seemed to only know her as being veiled."

Anne started picking up the breakfast bowls as the girls came back from their walk-about. Atifah jumped and took the bowls and cups from her. "It's ok! I'll take them," Anne protested.

"No! I help," Atifah said, taking the tray from Anne and walking out the door with it. "You don't work now. I work now."

"Whoa!" Anne raised her eyebrows as she watched the young girl strut out of the bedroom. "What do you think she meant by that?"

"My guess is she thinks you are the old wife and should be retired and put out to pasture," he said.

It dawned on Anne again that as young and vulnerable as this girl was, she believed she was married to her husband. In fairness, she *was* married to her husband. The road ahead was not going to be easy. Once again she briefly saw Atifah, no longer as Katie's friend, but as her husband's second wife. The flowing hair, beautiful porcelain complexion and model-like figure had a whole new meaning than it had merely seconds ago.

"She's married to you. In her mind she is married to you. How the hell do we tell her she's not?"

"Honey, let's not worry about it until we have more answers. Tomorrow I will contact our lawyer and the Sultan. We can get some proper perspective on this. For now, let's go for a drive, show her around and treat her like she is a visitor. Ok?"

After a long thoughtful pause, Anne relaxed. "I guess so."

MONDAY, 6TH

Mike and Roger pulled into work at the same time. Walking from the parking the two were quiet, neither of them feeling the need to speak. As they entered the office, Alan met them at the door with a concerned look. "Guys, we have a problem. Please come through to the boardroom. Barbara, hold our calls."

The two engineers dropped their cases and headed straight to the boardroom. "What's this about, Alan?" Roger opened the door and was welcomed by cheering and applause from the entire company.

Alan stepped forward and shook the hands of the engineers as somebody was taking photos. He raised his hands for quiet. "Thank you everyone. Sorry it's so cramped in here." Unique Engineering wasn't a big company. They designed and built flow systems for the oil and gas industry. The office comprised a design team headed by Roger, a sales team headed by Mike, a drawing office and admin staff. Altogether there were twenty-three people crammed into the smallish boardroom. The actual building of the units was outsourced to an engineering company.

Alan continued, "If our intrepid world travelers had been on time for work this would have been over by now." He breathed deeply. "On Friday, Mike and Roger signed up our biggest deal to date. I know it's early to be drinking, but I think we need to celebrate today …" Alan paused and beckoned somebody in from the side door. "Those who wish to have a champagne breakfast, please enjoy."

He continued, "As I was saying, these two have signed up a single deal which is equivalent to our turnover for the last three years."

A few smiles and nods. "News from the factory is they can push this deal through as a single job. This means economies of scale, something we have never had to deal with. Our gross from this job is going to be closer to four years gross profit." More nods of appreciation knowing bonuses would be good this year. By now the champagne had been handed out and the hot snacks wheeled in by the caterers.

"So! From now onward, you guys are going to be busy. Extremely busy and I am going to have enough cash to take a short holiday." A few laughs circled the room. "Seriously though, well done you two. You have outdone yourselves this time and I want to know, who'd you have to screw to land this deal?" A few more courteous laughs circled the room. Laughs saying it wasn't funny, but you're the boss.

Mike looked at Roger. "Screwing is if you want to sell a unit, Rog' had to marry somebody for this deal." Everybody laughed while he raised his glass. Roger glared at Mike but nobody saw.

Monday had started off on a pleasant break from the norm. All the staff were in high spirits. For a good hour the staff mingled eating breakfast, drinking and probing the engineers about their week. Everybody heard about the trip, but nobody heard about Atifah. After a while the crowd dissipated back to their desks and Mike and Roger followed.

Roger sat at his desk looking around as if acquainting himself with what was scattered around him. He smiled to himself as he thought of the twenty odd people crammed into the boardroom. Today was going to be a good day. His phone rang. "Macadam," he said in a professional tone.

"Mr Macadam." It was Barbara, the receptionist's voice. "There are two men here to see you."

"Thanks Barbara, I'll be there in a moment." He replaced the receiver. He looked around once more, tapped his fingers on his desk and stood up. As he walked into the reception area Roger realize he should have gone out the back way and down the fire escape. Standing in the reception area were two men, fully compliant with FBI agent stereotypes. Looking like something out of the Men in Black, both turned toward him as he entered and from the slight change of expression, both knew exactly who he was.

"Mr Macadam. Federal Agent Matthews." He removed his black glasses revealing a plus-minus thirty-year-old, cocky-looking individual with short, spiked, blond hair. He was of medium build, but sporting a slightly extended beer and doughnut gut, which looked to be more from lack of exercise than over-indulgence. "This is my partner, agent McClellan." Murphy removed his dark glasses as if on cue. He was a good foot shorter than Tony Matthews, but at least ten pounds heavier. He was striking by virtue of his head of carrot-orange, curly hair. His pale skin and ruddy cheeks rounded off the Irish look to perfection.

"Good morning Mr Macadam." No hint of Irish there. Only unadulterated Texan.

"Hello." Roger was starting to sweat again.

"We need to have a word with you regarding your wife. I wonder if you would be so kind as to come with us for a drive down town."

"Can't we talk here, the boardroom will be ..."

"Mr Macadam. I strongly urge you to come with us and nobody will have to be embarrassed by the scuffle that will break out if you force us to arrest you." The pseudo-Irishman was aggressive.

"Arrest me? Do you have a warrant?"

"I can have one within the hour."

"By which time we could have sat and spoken and you'd know the whole story."

"You know why we are here, Mr Macadam. How long did you believe you would get away with this charade?"

"How long?" Roger was taken a-back by the aggressiveness and became a little defensive. "I arrived in the country late Saturday night and you are here Monday morning, the first working day. If I'd thought the bureau would be awake on the weekend, I'd have popped in for a visit." Barbara's eyes were wide open. The switchboard was buzzing, but there was no way she would answer. She was taking mental notes for the report back to other staff members.

"Then you're not going to deny it? You're not going to tell us we've made a mistake or maybe use one of the other thousands of excuses we hear on a daily basis." McClellan seemed almost disappointed.

"Would it do me any good?" Roger was starting to calm down again. The confrontation was not as bad as the anticipation. What Roger had been dreading was almost a relief when it came.

Agent Matthews answered coldly. "Not really! No!"

"You wouldn't come here without having done your homework." Barbara's eyes darted back and forth between the talkers, dying to catch the slightest clue as to what everybody else seemed to know.

"You do realize bigamy is a felony in the US don't you?" Her questions were answered in an instant in a way she would never have dreamed. Barbara's jaw dropped to around the middle of her abdomen.

"Of course I do. This is a misunderstanding."

"Ah!" agent McClellan brightened up. "And the excuses start to flow."

"Not at all! I had every intention of resolving this issue. I would have liked the time to seek legal advice first." The switchboard was still buzzing and Barbara's mouth still hung open like the air intake of a sports car. "Could you answer that?" Roger snapped.

Shocked at suddenly being a part of the dialogue, Barbara looked down embarrassed.

"Of course!" she said.

Roger continued, "You're probably right. Maybe I should come with you. Would you mind if I let my colleague know? ... So he can inform my wife." Roger started to turn to walk to Mike's office.

"NO!" Agent McClellan was insistent and somewhat scary with his single word answer. Roger stopped in his tracks.

Agent Matthews raised his hand giving the calm down signal to his partner. "I'm afraid we'll have to accompany you. We don't know if there are any exits back there."

"There is an exit back there. Do you think I am going to make a run for it?" Roger looked at McClellan. "I think you watch too much TV."

McClellan's face hardened. "You obnoxious little punk, I ..."

Agent Matthews held up his hand again. "Mr Macadam. You have no idea how many people make a run for it."

"But they're probably guilty aren't they?"

"They're all guilty." Agent McClellan scowled at Roger, wanting to beat him to the ground, strap the cuffs on and drag him out screaming. "They're all guilty until proven innocent."

"What my partner means is at this point a suspect will be on high alert ready for fight or flight. We have to be aware of this and may become a little tense."

"I assure you I will not be running nor fighting and you are welcome to accompany me." Roger did not convince the FBI with his honest approach as both agents accompanied him to Mike's office.

"Mike!"

"Yes Rog!" Mike didn't lift his head.

"I'd like to introduce you to Agent Matthews and … Agent MacLaren." Roger was toying with McClellan and he knew it.

"McClellan. Agent McClellan." He was frustrated and getting impatient.

"Hi!" Mike lifted his head from his work.

"These gentlemen are here to arrest me for bigamy."

He looked at the two agents, then at his watch. "Did you guys wet the bed?" Only Roger laughed.

"Not to arrest, to question," Matthews replied, nodding slightly to acknowledge Mike.

Roger addressed his friend. "Can you see to it that Anne knows where I am and ask her to call my lawyer?"

"Sure bud! Anything else I can do?"

"I was …"

Agent McClellan stopped Roger. "We gotta go."

"Then I guess not," said Roger, calm and in charge. So unlike Roger. "But remember Mr McClellan, until you have a warrant, we don't gotta go nowhere. I'm accompanying you out of courtesy."

McClellan reached behind his back and withdrew a pair of handcuffs. At last, something physical. "Murphy! He's not under arrest. Put the cuffs away." He replaced the cuffs, visibly disappointed.

Mike, still not serious, said, "Ok Bud! I'll see you in three to five." The two friends laughed, even though they knew they shouldn't.

Roger called back to Mike as he was being led out the door. "Tell Anne to get Atifah back into her outfit in case this becomes public. We don't need her face splashed all over the news." Roger started to think through the likely effects of a possible arrest.

"Will do Bud!"

The minute Roger was out the door, Mike was on the phone to Anne forwarding the message to her and she in turn managed to contact the family lawyer who immediately left for the Houston FBI regional headquarters. He started the long drawnout process of tracking down Roger's location. As could be expected nobody had any clue as to where Roger had been taken. No arrests had been logged on the system and the field agents responsible could not be contacted. Meanwhile, Roger was drinking coffee given to him by Agent Matthews in one of the interview rooms. His partner was not in the room. Roger guessed he was sitting behind the large mirror, either filming, recording or aiming his gun at Roger's head in case he tried to run.

At first Roger had thought the attitude was part of a good cop - bad cop thing, but he soon realize it was more a case of mediocre cop - idiot cop. McClellan was the type of person you'd expect to have joined the force so he could grow his hair long, wear boots and carry a gun. His attitude riled Roger and this wasn't what he needed at this point.

"Is the coffee good?" Matthews started the ball rolling.

"Perfect! Thanks!" Roger lied.

"So! Mr Macadam. You know why you are here. Why don't you start from the beginning and let me know what this is all about."

"Sure! I have nothing to hide. The short version of the story is on Wednesday in Oman I saved the life of the Sultan of Oman. As a gift, he gave me the hand of a family member in marriage. I had no clue about this until I was boarding the plane to come home on Saturday morning. I arrived home on Saturday night so I haven't had time to find out anything about the status of the marriage. Hell! I only saw her face for the first time on Sunday morning."

"So! You're not living as husband and wife then."

"Hell no! This girl is the same age as my daughter. I don't think my wife would appreciate it too much."

"Which wife are we talking about here?"

"Funny!" Roger answered, aware of a change in Matthews's demeanor. A slight change, but the agent seemed a little more menacing. Maybe it had something to do with finding out he had no bigamy case to pursue. To worsen matters, his partner walked through the door, silently greeting his partner with a nod. Roger continued, trying to look confident. "I didn't expect you would be onto me this fast. What caused me to spark your interest so quickly?"

Agent McClellan spun the chair and sat opposite Roger looking directly into his eyes. "Since 9/11, the immigration people are on the lookout for all the rag-heads entering into this great country."

"Rag-heads?"

"Muslims! Don't tell me you hadn't realized your wife wears a rag over her face. Hey! Maybe she's not a Muslim. Maybe she's just fucking ugly?" McClellan was becoming aggressive but more worrying, his partner was no longer holding him back. "For reasons I cannot imagine, you or your new wife inspired the immigration official enough to pass your names onto the FBI. We carried out research on the young Mrs Macadam and nothing came up. Nothing ever does. Then we decided to find out whether you were a rag-head sympathizer."

Agent McClellan was on a roll. "When we don't find anything on the rag-heads, we look at who they're coming to visit." He paused, waiting for a response. None came. "That's you!" He was almost indignant. "And guess what our advanced people info system dug up about you. You're married and not to the woman you came through the gate with." The agent again waited for a response.

Slowly and in control, Roger turned and looked at the agent. "I thought we had already established that."

The tone of his voice infuriated the agent. McClellan sprang forward at a rate that surprised Roger. He pulled Roger from the chair and kicked between Roger's legs sending the chair backward, leaving Roger unbalanced and ready to topple backward.

Roger had always been light and quick on his feet and without even thinking, he managed to regain his balance. He stood up, infuriating McClellan even further.

"Do you think you can go on flouting the law indefinitely?" Roger could hear the anger in McClellan's voice.

Roger didn't help matters. "No! But I thought I might at least make it through the weekend." He turned to Agent Matthews. "Flouting? You teach your little agents big words."

This proved too much for the angry little man. "Why you…" McClellan swung his fist into Roger's midriff, doubling him up and knocking every bit of air out of his lungs. Roger was not a large man, but he did like to stay in shape. For the past few years he had been waking early and exercising. He enjoyed running when he was given the chance, but he religiously worked on his core muscles and made sure he did at least one hundred and fifty sit-ups and crunches daily. He did this for this exact reason, to have strong abs when he needed them. All those years of exercise amounted to nothing because he didn't see the punch coming. Roger fell to the floor scarcely able to suck air back into his lungs.

"What the hell is going on here?"

A welcome voice, but Roger was in way too much pain to appreciate it. Brad Wright, the family lawyer had walked in just in time to see Roger fall to the ground. Brad was no 'little grey man' type lawyer. He had graduated a few years earlier top in his class but more importantly at this point, Brad was a good six foot seven with shoulders almost as wide. Brad pushed through the agents swatting them aside like they were fluff on his jacket sleeve.

Brad reached down taking Roger's hand and effortlessly lifted him to his feet. He was no gentle giant. A good looking man, but not one you would feel comfortable meeting in a dark alley. He looked more like a person you would expect to see in the dock than the lawyer trying the case. Ignoring the protests of the agents, Brad pushed Roger toward the door. Roger stumbled, still not knowing what was happening and still battling to catch his breath. Brad turned to face the agents. They stopped dead in their tracks. He held out his hand. "Cards!" he said, daring the agents not to comply. Both handed him their contact details without argument. They both knew they had been caught crossing the line. Brad turned without looking back.

Once outside the building, he softened. "Are you ok?" he asked in a concerned voice which seemed way out of place.

"I'll be ok," Roger replied between gasps.

"Let's sit over here." Brad pointed to a bench. "What have you been up to?" He questioned Roger in a voice which sounded more like he was asking the question. "What the hell have you done to deserve this treatment?"

"It's a long story." Roger leaned forward on the bench still clutching at the painful area between his stomach and his ribs.

"Good! You pay me by the hour. Do you want to go somewhere and give me this story, or would you prefer to do it tomorrow?"

"No! We'll do it now. Here!" Roger was ready to explain the story yet again.

The street noise dimmed as the two men concentrated on the story. Roger spent the next hour relating the finest detail of the story to the lawyer while he took notes. At the end, Brad lifted his eyes from his notes and said, "So why the violence?"

"I have no idea. Maybe I pissed them off or something."

"You must have." He was thoughtful. "So how do you want to proceed?"

"How do you mean?"

"Do you want to lay charges against the agents?"

"As we speak, of course I do. I'm mad as hell, but maybe we should see how the bigamy thing plays out first."

"The two aren't connected ... legally speaking." Brad was still thoughtful and speaking slowly with no emotion, not even looking at Roger as he spoke. "I suppose you're right. You may still have to butt heads with the prosecutor and they're all on the same team. They are out to get you... physically if necessary... with no fear of recriminations. This is a bit worrying."

Roger felt a wave of anxiety course through his body. Something didn't ring right.

"Can I drop you back at your office?" The big man shocked Roger back to reality.

"No! Don't worry. I'll ask Agent McClellan to drop me off."

Brad was dumbfounded. He was fighting for a word, but none came. Roger turned and smiled.

-- o --- oOo --- o --

As Roger walked back in the office, Barbara caught sight of him and looked down at her desk.

"It's ok Barbara, you can look up."

"I'm sorry Mr Macadam, but I couldn't help... I was sitting right..."

"I said it's ok. It doesn't matter what you heard, my wife knows the full story and believe me, if I were doing anything wrong I wouldn't tell her."

She smiled a shy smile, looking a little relieved, but still longing for the story. "So why did they think you were a bigamist?" She couldn't help herself.

"Because I married a young Omani girl on Friday."

Her jaw dropped again. Roger smiled and carried on to his office feeling satisfied.

TUESDAY, 7TH

In the morning Roger was awoken by a loud banging on his front door followed by the door chimes ringing. He stumbled down the stairs and opened the front door. Agents Matthews and McClellan stood at the door. McClellan barged in grabbing Roger by the shoulder, spinning him around and pushing him hard against the open door. Pulling his hands behind him, he cuffed Roger's wrists while Matthews read him his rights.

Roger knew Anne had been awake so he called out. "Honey! Call Brad and tell him to meet me down at the FBI offices."

She rounded the top of the stairs in time to see the back of the agent's foot disappear round the corner. She called out, but Roger was already being walked to the black FBI vehicle. By the time she reached the gaping front door, the car doors were closing and the vehicle was starting up. She watched in disbelief as the vehicle sped away.

She hadn't exactly heard what Roger had said, but she had heard the word Brad and soon pieced the situation together. Anne located Brad's cell number and called.

"Hi Brad! It's Anne Macadam here. The FBI have pitched up and arrested Roger. He asked if you can go to the FBI offices."

"Mrs Macadam. Are you ok?"

"We're fine, but I think you need to go and rescue Roger."

"It'll be ok Mrs Macadam. I'm on my way."

-- o --- oOo --- o --

In the back of the agent's vehicle, Roger found himself detached from the situation and calm. He looked down at the way the morning sunlight glinted off the cuffs on his wrist, then rocked his head back in complete acceptance of what was going on. He closed his eyes as he rested back. Matthews negotiated the traffic in silence, while McClellan sat alongside keeping an unfailing vigil and ensuring that if by some miracle the cuffs dissolved, the car stopped, the door unlocked and he was able to run for it, he would not manage more than three paces before being gunned down.

Although relaxed about his current situation, Roger felt the stab of acidic anxiety in the pit of his stomach when he thought about what was going on around him. He knew, as focused as these agents were in their resolution to bring him in, it was a complete waste of manpower. The agents knew it too. If they had picked up a phone, dialed his number and asked him to come down to the office, he would have been there in a flash. What was the purpose of this aggressive show of power? Which criminals were slipping through the gaps while these agents were bringing him in?

"What the …"

His thoughts were interrupted by Agent Matthews's exclamation and the sudden screeching of tires. Roger was catapulted forward with the seat belt arresting his movement moments, before he was sent crashing into the back of the front passenger seat. His neck jarred as he jerked back into his seat.

Agent Matthews tried again. "What the hell …" He still didn't finish his sentence. Two men sprang from the black sedan which blocked the road. Black suits. Black shades. They could have been from the desks alongside Matthews and McClellan. Matthews jumped out of the vehicle and met the quick moving men between the two cars. An exchange of angry gesticulations took place ending in the new agent flashing his card in Matthews's face. By this time McClellan had lost interest in looking for a reason to put a bullet in his prisoner. He was out of the car and entering the fray.

Roger found the time to laugh at the ridiculous situation. McClellan's door was left open - leaving a getaway possibility for the 'perp'.

"Mind you," he thought out loud. "These guys are pretty pumped. I would be showered in a hail of bullets before I reached the door handle."

Roger watched as Matthews lost his fight. He saw the exact moment when the fight was decided, by an almost imperceptible drop in Agent Matthews's shoulders. He watched the proceedings with interest while the arguing continued on for another four minutes, but Matthews had lost even before he knew it. Now in charge, the new agent finished the direction he'd started toward Roger. He opened the door and reached in with surprisingly strong hands and dragged Roger across the rear seat. Rough, strong hands grappled at the cuffs, removing them and tossing them to McClellan. They were replaced in a flash by the agent's own pair. Once done, he pulled Roger out of the vehicle, the blend of testosterone and adrenalin coursing through the agent's veins helped him to decide to punch Roger in his mid-section in much the same way as McClellan had.

Roger was a little more ready this time. He took the blow in the stomach, but this time it didn't knock the wind out of him. He doubled over and pretended to be hurt. His mind was alert and active. Parts of his brain he didn't even know existed were racing. The agent, satisfied with the result, guided the felon towards his own vehicle. McClellan and Matthews jumped into their car looking disgruntled and sped off spinning the wheels in anger and frustration.

The two agents were smug, pleased with their conquest. The agents didn't say a word to each other, but both were 'basking in their own glory'. Roger was rough-handled into the back of the idling automobile. The first agent, the older of the two, was the one doing the rough handling and the driving. He was a big man and could probably crush skulls in the palm of his hands. He looked more like a cartoon crook than a defender of the peace. Roger could see his scalp through his cropped, light brown hair. His head was perched on massive shoulders. No neck was visible above his jacket collar. He whipped out his phone, unlocking it with five zeros, dialed and just said the words, "Got him," and hung up again. The other agent was seated next to Roger, looking him up and down. The younger man, about thirty-five, was nowhere near as large as the older, but he had a coldness about him which was far more intimidating than the size of the older man.

They pulled out into the road in the opposite direction to the one taken by Agent Matthews. Roger was intrigued. "Where are we …?"

"Shut up! Shut the fuck up." The cold agent waved his handgun in Roger's face and spoke with a shocking fierceness. "You don't talk. You don't say a word." Roger thought it best to comply.

The driver looked back in his rear view mirror and caught Roger's gaze. "You killed his sister. You and your bitch wife."

"What?" The word had barely escaped Roger's lips, when the barrel of the agent's pistol crashed into the side of his head. For a moment he thought he was going to black out. Lights flashed in his eyes and his head hurt like hell. He started to slump to his right. As he rolled forward, through blurred eyes, he could see the driver turning in his seat shouting obscenities at him, but he couldn't hear a word above the wild rushing in his ears. As his eyes closed, he thought he felt his body being thrown about and tossed backward and forward. He felt the agent next to him lunge, crashing into him and pinning his body against the door of the car with a force which made Roger think the door would burst open.

Suddenly there was silence. Blackness. For a moment Roger believed the agent had killed him. Then, as his head started to hurt again, he knew he was alive. Focus! He had to focus. He tried to move, but still found himself pinned to the door by the weight of the agent. He couldn't move.

Roger opened his eyes and pain flashed like strobe lights through his head. As his head started to clear, he could make out the sleeve of the agent's jacket in front of his face. Not gripping him but limp, unmoving. Blood ran down his immobile arm and dripped from the end of the finger. Puzzled, hurting and unable to move, he listened for the sound of movement, breathing. Nothing came. The agent was dead. He didn't know how but he knew it.

They were going for Anne. The agent's words rang through his mind. Roger found a new strength. He shifted the agent, pushing with all he had, his cuffed hands grappling for the door handle. The door popped open and Roger made an ungainly exit, his body sprawling out of the vehicle, leaving his trapped feet to be wriggled out one by one.

Looking back at the vehicle he could see both agents lying motionless, bloodied and crushed. He looked up at the face of the driver of the truck which had ploughed into the side of the vehicle. The numb horror on his face told the story of what had happened. The agents had jumped a light while concentrating on Roger and had paid the price.

Roger looked around at the pedestrians and they were all looking back at him. They were stunned at the horror of the scene. The truck driver sat motionless in his cab. He needed to act quickly. People had already started to move in. Maybe nobody had noticed he was cuffed. He felt frantically about the body of the agent and soon found the keys. Against the odds, he picked the correct key first time but still fumbled, trying to loosen the cuffs. An eternity passed before the clasp slid open and he was free.

He glanced around, like a wild cat trapped in a circle of dogs. The onlookers were closing in. What if he was tackled? He needed to get to Anne before the agents did. The dead agent's weapon lay on the floor, dislodged from his grip by the impact. It was imploring him to pick it up. He looked around again. One man had broken into a run. Roger reached down, picked up the heavy weapon and stood up. Without his having to raise the barrel, every person stopped in their tracks. A glance at the truck driver showed the horror was gone, replaced by fear.

It was a mistake to pick up the gun and he knew it. Somehow Roger was aware this was a pivotal moment in his life.

This mild-mannered mechanic in an instant, became an object of fear. They had all seen the cuffs and now they saw the gun.

"Stay back!" he called out using his best tough-guy voice. What the voice lacked, the handgun made up for. Nobody was going to venture closer. Roger pushed back into the car. Finding the driver's mobile phone, he slid it into his pocket and then turned and looked around. A small, old, red and rusted Austin Mini stood empty behind the black Ford. It was dwarfed by the black car and looked out of place, like it had driven in from the 1970s. The driver had seen the accident and climbed out only to freeze on seeing this 'felon' with a gun in his hand. A baby-seat in the back was occupied by a sleeping toddler.

"Whose car?" Roger said looking around at the crowd and pointing at the vehicle. The fierce abruptness in his voice shocked even him.

A young woman shrieked. "No! Please! My baby is in there."

Roger looked at the car and noticed the gun in his hand pointing at the car. He lowered the weapon. Calming down a bit, he gestured to the girl to come closer. "I'm not going to hurt you or your baby, I only need a lift home, nothing more. It's a short distance away."

"Take it! Take the car! Don't take my baby." The girl was hysterical. "Please!" She was crying.

"Don't be silly! How will you get home?" Roger didn't stop to think how stupid he was sounding. He didn't register he wasn't asking for a lift, he was hijacking a woman and her baby. "All I want is a lift home. I'm not a killer and I won't hurt you or your baby. I was arrested for bigamy not murder." All of a sudden bigamy sounded like a walk in the park. It's ok! I'm 'just' a bigamist. A wry smile crept across his face. Calmly and with purpose he spoke to the girl. "Please will you give me a lift home?"

The young girl was traumatized and sobbing uncontrollably. She edged toward her driver's side door, too terrified to move in a way that might be misconstrued. She stretched out her hand slowly toward her door like she was expecting a shock from the handle. She hadn't taken her eyes from his all the way. Roger made his way to the passenger seat. As she opened her door she spoke to Roger. "Please don't hurt my baby."

Roger felt for her. "I'm not going to hurt your baby. As soon as we are on our way I'll unload the gun. Will you be happier then?"

She didn't believe him. "Please don't hurt my baby."

True to his word, as soon as they were mobile and beyond the possibility of somebody being heroic, Roger loosened the clip from the hand gun and threw it down onto the floor between his feet. "See! Nobody's getting shot today." Roger laid his head back, folded his arms and closed his eyes. He started to digest what was happening. Less than a week ago he was a respected engineer. Now he was a bigamist, a hijacker and a criminal on the run.

He felt the vehicle slow and opened his eyes. "What's wrong? Why are we stopping?" Turning to her, he looked straight down the barrel of a tiny hand gun. A shiny little ladies handbag gun which looked like it couldn't hurt a fly. He knew otherwise.

"Out of my car," she said in a controlled and unnerving voice. Her voice was controlled, but her hand was still shaking.

Roger sat still, looking past the gun as if it wasn't there. "If you are going to shoot, then be sure you hit me in the temple and pray I don't have a finger twitch when I die. Maybe I won't pull the trigger."

She looked down, horrified to see the gun under Roger's arm pointing at the back seat somewhere in the region of the child. She stiffened. "You don't have bullets. I saw you throw them down."

"I threw down the magazine. There is still one in the chamber. Do you think I'm stupid?" Roger hated himself. He had become a criminal in every way. "Reach around and drop the gun on the floor behind you and drive. We have less than a mile to go and you'll never see me again." Roger's voice was earnest even if a little cold. "Your youngster will still be sleeping and you can be on your way. I told you I wouldn't harm you or your child." He stopped himself short of saying "Don't make me change my mind." The young girl's face drained white. He hated himself even more.

"What's your name Honey?" He tried to sound authoritative. She hesitated. "Your first name, I don't want to hunt you down or anything."

"Lorraine."

"Hello Lorraine. My name is Roger Macadam. I don't have time to tell you the whole story and you probably wouldn't believe me anyway. But please believe me, you and your child are in no danger."

Lorraine still didn't believe Roger. She drove on in silence. Terrified.

"Oh hell! I can't believe what I have become. Drop me over here Lorraine. You don't need any more distress."

The girl didn't need to be asked twice. A quick check for vehicles behind and a stop just short of Roger having to extricate himself from the glove compartment.

"You'll almost certainly be asked about this by the police," he said, starting to reach for the bullets by his feet. She stiffened. "Relax!" he said. He slid open the weapon revealing the empty chamber. "See! Nothing!"

"I'll keep these," he said holding up the small metallic case of death-dealing lead projectiles, "but I want to leave the gun with you. Please give it to the police when they come to question you." She sat motionless while he opened her gun and emptied the shells onto the floor. All she wanted was for this person to leave her car.

"Thank you Lorraine and I'm sorry to have done this to you." She turned her head and glared at Roger with as much hatred as anybody could deliver in one glare.

There was a brief silence as Roger contemplated saying something, but he punched down his half-closed fists onto his knees. He said goodbye and climbed out. He exited and moved behind the vehicle in case the girl decided to try to run him down or something. She didn't. She pulled away before he'd reached the back wheel.

Roger left the main road and headed down a side road on the way home. It was a bit further, but he didn't want to attract attention. He felt sure people were looking at him, but nobody could know of the arrest yet. He only had a couple of hundred yards to go. He walked at a brisk pace, but was sure not to attract attention by running. Even at a brisk pace it was hard to be nonchalant. Still he felt people were staring at him as he walked.

As he passed a parked vehicle, he glanced at his short, stumpy reflection in the curved glass of the parked Toyota. He gasped in an instant of heart-stopping horror. He looked around in panic as eyes glared at him from all angles. Looking back in disbelief, Roger adjusted his position trying to see a clearer picture. A look in the side mirror backed up what he already knew. The side of his head, neck and shoulder, were covered in blood. Roger put his fingers to the side of his head where he felt his short hair matted in congealed red gel. If Roger had been given the chance to have breakfast, it would have hit the sidewalk. He felt around in the mess for wounds, but soon realized this was the agent's blood. He stumbled on as he tried to straighten his thoughts. So much for trying to look inconspicuous. He looked like something out of the The Texas Chainsaw Massacre.

An onlooker stepped up, about to query his wellness, but Roger brushed him off. "I'm fine. Really. You should see the other guy." He pushed on not looking back. No longer worried about looking inconspicuous, he broke into a gentle jog. After looking around for any sign of anybody staking out his house, he went inside.

The house was in silence. "Anybody home?" he called out.

"Hello!" The answer from the top of the stairs. He knew it was Atifah. She met him at the top of the staircase dressed in her loose fitting, full, body-covering abaya. At this point she was not wearing the scarf. When she saw him covered in blood she let out a gasp. For a second it looked like she might faint, but she steadied herself on the handrail.

"Your face! What is wrong?" Horror was etched across her brow as she looked at Roger's bloodied face. Roger couldn't stop to examine the situation.

"Where's Anne and Katie?" he demanded as he headed toward the shower.

"They left," she said. "To town to find you." She was still looking at the sight of a dishevelled Roger becoming more flustered at what she saw.

"Did they say how long they would be?" He was reaching for the telephone and started dialing Anne's mobile. As usual, when you have a real need to speak to somebody, the cellular industry lets you down. As communication methods go, the mobile was not Roger's favorite.

"No! Only that they were going to the FBI offices with your lawyer."

Roger's mind was in turmoil. So much so, he didn't initially realize Atifah was talking in perfect, unbroken English. He turned and was startled by her closeness. She had followed him into the bathroom and was standing a short distance from him. Although he still hadn't noticed the absent accent, he knew something wasn't right. He tilted his head as if deep in thought, but his thinking was incoherent. She had a towel in her hand and reached out to dab the blood from his head.

"No! I'm fine. I'm going to have a shower. I'm not hurt."

"What happened? How did…"

"I was involved in a car wreck. This is somebody else's." He pointed to the mess on the side of his head.

She stood.

"Can I shower?" he said, starting to lose his patience a little.

"I'm sorry!" She looked down embarrassed and backed out of the doorway.

"Is your outfit compulsory?" Roger waited for a response, but she simply looked back, perplexed.

"Your burkha. Is it compulsory or can you dress Westernized to go out?"

She didn't feel the need to correct him on what she was wearing. "It is personal preference. Qaboos suggested I wear it at all public gatherings. He wanted to ensure I could move around with a degree of anonymity when I'm not wearing it."

"Can you change into denims or something? Something Western-looking. We're going to take a ride and I need us to be as unnoticeable as possible. If you need clothes, take something from Katie's closet."

"I have other clothes. I'll be in my room." Her accent had returned a little. She bit her lip and glanced up at Roger. Too late! It suddenly dawned on him that the shock of seeing him covered in blood made her lose concentration and she had failed to maintain her facade.

Roger climbed into the shower and started the water. He adjusted the temperature, then leaned onto the wall and watched as the red liquid washed off his body, streaming down the drain in the corner of the shower floor. His thoughts were far away, thinking through the crash and what the agents had said to him. They must have been mistaken. How could he and Anne be responsible for the agent's sister's death? There must be a misunderstanding. Coming back to the present and realizing he was watching blood run off his body, he grabbed the soap and started scrubbing his hair, face and body.

Once he was convinced he was clean, he relaxed a little and once again started digesting the events of the morning. His mind slowly worked its way round to the point where Atifah had spoken in perfect English. He turned off the water and slid open the glass shower door. He paused, deep in thought, before exiting the shower cubicle and drying off. He wrapped the towel round his waist and tried the phone again. It was still busy, unavailable or whatever else that stupid sound was supposed to mean. He grunted and slammed the handset down. He puzzled again over the short conversation before the crash, but it made no sense. If somebody believed he'd been responsible for a death, it answered the question as to why he'd been 'stolen' from Matthews and McClellan and treated to such violence. In a strange way Roger found this little excursion from daily life a little exciting and far less scary than the old Roger would have found it.

He knew he was now 'on the run'. It wouldn't be too long before the FBI dropped round for a visit. He needed to speak to Anne urgently. He couldn't be at the house when the FBI arrived. He called Atifah who came down the steps wearing long denim pants and a long sleeved tee. Her hair was tied back and covered with a bandana. She was looking nervous. She knew she had been caught out and was expecting a confrontation from Roger. It surprised her when it didn't come.

"Do you have the phone Qaboos gave you?"

"It's in my room."

"Bring it and bring a change of clothes too," he said heading for the door. "And hurry. We need to leave now." He was more abrupt than he should have been.

Atifah retrieved the phone from her room, along with a change of clothes and her toiletries. She walked outside to find Roger had already backed his SUV out of the garage. He leaned over and opened the door to allow her to climb into the vehicle. She looked at Roger, trying to glean as much information about his mood as possible, while she adjusted her safety belt in a tense silence. Roger started reversing into the street, but then stopped. They will be looking for his vehicle, especially after they visit his house and find the vehicle missing. The neighbor's Mercedes was parked in his driveway. There was no sign of the neighbor. Roger reached across and took a small toolkit from the glove compartment. Taking a screwdriver with him, he slipped out of his vehicle and removed both licence plates.

A quick check up and down the street to see whether anybody was looking and he set off in stealth mode, keeping below the line of sight of the neighbor and running as silently as possible. Of course, if the neighbor had looked out of his window he would have seen Roger, but for the time being Roger had luck on his side. He removed the neighbor's plates and replaced them with his own and then, getting back to his vehicle, attached his new plates. Roger justified this in his mind, knowing it was a temporary trade. He needed to let Anne know what was going on. He needed to let her know she was also being hunted. He reversed out and pulled off into the street.

They travelled in silence. KIKK radio was playing as they approached the city. Roger preferred to listen to the news, rather than music. He wasn't listening at this point, he had too much on his mind, but a news report attracted his full attention. He adjusted the volume and listened, stunned as the news report unfolded.

"… drama today as a prisoner made a daring escape from custody by hijacking a woman and her infant at gun point. The carjacker allegedly took the agents' firearms as they bled to death in their vehicle. He then used the firearm to threaten the life of a passerby and her child in a daring hijacking. Lorraine Peters had this to say."

"… He pointed the gun at my son. I was so scared. He was cold. His eyes were dead, like he had no feelings at all."

"We don't yet know what the prisoner was wanted for, but rest assured, this reporter will keep you updated as we learn more. Back to you in the studio."

Roger had failed to breathe while he was listening to the report and he gasped as his peripheral vision started to fade to black.

Roger now knew he was unable to walk into the FBI offices looking for his wife. He would be arrested long before he saw her. He couldn't go home either. He was sure they would be there waiting for him. Roger would hand himself over once he had spoken to his wife. This was a big misunderstanding. He wanted to clear his name. He needed to ensure Anne was not caught up in this.

Roger stopped at a convenience store and bought five cheap prepaid cell phones. The senate was looking to control prepaid phones and he felt sure he was about to help the decision, but for the moment he would use these phones to keep in contact. He fired up the first phone. "Just in case," he thought. In case of what, he wasn't sure.

Roger pulled off the road into a multilevel parking garage. He took his ticket and drove up to the second floor where he found an empty bay and stopped. He took his phone from his pocket and tried again to dial Anne. This time he couldn't find a good signal.

"I hate these phones," he mumbled, more to himself than anything else. "Come! Let's take a walk."

-- o --- oOo --- o --

Down at the FBI office, Anne was still doing the bureau dance. She had been moved from one person to another and still had not managed to find anybody who knew her husband. Katie trailed behind as her mother who strutted from person to person. She approached yet another doorway and tapped on the door.

"Come in!"

They opened the door and entered.

"Hi!" Anne smiled but only on the outside. "I was given your name by somebody downstairs. They said you might know where my husband is …" She looked down at the name plate on the desk "… Umm! Mr Matthews."

"Who might your husband be Mrs …" He waited for a response.

"Macadam. I'm looking for Roger Macadam."

"Ah! Mrs Macadam." He sat back in his chair. "I am filling out my report about your husband. Why don't you take a seat?"

"At last, somebody who knows something." A wave of relief swept over her. She had told Brad to meet her at the FBI headquarters. Her phone sprang into life. She waved her phone at the agent. "Do you mind if I take this?"

"Carry on!" he said, but she could see he was a little annoyed.

"Hi Brad!" A pause … "we're on the fourth floor, room 414." She spun around to check the number on the door. Another pause and then - "Ok! We'll see you shortly."

"My lawyer." She spoke as if she were introducing him.

"You'd like to wait for him?"

"Might as well. He won't take long."

"Would you like coffee?" he asked. She shook her head. Katie, standing behind, shook her head as well. The agent stood and poured himself a cup. He sat down as Brad's frame filled the entire doorway. He ducked his head as he came in through the door.

"Agent Matthews! We meet again. You'll be happy to know my client will not be pressing charges at this point. However, your conduct has been …"

"Sit down … can I call you Brad?"

80

Brad sat, nodding confirmation.

"I don't know the full story yet, but your client and your husband ma'am…," he nodded in Anne's direction, "… is in a lot of trouble."

Anne sat forward in her chair. "I would hardly call an accidental, bigamous marriage a lot of trouble. I'm sure given enough time he would …"

"Mrs Macadam." The look on the agent's face meant business and Anne stopped talking. "I was assigned to bring Mr Macadam in based on the charge of bigamy. I thought it was not necessary as he had shown no flight risk, but we have to follow orders." Agent Matthews sat on the corner of his desk and took a sip of his coffee. Brad and Anne looked on expectantly. "On the way over here I was stopped and had to hand your husband over to a couple of special agents from Homeland Security."

"What are you talking about?" Brad stood up.

"Sit Mr Wright! We're not at the bad part yet."

"Is this handover allowed?" Anne interjected at the same moment Katie spoke.

"Is Daddy ok?"

"Yes it is!" Agent Matthews said to Anne ignoring Katie's question. He held up his hands pleading for a pause in the questions. He continued. "The agents had the proper authority and all the paperwork was in order."

"Where is Roger now?" Anne was starting to worry.

"I'm not altogether sure, but I will find out."

"The bad part?" Brad's voice was insistent and his demeanor a little scary.

"Homeland Security is a free department. They're not constrained like the rest of us. If Homeland wants to arrest without a warrant, they can. Congress has given them free reign in the name of national security. The agents cited national security for the change in orders."

"National security? For bigamy?" Anne couldn't hide her frustration. "It's not even bigamy. Believe me! I would hand him over myself if I thought …"

"Calm down Mrs Macadam. I said I don't know the full story yet, but I will find out."

"Tony. A moment." Agent McClellan had stuck his head in the door.

"Excuse me!" Matthews nodded to his guests and left the room.

"What's going on Brad?" Anne was tense and held her head in her hands.

"I don't know. There was something about this case from the beginning. The Feds were taking way too much interest considering the facts. Wait here, I want answers." Brad left the room.

As he rounded the corner the agents stopped talking and spun around to face the big lawyer. "What's going on guys?"

"Mr Wright. Please wait for me. I will be with you in a moment." Brad backed off sensing the tension between the agents.

Brad re-entered the small office and sat down. Matthews followed closely behind. Circling around, he sat down again on the corner of his desk. "Mrs Macadam. Your husband was in a lot of trouble," He emphasized the 'was'. "But now, to put it bluntly, now he's in a shit-load of trouble."

If the agent paused for effect, it worked. Both Brad and Anne were fixed, waiting for the next words. "Mr Macadam is on the run. He is classified as armed and dangerous."

"What the hell are you talking about?" Brad was on his feet. "Roger is not a dangerous person. You need to retract that classification immediately, before somebody gets hurt."

Anne stood looking up at Brad. "What does this mean?"

Brad wasn't listening to Anne. "If anything comes of this heads will roll." Anne was in a daze. She looked from one man to the other. Brad continued. "How did this happen. For goodness sake the guy is an engineer, not Rambo."

"The Homeland Security vehicle was involved in an accident. Both agents were killed. Mr Macadam lifted the agent's weapons, hijacked a passerby and escaped."

"Hijacked? That's not Roger." Anne sat again. "He's never even shot a gun. He hates guns."

"Matthews! Are you sure you have your facts straight?" Brad quizzed the agent. "No mistakes?"

"No mistakes. I'm sorry. I wish I could tell you more, but for the time being you know as much as I do." He turned around and sat down on his chair. "Mrs Macadam, I cannot overemphasize how urgent it is for Mr Macadam to hand himself over to authorities. He has been labeled as armed and dangerous. It's not good news, especially if he doesn't know how to handle himself. Within a few hours, every cop in Texas will be on the lookout for him and you know we have trigger-happy cops down here."

"There's been a mistake Mr Matthews." Anne spoke quietly and with purpose, pleading for common sense. "My husband is not armed and dangerous."

"Then have him come in Mrs Macadam. Once he's here, everyone will know he's not armed and dangerous."

-- o --- o0o --- o --

Back at the parking, Roger and Atifah walked side by side. He thought a walk to the top floor would allow them time to talk and see a signal on his phone at the same time.

"So! What's the story Atifah? You could hardly speak English on the plane, but now you are fluent? I think you may even have a slight British accent there if I'm not mistaken."

"You're right. I was schooled in the UK and I read my degree at Oxford." Atifah's head was down like a child, caught cheating in an exam.

"Why the lies then? What were you hoping to achieve by …" He trailed off but she knew where he was going.

"I don't know." She kept looking down ahead of her as she walked. "Qaboos wanted me to be sure you thought I couldn't understand any English." She was thoughtful. "He didn't want you to say no. He didn't tell me when I should drop the charade."

"But why?"

"I don't know. He didn't tell me the whole story, but he must have thought I was in danger to take such drastic action. Maybe he wanted me to leave under a different name."

"There must have been an easier and less permanent method of hiding you than … are we even married?"

Atifah hung her head. "I don't know. It is not permissible under Islamic law for a woman to marry a non-Muslim man. Nor is it allowed to trick somebody into marriage."

"So we're not married."

"I don't know," she repeated. "It is also not permissible for me to be alone with you if we are not married. The ceremony was correct to the best of my knowledge, but I don't know what our status is. Either way it looks bad for me. Qaboos must have had a strong fear to take such drastic action."

"Are you able to return home, ever?"

"I think so. Why?"

"At the airport Hussein told me you would be stoned to death if you returned."

Atifah laughed a shallow laugh keeping her eyes down. "I think he said that for your benefit. I have heard of it happening in other countries, but I don't believe it has been done in Oman for many, many years."

"Why would you agree to such an arrangement? You are young and beautiful. You could have anybody you want." She glanced sideways at Roger for the first time, since they had left the house. "Surely you must have known this marriage could never be a permanent thing."

"For one thing I didn't know you weren't Muslim. Besides, Qaboos said it would be best for me. I gather he couldn't trust anybody until you came along." They walked a few more paces as they both took in the enormity of the situation. "A few days before the wedding Qaboos ordered I be moved to the palace with him and I was forbidden from leaving. I don't know why."

"To protect you?"

"It must be. Reading between the lines, I thought maybe I had been threatened, but Qaboos was never one to burden others with his problems."

"Maybe it was the same crowd that tried to take him out in the streets of Muscat." Roger was thinking back to the start of this episode. "So it explains why he wouldn't tell me about this until we were at the airport."

Roger felt as though things were starting to fall into place. These last few days had been the craziest he had ever known. Once on the roof he checked for signal on his phone and tried again to dial Anne. To his amazement, the phone started to ring.

"Anne! Where the hell are you?" Roger was happy to hear her voice on the other end.

"Roger! What's going on?"

"It's a long story. Where are you?"

"I'm at the FBI offices with Brad. Honey! You have to come and give yourself up. They think you are armed and ..."

"Honey ... Honey!" Roger needed her to listen. "Listen to me Honey! You need to talk to Brad privately. I think the Feds are after you too. One of those agents said you and I had killed his sister."

"That's crazy! Where are you now?" The situation started to sink in and she became decidedly worried.

"Can I speak to Brad?"

"Sure! Honey, be careful."

"I always am, Beautiful. Love you!" Roger longed to see his lady, but he had resigned himself to the fact that he wouldn't see her for a while. This scared him a little. He tried to sound upbeat anyway.

Anne passed the mobile to Brad. "He wants to speak to you."

Matthews interrupted. "You seriously need to tell Mr Macadam to hand himself in. His picture is going to be all over the place in a short while."

Brad paused as he took in the agent's words and then put the phone to his ear. "Hi Mr Macadam."

"Hi Brad! Is Matthews with you?"

"Yes!"

"Ok! Then it hasn't filtered through to his department yet."

"What?"

"I was handed over to …"

"I know! Homeland Security!" Brad saved him the story.

"Ok! I didn't know who." He paused a moment then continued. "Shortly before the accident one of them mentioned that Anne and I were responsible for his sister's death. I have no clue what he was talking about and a small truck made sure I didn't find out. You need to protect her at all costs. Do you understand?"

"Sure Mr Macadam. They're a tough nut to crack though. They have free reign and do as they please."

"So I've heard! Look after her Brad. I'm counting on you. Whatever the cost!"

"Music to my ears!"

"Shut up and let me speak to Anne again."

"Hi Love!" He was missing her even though he had seen her only a few hours ago. "Listen! I have been home and I have Atifah with me. I have taken money from the dresser. I need to find out why Homeland Security is after you. If I hand myself over I won't be able to find out."

"Roger! They're saying you are armed and dangerous. You have to hand yourself in or you'll be hurt - or worse!"

85

"I can't do that, Honey! I would have been happy to until they implicated you. I will be calling them as soon as I have finished speaking to you. When I have answers. I will hand myself in – no problem."

"Roger! Be careful."

"Careful is my middle name Honey. As soon as I have answers they can come and pick me up. I will then call Brad and we can put this stupid episode behind us."

As soon as he hung up, he dialed Mike. "Mike!"

"Rog! What the hell is going on? I was listening to your story on the radio. Hijacking?"

"Mike. I have no idea what is going on. I am now being chased down by Homeland Security. All this for bigamy sounds suspect to me."

Mike laughed. "My buddy the hunted man."

"I don't know where this will end up. I need you to do something for me."

"If you don't make it you want me to marry and take care of Anne?" Mike took nothing seriously.

"Mike … focus! I think I am in deep trouble here and I need your help."

"Sorry Bud! What's the problem?"

"The Homeland Security agent mentioned that Anne and I had killed his sister. I don't know what is going on, but these guys were not playing games. If they catch me I'll be taken off to who knows where and held without trial."

"They can't do that?" Mike was shocked at the stress in his friend's voice.

"Yes they can. They can do it in the name of national security. They can do what they want."

"National Security?"

"I don't know Bud! Homeland Security don't mess around with bigamy cases. These are the big guns. If I am not caught or dead in a few hours, they will be tapping Anne's phone, your phone, and everybody I know. Once they cast the net I don't know what will happen."

"Rog! I'll do anything. How can I help?"

"I'm going to wait it out a little before handing myself in. Only 'til I know what I am dealing with. I need a contact Mike and you're it."

"Ok! I think!" Mike was a little puzzled. He could contact him any time.

"I don't think there has been time to set up tracing yet, so I'm going to text you from another number with an arbitrary message from an ex-lover or something. You'll know it's from me. Don't use voice, only text. Don't use my name, or any other name we know. Try to keep it looking innocent, but I need you to stay in touch."

"Sure pal! Do you think it's necessary?"

"I hope not. I don't know what's going on, but this little bigamy issue just became bigger."

"So it's bigger than bigamy?"

"I guess so! This is real cloak and dagger stuff. Oh! And also I want you to take Anne and Katie to your place and look after them for a bit."

"No problem. I'll go there right now."

The two said their goodbyes and hung up. Roger turned to Atifah. "Right! Let's move out of here." The two headed toward the steps and back to the parked vehicle. "We're going to find somewhere to stay tonight. I don't think I can go home."

Back in the vehicle, Roger switched on the ignition as the following words were being spoken. " ... on the run with his second wife, apparently related to the Sultan of Oman. Both are alleged to be involved with the Omani branch of Al-Qaeda, but their level of involvement with the September-Eleven attack has not yet been established." The words faded to insignificance as Roger turned in disbelief to Atifah. His mouth hung open while he scanned her face for the slightest sign this might be the truth.

She understood the situation perfectly. "It's not true! I don't even think Oman has a branch of Al-Qaeda. It's not true Roger. I give you my word. In Oman, the authorities arrest and hand over Al-Qaeda people."

Roger sat in thoughtful silence for a long tense moment and then he spoke slowly. "They weren't talking about Anne, they were talking about you. Is this why you had to escape Oman?"

"No!" She was adamant. "It's not true. I would never..." She cut off her sentence sharply, angry at Roger's insinuation. He hadn't seen this much emotion from Atifah. He realize he'd hit a nerve. He knew she was telling the truth.

"Ok!" He spoke softly trying to calm the tension. "Ok! Let's go for a drive and find somewhere to stay tonight." They moved off in a strained silence.

After killing time for a few hours, Roger headed out of town toward the Bear Creek golf course. Although he had never stayed in any of the hotels in Houston, he knew which ones had a good reputation. The La Lucia was a quaint hotel on this road and he knew the hotel had internet access. He pulled into the parking lot and parked the vehicle centrally to reduce the chances of standing out, either from the road, or from the lobby. He instructed Atifah to go ahead and book in as Mr and Mrs Costopoulos. The Greek name would allow for Atifah's Mediterranean look. He would follow later and go straight up to the room. He would wait a while until the night staff came onto shift.

He gave Atifah cash so she would not be required to present identity documents or swipe credit cards. In the meantime, Roger headed back toward town. He selected a dingy downtown motel and checked around the building for all the vantage points. Then, after checking for a secure point across the street, he walked in casually and booked a room for the two of them. He swiped his card, made an excuse for having to leave and walked out across the busy street to a diner a short way off. He settled into the padded chair to watch the front of the motel.

"Coffee … please." He assumed the thickset waitress's blank stare was a question. Her expression changed from blank to frustration when he actually wanted something. She turned on her heel and headed behind the counter where, after a few moments, she emerged carrying his large cup of thick black poison which after tasting, wasn't as bad as it looked.

Roger thanked the girl and settled back in his chair to drink his coffee. After about an hour and a half, Roger decided these guys were not as good as in the movies. He drained the dregs of his second cup, swallowing the bitter liquid. He stood and dropped the cash to cover the coffee plus the statutory fifteen percent then, after a moment's thought, dropped an extra dime for the bubbly personality. He headed for the door and stepped onto the street, pausing to adjust his eyes to the fading light. As he did so, a movement from the motel caught his attention. Nothing glaring and nothing he could immediately see, but something wasn't right.

He stepped forward and headed toward his vehicle parked about three blocks away. He paused and looked back as three dark suited men entered the motel. The urge to look and see if they had come for him was soon overcome by the urge to drive away fast. Now he knew the government was serious and he was being watched.

-- o --- oOo --- o --

"You need to come one hundred percent clean with me now." He signalled for Atifah to sit on the comfortable looking hotel bed. He spun the chair around and sat looking into the face of the young girl. The anger had passed and the vulnerability was back.

"I understand why you thought the way you did, but other than pretending not to understand English I haven't lied to you in any way." She looked down at her hands turned palm downward on her jeans.

"I believe you." Roger was genuine. "A few days ago I might not have believed you, but today I do. There is something strange going on. While I was out I did a test. I used my credit card then sat back and watched. They were on me ... us, in about an hour and a half." He paused deep in thought, blank and emotionless. "We are being watched and they are out to catch us. We are wanted people and they believe we are armed and dangerous. Do you understand what it means?"

"Of course! We have movies in Oman." Atifah was also blank and emotionless as she spoke, numbed by the prospect of what might lay ahead. They were both searching their minds for a clue as to what was happening. They found nothing.

"I need you to contact Qaboos and find out what's going on." She reached for her bag and the Omani phone. "Not now! Wait 'til tomorrow when we're on the road. I have no idea whether they can trace the call. I don't know what they're capable of. Only what I have seen in the movies. We have to stay as invisible as we can."

"Do you think they know this number?"

"I don't know what they know." He stood up. "I'm sure if it was me I'd have a list of all the phones of Omani origin in the country, or I'd be watching the calls going out to Oman. Remember, you have to set up international roaming, so they can easily find out Omani numbers. Maybe you should switch your phone off and remove the battery while we're not moving." He paused while Atifah stripped the phone of its power source. "What I do know is they followed my credit card. I also know we need answers." He

89

pushed the chair back under the desk and crossed the small space to settle in the arm chair in the corner. "We'd better get some sleep. I think we have busy and difficult times ahead."

"Are you going to be alright in the chair?" She was concerned for him. He thought it was sweet.

"I'll be fine," he grinned a broad grin at the girl. "I'm a tough engineer."

She looked at the slightly built 'old' man and grinned back, thinking he didn't look at all tough.

As Roger settled he felt in his pocket. He still had the phone he had taken from the agent. He panicked. What if it contained a tracking device? He whipped through the menu options on the phone to set a new PIN. When he was prompted for the old PIN, he remembered back to the five zeros the agent had used to unlock it and he tried. The phone prompted for the new pin. Roger smiled as he cancelled the process. He wondered if the agent's login to his online banking would have the same password. Katie would have been proud of her mobile-literate father. He switched it off and removed the battery. He soon fell asleep.

WEDNESDAY, 8TH

Roger was up early and on the internet using a PC in the lounge area of the hotel. His first stop was Google. Roger had heard of various sections of the government using non-traceable phones. Since he didn't know about this, he entered the search 'non-traceable cell phones'. To his amazement, he quickly learned that non-trace-ability was not only possible, but readily available.

He read the words of an article suggesting you can pull out the battery to render it non-traceable between calls. He gave himself a mental pat on the back. The chances were they didn't know he had it anyway.

He arrived back at the room to find Atifah up and around. She smiled as he opened the door.

"Good morning!" he said as he caught her radiant smile. He shut the door behind him and came inside. "You're awake early again. Praying?"

"'Morning!" She seemed relieved to see him. Roger had left before she'd woken up. "Islam dictates we must pray five times a day. One of those prayers, fajr, must occur near the dawn so we always wake early."

Roger closed the drapes after Atifah had opened them. He switched on a lamp in the darkened room and looked for the TV remote. Roger had never been one to watch TV in the morning and he had always given Katie strict instructions about what watching TV does to your brain. "There is no place for TV in the morning," he had always preached. "It's not good for a family to have one member sitting and watching TV." She had never known any different. "I want to watch the news." He justified the TV more to himself than to Atifah.

There was a knock at the door. The two froze. Roger pressed his finger to his lips telling her to keep quiet. "Who is it?" he called out in mock sleepiness which he had to admit, wasn't too bad.

"Room service Mr Costopoulos. Mrs Costopoulos ordered breakfast in your room."

"Hold on!" He gestured for Atifah to go to the door. After all, she had booked in and there seemed little advantage to the staff seeing him at this point. He took off the shirt he was wearing and threw it on the end of the bed and as she climbed out, he climbed in and covered up to his neck making a single blanket shuffling sound. "Clever!" he thought to himself.

She darted for the small bathroom and wrapping a towel around her head turban style, opened the door and let the young man into the room. The trolley was pushed to the end of the bed. He looked to head toward the drapes but Atifah stopped him. "I'll open them. Don't worry."

The attendant thanked her as she pushed a note into his palm, one she had extracted from Roger's wallet on the desk.

"Thanks Ma'am," the young man said, as he left the room. Roger laughed inside when he thought of the man, probably her age, calling her Ma'am.

"Thanks. You were great!" he said as she pushed the trolley alongside the bed. "Ma'am. What's with the towel?" Roger enquired.

"Islam is very strict on awrah. There are rules about what women and men for that matter, may show." She sat next to Roger, blocking him from getting out of bed and passed him the various items from the breakfast tray. "Awrah, the part we may not display to anybody but our husbands."

"Thanks again," he said, suddenly remembering this girl was possibly married to him.

Roger had always served the women in his life as best he could. He found it enjoyable to prepare breakfast for Anne and Katie, even though neither of them expected it from him. This felt different. It seemed as though Atifah wanted to serve Roger in the same way.

"Can you eat all of this?" He waved his hand over the tray. "How will you know if it is halal?"

"It isn't," she smiled as she spoke. "Bacon cannot be halal. The correct term is zabiha. A large number of Muslims do insist on meat slaughtered by Muslims, but many of us are happy to eat meat slaughtered by people of the book."

"The book?"

"Yes. Jews and Christians."

"So you don't insist on halal or zabiha food."

"No. My family do, but I spent ten years in London. I cannot eat pork though and I would always choose to eat zabiha if the choice was available."

"Come and sit in bed," he said pointing to her side of the bed. She looked at Roger with a hint of puzzled bewilderment in her eyes. "God! I'm sorry! I didn't mean …" He broke off his sentence not wanting to go any further. "I meant I would pass you your breakfast." He felt awkward and not unlike a teenager caught with a Playboy. Atifah realize he'd seen the uncertainty in her eyes. She stood purposefully, walked around the bed and sat down next to Roger demonstrating her complete trust in him.

They ate in silence while Roger passed her the various breakfast items. He spread the jelly on his toast, then placed it on the tray. He had to break the silence. "All right!" he said in an abrupt voice, shattering the silence. He hadn't meant it to sound as fierce, it seemed to slip out without his control. He softened his voice. "I have a lot of faults, but please don't ever think of me as some kind of pervert. I'm not." His mind wandered briefly to his occasional thoughts of the last few days. "At least I don't think I am."

She laughed a small forced laugh. "I didn't see a pervert." She paused almost wanting to leave the sentence there but then added, "I saw a caring husband."

Roger sat for a while in stunned, sobering silence. This felt more awkward than being a pervert.

After they had eaten the two sat in virtual silence, neither wanting to move and give the impression they were trying to escape the awkwardness of the situation. Eventually, Atifah made the first move and excusing herself, retreated to the sanctuary of the bathroom. As the door clicked closed Roger relaxed, glad the tension was over for a while.

There was no news, so he clicked through the channels until he found CNN. Within seconds of locating the channel, he heard the anchor announcing the headlines. He reached for the remote again.

"In your headlines. The Houston man, on the run from the police for his alleged involvement in 9/11, is believed to have killed a desk clerk at a Houston motel last night. We cross to Elaine Hodges on the scene."

"What the hell…" Roger's jaw hung open in disbelief.

"Thanks Ken." The image on the screen behind Elaine showed the motel, pretty much from the angle Roger had sat watching it last night. Elaine was a thirty plus reporter. She was petite with blond hair and a pretty but angular face, not unlike a cartoon mouse, but hardened from long hours, hard work and ten odd years of smoking. "Last night this motel was the scene of a tragic horror. Roger Macadam, currently being sought by the FBI for his alleged involvement in the 9/11 attack, booked in to stay the night. It is alleged he shot the desk clerk in the back of the head execution style. The motive for the murder is unknown.

"Police are still waiting for ballistics test results to confirm this was the same weapon taken from the dead bodies of security agents who were transporting Macadam at the time of his escape.

"In a little over a day Roger Macadam and his illegal, bigamous wife have gone from being wanted, to being number one on America's most wanted list." The picture changed to an image of him while Elaine spoke in the background. "The FBI is offering a staggering one million dollar reward for information leading to his arrest. The FBI has warned Macadam is armed and dangerous. Do not try to apprehend this criminal."

The camera zoomed back to Elaine. "Details are still sketchy around Macadam's level of involvement in 9/11 and Al Qaeda as Homeland Security is tight-lipped on the matter, but rest assured this reporter will find the details. Back to you in the studio Ken."

"Thanks Elaine. Nasty things going on there. In other news today …"

Roger was no longer listening. Thoughts swarmed through his head like a thousand hornets. His mouth was dry. What had seemed like a game with serious challenges, had become a life and death struggle and not only for him it seemed. Something big was going on.

Staying out of sight was no longer an advantage, it was imperative. Atifah entered from the bathroom. She saw the grey look on Roger's face and knew something was wrong. She stopped in her tracks.

"You heard?" He wasn't sure how long she'd been standing there.

"No! What happened?"

"Somebody was killed last night and they think I did it." Her mouth opened as if to question, but she opted not to. Roger continued, "I told you I booked into a motel last night after leaving here."

"Yes!"

"They pitched up an hour and a half later. A desk clerk was shot and they're saying it was me. You and I are wanted for murder as well now."

Atifah sat down, overwhelmed with this information. "You didn't do it?" she half asked and half stated.

"Of course not, but they know I was there last night. I used my credit card." He walked to the young frightened girl and took her hands in his. She was struggling to hold back tears from her terrified eyes. "They still didn't have a picture of you, but I suppose it's only a matter of time. We need to disappear, soon. We need to speak to Qaboos and we need somewhere to stay. Once we have spoken to him, we can think about what we will do next. Are you going to be ok?"

"I don't know," she said, by now sobbing openly.

"Listen! We need to walk out of here confident and strong, like nothing is going on. We are innocent of everything here. We need to sort this out. Ok?" He prompted her for an answer. "Ok?"

"Ok!" she said without much conviction, but feeding off the apparent strength of the older man.

Roger wasn't somebody to lie in these circumstances. Generally, he was a typical engineer and would blurt out truths to the detriment of all those within hearing distance. This situation was different. This girl needed to hear something positive. "Everything will be fine." He took her hand and squeezed it gently. She looked up at him and smiled a faint smile, but a smile nonetheless.

-- o --- o0o --- o --

Anne had taken the day off work. She went home from Mike's place and gathered what she needed for herself and Katie and bundled it all into suitcases. She was about to leave, when there was a knock at the door. By this stage, Anne had developed a grim, but fatalistic acceptance, of the events to date. She had been watching the news and knew this was spiraling way out of control. Maybe her acceptance was because things had escalated so fast into a situation so ludicrous, she could do nothing but accept it. She feared for her husband's safety, but knew this story needed to play out further. She reluctantly agreed with Roger. Getting arrested and shipped off to jail without the need for a court hearing, would mean months could pass before the situation was resolved.

"Hello Mrs Macadam." It was Agent Matthews.

"Come in Mr Matthews. I'm sure you know Roger is not here," she said, showing her distaste for what was happening to her family. Tony Matthews entered the main lounge area and following the silent gesture from Anne, sat in the comfortable lounger.

"I'll cut straight to the chase Mrs Macadam. Your husband is worsening the extent of his trouble with each passing hour …"

"You think I don't know that!" Her voice raised a notch, sharp with frustration. "Of course he is, but what are his options Mr Matthews?" She implored him to deliver a viable option to solve the crisis. "If he hands himself in he could be locked up for months without trial under the Patriot Act. You know that!"

"This is true, but while he is on the run his life is in danger. People out there will shoot on sight and …" He trailed off not wanting to state the obvious. "He must hand himself in Mrs Macadam and let us resolve this issue. We can protect him if we have him here."

"With all due respect Mr Matthews, you didn't protect him for long while you had him did you?" She continued, "Do you believe he did these things? You've met my husband. Does he strike you as somebody having anything to do with something like 9/11?" Her voice had lost the frustrated anger and had developed tones of pain and desperation.

"It's too early to tell for sure at this stage, but off the record, no, I don't believe your husband is involved in anything like the 9/11 attack." Her face showed the pain she was feeling. "We were given the instruction to pull out all the stops in getting after your husband on the bigamy charge, but he …"

"But he had no control over his marriage. I have seen the video. Did you bother to ask him for an explanation of the situation? Was he even given the chance to explain, or did you go in with your head down and your blinkers on, wanting him to be guilty?"

"Yes! Guilty as charged Mrs Macadam. We follow orders and we deal with innocent-looking people every day. Terrorists, drug dealers, rapists and murderers. We deal with a wide range of people and the vast majority turn out to be guilty. Not all of them, but we find the majority are guilty. A few of the guilty ones walk free and a couple of the innocent ones end up in jail. If I have been hardened to the point that I assume people are guilty before the court does, then so be it. I'm not going to apologize for doing my job. I don't have the luxury of being selective, that's for the court to do." He stood up, wanting to create impact. "Mrs Macadam, you need to tell your husband to come in. We will try to work with him to resolve this, but we can't do it while he is on the run."

"No offense Mr Matthews, but I don't believe you have my husband's best interests at heart when telling me to bring him in."

"A fair comment under the circumstances, but I swear you will never be more wrong." She stood up and followed as he started to move toward the door. "Not only do I want to clear your husband, but I want to find out what is behind these allegations and find the guilty ones involved. Goodbye Mrs Macadam. Call me if you can think of anything helpful."

He left Anne feeling empty and frustrated. She wanted answers and he had raised more questions and uncertainty.

-- o --- oOo --- o --

The two wanted criminals managed to escape the hotel easily. It was early and the bustle of the breakfast rush was still an hour away. Roger had phoned the front desk and confirmed everything was settled. They then left at different times. One thing he knew, he needed to blur the lines of what people were looking for, much like the spots on a leopard blurs its edges in the forest. The public would be on the lookout for Roger and his 'wife'. It was important to be seen together as little as possible.

On his way out, Roger picked up a complementary newspaper to keep abreast of the latest happenings. Other than what looked like an almost life size shot of Roger's face on the front page, there was nothing new worth noting. They still had no picture of Atifah, which was a relief.

At his vehicle, Roger opened the door for Atifah. Then keeping low, he exchanged plates again with the vehicle next to him. He thought by now the neighbor may have seen his changed plates. Roger thought a change in vehicle would also be worthwhile. His SUV tended to be easy to spot, but for the time being he needed to be on the road.

Once mobile, Roger instructed Atifah to contact Qaboos. She retrieved the Omani cell phone from her bag on the back seat, replaced the battery, selected the number and held the phone to her ear. What followed was an emotional outburst of frustration built up over the last few days. The high–paced hybrid Anglo-Arab dialog allowed Roger to understand nothing of the content, but the sentiment was all too clear. Between the tears and frustration, he could sense the hurt in the girl's voice and the anger at being landed in this situation.

After a short while she quieted down and held out the phone to Roger. "His Majesty would like to speak with you."

Roger started to take the phone, then hesitated. Not wanting to attract any undue attention to himself by talking on the phone while driving he withdrew his hand. "Put him on speaker phone."

With a single deft movement, only possible to people of the cell phone generation, Atifah had the speaker phone on and held the phone between the two of them.

"Your Majesty! Can you hear me ok?" Roger said in a voice too loud for the situation, then without giving him chance to answer. "You are on speaker phone."

"I can hear perfectly Mr Macadam. No need to shout." The voice was clear. "Firstly, I want to apologize for deceiving you. It's not my nature to deceive. Especially to deceive somebody who risked his own life to save me." There was a pause as if the Sultan was waiting for affirmation, but 'that's fine', or 'no problem' was not going to emanate from Roger at this point!

"Mr Macadam. Let me start by saying I love Atifah dearly and I would entrust her to nobody else but you. The fact that you are both on the run together proves I judged you correctly."

Roger was not impressed by the compliment. "What is going on Your Majesty and why am I now wanted for terrorism as well as murder?"

"Roger! I don't have a clue." The Sultan spoke slowly. "I will tell you what I know, exactly as I know it. A couple of weeks ago there was an article in an American newspaper suggesting a huge oil deposit had been located near Salalah."

"I read it. It was the week before I flew out to Oman."

"Correct! There was no truth to the article, but directly following the article, I started to receive death threats against members of my family, especially Atifah."

"Hence you wanted to get her out, silently."

"Correct again! But I still didn't realize the threats were coming from Americans."

"Americans?" Roger was shocked. "How do you know it was Americans?"

"My intelligence department did a cleanup of the area where you saved my life. The attackers were a combination of Americans and Arabs"

"It would explain how they found me so quickly after I arrived home."

"It didn't stop there. After I moved her to the palace, I received a call telling me to check her room. The caller told me exactly where to find a small bomb. I panicked. It was in her room and set to detonate while she slept. It could only have been placed there by somebody from my own household or staff. I would never allow it to happen. I could trust nobody until I met a man willing to die to save another man's life."

Roger remained silent.

"It's worse than I originally thought. Whereas I thought the American involvement was mercenary, what you have said leads me to think it may be governmental. This is most worrying." He sounded worried. "If the government is involved, then there is no point in me sending you a plane to rescue you. They will be guarding every airport and you can be sure, our air space is being watched too."

"Is there nothing you can do for Atifah? Get her somewhere safe or something. She is too young to be involved in this."

"Don't worry about Atifah. She is much stronger than you think. I will see what I can do from my side. There are people in your country owing me favors but remember, Omani citizens will be watched. You don't want to be in an Omani house if your government clamps down. No! The best thing for you is to do what you are doing. You and Atifah need to stay away from people and not be seen."

"Look! We need somebody to do some digging. We need help here."

"Anything I can do I will. I give you my assurance, the last thing I want is for something to happen to you or Atifah. I will be in touch with respect to finding a safe house, but I don't think it is going to be easy. Can I speak to Atifah again?"

Atifah and the Sultan exchanged a few words and she hung up the phone. They drove on in thoughtful silence for a while. Roger was starting to map an image of the situation in his mind, but he didn't like what he saw.

"So!" Roger said after a while. "Not too much better off are we?"

"Not really!"

"Did you ask if the marriage was legitimate?"

"I didn't. I'm not sure I want to know." Then after a pause. "Where are we going?"

"Mike has a cabin up near Conroe Lake. We'll spend the night there and try to plan our next move."

-- o --- oOo --- o --

On the way up to the lake they stopped at a shopping mall where Atifah bought supplies. All the while, Roger lay down and pretended to sleep on the back seat. She purchased a few changes of clothing for both of them, food, a dark hair dye and hair gel. Roger had always worn his greying hair flat on his head. Now he would dye it 'auburn flair' and gel it up into a spiky look. Atifah also bought clothes typically worn by younger adults, including a hoodie and shades for Roger and a few 'far from Muslim' items for herself. If nobody knew what Atifah looked like, the two could pull off a younger couple provided nobody saw his face. He was impressed with her thinking process. She was blurring the lines well.

She climbed into the driver's seat and started driving the car out of the parking. "She drives!" A muffled voice came from under the hot blanket in the rear of the vehicle.

"She drives well so relax," she answered.

"Is she licensed to drive in Texas?" came the muffled reply.

"She has a British license, an Omani license and an international license issued in both places. I may be a murderer and a terrorist, but I would never drive without a license."

"No more questions for her then." Roger half relaxed looking out from under the blanket at the beautiful young driver. So much confidence, yet so much to fear.

"Besides," she continued, "we're wanted for a lot worse than driving without a license." Roger laughed in agreement.

For a moment things became tense when the driver of a police car pulling into the mall parking, looked into Atifah's eyes.

She had seen the cop pulling into the parking ahead of her. Roger was still hidden. "Police car ahead!" she spoke without turning her head.

"Keep in mind they don't know you. You are a beautiful woman to them. They are looking for me. Relax and charm them if necessary." He spoke from under the blanket.

"He's looking at the number." She spoke through gritted teeth.

"Relax. Just relax."

Roger held his breath as he watched Atifah pull forward, turning her head briefly to the side and smiling at the police officer

100

saying, "I caught you looking at me", rather than, "I'm on the run. Arrest me!" Aside from the policeman incident, the ride to Mike's cabin was uneventful and relaxing, under the circumstances. Roger and Atifah were beginning to feel somewhat relaxed with each other and were starting to make small talk. Putting aside the fact that they could be shot on sight, things appeared normal.

As they approached the cabin Roger again climbed into the back seat and hid under the blanket. It wasn't necessary, as not a soul was to be seen. From the outside, the cabin was rustic and appeared to fit well in the vastness of the forest surrounding it. The closest trees were about one hundred feet from the cabin, pretty much in a circle with two exits. The dirt road along which they had driven and at the back, a footpath which headed down the hill toward the lake. Off to the left of the cabin was a car shelter, overgrown from disuse, but apart from that there was nothing around. Atifah ignored the shelter and pulled up close to the front door, enabling a speedy entry into the small cabin.

Once inside, the rustic nature was even more apparent. The rooms were small, but well furnished with more than adequate comfort for anybody not wishing to 'rough it', yet rustic enough to engage the senses into believing you had left the city behind. Through a large window at the back of the lounge, the footpath could be seen going in an almost straight line through the trees down to the water. This image, more than anything else, had sold the property to Mike. He would often spend weekends here fishing until late in the evening and then be up early enough to catch the first rays at the water's edge.

The lounge area stretched the whole width of the modest building and then to the left there was an open plan kitchen, a narrow passage to the two tiny bedrooms and a bathroom. It was no mansion, but Roger had been here when a small party slept over. With fold out beds and camp beds stored in the closet, this little house had slept eleven at one time.

Although the light was starting to fade, Roger proceeded from room to room quickly and closed the drapes, conscious of not standing in the windows while doing so. If anybody were walking through the trees they would clearly see him through the glass, which was oversized for a small cabin. It had been Mike's desire to be able see the view, both the wood and the trees as it were.

Roger headed out to the SUV grabbing the bags in one movement and slipping back in through the door in another. "We'll keep the door locked. If anybody knocks I will move to the bedroom and you can tell whoever it is, Mike has a headache and is sleeping."

"No problem!" she answered.

Roger looked through the bags. "Firstly though, I need to dye my hair."

"Ooh! Good! A makeover." Atifah clapped her hands. Every now and then her youthfulness would shine through, but in her tight denims and long-sleeved tee, she was looking far less like a child. "I want to help you," she said grabbing the dye from Roger and heading toward the small bathroom. She turned and pointed to his greying hair. "I can see you are not experienced in this area." She smiled a relaxed, friendly smile.

The bathroom was cramped, fitting both a shower and a bath. Atifah was already inside opening the box and tipping out the contents. "Take your shirt off and lean over the bath."

She was in control and loving it. She was on her own turf. She turned and pushed Roger toward the bath. "C'mon! Hurry!" He obeyed, enjoying the playfulness as an escape from the worry which he tried his best to hide. "Shirt off and bend over the bath," she commanded again.

He waited, poised over the bath while Atifah squeezed tubes of brown goo onto his head. She worked swiftly, brushing the dye paste through his hair with a small brush.

"Ok!" She signaled she was finished. "You need to wait a while for the dye to take, then we'll wash it out. I'll make coffee if I can find it."

She did find the cups and made instant coffee for the two of them, which they enjoyed more than they would have expected. After several time checks, she looked at her watch. "It's time. Let's wash it out."

Roger headed to the bathroom again. Leaning over the bath, he opened the faucet running the cold water. There was no point in running the hot water as there was none.

Roger grunted as he thrust his head under the icy cascade. "A bit cold is it?" Atifah laughed. "Look! You have little bumps all over." She ran her soft finger over Roger's back which felt like a feather on his skin. Roger reached for the bottle, but it was already gone. "Stay still!" Atifah commanded, seeing him starting to move. Next she reached across him and started washing his hair. He was acutely aware of the warm, soft hand she placed in the center of his back, in order to steady herself while reaching to wash his hair. He noticed a tingle of excitement in places where he shouldn't be excited.

"I can do this," he said, trying to escape the unwanted emotions.

"I've done it!" she announced unaware of the turmoil in Roger's head. She leaned harder on him as she reached to wash the excess dye from the plastic glove on her hand. At the same time she slid the other hand across his back to his side and guided his head to the gushing water. This time Roger didn't even notice the icy water on his head. He was aware only of the soft, warm hand on his side and the illicit excitement growing in him.

He grunted again, but this time the cold had nothing to do with it.

The remainder of the procedure was a blur. He vaguely remembered leaning on the edge of the bath. He was excited by the way she leaned against him while she washed his hair. He wasn't sure if he'd purposely moved his head from the stream of water so she would again slide her hand down his side, pulling him toward the stream. He closed his eyes tight and started humming an indiscernible song which allowed him to focus away from the girl. It seemed to work.

"I can do this," he repeated.

"Ok! But rinse properly. All round your face as well." He wasn't sure whether he was relieved, or disappointed, but he rinsed his hair out and dried it on the towel. He stood and for the first time, looked in the mirror.

"Oh my ..." he looked at the young man looking back at him from the mirror. The dye had knocked ten years off his appearance. Only the grey speckled eyebrows and grey beard stubble gave away his age. He saw Atifah's jaw drop when she walked into the bathroom.

"Wow! You look almost human," she said, laughing. "You'll have to lose the stubble on your face though."

-- o --- oOo --- o --

"What now?" Atifah asked after they had eaten and they sat motionless, staring at nothing. She was startled by her own voice as it pierced the stillness.

"It's been a long day. I've switched the hot water on to have a warm bath and then bed. Can I pour you another coffee?"

"No! I meant what now? What about tomorrow?"

Roger became serious again for a second. "To be honest, I don't know. I want to travel back to the highway that circles the city and try to get hold of somebody at the FBI. Then you need to buy a car for us to drive. Until we see your picture on TV, you are going to be our face."

"Of course!"

"And also …" he paused getting her full attention. "I think you need to have your hair cut shorter."

"My hair!" She sounded horrified.

"I think so. These people are serious and if you cut it after they release your pictures, I will have to cut it for you and you don't want that." He paused again. "I'm sorry, but I think it's best."

"You're right." She was visibly saddened.

"I am unfortunately. You have beautiful hair but …"

"I know. You are correct. I will cut it tomorrow." Atifah was sad. Her hair was long and luxurious and she didn't want to cut it.

THURSDAY, 9TH

Roger woke early before daybreak. He wasn't sure whether something external had woken him, or whether it was his internal alarm. He lay in the near total darkness listening hard. Somewhere way off he heard the sound of voices. He could not hear any content, but he could definitely make out male voices.

Looking at the bedside clock told him it was 4:33. He slipped off the bed, crept along the short passage and across the lounge area feeling his way to avoid hitting the furniture. He stopped next to the window closest to where he thought the voices might have come from. Keeping low he moved to the corner of the window and carefully moved aside the drape. He knew that in the near total darkness it was unlikely anybody would see the movement. He moved the fabric enough to see outside, but could see nothing in the darkness.

He froze as he heard the voices again in a low tone, now closer than before. For a while he stopped breathing. Listening, he thought he could hear a conversation between two people. It was probably nothing to worry about. This was confirmed as one of the speakers burst into laughter. It was probably a couple of guys headed to the water for a bout of early fishing. Roger relaxed and congratulated himself for waking up at the sound of such distant and almost inaudible voices.

He closed the drape, stood up and felt his way for the light switch. There was an unimaginable contrast between the total darkness of the country morning and the glare of the fluorescent tube as it flickered into life. He instinctively covered his eyes.

He turned, forcing his burning eyes open and was startled to see a human form not three feet from his nose.

"Did I wake you?" he asked, his eyes adjusting so he could see the girl rubbing her eyes from the shock of the light going on.

"No! I was awake. I heard you moving. I thought you were going to leave me here."

"Leave you?"

"Well I…"

"I think you need to understand me a little better. I won't leave you unless I tell you I'm going to leave you and only then if I think the situation requires it. We're partners ok." He reached out and lifted her chin so she was looking into his eyes. "Partners?" he said looking deep into her unusually pale greenish brown eyes.

Once she acknowledged, Roger turned and walked over to the television and switched it on to catch up on the latest developments. It seemed there was no change in their status. Another life-size image of his face and more news content making him appear to be a deadly killer on the run, but still no image of Atifah. According to the report, the police were hard on his trail and an arrest was imminent. He hoped it was wishful thinking on their part.

The two of them didn't bother going back to bed, but did the usual morning routine: bathing, praying, eating and then a quick whip around to clean up and ensure their existence at the cabin was hidden. Roger stepped outside again, vulnerable in the near darkness of the early dawn, but consoled himself with the thought that if anybody knew he was here, they would have already been here by now. He bundled up the trash for dumping to remove any hint of their existence at the cabin. He also washed out the bath and packed the towels into the SUV. Who knew what these people were capable of?

When they were ready to leave, Atifah paused at the doorway. "We are leaving, but are we going somewhere in particular?"

"Not really. I don't know where we should go, but I think we should keep moving."

"We are secluded here. Nobody can see us."

"I agree," Roger could feel the anguish in the girl's voice. She was already tired of running, "But my guess is they are researching for me in a big way and that includes investigating Anne and Mike too. Sooner or later they will know Mike has a cabin and send somebody round to have a look. It may be today, it may be two weeks from now, but I don't want to be here when they arrive. There's nowhere to go to get away."

"You're right I suppose." It wasn't even light outside and Atifah was dejected already. It was going to be a long day.

Roger knew the longer they could go without being seen, the better. They needed to get going and they needed to change cars – urgently. Walking outside, Roger locked the door behind them. "I think we should head for San Antonio."

"Ok!" She hadn't a clue what he was talking about.

"But first we need to dump the trash and the plates. We need to hang around town long enough for us to buy a new vehicle."

"And for me to cut my hair." Her voice was quiet as she said the words.

"I didn't want to bring it up."

"It'll grow back when this is over," Atifah consoled herself.

When it's over? Roger tried to see the route between here and 'when it's over'. He could not establish a clear picture in his mind. There were huge, terrifyingly dark patches between them and the end point. Roger had already decided he needed to do something to force their opponent's hand. He, as yet, didn't know what to do, or how to do it. He didn't even know whose hand he should be forcing. He was hoping things would happen naturally. Amazingly, Roger felt in control of the situation. He knew the country was looking for a grey haired Roger and he was a brown haired Roger. The country was looking for a bigamous Roger and his second wife. He would ensure they were not seen together unless it was an absolute necessity.

At the first opportunity they stopped in the half light of the morning and Atifah threw the trash into a roadside garbage can. While she was busy, Roger slipped out of the car, removed his two plates and swapped them for those on the vehicle behind him. This process was becoming slick and he gave himself an imaginary pat on the back for the speed with which he was able to complete the task.

Heading back toward town, Roger drove in the half light and when the traffic picked up he found somewhere to stop and change places. He then spent most of the journey lying across the rear seat talking to the side of Atifah's head. At his request, Atifah turned on the radio to keep up to date with the latest information.

"Where is San Antonio?" she asked as she climbed into the passenger seat.

"It's west of Houston along interstate ten." As if it would mean anything to her. "Two-twenty, two-fifty miles. I'm not sure." He knew Atifah didn't like to be on the road. She probably had good reason as they were sitting ducks on the highway. The upside to being on the interstate is you are a vehicle, not a person, and you could travel for hours, see thousands of vehicles, and not a single face.

"How long will it take?"

"I don't know. Probably three to four hours I guess. I've never been there."

"You've been all the way to Muscat, but you haven't traveled around the corner to San Antonio."

"There are lots of places I haven't been and quite a few of them are in Texas."

"Why San Antonio?"

"We need another car. If the purchase becomes public, I want the authorities to think we are on our way somewhere."

"So we're not on our way anywhere?"

"Nowhere specific, but San Antonio could be on the way to Mexico. If we can divert man-power to watching the border, it leaves less man-power to find us."

Roger listened to the radio news when he heard mention of his flight but again, there was nothing new. The federal police were still hard on his heels and an arrest was still imminent. Then new news surfaced which he thought was probably related, but it was not reported as such.

"… the Al Qaeda training camp is situated about eighty miles outside of Muscat, the capital of Oman. Omani nationals undergo rigorous training which includes weapons and explosives training. They prepare themselves in the mosque daily, longing to lay down their lives in support of their religion." The report ended and switched to a story about a baseball team captain and his sex life.

"What is going on Roger?" Atifah shook her head from side to side in disbelief. "There is no such camp."

"I don't know what's going on, but I think I'm starting to see a picture."

"What picture?"

"On the surface, it looks like we, America, are looking for a reason to go into Oman. Similar to the Iraq situation where we waited for something like 9/11 and then jumped on the opportunity to invade. I think Qaboos guessed this and wanted you out of the country." Roger looked straight ahead as he talked, his face was etched with concern. He was deep in thought when he spoke. "They know they can't play the weapons of mass destruction card, so they are searching for something else." He was thinking aloud and not talking to Atifah. He paused while the scenarios spun around in his mind. "I think we are part of their plan … but how? … and why?" She didn't answer, but he hadn't wanted her to. For a while he didn't even know she was there.

-- o --- oOo --- o --

Not far from their current location, an early morning strategy session was taking place at a makeshift Homeland Security office in Houston. The meeting was being led by one Major T. S. Crane. Crane was a thorough-bred military man with marine-style cropped hair and granite hard features tempered through service in a number of wars. At fifty-five, Crane had taken this job to spend his twilight years with his wife. She left him within six months of his being home. This hadn't helped his sunny disposition.

He was not a big man, but was as hard as nails. Many under him had feared him, some without ever having contact with him. He rarely smiled and under these conditions there wasn't going to be a smile anytime soon.

"Tuesday he was in our hands. It's now 07h30 on Thursday. Why has this man not been apprehended? He's an engineer for God's sake, not a fucking marine!" Crane barked at the agents seated around the table. He waited for an answer, but then cut off the first agent daring to open his mouth. "It's now 07h30. We have one hour to come up with a plan to flush this pussy out of hiding. I want him here, dead or alive, before anyone leaves here today. Is that understood?" He looked around the table as the agents glanced at each other. This was the first time any of them had met. Some of them had arrived the evening before but the majority, including Crane, arrived this morning. Crane flew in on the early flight from DC, handpicked by his superiors for the task at hand. "UNDERSTOOD?" He slapped the palm of his hand on the desk sending a shock wave reverberating through the agents as they jumped in their seats. They all gave him an affirmative.

Crane's team, handpicked from various locations around Texas, numbered eight, one woman and seven men – all younger than thirty-five. All of them knew of Crane, but none of them knew he would be leading them until he had walked in the room earlier. "Who did I speak to last night regarding the dead agent's phone?"

"That was me," Agent Derrick England raised his hand signaling his whereabouts.

"And who the fuck is me?"

"Derrick England."

"So Agent England, you're the computer guy are you?"

"Yep! I did ..."

"Has the phone come on line yet?"

"Err! Not yet, No!"

"Then why is your ear not stuck to a phone dialing right now? I told you I want to know as soon as it comes online, not half an hour later when you decide to try again."

England was indignant. "I didn't dial the phone, I ..."

Crane glared at the agent. He spoke slowly and with an undertone of nastiness. "I remember specifically asking you to keep trying through the night – did I not?"

England was getting trampled, but he wasn't a soldier. He didn't have the levels of blind submissive obedience beaten into soldiers. He stood up, glaring at Crane. "I thought it might have been a waste of time dialing and redialing a phone that was switched off. I sent the phone a text message. I'll be notified when it gets delivered."

Crane glared back at England, but knew the nerd had won. "I can see you and I are going to get along just fine." Then under his breath, "I hate fucking civilians."

He turned to the whiteboard behind him. "Right, what have we got?" He scribbled as he spoke. "Tuesday, Macadam is uplifted from the Feds. Shortly afterward a truck slams into the side of our guy's vehicle and Macadam stages his escape. He steals a weapon and phone, hijacks a vehicle and drives home. He lets the driver and her kid go unharmed. He then gets in his car and disappears. He resurfaces briefly, still in Houston, at a motel, whacks the desk clerk and then disappears before our guys get there. Which of you discovered the clerk?"

Blank looks all round. "I think we all arrived this morning from all over the state." Terri Wilson was the only female on the team. She had a 'Miss Congeniality' look about her, before the makeover and pageant. There wasn't much 'girly' about this girl, but she was attractive enough to turn heads. She held her own with the boys and then some. Agent Wilson had received top honors at the police academy and was snapped up by Homeland Security after solving a couple of high profile cases early on in her career.

"Wilson, is it?" Crane didn't like girls in service.

"Yes Sir."

"Wilson, what have I missed?"

"The hijack victim told police Macadam left the weapon in her car and she handed it to the police. It has since disappeared. I read it in the case file, Sir."

"Interesting." Crane made a note on his whiteboard. "Thank you Wilson! Has anybody been out to quiz the staff at the motel?"

"According to the police report nobody saw anything, but there was one old guy drinking coffee at a diner over the road claimed he saw Macadam watching the motel from the diner. Then he got up and left at around the estimated time of death of the clerk. He was on his own and walked in the opposite direction to the motel." Agent Tim Crosby spoke for the first time.

Tim was another detective prodigy. He had joined the Texas Rangers from school and was soon spotted for his quick eye and attention to detail. Tim was of slender build, about twenty-five years old and not at all what you would expect of a donut-eating detective. He was a good looking young man, but not a 'life of the party' type of guy. Tim was from the Austin office, along with Johnny Mills. Agent Mills was the ultimate marine. Everything about him screamed US Marine! He was of medium height, but looked as wide as he was high. Mills brought two abilities to the team. He could mercilessly kill a man and feel nothing. Secondly he was a crack marksman. He could ruthlessly kill a man from a distance as well.

"That all?" Crane had been writing and drawing lines and arrows while the agents were talking.

"All we have Sir."

"So if he walked away, who killed the clerk?" Crane was puzzled. "Are any of you from this office?" He looked around as the agents shook their heads. "Strange!"

His bewilderment was shattered by the sound of England's phone beeping loudly. Derrick whipped his phone open. With a big smile he shook the phone in the air. "Delivered!" he said triumphantly.

-- o --- oOo --- o --

As they neared town, Roger pulled off the road and they swapped seats. Still later, as the traffic built, he climbed into the back seat and gave instructions from there. Pretty soon they were on the 610 traveling clockwise around Houston. Roger leaned across and retrieved the dead agent's phone from the glove compartment.

"Here goes!" He switched on and the phone fired into life. Roger sat and watched as the screen flickered. Once he had entered the PIN code and the phone had stabilized, he started the process of pawing through the maze of menu items looking for contacts or something to give him a clue as to who the owner of the phone had been. While he was looking, the phone buzzed informing him of the arrival of a text message. Opening the message, he read the word 'Hi'. It came from an unknown number.

Roger was about to continue searching through the contacts when the phone sprang into life.

"Hello."

"Mr Macadam I presume. Agent Crane here."

"Hello Mr Crane."

"Mr Macadam, I'm going to cut to the chase. I want you to hand yourself in at my office. I have a team of eight top agents sitting here with me and we're about to start our day. Our sole purpose is to bring you in dead or alive. I'm sure you would prefer the alive option. Bring yourself in Macadam and we can all go home this evening."

"I'm sure you've seen the news this morning, Mr Crane. I'm wanted for murder. Now both you and I know one of your agents killed that kid."

"Why do you say my agents?"

"I watched from the diner across the street as three agents entered the motel."

"Interesting! But just so you know, my team arrived here this morning, so it was not one of mine. If it's your intention to run Mr Macadam, I assure you we will find you and you probably won't like that outcome."

"It's never been my intention to run Mr Crane, only to keep out of your way."

"You can't keep hiding. Sooner or later you'll make a mistake. Everybody makes a mistake eventually."

"Maybe, but while I'm talking about intentions. Let me see what your intentions are …"

"Isn't it about time to turn off the phone so we can't track you?"

"Now would you be saying such a thing if you were able to track me. I already checked, no IMEI number on the phone. Besides, I can tell you where I am, I'm somewhere on the 610, but within two minutes I will be off so it won't help you."

"I don't know what an IE… whatever number is, but I'm impressed."

"Thank you! Now, as I was saying, here's my proposal for you. Go on air this evening and tell America my new wife and I are innocent of the crimes you claim I committed, except of course the bigamy thing, which I had no control over and I will hand myself in tomorrow."

There was silence while Crane thought about what Roger was saying. "You know I can't do that until you hand yourself in."

"Ok! So now we know what your intentions are, let me give you mine. I am going to keep clear of you for a while longer, until I have figured out who is trying to screw me over and why. Once I have figured it out I will broadcast it publicly and then hand myself in. Simple!"

"But you can't escape us, our eyes are all over. Even the public is on the lookout for you. It's a matter of time."

"Then for my sake let's hope it's time enough. I'm sure it will be easier to find answers out here than it would be locked up in Guantanamo Bay."

"I think Guantanamo is going to close down."

"Wherever you decide to house terrorists without trial out of the public eye will simply be another Guantanamo Bay. Besides, Obama will never close it down. It means you would have to find somewhere to hide the inmates."

"So! It's business as usual then. You run, I find."

"Looks like it."

"So I'll see you around. Mr Macadam."

"Not if I see you first. Mr Crane."

Roger pressed the red phone on the phone's keyboard and hung up. From what he had said, it seemed as though Crane and his team had been brought in recently and were probably not the ones responsible for the execution of the desk clerk. He needed to find a way to flush out those responsible without running into Crane. Life was going to become complicated. He dismantled the phone, removing the battery just in case.

-- o --- oOo --- o --

"You need to go and buy us a car," Roger blurted out after about a minute of silence in the vehicle. Neither of the two were garrulous types, which worked well. They would be in each other's company for a long period without saying anything. Normally, Roger found this uncomfortable, not because he wanted to talk, but because he felt the other person wanted to. He would find himself trying to force a conversation, but with Atifah they both seemed content with the silence.

In this instance, the sudden outburst seemed to startle both of them. She recovered quickly. "Ooh! Shopping!"

"Don't get too excited, we're going to be looking for a real wreck. I need more money before we buy anything decent."

"Ok?" She wanted to know more.

"Take the next ramp and head toward Katy. We'll stop off at the library there and use the internet."

"What am I looking for?"

"The best bet is to go to Google and search for something like private-sale-car-Katy. Then write down a bunch of cars. Look for recent posts. We're looking for something understated and common on the road. Maybe a Ford Taurus or a Chevy Cavalier or Lumina. Maybe a Thunderbird. Not too small, we may need a little power at some point and not more than 120,000 miles on the clock."

"How much do you have to spend?"

"Look for cars up to two thousand, but I'd prefer to spend less."

As they approached the library, Roger assumed his position on the floor in front of the rear seat and covered himself with the blanket. Atifah pulled her hair back into a ponytail at the back of her head, took a deep breath and exited the car, locking it behind her. The bleep of the alarm reminded Roger not to move. He lay there for what seemed an eternity, hot and sweaty under the blanket. He heard several groups of people, mostly youngsters, as they passed by his vehicle on their way to or from the library.

Eventually he heard the double bleep as the alarm was disarmed and Atifah climbed back into the SUV. She started the engine and reversed out of the parking in what felt to Roger a quick movement.

"What's wrong?" he asked from below the blanket.

"A creepy looking guy was looking at me strangely."

"What was he wearing?"

"I don't know, I only saw his eyes. Maybe denims and a sweat shirt."

"Color shirt?"

"I don't know, but dark. Brown or green I think."

"How old was he?" She was starting to realize she should have paid more attention.

"Old! In his forties."

"Nice!" thought Roger, but he said, "Keep checking as you drive away and see if he comes out of the building."

After a short while Roger assumed he hadn't come out of the building and spoke.

"Looks like it was an admirer," he said. "You're a pretty girl. You may be used to being covered, but people are able to see you now."

"I wasn't covered the whole time, only on formal public occasions."

"You should try to be more observant. If you see something strange ensure you remember the person. Your life may depend on it."

She looked disappointed with herself. "I understand. It was stupid of me."

"It wasn't stupid. It's new, that's all. We have an entire country looking for us. We need to be alert to stay ahead and we need to stay ahead to stay alive."

Atifah had noticed a change in Roger. Not a mood change, but a change in presence. He seemed like a different person, even though he looked the same. Whereas he had been a quiet person, fading into the background, Roger now commanded attention and grabbed control. He appeared to be more relaxed as America's most wanted, than he was as Roger Macadam, the chemical engineer.

"Anyway," he said in a tone aimed at diffusing any tenseness. "What do you have for us?"

"Ok! There are twelve cars I've printed out." She handed the pages backward and Roger, still on the floor, took them and started paging through. "I'm driving in an unknown direction here. Where should I be heading?"

Roger lifted his head and looked around. "Take a left further up. There should be a sign for the Forbidden Gardens. We'll stop in the parking there and look through these."

Atifah positioned the car where it was least visible and then they started discussing the cars in the pile. Roger short listed three of the vehicles and handed Atifah the phone. "Call Eric … what was it …Waldorf. Find out if the vehicle is still available and ask him when you can go and see it."

Atifah dialed the number and listened while the ring tone sounded. Roger spoke quickly while she waited. "You're a Londoner. Here on a long holiday."

She turned as if to ask what he was talking about, but then realize at the same moment as Eric answered his phone.

"Hello!"

"I'm lookin' for Eric?" in broad Londoner.

"You found him." Eric was almost singing into his phone.

"Hi Eric, My name's Joan." Her cockney was impeccable. "I'm in Texas for a couple o'months an' I need a car. Is your Taurus still available?"

"It is. Would you like to come and have a look?"

"That'd be smashin'. Is the car runnin' properly? I'm not a good mechanic."

"The car is a daily runner. It's been around the block a few times and it comes with the Ford guarantee of a lifetime of rattles and squeaks, but it's in good shape and it'll see you through the next few years no problem."

"When can I stop by?"

"Anytime! I'm here all day."

"Can you give me your address?"

Eric read out his address while she wrote it down. She hung up the phone. "First one done," she said. "We can go anytime."

"You were great! Let's go right now. Luv!" He tried a bad English accent. Atifah laughed at his attempt.

"Was it bad?"

"Worse than bad! I was being kind."

Atifah pulled out into the street again heading for Eric's house, following Roger's instructions as he read off his map in the back seat.

-- o --- oOo --- o --

Atifah drove past Eric's house, while she and Roger did a cautious recon of the area. The Taurus stood in the driveway, clean and polished as they all are when they are being sold. She pulled over about a hundred yards or so up the road and turned to Roger.

"Ok?" she asked awaiting instructions.

"First thing you will need to do is take the car for a drive. See that everything is working. If you hear any funny knocks or sounds then when you get back, tell him you have other cars to look at and say you'll get back to him. I'll follow you from a distance to make sure he's not some weirdo. When you turn back into this road again, I'll hang way back until you turn into his driveway."

"Do I need anything?"

"He will probably want to see your international license before he lets you drive. I hope you have the English version. Take the cash and if you think it's a good deal, then give him the money.

He may give you the title document and a 130-U form for you to use. And also, he must give you a vehicle registration receipt. We should at least make the transaction look authentic."

"Title, 130-U and registration receipt. Is that all?"

"Money!" He handed her a small wad of bills. "Try get a better deal if you can. I've dealt with enough Middle Easterners to know you probably can."

Atifah smiled as she climbed out of the vehicle and began a confident walk toward Eric's house. She stopped in her tracks and turned back toward Roger. His senses went into overdrive. What was wrong? She hurried back to the vehicle and opened the door. "What was my name again?"

"I think you said Joan." Roger laughed.

"That was it. Joan!" She looked relieved.

"If he notices your name is not Joan on your license then tell him Joan is your nickname."

"Right! Joan Macadam." She reassured herself, then closed the door, slid on her dark shades, spun on her heel, and headed toward Eric's house.

-- o --- oOo --- o --

Back in the SUV, Roger listened to the news. Again, he heard of the Al Qaeda training camps in Oman. He heard of the Omani links to organized crime. He heard of how a diplomatic mission had landed at Muscat to discuss the disarming of the Al Qaeda forces within Oman. He heard of how the meeting failed, broke down, how the parties had stormed out, but mainly how the Sultan's representatives' rejection of the demands of the international community had bordered on violent.

It was déjà vu. He'd seen this all before. Firstly with Afghanistan, the supposed location for Bin Laden, and then in Iraq with their non-existent weapons of mass destruction. The difference was, this time he knew the truth. He couldn't specifically vouch for there being no training camps in Oman, but he believed even the Sultan and his family had no knowledge of those camps and he certainly didn't see the Sultan as violently rejecting anybody.

-- o --- oOo --- o --

"You must be Joan," Eric said when she greeted the man in the doorway.

"That's me! Did my accent give me away?" Eric was in his late forties and a little large around the middle. His fair hair was beginning to grey at the temples and his red cheeks spread into a broad grin as he looked this babe up and down. He looked soft and flabby, like somebody who had spent too long watching too much television and eating too many TV dinners.

"There's the car," he said, awkwardly pointing toward the Ford standing in the driveway and shining in the sunlight. He knew she had walked past it a moment ago.

"Looks nice from the outside. Can we go for a spin?"

"Of course. I'll bring the keys." Eric disappeared for a nanosecond and reappeared, his expression showing his happiness that the babe was still there. "Do you want to drive?"

"Sure Luv! Why are you selling it?" Atifah was concentrating on keeping the accent going.

"I've bought a Porsche. A real nice, red cow catcher." Eric burst into a fit of loud cackling laughter and then stifled it as he realize Atifah wasn't laughing. He passed the keys to Atifah. "It's a SHO V8 3.4. It's got great acceleration. I bought it new and you can see I have looked after it."

"It does look lovely. Why seventeen-fifty? It looks like you could sell it for more than that." Atifah had no idea of prices, she was probing for anything wrong.

"They offered seventeen-fifty as a trade-in. I need to sell quickly and I would much prefer to give it to you than to them." He waved his hand in an arc, pointing to the general population, but referring to the motor dealer. "They will sell it at a huge profit. Besides, it's old and it has done a big mileage, but it's not using much oil or water." He watched as Atifah climbed in the vehicle and then he climbed in next to her. "Oh! The CD changer is not working. There's a CD in there, but I couldn't eject it. I'll throw in the CD for free." Another loud cackle followed.

Atifah turned the key and the dashboard flickered into life. She noticed the wear on the wheel. She turned the key again and the V8 purred into life. "Wow! What a nice sound." She maintained her English accent well.

"It's stock standard. I didn't do any work on it and there are a few rattles in the dash." As if on cue, something around the middle of the car started rattling but soon subsided. Atifah selected reverse and eased the car backward into the street. Pretty soon they were cruising along the street with typical Ford-like ease. The automatic gear changes were smooth and almost indiscernible at low revs. A hundred yards behind, she saw Roger's SUV pull out from the parking and start to follow.

"I don't know where I'm goin'. Can I go right up ahead?"

"Take the next four rights and we'll be back where we started. You can take it a bit further if you want." As she turned to the right and started going up the slight hill, Atifah pushed the pedal and felt the car ease effortlessly forward. She liked this car.

"I'll take it," she said without even feeling the urge to haggle. She was sure this was a good deal. "So I can phone the others and cancel the appointments." She lied convincingly.

"Great. I couldn't think of a nicer person to sell it to."

After pulling into the driveway again, Atifah dug in her small handbag and pulled out the notes. After counting off the seventeen-fifty, she handed a bundle of notes to Eric who was beaming at this point for having spent time with the hottest lady he'd seen in ages. "Would you like to come inside while I write your receipt?"

"No! If you don't mind, I want to see how this car works." She didn't want to chance getting too close, or being recognized later on. "If you don't mind," she said, knowing she could probably ask anything of Eric right now. She felt sorry for him. He seemed lonely.

"No problem. I'll get the paperwork."

Eric disappeared for a while and returned holding official looking documents, the car owner's handbook and other scraps of paper. Once all the exchanges were made, Atifah said her goodbyes and reversed out of the driveway slowly heading back toward Roger. Seeing the deal was done, he spun the SUV around and with Atifah following, headed back toward the Forbidden Gardens to use the convenient parking and to check out the car he'd bought.

"You were great! Let's have a look at this." He stepped out of his vehicle and spun around the hood keeping as much vehicle between him and any potential onlookers as possible. "This looks great. Does it run ok?"

"It seems fine." She was smiling at being given praise for successfully concluding the deal.

"This is nice. I'll let you choose the next car I buy too." She smiled again. Roger threw his right arm around her shoulder as she stood next to him and hugged her in tight to him as he'd done to Anne or Katie. Her smile faded as she spun in close to Roger. To steady herself, she raised her hand and placed it high on Roger's chest, almost on his shoulder. For the briefest moment, the two came face to face, staring into each other's eyes. For one brief, tense, magical and exciting moment, the world faded around them. They were only aware of the other's eyes.

Roger shattered the moment as thoughts of Annie, Katie and old men and young girls flooded his head. For a second he was dizzy and while regaining his senses he heard himself apologizing to her. Atifah also regained her composure, more than a little shocked at the rush of sensation that swept over her.

"No need to apologize. I'm not hurt." Brilliantly diffused, but it didn't work. They both understood. The damage was done. As much as Roger would later write off the moment in his head as the time spent together, the circumstances and numerous other things, they shared an undeniable moment. One which would haunt his thoughts for several days to come.

She continued, "I think it's time for my hair."

"I didn't want to mention it, but you're right. I think I'd like to dump the car first." He thought for a second. "We'll drive back to town and then take the I45 north for a while. You can follow me in the Ford. We'll find a small town to stop and do your hair. We'll leave the car there then head back this way again."

"A lot of traveling," she looked tired.

"A couple of hours. Far enough to make them think we're headed for Dallas, should we be spotted." He started to head for the SUV, but turned. "If we are separated for any reason, go back to Mike's house at the lake."

"I would never find my way back there." She was tired and feeling irritable and still a little uncomfortable from the 'moment'.

"Head back to Houston and ask directions to Lake Conroe, that's C-O-N-R-O-E. Take the Lake Conroe turnoff the freeway and follow the signs. When you can see the lake, look for the *Welcome to Lake Conroe* sign and from there go right – left – right – right. You should be on the little dirt road up to the cabin."

"Right – left – right – right." she confirmed, picturing the turnings in her head.

"Here!" He handed her one of the bought cell phones and wrote down the number of another. "Don't use it unless you have to. We don't know whether these phones are being tracked." He knew the possibility existed that the shop assistant might have called in the purchase if he recognized him. "If you have to, use it when you are on the highway and moving. As soon as we have finished talking throw the phone out onto the road and keep driving. I will give you directions and we'll meet. If for some reason ..." He trailed off. "If I can't get there, use your phone and tell Qaboos to rescue you."

Her head was spinning with the instructions. "It's just in case. We'll be fine." Roger reassured the girl. He hoped he believed it.

-- o --- oOo --- o --

"Ok! Macadam is still in Houston." Crane leaned back on his chair and replaced the receiver on the phone. "I want you all ready to roll as soon as we hear anything. This man is not running." He scratched his head while everybody looked on, waiting for direction.

"Wilson. You and Crosby are the detectives. I want you to go and find out what you can about the woman. We need a picture on the news pronto." He turned and stuck the picture of Roger's face on the whiteboard and then drew an outline where Atifah's picture would go. "I need this spot filled," he said talking to himself more than to the others.

He spun around. "You and you." He pointed to Agents Caleb Johnson and Dwight Roberts. Caleb was a large African American and Dwight Roberts, a young red-headed agent. Caleb had grown up in Houston and was currently working on immigration issues in San Antonio. He hadn't wanted to be involved on this assignment, but orders are orders. He was huge. His muscled, two hundred and seventy pound frame and cropped hair made Caleb look as much the marine as Mills looked, but he'd never served. Agent Johnson was chosen for this assignment because he had knowledge of immigration. He had previously caught several offenders in a quick and efficient manner. Caleb had a calm disposition and under most conditions was not rattled easily.

Dwight on the other hand was the polar opposite of Caleb. A young, carroty red-headed and ruddy faced agent whose hyperactive terrier-like tenacity and sheer dogged determination had earned him not only results, but the nickname 'Louis'. The shortened version of Louisiana Pit Bull. Agent Roberts was from Estelle, Louisiana, but always told people he was from New Orleans. He now lived in Dallas and had made a name for himself by cracking open a terrorist plot involving at least half a dozen high profile terror suspects. His knee bounced up and down under the table while he waited for the go signal from Crane.

"Get your heads together with the geek over there and see if you can track down a credit card transaction, a phone call … anything that will give us a direction. We need to know where we can start looking for this man. Give me something!"

Crane sat deep in thought as he thumbed his way through the few pages of the case file. He looked up to see all the agents looking at him expectantly. "What?" The agents looked at each other, then back at Crane. "GO!" he shouted. The five of them left in a hurry.

"Ok! The rest of you move in closer." Crane waved them in. "We are going to find a way to flush this bird out of hiding and we're going to do it today.

"Macadam has a wife and daughter. Have they had contact with him?"

"Not to our knowledge sir," Agent Sam Kozlowski answered. Kozlowski was a third generation Pole in America. He was a stout round faced agent, looking like he was always about to burst into a fit of laughter. The roundness of his face was accentuated by a Beatle style fringe on his forehead. Sam's claim to fame was cracking a case concerning a bunch of resident Russians supplying arms and ammunition to Robert Mugabe and other African tyrants. It had been assumed the Russians had been working with the Russian Mafia and so were tracked for months after Sam had cracked the case. It turned out they were a bunch of Russian 'entrepreneurs' making a quick buck. Nonetheless, it had taken serious work to track them down in the first place and this had not gone unnoticed.

"Macadam's family has moved in with Mike Parker, Macadam's friend from college days. The Feds have been watching them. We have the phone tapped and nothing is happening."

"Have they been in the house the whole time?"

"They were followed into town for a couple of hours on Wednesday evening, but they had a shake and headed back home again."

"Ok! I think Macadam isn't going to be an average case. This man is not stupid and has not even shown his face. More interestingly, he's not running. He knows his friends and family are being watched." Crane rubbed his ear while he thought. "Nobody can keep going forever without making a mistake. We need to be ready. What about Parker? Is he linked to any terror groups?"

"Nothing known, sir." The agents had already been through the case files. "Even Macadam has no known links to Al Qaeda, or anybody else."

"So why is this man the most wanted man in America at the moment?"

"Macadam was in New York on business on September 11, 2001."

"Oh! I can see the link." Crane was sarcastic. "So were thousands of other business men and women."

"He was also on business in Nairobi on August 7th 1998 and in Oklahoma City on April 19, 1995." Agent Mills proved he could read the report as well as shoot people.

"Ah! Now there's something interesting. Are there no links to McVeigh, Militia, the Neo-Nazi's, or anybody else involved in any of those attacks?"

"Not according to reports sir."

"I wonder what the odds are of being in those places on those days. You two man the phones. Barnard, come with me. I think I would like to pay the legal Mrs Macadam a visit. Is she still at Parker's house?"

"According to the report sir." Chris Barnard was named after Doctor Christiaan Barnard of the heart transplant fame. Both of his parents were renowned mathematicians and Chris, being the black sheep of the family, failed to achieve the family average of 98% and had to settle for a little above 95%. Accordingly, he settled for a life outside of academia and started work for the bureau as a strategist and situation modeler. He was nonetheless, well known as being one of the best in the business and this helped to reduce his parents' disappointment at his reluctance to enter academia. Chris was a great mathematician and looked the part. He had the glasses, the hairstyle and the clothing that screamed – "Hey! I'm a mathematician." He was the youngest member of the team.

-- o --- oOo --- o --

The two cars headed back toward town, then via the outer ring road to Interstate 45 and toward Dallas. Roger was driving the SUV and he kept constant check on the white Ford traveling behind. He led her off the I45 and onto 75, then drove toward Madisonville.

Madisonville, a small town in Madison County, is a typical ranching town. Although he had never visited Madisonville, Roger soon located a hairsalon for Atifah to have her hair cut. She was not enjoying the prospect. Roger gave her cash and took the spare keys for the Ford. He was going to dump the SUV and walk back to the Ford to wait for Atifah. Once again, Atifah had parked the vehicle in a bay against a wall, reducing the likelihood of somebody looking into the front of the car.

As soon as he saw where she had parked, Roger exited the parking and headed back toward the highway. As he pulled out of the mall parking, a police car passed him going in. Roger kept looking forward, but out of the corner of his eye he saw the movement of the cop's head as he looked at Roger. What he didn't see was the puzzled expression on the face of the cop. The policeman had looked at Roger by accident and he knew he'd seen him, but he couldn't picture where. Roger looked back to see if the car would turn around, but he was relieved to see it drive straight on.

On the way in from the interstate, Roger spotted a possible dumping point where he could take the car off the road without being noticed. He hadn't been able to see around the thicket, but if it was the same there as the rest of the terrain, then there was no one there to watch him drop the vehicle off. At the desired point Roger turned into an open gate and took the small, dusty, dirt road rounded behind the thick group of dry, twiggy trees. He was pleased to see nothing but miles of flat land on the other side of the thicket. He wasn't sure where the road headed, but it was far enough for his requirements.

About a hundred yards along, before the road became visible to passersby, Roger turned off the road and headed into the thicket between the trees. The branches scratched and scraped the sides of his vehicle as he bounced forward making slow progress over the rough, rocky ground. He came to rest in what looked like the dried up pan of a small lake, only a few yards across, in the middle of the trees. It was better than he had expected. The vehicle was hidden from all sides and above.

Roger had already packed what he needed into the trunk of the Ford, but he did a quick look around to check if anything had been missed. Satisfied, he left the vehicle and keeping to the fields made his way back toward town.

In the heat of the midday sun, a few heads turned to look at the man walking through the open land, but he was far enough from the road to prevent any passerby from having an overwhelming desire to stop and ask if he needed a lift.

Approaching town, he knew it was necessary to move back to the roadside, but at least the presence of a sidewalk indicated it was acceptable for people to walk there. As he neared the road, Roger pulled up the hood of his new 'hoodie'. He was sweating like an athlete, but nobody turned their head to look at him. People were no doubt wondering what idiot would be wearing sweats in this weather, but through his shades he could see nobody had looked into his face. The disguise was working well.

Pretty soon he rounded the corner into the parking and could see the Ford still parked in the same spot. It was over an hour later and she was still busy with her hair. Roger settled down in the passenger seat of the Taurus, opened a couple of windows, laid the seat back and relaxed. He wasn't worried. He had a wife and daughter. He knew from years of experience about the complexities of a haircut and how they were way beyond the comprehension of any man. Even the cuts leaving the wearer looking identical to her pre-cut look could take hours and cost the earth.

After a further hour and a half he awoke to the sound of the door being opened. Atifah climbed into the driver's seat. Her short blond hair bordered on being spiky, but she was still as stunning as ever. She looked as different as could be imagined. He tried to say something, but the dusty dryness in his mouth and throat, allowed only the emission of a weak hiss, followed by a choking sound.

"Don't say a word!" She feigned a pout. She had been angry and frustrated. Years of growth had been hacked off in a matter of seconds. The couple of seconds had stretched into over three hours and what she had originally thought to be a hack job had turned out to be a masterpiece. Even she had to admit it looked pretty good!

Licking his lips and swallowing a few times, Roger managed to squeeze out a single word – "Beautiful!"

She turned and smiled a broad smile "Ok! It's not so bad." She ran her fingers through the short blond spikes and laughed out loud. "I hope the saying is true and blonds have more fun."

Roger hissed another "beautiful!", which was quickly followed up by "water!"

"Sure! I'll go and buy something." Atifah jumped out of the car and headed for the store. She had a newfound skip in her step. She collected a couple of sodas, four bottles of water and a few snacks. She paid for them and left.

As she rounded the corner she stopped in her tracks. A policeman was staring into the empty Ford. He had seen her coming and looked up at her. He was as taken aback by what he saw. The officer smiled. She was a good few yards away so the officer half spoke, half shouted to her. "This your car ma'am?"

"Yes it is." She had no idea of how the car sat legally, but she wasn't about to start debating the issue.

"Sorry to alarm you ma'am." He had noted the shock on her face. "I was walking past and saw your keys in the ignition." He saw her relax. "I thought I would hang around 'til you came out. You don't know who might be lurking around."

"I suppose not." She was putting on her English accent again. She spun the other car keys around her finger and brought them to rest in the palm of her hand. "I must've picked up the house keys. Thank you officer."

"No problem ma'am. Try to be more careful or you'll come out and your car will be gone."

The officer's admiring eyes made her feel good. Bad, but good. She knew her new image made her look good. All told, the hair was less of a stumbling block than she had expected.

The policeman turned to walk and then thought better of it. "I know you're not from around here. Are you going to be in town long?"

"No! Sorry! I'm on my way to Houston"

"Pity!" he smiled. "The good ones are always passing through." He took one last lingering look at the girl in tight denims and bright, long-sleeved t-shirt. He waved a resigned wave, got in his car and drove off.

This attention was not normal to Atifah and although her head was telling her it was wrong, she knew the circumstances required it. She felt guilty as she enjoyed every moment. She watched as the young cop drove off and was certain he was looking at her in his rear view mirror.

The moment was gone. Where was Roger? She looked around, worried, trying to remember the instructions should they be separated. To her relief he came from around the corner of the building. "Looks like I'm not the only one saying your hair looks good." She smiled a wide smile and handed Roger a soda. "Thanks!" he said as he cracked the seal on the lid. "I need this."

"Why were you out of the car?" she asked as she opened the door.

"I saw the cop car driving in. I recognized the driver as the one I passed on the way out. I think he recognized me, but I can't be sure. I didn't want to risk being seen in the Ford. Not yet. You were great by the way. You handled the situation like a star." Roger gulped down the soda as he sat in the passenger seat and Atifah sat behind the wheel. The cold liquid felt good in his throat.

Roger had the sunvisor down and in the makeup mirror he noticed a large black Ford sedan pulling in through the entrance. The hairs on the back of his neck stood up. He watched as the two men in dark suits and shades drove slowly into the parking area, looking around with purpose. He knew these were agents. The cop must have called it in once he arrived back at the station and then maybe popped back to double check.

The cop had seen Roger pulling out, so there was no way they thought he was still here, but he couldn't risk being seen in the new car. "We have company."

Atifah turned, frightened by the tone in Roger's voice.

"Relax! Don't look round. Use your mirrors."

They watched as the car glided slowly past and pulled up next to the police car which had parked across the other side of the parking area near the exit. The cop stood next to his car and walked around toward the agent's car as Caleb Johnson and Dwight Roberts walked to greet him. They all met between the two cars, greeted each other politely and began talking. There was gesticulating which Roger read to mean something to the tune of how he'd seen Roger going out while he was driving in. The following appeared to be an explanation of how he hadn't initially recognized Roger until he was back in the office. He called the contact number straight away.

Agent Johnson looked at his watch considering how he might have been trying to estimate the distance covered by Roger since he was spotted. The direction he was traveling and the quick calculation accounted for the disappointed look on the agents' faces. They realized Roger could have been well on his way to Dallas or Houston by now.

As Roger watched, another black sedan rolled in slowly and parked alarmingly close to Roger, but the agents inside were intent on the conversation going on across the parking and paid no heed to the white Ford. Roger was relieved he was rid of his car. He realized he'd held onto it way too long.

The agents and the cop shook hands and the cop climbed into his car and pulled out, heading in the direction of the interstate.

The agents locked their car and made for the shops. The second black car pulled out and looked like he might have been following the cop.

"Wait here!" Roger said to Atifah. She started to say something, but Roger had slipped out of the car and crept around the side of the building again. The entrance to the building wasn't close to where they parked, but he thought it better not to risk being seen in the white car by anybody. He'd thought about ducking, but knew how the sight of someone ducking can catch your eye, whereas the sight of somebody getting out of their vehicle and walking away is an everyday occurrence. Roger headed around the corner and hid there in the shade. He looked back and saw Atifah sitting in the driver's seat of the car. She was getting good at looking inconspicuous.

As he was watching her, he saw an almost imperceptible change. Her eyes widened and she glanced at Roger. Something was wrong. Roger overcame the desire to stay and find out what had worried her and he took off. As he moved he slipped the hooded jacket off over his head and dropped it under a few small shrubs.

If he was caught and they started questioning passersby, he might have been seen getting out of the vehicle and he didn't want anybody to be able to tie him back to the Ford and Atifah. Putting on his shades, he entered the back entrance of the mall. It felt like forever since he had been around people and as much as he hated shopping malls, it felt good to see people up close again. The warm fuzzy feeling was soon shattered by paranoia as he soon felt everybody looking at him. The glance of a passing geriatric felt like an electric shock and the man stepping in front of him was about to tackle him to claim his bounty. It took massive amounts of self-control to simply keep walking. Logic told him nobody would recognize him, but his emotions urged him to run out of there.

Sitting at a table in one of those interior sidewalk cafés a middle-aged man was reading something on the inside of a newspaper. He held up the paper allowing the rest of the mall to view an almost life-sized picture of Roger on the front page. Thankfully, true to form, the public was way too busy with their own lives to worry about whether a killer was walking among them.

To escape the mainstream flow of people, Roger took the flight of stairs, went through a pair of glass doors and entered into the office suites area. He was in a grey passage with white doors spaced at uneven intervals along both walls. It was lunch time so most of the doors were closed. At the opposite end of the passage a fire escape was visible as the sun shone brightly through the frosted glass. Roger, in his normal, careful way, strolled to the end of the passage and examined the fire escape, just in case. It was locked, but where a small glass tube had once prevented people from using this as a general exit, there was a gap. The door was easily opened, but he was sure it wouldn't be needed. He went through the swing doors at the other end of the passage, where from the door he was able to look down over the ground floor of the mall. The two agents stood out like a pair of black flies on a white sheet. Their sunglasses, black suites and stern demeanors clearly highlighted them as FBI agents and not only to Roger. The glances from other pedestrians showed they too had spotted the agents. Roger grinned to himself. "Incognito?" he thought.

As he watched, the two agents approached the same steps he'd just walked up. There weren't a lot of routes they could take other than this passage and Roger decided on a hasty retreat. He made his way to the fire escape. The agents moved faster than he had anticipated and he heard the door behind him open.

Roger made two crucial errors. Firstly, instead of simply continuing to walk down the passage, he became alarmed at the speed of the agents and he turned to look at them over his left shoulder. He caught the eyes of the young red-headed agent. His second error was his failure to realize the light from the door at the end of the passage caused him to be an unrecognizable silhouette to the agents and they could not see who he was. Without realizing what he was doing, he picked up his pace. The agents noticed.

"Excuse me!" Caleb Johnson called out suddenly on high alert. Roger kept walking.

"Sir?" No response. Roger kept heading for the door.

"FBI! Stop!" Only a couple of yards from the exit, Roger stopped close to an office door on his left, his mind racing.

"Damn!" Why had he broken cover? Thoughts of what he should have done passed briefly through his mind, but were soon lost in a mesh of thoughts about what he would do next. He might reach the door before they could shoot, but what then? He had no idea what was outside the door. Once outside, how far would he need to run before he reached cover? He needed a diversion.

Roger turned slowly away from the door on his left to face his captors. As he turned he tapped on the door with his left hand, hoping somebody was inside. From inside he heard a muffled – "Come in, the door's open." Music to his ears, but he hoped the agents, who were still some distance away, hadn't heard this response.

"Well now! Ain't this a pain in the ass?" Roger stated the obvious as he raised his hands, seemingly oblivious to the receptionist's call.

The agents still didn't realize who they had captured. They advanced on the suspected terrorist slowly with their hands at the ready. As they neared Roger, the younger agent's puzzled look turned to recognition. "Macadam?"

"One and the same. Nice to meet you gentlemen." Roger shifted uneasily looking at the walls, the floor, the ceiling; all the while he was willing the person inside to come to the door.

Johnson spoke "I don't believe it. What are the chances!" He was smiling.

The door handle clicked and Roger knew it was time. The agents heard the click and their eyes widened in horror. Agent Johnsson started to shout to the person to get back inside, but it was too late. Roger jammed his shoulder against the door smashing the door into the receptionist's face as she attempted in vain to get out of the way.

He swung around behind the dazed woman and jabbed his fingers hard into her back, holding her across her shoulders with his free arm. He pulled her back into a corner.

"Be quiet!" he commanded in a quiet, hissy voice.

He had expected the agents to follow him in, but the doorway stood large and empty.

"Inside. Both of you." Out of the corners of his eyes, Roger saw brief movements as office staff looked to see what was going on then realizing, ducked out of sight. "Or she gets a bullet in the liver."

He waited about a second, but didn't want to give them the chance to get their minds straight.

"Now!"

Agent Johnsson answered, "Alright Macadam. We're coming in. Don't do anything stupid." The agent filled the doorway as he came through, his weapon pointed at Roger's head.

"Both of you. Now!"

Johnsson hurried inside and Roberts followed.

Roger shielded himself as best he could behind the silently sobbing girl. "Somebody in the back office is dialing 911 as we speak, so I don't have much time. Let's not put these people's lives at risk by making me desperate. Do exactly as I say and nobody has to die today."

"Both of you place your weapons on the floor and slide them over to me." The two agents looked briefly at each other. "C'mon guys. Time's a wasting. Don't think, just act."

Johnsson started crouching slowly and Roberts followed a split second later, sliding the handguns to within two feet of the woman's shoes. "Good boys. Now. Both of you down on your stomach, arms stretched way out in front of you." They reluctantly complied.

Once they were fully prostrated, Roger used his feet to slide the weapons into the corner behind him. "Both of you, use your left hands and get your cuffs out and cuff your right wrist. Nice and tight." Once again the agents complied.

Roger spoke to the girl. "I'm going to let you go now. I want you to bend down the other side of these two guys and one at the time, they're going to place their hands behind their backs and you're going to put their cuffs on them. Understand?" She nodded. He released his grip on her shoulder and as she hesitantly moved forward, Roger slid down the wall picking up the agents weapons.

Firstly she cuffed agent Johnsson, then at Roger's instruction, Agent Roberts linked his arms through his partners and they were shackled together to the leg of the receptionist's desk.

Roger reached into the inside pocket of Agent Johnson's jacket. "Where's your phone?"

"Right side pocket."

"Is Crane's number in here?" He wanted to have a chat with Crane.

"Under 'Crane'."

"Agent? …" Roger asked the big guy for his name.

"Johnson. Caleb Johnson."

"Caleb. You should be looking a lot happier. You're alive and well. I'm no killer guys. Remember that if I happen to end up in your sights. Ok?"

Roger stood up. "Gentlemen, I'm going to take my leave. I'll see myself to the door." He raised his voice so everybody could hear. "I'm leaving now. If you're all good and keep your heads low, you'll live to tell your families what an exciting lunch time you had.

If I notice so much as a hair on your head in the window, I'll put a bullet in it. Understand?"

There were no answers, but he was sure they'd all heard. "Remember. I know where you all work and I can come back." It was his final attempt at being intimidating. He loosed the clips on the agent's weapons and sent them spinning to the end of the passage. The weapons he kicked to the other end. He slid back the bolt of the fire escape door and exited the building.

The door shut behind him, but he was already at the bottom of the steps. He hurried around the back of the building, keeping close to the wall so he would not be visible from the first floor. He rounded the corner, picking up his hoodie from the shrubbery in one fluid movement and climbed into his waiting getaway car. Atifah looked a little anxious, but Roger was calm and in control.

"Like a thief in the night," he said, exhilarated by the events.

"What?" she asked, unaware of how close he had come to being caught.

"I'll fill you in on the trip. It's getting late. Let's head for San Antonio. Do you want me to drive for a while?"

"No! I'll be ok for now. Maybe you can take over after Houston."

-- o --- o0o --- o --

"Good afternoon Mrs Macadam. I'm Agent Crane from Homeland Security." He held up the official-looking shield where Anne could see it. "Do you mind if I come in and talk. I'd like to ask you a few questions."

"I've already spoken to the police, the FBI and probably half of your department too. I think you can go and read all the reports. There's no point in wasting time telling you the same thing again."

"I understand your frustration Mrs M..."

"Do you?" Her voice raised in anger. "So your wife is implicated too, is she? She's been labeled armed and dangerous and had her face splashed all over the television has she?"

He paused. "You're right. I don't understand. I could never understand what you're going through."

"Damn right you don't understand," she softened, falling for the sweet talk.

"I'll tell you what, any question you've already been asked, you don't have to answer. Answer only the new ones."

"Come in Mr …"

"Crane! Tom Crane." He moved inside, looking around as if he half expected Roger to be waiting inside.

"Have a seat Mr Crane and …"

"Oh! This is Barnard." Crane was almost dismissive of the younger agent. "Mrs Macadam. I want to warn you up front …"

"Anything I say can and will be …"

"No! I wanted to warn you I'm an ex-marine. Diplomacy is not my strongpoint. I don't pretend to be a diplomatic person and I will probably insult you or say something heartless at some stage. Please bear with me. I am here to gather information. Nothing more." He paused briefly.

"Do you know where your husband was on September 11, 2001?" Crane didn't waste time.

"He was in New York on business."

"It never struck you as strange he was also in Nairobi on August 7 1998 and in Oklahoma City on April 19 1995?"

"Not at all! He doesn't decide where he is going. Alan tells him where to go and how long to be there. He wasn't close to any of the blasts, except Nairobi where he heard the blast from his hotel. He was also caught in the crossfire of skirmishes in Kuwait and now recently in Muscat. He goes where there's oil and where there's oil, there's somebody protecting it from somebody who wants it. It's time he got out of the game."

"Ok!" Crane showed no interest in her opinion. "His boss, Alan Foggarty is that right?"

"Yes! Alan, or at least his PA is the one who does the cold calling on these companies and sets up the meetings. Maybe you should be asking them these questions. Besides, you do realize Mike was also at these locations, at the same time."

"I do Mrs Macadam and I'll definitely be talking to Mr Foggarty and Mr Parker." Crane was deep in thought as he scribbled notes down in a book on his lap.

"Is his partner always with him?" Chris asked in a matter of fact way which resulted in a disapproving glare from Crane.

"Most times. I'm sure he was there in all those particular cases. Mike usually goes ahead of Roger to begin the sales process, then Roger follows when there is a glimmer of hope of the sale going through!"

"And you've known Mr Parker a long time?" More glares from Crane as agent Barnard started taking over the interview process.

"Years! The two of them were at college together."

Crane cut in. "And no chance of Parker being linked to militant Islamic groups?"

"Hell no!"

"Nazis?"

"Nazis? I didn't even know there were Nazis?"

"Oh there are Nazis. Neo-Nazis, ultra-rights. McVeigh was linked to them and a group called Militia."

"McVeigh? Of Oklahoma?"

"The same."

"Where are we going with this?" She was getting annoyed. "I am one hundred percent certain that neither Mike nor Roger was involved in any of these activities. I can tell you with absolute certainty, Roger has never killed anybody. He hasn't even thought about killing anybody."

"What can you tell me about the woman?" Crane changed tack.

"Atifah, Nothing!" Anne was matter of fact. "Almost nothing. She's young and beautiful. Under different circumstances, I'd probably like her a lot."

"Different circumstances? So you don't like her?"

Anne laughed. "Roger introduced her as his wife. It's a bit of a shock."

"Do you think she and your husband …" he trailed off.

"You don't know Roger. I trust my husband in every possible way. He's not an outgoing person and the majority of people would find him boring, but I could count on Roger to donate both his kidneys to me, or Katie if the need arose. He'd cut them out himself."

Crane feigned shock at the thought. "Do you have a photograph of her?"

"Come on now Mr Crane. You don't expect me to hand over photos and increase the probability of you putting a bullet in my husband do you?"

"I can get a court order."

"If there are any they'll be destroyed before you get back here with a court order. Let's understand something Mr Crane. I will cooperate with you to the extent I have to, but don't expect me to hand over my husband to you and don't expect me to increase the possibility of someone taking a shot at him. It won't happen."

"Fair enough Mrs Macadam." He appreciated her honesty and frankness and decided he liked Anne. "I can't say I'd act differently. I have nothing more." He looked at Barnard who shook his head indicating he had no more questions. They both walked out thinking the visit had raised more questions than answers.

His phone rang.

"Johnson. What have you got? ... Madisonville? No. Go! Speak to everybody. We want a description of the girl... take Roberts with you and I mean talk to everybody!" Crane gave a half wave as he made his way out into the yard. "Do we know what he was doing there? Speak to the black and white. You need to speak to everybody. Shop and office staff. If nobody has seen him, then stand at the door and talk to people coming out the center. We need a description of the girl."

He hung up still standing outside the front door. Then after a few more clicks. "Wilson! Speak to me. ... Crap! Ok! Leave it. I want you and Crosby to head over to Macadam's employer and find out why he was in the same locations as the terror attacks ... he's been spotted in Madisonville. Maybe on his way to Dallas I think ... it's not confirmed, but it looks positive."

-- o --- oOo --- o --

Roger related the story to Atifah while she drove. He saw a deeply scared little girl as she processed the information and realized how close she had come to being alone and wanted in this big country. She didn't even want to go on to processing any 'What if ...' scenarios.

"We're going to have to be careful about putting 'this' in public." Roger waved his hand in front of his face. "I was recognized while I was driving. It was slow driving, but I was still moving. I'm more recognizable than I thought." Then not talking to anybody but the universe in general. "The cops now know I have dark hair. I will need to be extra careful."

"It was the same policeman I talked to." She was going through the meeting in her head. "If only he'd known."

"We're ok until your photograph hits the TV. Then we may have a problem." He paused. "For the time being though, you're our public face."

"I think I can manage."

"I know you can. You're doing a great job." She had handled herself well and with careful thought in pressured situations. He knew there would be more pressure as time moved on, but he was confident, if they kept their heads, at least better than he had when he'd been seen by the agents, they would be all right. His mind wondered to thinking about how many terrorists and criminals had justified holding people at gun point in the way he had, for their own selfish needs. He'd hurt the receptionist and not given it a thought.

He picked up the agent's phone and dialed Crane's number through the contact list.

"Talk to me."

"Mr Crane I presume."

"Who is this? …" Crane's voice trailed off.

"Roger Macadam."

"Macadam?" Crane was confused.

"I've had an accidental run in with two of your team. They forced me to play my …"

The reality hit Crane like a clap of thunder. "Where are they?" Crane's shoulders sagged as he thought the worst. "If you've …"

"Relax Crane. They're fine. Maybe a little embarrassed.

Not sure of the situation, Crane pictured himself having to visit the agents' families. Something he'd done too many times. "Are they …?"

"They're fine," he repeated.

Relief and anger started to flood into the agent's mind, but he was still confused. "Where are they?"

"I said they're fine." Roger could hear the disbelief in Crane's voice. "I let my guard down a little and we had a chance meeting. You'll be getting a call from them I'm sure. I didn't want to risk the motel scenario again, so I left them in a public place." It hadn't entered his mind at the time, but he had thought about it with relief afterwards.

"What do you want?" All the niceties out the way. "Why are you calling me?"

"To let you know your boys are alive and well and to let you know I had a gun on both of them, but they're both ok."

"So!" Crane still wasn't understanding what Roger was saying.

"To let you know I had both of the agents' weapons in my hand, but I left them both at the scene."

"So!" Crane insisted.

"So! Sooner or later we may be in the sights of one of your people. I'd like to be offered the same courtesy I gave your boys. Make sure they know we may be on the run, but we're not killers. You have the wrong person."

"Hand yourself in and it'll be over."

"And then what Crane? Then what happens? I'm locked up and have to prove my innocence while I'm inside. We've had this conversation Crane. You know I can't do that."

"And you know I can't take off the armed and dangerous label while you're on the run."

"Listen to me Crane, there's a young girl here who has her entire life ahead of her. Whatever the outcome for me I want you to assure me ..."

"I can only assure you of one thing. I will catch you and the girl. It's what I do. You can't keep running forever."

"I don't intend to. Only 'til I've cleared my name... our names. Then I'll be handing myself in."

"Why don't you simply come in? We can sort out the details then." Crane didn't even try to hide the condescending tone in his voice.

"Which of your people shot the bellhop?"

"My people didn't."

"Then there's more here than you and I, isn't there?"

"So you didn't kill the boy either?"

"I've already told you I didn't Crane. You need to pay attention."

"I don't need to listen to you. You're not my buddy, you're a perp on the run. Understand you are not giving me much to believe."

"I'll give you something to believe," Roger was thinking. "But you will have to act fast or another innocent person could die. Have your team ready to move this evening. I will call in a location

137

to you and then you move your people in to stake out the location. If you're not fast enough, you could end up with another bellhop problem."

"Your card has been frozen."

"No doubt, but I'm sure your guys are still on the lookout for me using it. These phones are encrypted or something, aren't they?"

"How do you mean?"

"There is no point in doing this if somebody is tapping your phone. This has to be between you and me only."

"Yeah! Our phones plug into some private cloud thingy, which means they can't be traced or listened to." Crane paused while he thought. "So you're going to swipe your card, which we'll pick up and come to stake out the place where you swipe it."

"Better! I'm going to give you the heads up before I even arrive at the place, so you can be on your way early."

"How do I know this isn't a trap?" Crane was thinking through the possible outcomes.

"I could've shot your two agents today. I'm no killer."

"S'pose so."

"You're not going to have the chance to set up surveillance properly. If it doesn't go according to plan, you need to get in there and protect the staff. I don't want this on my conscience."

"No problem!" Crane felt a little uneasy about the situation, but was sure it could be contained. "So let's get this straight. You're going to phone me and tell me where you will use your credit card."

"Yep!"

"Then I'm going to rush my guys out there and stake the place out."

"Correct!"

"And you think somebody will pitch up and whack the desk clerk?"

"Possibly! It happened before."

"What if nobody pitches up?"

"Then we're back to square one. I run, you follow."

Both of the men sat in silence for what seemed like an eternity as they thought through the process, examining the margins for error at each stage. They disconnected their phones simultaneously without saying another word to each other, both oblivious to the person on the other end of the line.

-- o --- oOo --- o --

When Roger terminated the call, he sat quietly for a while thinking. His thoughts were disturbed by the mention of Oman on the news. He reached over and turned up the volume.

"… are massing in southern Italy, Greece and India. The strike force is estimated to be twice the size of that which crippled Bagdad. US, British and Indian ships are en-route to the Arabian Sea. The Department of Defence, today confirmed the mobilization of over one-hundred and twenty-thousand US and international troops. They are being flown to the Gulf region as we speak and are due to set down within hours."

Roger and Atifah sat in stunned silence as the news unfolded.

"US Defence Secretary, Robert Gates, said today, that it was time that terrorist states and states that harbor terrorists, should be made to pay for their part in world instability. He went on to say that any proponent of terror, was an opponent of America and that ridding the world of terror was the first step to introducing a new world order of peace and security.

"Al Jazeera TV reported that a letter had been received from Al Qaeda stating that a declaration of war with Oman by America, will be a declaration of war with America by Al Qaeda. The writer of the letter issued a warning that no American will be safe to step out of their home and no American will be safe in his home."

Atifah started to talk. "But …" She stopped as Roger raised his hand.

"In local news, at least three Omani homeowners were chased from their homes by their respective communities, with one of the families being beaten by members of the community. This was captured on a cell phone camera and the footage can be viewed on www.cnn.com."

She could no longer contain herself. "What is happening? Why are these people being beaten?"

"Why are we being hunted? There is something going down and we're right in the middle."

"What can we do?"

"First of all, call the Sultan and tell him to do everything in his power to avoid this and I mean everything. He has to publicly invite the international community to inspect his land. He has to avert any attack. Maybe the US wants Oman as a stepping stone into Saudi. I have no idea. He must do it publicly so the whole world knows or Muscat will be a dust pile within a few days."

-- o --- oOo --- o --

"Mr Foggarty. You have two people here to see you." Barbara's voice was flat and emotionless. She was hesitant as she looked up at the two people dressed in black before her. She knew this was something to do with Roger. Both agents had their eyes hidden by dark sunshades.

She didn't move as she relayed Alan's message to the agents. "Please take a seat. He'll be right with you."

Agent Crosby thanked her courteously. They both moved to the side and were talking in lowered voices when Alan came through. He was visibly shocked when he saw the two. "Uh, can I help you?"

"Mr Foggarty! I'm Agent Wilson, this is my partner, Agent Crosby." She held up her badge. "Homeland Security!"

They carried out the usual formalities and then Agent Wilson began. "We're investigating the Macadam case. Can you spare us a few minutes?"

Foggarty wanted to dodge this as much as possible. "I do have a meeting this after …"

"You sent Macadam to New York on September 11 2001." She paused for a second, but not long enough for Alan to speak. "On April 19 1995, he was in Oklahoma City and on August 7 1998 you sent him to Nairobi. I think it might be worthwhile you having a chat with us."

"I didn't …"

She stopped him by raising her hand. "We don't need a court order to take you in for questioning." She softened. "We'll only take a couple of minutes of your time."

"Sure! Come through!" He glanced at Barbara. "Hold my calls."

"Please! Have a seat."

"It's simple Mr Foggarty. We need to know why you sent Roger Macadam to those destinations. And why on those dates?"

"I don't remember why I sent him. It must have been to quote on equipment. We generate leads and react to enquiries."

"What equipment?"

"We manufacture and install fluid moving equipment. We mostly sell to the oil companies, but we have made sales in other industries."

"Which companies did he visit on those days?"

"Offhand I have no idea, but I can probably find it. I would need a couple of days."

"We don't have a couple of days Mr Foggarty. Can you look it up now?"

"Now? No! You want me to find out where he was in '98. Fourteen years ago. I can't open his email can I? I don't think we had email then." Agent Wilson twitched the corner of her mouth downward as she thought about it.

"Ok! Mr Foggarty. We'll stop by tomorrow to see if you've made any headway. Thanks for your time."

"Wait a second!" Alan thought about something. He picked up the phone. "Barbara! Please will you have a look in Roger's filing cabinet? I'm sure he has a box in the bottom, where he keeps all his old diaries." He paused. "Thanks."

"It's a long shot, but worth a try." He smiled at the two expressionless faces in front of him. "Would you like coffee while we wait?"

"No! ... Thanks," agent Wilson answered. Agent Crosby shook his head. Terri Wilson continued,"Maybe you can tell me a bit about Roger Macadam?"

"Like what?"

"As a person, what makes him tick?"

"Family! Nothing more, nothing less. Sure, I send him away a couple of times a year and he always goes willingly, but I know his family is everything to him. He's a brilliant, brilliant engineer and I'd hate to lose him. It's always a balancing act with him. If I ask too often, he'd walk away in an instant. Money, power, nothing would attract him to stay if I keep him from his family. The best bonus I can give Roger is time off. He loves to go home to his family."

"Strange he ran so quickly with this other woman then?" Crosby asked.

"Depends on how he views the alternative, doesn't it?"

"You mean getting caught?"

"No! I mean handing himself over." Alan paused as if to dramatize his words. "His family is his central point. If he thinks he can solve this issue before you do, there's no way he will ever hand himself in."

Barbara entered the room carrying a large and seemingly heavy box. Agent Crosby jumped up to help and took the box from her. "There's another one there, call me if you want me to bring it in." Barbara was looking a bit red faced.

"Thanks Barbs." Foggarty didn't look up. He was intent on the box.

Agent Crosby tipped the box on its side and a pile of diaries of various shapes, sizes and colors tumbled and slid out.

Immediately, a black diary was visible with 2001 emblazoned in gold on the mock leather cover. "Bingo!" Wilson reached for the book. She thumbed through it, half expecting to see a history of Roger Macadam, but was a little disappointed to see mostly blank pages with the occasional entry saying things like 'meet H Goss – Goss Enterprises'.

Occasionally the entries would be annotated with an address or phone number. It was clear Roger used the diary as a reminder of forthcoming events, not an historical recorder.

She found September and the days around the 11th. She read out, "Meet G Taylor – Harrow Foods". She flipped the page to see if there was more. "That was September 10 at 11h00, the Monday before 9/11."

"I remember! Harrow Foods, outside New York. They manufacture, or purify, or do something with vegetable oil. A subsidiary of Heinz I think."

Crosby was already scratching through the pile for the '95 and '98 books. "Ninety-eight." he said letting everyone know he'd located the book. "And ninety-five." He handed the diaries to Agent Wilson.

She found the entries in both books, then flipped out her phone and dialed a number. She spoke abruptly, "England! Wilson! We're coming back to the office. Can you find out what you can about Harrow Foods in New York, Africa Engineering in Nairobi and Paton Tex in Oklahoma City?" She paused while Derrick England questioned her. "If I knew I wouldn't be asking. Find out what you can. Are they real companies? Who owns them? What do they manufacture? Use your imagination." She closed her phone, frustrated at Derrick England's obvious inability to think for himself.

"I'd like to keep these," she pointed in the direction of the spilled books. "And the other box too."

"Sure! No problem!" Alan was pleased with himself for thinking of the diaries. "I don't think you'll find much in them. Roger only used them as a reminder."

"I think it would be worth a look anyway." She motioned to Crosby to go to the receptionist to retrieve the other box. He nodded and left the room. "Mr Foggarty. I don't think you should disappear for the time being, or you may find yourself on America's most wanted too."

"But I …"

"Keep us informed where you are at all times and don't give us reason to think you may be running. Here's my card." Gut feel told her Foggarty had no involvement. It was her way of putting fear into people. She picked up the box effortlessly after replacing the diaries from the floor and left through the office door. She nodded to Barbara on the way out and the two agents left the building through the main doors.

-- o --- oOo --- o --

Roger was thinking, not only of the risk to him, but also of the staff and the agents. Lives were at stake and he needed to be sure he covered all the bases.

"Change of plan," he said to Atifah. She glanced over at him confirming she'd heard. "We need to find somewhere to sit out the afternoon. Also, I think I need to buy a camcorder or something."

"Ok!" she guessed there was more detail to follow.

"We can't go back to the same hotel. You've changed a bit since we were last there."

"Oh! The hair."

"It might draw attention if a very different Mrs Costopoulos books in. We'll find another hotel."

Atifah found herself looking forward to the prospect of relaxing in a decent bed again. She didn't like traveling. Roger on the other hand was enjoying being chauffeured around.

"When you reach the interstate, head towards Dallas. We'll drive up the I45 for a bit."

"Will we need more gas?"

Roger looked over at the gauge. "Nah! We'll be ok for now." He slipped his wallet out of his pocket to examine the money situation. "Damn!" he said to himself as he thumbed through the small pile of notes. "We're going to need more cash. Let's find a bank before we go. I think we passed one on West Main Street."

"They'll know if you use the card."

"It's ok! They know we're here anyway. Better to confirm what they already know, than tell them where we're going."

"True!"

Roger instructed Atifah to pull up outside a small supply store. He counted out a few notes, placing them in her hand. "I need a small rucksack and buy us both a pair of sneakers. We may need to do some walking. I'm a size 9. You can get any pair, but I need one of them to come in a box. I need a roll of duct tape. About six foot of plastic covered mains wire. Oh! And one of those carpet knives people are always cutting their fingers off with."

Atifah didn't bother to ask. She took the money and headed for the store. After a short while, she emerged with a large bag in each hand. She passed the bags to Roger as she climbed into the driver's seat. He thanked her and set about digging in the bag. He opened the men's sneakers and threw them into the back seat. He deftly stripped the plastic coating from the wire flex and cut the inside wires into a few smaller pieces.

Atifah started the car and waited. "Do you want me to drive?"

"Not yet. While I'm working on this won't you take a walk and see if you can find somewhere to buy a camcorder? We need one we can charge in the car, or an adapter, or something." She looked puzzled. "Tell them you want to charge it in the car. They'll know."

She switched off the engine and held her hand out. Roger stopped what he was doing and looked up at her and smiled. "Oh! I suppose you need cash." He took out his wallet again and handed her more cash. "We don't need to video the pimples on the astronauts in the space station. Get a bottom of the range camcorder. But tell them we are using it at night."

"No problem," she said, but Roger already had his head down and was working on his little project before she closed the door behind her.

After a while she opened the door and climbed into the vehicle again. Roger looked at the small box she was carrying and read out the contents. "Perfect!" he said. "Exactly what we need. Let's plug it in and start it charging."

Back at his project, Roger doubled over the wires and placed them in the box so that they were partially exposed. After replacing the lid and binding the box closed with duct tape, he slid the box into the rucksack, closing the clasps.

Roger sat back and closed his eyes as if meditating. After a short while, she started getting a little impatient. Atifah asked again. "Do you want me to go to the ATM?" She glanced down the street at the ATM as if planning her passage.

"Not this time. I'll go."

Shocked, she spun her head back toward him. "You might be seen!"

"I will be seen. The ATM will have a camera. We don't want them to see you using my card."

She sat in puzzled silence, not knowing what Roger was about to do. He grabbed a few pieces of paper from the glove compartment and checked whether they contained anything written on them. Satisfied, he scribbled something on the paper, folded the sheets in half and turned to the girl. "Ok! Pull the car round the corner and let's take a short drive."

She reversed into the street and pulled out turning down a small lane. Roger's head spun back and forth surveying the roads and buildings around about. At his direction, she made a figure-eight route around two blocks. All the while Roger was expressionless, much like he was when designing intricate process control systems. His eyes scanned up and down the buildings. Satisfied, he smiled. "Pull up around there and find a parking out of sight of the bank."

"Perfect!" he said as she pulled into a roadside parking.

He took a deep breath. "Wish me luck. Keep the engine running."

She half shrugged her shoulders and smiled at Roger, showing him she had no idea what he was talking about. "Good luck! Are you sure you don't want me to go?" She was still oblivious of his intentions.

Roger laughed. "No! This one I have to do alone."

She watched as Roger crossed the street and disappeared round the corner. She smiled and shook her head as she watched him go.

Roger entered the small banking hall and looked around. The place was nearly empty. One teller sat looking at her fingernails, another shuffled papers to her left, and a third was dealing with a young woman while her child played on his knees on the floor, sliding around his mother's feet.

An armed security guard sat on a plastic chair inside the doorway. Roger greeted him as he entered. His greeting was answered in an equally courteous manner. Roger's rucksack was slung over his left shoulder and in his right hand he carried a cell phone. The young girl looked up from her nails, a little disgruntled, as Roger approached her counter, but broke into a smile as her teller-customer-focus training kicked in.

"Good day, Sir! How may we assist to you today?" It was like she was reading from a prompt card.

"Hello!" Roger replied in a relaxed manner. "I'd like to …" He patted his shirt pocket as if looking for something, then his left hip pocket. "Sorry! I think I've lost it." He slipped the rucksack from his shoulder and placed it on the high counter in front of him. The girl was beginning to display a hint of frustration when he said, "Ah! Found it!" He pulled the piece of paper from his right pocket. "I don't have my glasses. Would you mind reading this for me?"

The girl leaned forward, took the piece of paper from his hand and started to read. The color drained from her face as the words on the paper sunk in. It read: "Keep calm and do not alarm the people around you. There is a bomb in this bag which will go off if I hit the button on my cell phone." She looked up horrified, firstly at the bag, then up at Roger. He smiled and showed her the cell phone in his hand. She looked down again at the piece of paper in her hands, which by now were quivering as she read. "Do not try to alert anybody or set off the silent alarm as the electrical current in the switch will set the bomb off and everybody will die." He knew this was probably impossible, but hoped she didn't.

She read on. "My account has been frozen by the bank and I need cash. Please hand me $20,000 which you can take from my savings account – details below." She looked up and glanced sideways toward the security guard, but Roger had positioned himself in her line of sight. She looked at Roger's now stern eyes. He shook his head and mouthed the words, "Don't be stupid!"

She hesitated again, but quickly realized she was on her own. The child still played on his knees on the floor and was hogging the attention of everybody in the bank with his innocent laughter. Everybody smiled as they watched the child, but for the teller, time stood still. She slowly opened her money drawer. She counted off four bundles from the back of her drawer and pushed them toward Roger. As he reached for them he handed her another piece of paper. She read in silence. "Take the bag – it's safe – and place it by your feet." She looked at Roger with wide, horrified eyes and in tiny, almost imperceptible movements shook her head. She didn't want to touch the bag. Roger leant forward placing his right hand with the cell phone on the counter top. In movements just as small, Roger nodded his head telling the girl in no uncertain terms, she would place the bag by her feet. She obliged, picking the bag up with shaking hands and leaned forward placing the bag on the ground.

"Oh! One last thing …" Roger's voice took her by surprise and she looked up at him, startled. He slid a third piece of paper across the shiny counter top. Again, the terrified girl reached across for the note. "I'm leaving now. If I see anybody follow I can detonate from anywhere. You can call the police after I'm gone and you can give them these instructions: They can open the box to disarm. There are no booby traps."

"You've been an absolute star," Roger said to the girl. "And don't worry about it. It's safe."

The girl didn't believe him and wanted to scream, but the left side of her brain kept her from being stupid. She watched in horror as Roger turned and started walking away. She wanted to run away from the bag at her feet. As a reminder to keep still, Roger turned to her and waved good-bye using his right hand with the cell phone cradled in his palm. He reached the door, greeted the security guard and left.

He walked swiftly, but not fast enough to attract attention. As he crossed the street he battled with the urge to look around. He felt more comfortable as he rounded the corner and even more so as he climbed into the car and sat down next to Atifah. "Ok! Let's go. Turn right at the end and drive."

"What happened?" She still had no clue.

"I held up the bank." Roger was speaking almost with pride. There was gloating in the tone of his voice. He'd enjoyed this experience. The adrenalin was coursing through his veins and he was feeling powerful and in control. He stifled back the urge to scream out obscenities at the bank and its personnel.

"What are you talking about?" Atifah was shocked and dismayed. "You held up a bank?"

"It was GREAT!" He couldn't resist any longer. The 'great' bellowed from his throat.

"Great! What do you mean, great?" She couldn't believe what she was hearing. "Now to add to it all we've become bank robbers too?"

"No! I didn't rob anything." Roger came crashing down as he realized she was not enjoying this as much as he was. "My account has been suspended. I had the money in my savings account. We've been saving for a while." Suddenly, she'd brought the reality back and he wasn't sure whether he was justifying his actions to her or to himself. "Look! We needed the money. I can't simply go home and pick up cash."

"Neither can I, but I don't think I would have held up a bank. What did you do? You don't have a gun, do you?"

"You know I don't." From king of the castle, Roger had become the troublesome knave. "I told the teller I had a bomb."

She sat with a deadpan face in silence. After what seemed like an eternity, she spoke, "What do you think those people suffered through, thinking they could be killed at any moment?"

Roger sat in silence. He knew the question didn't need an answer. "You're right!" he repeated to himself. "You're right!"

As he thought about it, he realized he'd enjoyed the experience way too much for comfort. Thinking back, what if she'd caught the guard's attention? What if she'd panicked or frozen? What if things had been different? What if he'd had a gun? Would he have been willing to use it on those innocent people?

"Damn! I've become what they're saying I am."

"You have and you're enjoying it." She wasn't pulling her punches. "You've become somebody else. Somebody I don't like!"

Roger was about to start talking. He was about to tell her he didn't care whether she liked him or not, that he thought she was getting a bit ahead of herself, deciding who he'd become and she had not known him long enough to form judgments. Of course. She was right. This little girl was wise and she was strong enough to say what she thought, without fear of how he'd react. Roger liked her more and more.

"You're right on all counts. I apologize." He was sorry. He had failed to think through all the possible outcomes. He had placed both Atifah and himself at risk and through him, his family. "I've become a monster. I did enjoy it. It gave me a rush."

"Thank you for the apology," she spoke quietly, "and I accept. I think we should talk through things before we do them from now on."

"Of course! Dear!" Roger said. She showed no reaction to the ill placed humor. "Let's buy food, then find somewhere to hole up and rest."

"The best idea you've had all day."

"First, I need to have a look at the camcorder."

"Is this another 'need to know' mission?"

His gaze softened. "Not at all!" Roger proceeded to explain his conversation with Agent Crane. "So! I would like to set up a camera to monitor in case things go wrong. I don't want our name dragged further down."

"How are you going to record without getting caught?"

"I don't know at this point. We'll see when we find the correct place."

-- o --- oOo --- o --

"People! Listen up!" Crane spoke to his crew. "Macadam is going to be in contact with us. He's setting up a sting. He reckons he's innocent and he wants us to catch the bad guys. I need you all available this evening."

"Where are we going?" Terri Crosby had moved in closer.

"Not sure yet," Crane muttered under his breath. "Macadam said he is going to use his credit card, but will let us know before he does."

"It could be a trap," Mills interjected. "I don't want to walk into a trap."

"It could be! You'll have to have your wits about you. You all know the rules. I want Macadam alive, but if he gives you reason to take him down, then so be it. Take them both down if necessary."

"I don't think it will be a trap," Crosby spoke again. "He still feels ahead of us. It'll be worse when we close in on him."

"Are you starting to like this guy Crosby? Be sure you all know, he gets the benefit of the doubt, but if the need arises don't hesitate to shoot."

"Do you think we'll see him?"

"I doubt it. This guy's as sharp as a sewer rat and twice as nasty."

"Then why are we entertaining him by going?"

149

"Because! If he's telling the truth the hotel staff will be in danger. We saw what happened at the last place he used his card. We at least owe it to them to be there. So here's the deal. Nobody goes home. We wait for something to happen and then we move quickly, hopefully quicker than Macadam thinks we'll be."

"Can we use a chopper? Maybe we can have a headstart on him." Sam Kozlowski spoke from his desk.

"We could, but he would hear it coming. Let's split the team. Half of you in the chopper the other half will drive when we know where we are going." Crane sat for a while in silence then said, "He's probably going to stay close to the interstate. Find a map showing Houston to Dallas."

-- o --- o0o --- o --

The two traveled up the I-45 bypassing Centerville and turned off into Buffalo. The town of Buffalo appeared smaller than Madisonville with a lot of trees around. It was the type of place Roger could live. He looked around and marveled at the small town with the square fronted buildings, like the set of an old Western movie. He had often thought about the prospects of throwing in the towel. Saying goodbye to the engineering life to buy a house in a small town like Buffalo.

As they approached Buffalo from the interstate, he found himself trying to imagine the herds of bison that once roamed the area. The town was dusty and rough, but friendly. He found it inviting and relaxing. He liked the prospect of being able to walk anywhere in the town.

Once the fantasy was gone he started to notice the lack of movement in the streets. He felt a little uneasy. This looked like a place where everybody knew everybody. For a while he felt the locals were looking at their car. The roads were devoid of moving traffic and for a while it seemed they were the only moving vehicle. Pretty soon, as the panic subsided, he noticed movement and realized people were going about their business and nobody cared who they were. Cursing himself for being paranoid, he guessed Buffalo must have a steady stream of visitors doing the journey from Dallas to Houston. The town lay close to the interstate and was a convenient midway stopover to relieve the pressure of the sodas consumed in the first half of the journey.

Atifah drove slowly through the main street of Buffalo. They were looking for a hotel with cover from where they could overlook the lobby and video proceedings. Pretty soon they decided the Wild Horse was the best option. It was secluded and after dark they would be able to set up the camcorder, either in a large oak tree, or in the shrubs opposite depending on the available light from what looked like a large floodlight. Only darkness would bring the answers.

"Ok! So what should we do until it gets dark?" Roger turned to Atifah.

She smiled, "I would love to go into the hotel, have a nice bath and lie down on a wonderful comfortable bed."

"That would be good wouldn't it?" Roger reflected on the situation and realized his body was aching and would welcome a soft bed. His thoughts wandered to a holiday he'd spent with Anne a few years earlier. After a long, battering drive they had climbed into a warm bath together and lay there in each other's arms, too tired to move. He'd woken up first with his beautiful woman lying on his chest, sleeping. The still water close to their bodies had remained warm, but as Roger moved his foot the water swirled around their feet. What had been a warmish cocoon, suddenly became an icy torrent around their feet. It shocked them both to reality and the more they moved, the more the water swirled, freezing the couple into motion. He remembered how they'd jumped out of the icy bath and wrapped their naked bodies in thick warm towels, laughing. They jumped into the big bed to warm up. He came back to the present, a little sadder than when he left. "It would be really good."

"We still have a few hours before we can go to bed." He was still a bit vacant, trying in vain to reconjure the emotions he'd felt, a moment prior. They were gone.

Eventually, out of his half trance, he spoke. "In the meantime why don't we find something to eat?" He turned and pointed. "I think I saw a little takeout place back there. Then I think we'll take a drive out of town and find a place where we can stretch our legs and relax for the afternoon."

-- o --- o0o --- o --

After a short drive through the oak trees, Roger spotted a place where they could pull off the road. It was a scenic spot next to a small creek. Atifah eased the vehicle across the rough gravel surface and pulled up next to an old tree. Roger looked around but saw nobody. They both climbed out of the car and stretched their arms in unison. Roger turned to look at Atifah over the roof of the car with his arms stretched above his head. They looked at each other and laughed. Both had their arms in the same position. The sudden connection made Roger uncomfortable and his thoughts shot back to the 'moment'. He ducked his head into the open door, to pick up the boxes of takeout and then signaled her to follow him down to the creek.

The sun shone through the trees giving a bright, greenish glow to the sparkling water surface. After eating their lunch the two of them lay back on the grassy bank and for a while, simply forgot they were on the run from the entire country.

"It's not a bed but it's the best we have," said Roger with his eyes closed as he lay there soaking up the warm Texan sun. He opened his eyes as a shadow passed in front of his face. Atifah's face was inches from his. She leant forward and kissed Roger briefly on his lips. He was startled but didn't move.

"Thank you for getting us through this." She had been thinking about what she'd have done without him and realized he'd been taking good care of her, when there was not much reason for him to do so. "I am sorry for the way I spoke to you after the bank."

"Don't apologize! You were right and besides, it's not over yet. I think it's only the beginning."

"No! You were right. We needed money and you can't walk into the bank and draw it." She still lay to his right with her face a little too close to his. "I was selfish and was thinking of my own situation and what would become of me if you were caught. I didn't even think of what would happen to you."

"We're under more pressure than most people will feel in a lifetime. I think we can forgive ourselves a little don't you?"

"Then forgive me for this." She lay down on her side next to him with her head on his chest. He fought back his initial desire to move her aside and sit bolt upright. He realized she probably needed comfort and reassurance, so let her lie there with her eyes closed. After a short while he lowered his guard and drifted off to sleep, warmed by her closeness and the afternoon sun.

-- o --- o0o --- o --

When Roger woke he could still feel the weight of her head but now on his stomach. She had shifted onto her back. Disgust and horror flooded his head as he noticed the gentle curve of her stomach under the palm of his right hand. Scared to move, he became aware of the almost negligible movements as she breathed long, even breaths. Relief. She was asleep. As he slowly lifted his hand, she stirred and woke. Roger was embarrassed. He knew she had felt his hand on her stomach and the movement of his hand had woken her. She turned back onto her side looking up at Roger's face.

She was smiling. Roger couldn't read the smile. He couldn't look into her eyes. "I'm sorry!" he said slowly. "I didn't know … I was …"

"For what?" she interrupted. She knew! He could see she knew.

Roger was in an awkward place. She was being kind to him. She knew. What do you answer to right the situation? "My hand was … I mean, I was …"

He was stumbling. She came to the rescue. "I'm feeling much better. I needed sleep." She sat up and stretched. "I suppose we must get going."

The sun had sunk lower in the sky. The weather was far from cold, but she was right, they had work to do. Besides, it gave Roger reason to clear the thoughts of castration and self-mutilation out of his head. How could he have allowed it to happen? She stood and started moving toward the car. "Wait!" Roger called her back. He had to set the record straight. There had been too many 'moments' for his liking. Things were getting uncomfortable. "When I woke up I had my hand on your stomach. I apologize. I didn't know about it and it meant nothing."

She smiled. "Oh! It meant something." Roger's face took on a puzzled look as he waited for her to continue. "It meant you were fast asleep." He relaxed and grinned. "Roger!" She was sounding sincere. "I trust you! I wouldn't lie with my head on your chest if I thought you were going to grope me in my sleep." She smiled down at Roger while he sat on the grass. "I have never laid with my head on a man's chest and I've never had a man's hand on my stomach. I'm not afraid to tell you it meant something to me. I hope you will allow me to enjoy it without feeling guilty."

Roger stood up. He took her hand. "Of course! I'm glad you enjoyed being handled by an old man."

She laughed. "You're not old and besides, whether you like it or not, we're probably married. My body belongs to you." She laughed again as Roger's eyes widened in shock. He looked at her and laughed as he realized she must have been joking.

Trying to appear unfazed and nonchalant, Roger looked the girl up and down. "I'll keep it in mind." He wasn't at all convincing and she knew she'd ruffled his feathers. She laughed again.

They still had time to kill, so Roger stayed at the creek while Atifah filled up at the gas station. Once again her short blond hair and Halle Berry body didn't fail to attract the attention of every male over the age of nine. It's something Roger had thought about. If the FBI managed to locate pictures of Atifah she would be instantly recognized because everybody looked at her. At least for the time being it was distraction enough to prevent him being seen should the occasion arise. Roger had one of those forgetful and unnoticeable faces and an even less noticeable body.

He spent his time alone planning the evening and running through various scenarios in his mind. He needed to give the agents time to drive up from Houston before using the card. What if Crane placed agents up and down the interstate and they turned up before he was ready? What if they arrived too late putting the lives of the staff in danger? These thoughts were still swirling around his head when Atifah returned from filling up the car.

"Everything ok?" he asked.

"No problem," she said as she climbed out of the vehicle.

"Ok! Let's go over our plan." She sat next to him as he spoke. "Once it's dark enough we go back to the motel and confirm we can see a decent view of the lobby from somewhere."

"Check!" She ticked off an item on an imaginary list in front of her.

"Then we try to set up the camera in the old oak tree opposite. We may need string to attach it."

"String ... Check!"

"Then we'll call Crane and tell him where and when."

"I'm not sure I fancy this idea. It's like inviting a wolf for lunch."

"Don't worry! We're not going to sit in the tree waiting for him. I think we'll be far enough to be safe. There must be a good few hours recording time on the camera so we'll let it run and pick it up in a few days. As long as it's well hidden, it'll be safe!" Roger was his usual focused self, talking to the universe while deep in thought, rather than addressing her.

Atifah also became more serious as she started to go through the actions in her head. "What if they have a CCTV in the hotel and catch me using your card?"

"I'll pay for the room." He felt it was the safest way. During the transaction, Atifah would be parked a short way off at the other end of a small road. If he was recognized by the desk clerk, he'd pull the cell phone and bomb ruse again. He didn't have such a good looking bomb this time, but he had the takeout containers. He must be able to do something with those.

"You may be recognized." It was like she had already had this conversation today. "And you are not going to threaten to blow anybody up are you?"

"Only if I am spotted and it gets dangerous, otherwise you'll be waiting at the end of the roadway with the engine running and I will calmly meet you on the other side. We'll drive off serenely and sedately."

"Hmmm! Why can't I picture it happening?" she replied.

They headed back to the hotel and found their way round to the far end of the small roadway. They found a great hiding spot for the car and Roger did a practise walk along the road so he could map out potential threats in his getaway should the road prove to be too dark after the sun had gone down.

He followed the wires feeding the floodlight down the side of the old building and into the ground. After digging a hole with a small iron bar, he nervously snipped through one side of the circuit with the wire cutters from the car tool pack, cutting the power to the lamp before it came on in the dimming light.

A short while later the other lights in the area started flickering into life and to his relief the floodlight remained in darkness. A bonus he hadn't yet noticed, a floodlight in the tree itself lit up the motel. There was no way he would be seen placing the camera in the tree by somebody looking into such a bright light.

In the half light, he approached the tree and looked at how he would scale the monster. In only a short while he'd planned his ascent and descent and filed the routes safely in the back of his mind. He then took a quick walk around the hotel and noted several ground floor rooms were in darkness along the small road to the right of the building. He would aim to take one of those rooms for easy and hopefully, unnoticed escape.

After disconnecting the camcorder from the charging cable, Roger loaded the DVD into the side of the unit. The small camera buzzed and hummed as it set up the DVD for recording. With Atifah looking on, Roger scaled the tree. There was more light than he thought there would be, and more than he would've liked, but the roads were quiet. The light from the floodlight facing the hotel hid him in the tree. Using his duct tape, he attached the camcorder to the thick, sturdy, coated wire feeding the floodlight in the tree. It wasn't straight, but with a bit of fiddling he was able to zoom and fill the view finder with a reasonably full image of the lobby of the hotel. Roger pulled off a leaf from the tree and with a small piece of tape, covered the small red LED, then turned the recorder off, not wanting to waste the battery.

He found his way down the tree and reaching the bottom, he checked his watch. "Are we ready?"

"As ready as we can be." Atifah was still not sure she liked the idea of Roger doing the transaction, but it made sense.

"Ok! Let me call Crane." He cradled the agent's phone in his hand as he processed the plan in his head again. Satisfied, he dialed the number.

"Macadam! I didn't think you would call," Crane's voice filled the handset.

"I told you I would."

"Where are you?"

"Madisonville," Roger lied. "When your guys are halfway there give me a call and I'll tell you where I'll use the card."

"Ok! I'll dispatch them immediately." Crane was lying too. He had gambled on the possibility of Roger staying close to the interstate. He had his team stationed at strategic points all along the interstate.

In the vicinity a small helicopter took off and headed for Madisonville. When he saw the lights crossing the skyline headed in that direction, he thought it could well belong to Crane. He would have to reduce his time and be in and out a lot quicker than he had anticipated.

-- o --- o0o --- o --

"They're halfway." Crane had called Roger on Johnson's phone. Roger guessed all the agents were probably poised ready to take him down at each of the hotels in Madisonville.

"Good! Ensure they're not late."

"They won't be." Roger could hear the confidence in Crane's voice.

"Ok! So they should be here within 30 minutes if they are driving fast. I'll call you back in 15." Roger hung up. He checked his watch. He sat in the open space looking at the Wild Horse. He knew he was on a precise schedule. Precision was essential. There was no margin for error.

Once the fifteen minutes passed, Roger called again.

"Crane!" The agent answered as if he wasn't expecting the call.

"In five minutes I will be using my card to book into the hotel. It should give you enough of a headstart on anybody else."

"Wait!" Crane shouted. He had thought Roger was going to hang up again. "Which hotel are you going to book into?"

"The Wild Horse."

"The Wild Horse?"

"The Wild Horse Inn, Buffalo."

"Shit!" Crane gave away his plan. "I'll need more time." He was clutching at straws. Roger could hear the desperation in his voice and he could hear the papers shuffling in the background as Crane tried in vain to signal somebody to move his team.

"Sorry! No can do. I'm on a deadline." He hung up.

Atifah was already waiting on the other side of the dark ally in the car. Recalling his footholds, he scrambled up the old oak and started the camcorder recording the lobby of the hotel.

Back on the ground he checked his watch, then working his head back and forth, clicking the tension from his neck, he walked up the narrow sidewalk away from the hotel and approached from a different angle. As he advanced, he felt the surge of adrenalin kicking him into 'fight or flight' mode. He felt the slight burn in his stomach as nervousness started his digestive system working overtime, ready to feed the muscles as needed. Taking a deep breath, he strode into the foyer with his makeshift bomb-like object stuffed into a shopping bag in his left hand.

"Hi!" Roger stood at the desk before the clerk realized he was there. He lifted his head from his Sudoku puzzle.

"Good evening."

"I'd like to book into a room for the night. East side. Ground floor if possible."

"Sure." The young boy reached for the keyboard of the computer in front of him. After tapping a few keys in response to Roger's answers, the laser printer sprang into life. "Sign on the bottom and I'll get your key."

Roger signed while the boy turned around to retrieve the key card from a row of hooks behind him.

"Can I pay now, I will be leaving early." Roger held out his credit card.

"I'll be here all night." He reluctantly took the card.

"It's no problem. I'll probably wake up late and be in a rush. I'm not going to order room service or anything."

Roger watched as the youngster swiped the card a few times. "We have a problem with your card." The clerk looked up at Roger and passed back his useless card.

"It happens in a few places. Do you have an ATM nearby?"

This was going to be quicker than he thought. After confirming the presence of an ATM, Roger was able to leave through the main door. He walked in the direction given, crossed the road and disappeared into the darkness opposite the hotel. He heard the distant helicopter approaching through the night sky even as he crossed the open land behind the large oak. He navigated the dark alley and soon he and Atifah were headed south on the I145 toward Houston.

The mission was accomplished. The two sat in tired silence, while Roger navigated the straight highway. Bypassing Houston on the ring road he once again headed back along the I10, destination – San Antonio. He wasn't going to try to drive all the way there. He wanted to find somewhere to sleep, but he drove well into the night.

Atifah had crashed and was sleeping long before he reached the four-level to Interstate 10 and she was still out cold as he passed the signage to Katy. He made the decision to stop at Flatonia and within moments of leaving the interstate, he pulled into the parking area of a small countrystyle hotel. It looked welcoming and the inviting glow from the entrance was calling him. The thought of sleep overwhelmed all else.

Roger pulled up a short distance from the entrance, out of view of anybody inside. He looked over at the sleeping girl, guilty for her involvement, even though he had no reason to. He gently shook her shoulder. She jumped and immediately shook to life.

"Sorry! I didn't mean to startle you."

"It's ok! Where are we?"

"It's a hotel in a little town called Flatonia. I've never heard of it."

She rubbed her eyes as she sat up. "You want me to book in?" She was already up to speed, moments after the shock of being woken.

"'Fraid so!" Roger dug into his wallet and gave her enough cash. "You can use the same story as before. Book in as Mr and Mrs and tell them I've gone to find a drug store or something and I'll be along soon." He looked along the building and pointed. "Try to get a ground floor room along there, then when you're inside, flash the light, then open the window. Leave the light off after you flash it just in case."

"What if those rooms are already taken?" Thinking ahead! Roger liked that.

"Then we'll need another plan. Take this phone." She held out her hand to take the phone, but instead of handing it to her, he switched on the phone and watched the thing boot up. Realizing he was not going to pass it to her, Atifah placed her hands in her lap. Roger placed the two agents' phones side by side. After a time and a little laboriously slow keyboard clicking, he dialed a number and the dead agent's phone sprang into life. Quickly he killed the noise and hung up.

"Use it if you need to." She took a deep breath and climbed out of the vehicle.

Heading for the hotel entrance she turned briefly, smiled her beautiful, white smile and headed into the building. The interior of the hotel was typical of a Texan country hotel. The night clerk looked happy to receive a patron so late into her shift.

"Good evening or is it morning? My name is Michelle. Do you want to book in?" The clerk flashed her broad smile at Atifah.

Atifah smiled back, enjoying the sound of another young woman's voice. "Yes … please and I have no idea of the time. It feels like 4.00 am." Michelle smiled.

"You're booking in? Alone?" She slipped the two questions together into one breath.

"No! My husband will be along in a while. He's gone to find a drug store."

"No problem, let's book you in."

"Could I have a ground floor room. Maybe over that side?" She motioned to the direction Roger had alluded to.

"No problem! We're not too busy in the week. Tomorrow night will be a different story though." The girl spoke as she tapped on the keyboard.

"At this point, we're passing through. We'll probably be gone in the morning."

"Ah! Pity! I thought you would be staying the weekend. We have a sparkling pool out the back and they forecast great weather for the weekend." It was more of a pleading than information.

"We'll see what happens." Atifah was making conversation but then on thinking about it, she said, "Actually, can I book in for the weekend? If we change our minds, we'll let you know."

"Sure! No problem." The clerk almost looked relieved. She might have a young couple to talk to for her weekend shift.

A few more questions which were clinically answered by Atifah and she was soon being led to her room. The clerk opened the door and switched on the light. She seemed to take forever fussing around, enjoying the rare opportunity of having a talking partner.

"I take it your husband is lost."

"Must be! We don't know this town at all. I expect he'll be back soon."

"Don't worry. I'll keep my eyes open for him and tell him where to find you." Atifah cringed knowing she probably wouldn't be happy until she had seen Roger walk into the hotel.

After saying her good nights the clerk left, satisfied with her effort at making a new friend. Atifah shut the door behind her, locked it and then flicked the light once before switching it off. She felt her way to the window, unlatched it and slid it gently upward. Roger was already waiting and slipped inside. Atifah switched the light back on. Once he was inside, she started to explain why she had taken so long. He brushed it off. There was no need for explanations.

"I've booked us in for the weekend in case we need a home base for a day or two. Ok?"

"Sure! We can always cancel the booking if necessary."

In almost no time Atifah was showered and in bed. Roger came out of the bathroom and settled with a blanket in the chair. This chair was nowhere near as comfortable as the last one and he was soon shifting back and forth. Eventually, realizing his battle, Atifah sat up in the darkness. "You can have the bed. I'm younger than you."

"Don't even think about it. I'll be fine." He was lying to her. His back didn't feel fine at all. Another half an hour passed and it dawned on Roger, he wasn't going to sleep in the chair. Atifah also tossed and turned each time he moved in the squeaky chair.

Eventually she called him from across the darkness. "Roger!"

"Uh huh!"

"Please use the bed. There's enough space for both of us and I need to sleep."

Seconds later they were both sleeping soundly.

FRIDAY, 10TH

Roger opened his eyes, surrounded by the half-darkness of the hotel room. Atifah was lying close. He could feel the warmth from her steady breathing on his arm. She had slept right through her dawn prayer. He squinted at the pale glow from the backlight of his wristwatch. 06:17.

He was feeling good. He'd had a good sleep and there were no embarrassing embraces to wake up to. They'd both kept to their own sides of the bed, even though she had turned towards him in the night.

Roger slipped out of the bed doing his best to not disturb the sleeping girl and headed for the adjoining bathroom. After a quick wash and freshen up he was ready to take on the world.

He phoned the front desk and ordered one full breakfast and one vegetarian breakfast to be delivered to the room.

"Thank you!" Atifah mumbled as she opened her eyes.

"For what?"

"For ordering breakfast." She stretched her arms above her head. Roger could see she too felt refreshed. It was a good morning and this was going to be a good day.

Breakfast arrived. Roger grabbed a towel and jumped into bed, pushing Atifah out to answer the door, at the same time thrusting the towel in her hand. She feigned anger and leapt out from under the duvet wrapping the towel around her head as she did.

"Thank you!" She took the tray from the person at the door and placed a small value note in the palm of his hand. He thanked the girl and left.

"You're so lazy!" she joked.

"Lazy has nothing to do with it. We want to be able to finish our breakfast without a visit from the FBI don't we?"

"Ha!" She waved her free hand dismissing Roger's excuses. "But thank you for the towel." She smiled, amazed he'd remembered she would want to cover her hair.

"No problem. I don't understand why you want to cover yourself, but I do understand you do."

"Thank you," she repeated, deep in thought.

Roger jumped up and took the tray. "Right m'lady! It's your turn to be waited on." He signaled her back into the bed.

She smiled and jumped under the duvet, once again removing the towel from her head.

"So if you don't know if we're married or not, why don't you cover your hair when I'm around?"

She shrugged as she took the plate of food. "I don't know whether we're married or not. Besides, we've shared a bed. I think I would prefer to be married to the wrong person, than to share a bed with somebody I'm not married to"

Roger couldn't understand the logic and soon stopped trying. After a relaxed and enjoyable breakfast, Roger leaned across and picked up the remote. He switched on the TV and clicked to the news channel. He left it playing quietly, while he continued eating. After only a short period, Elaine Hodges, the reporter with the terrier-like disposition, started reporting.

"America's most wanted terrorist has struck again."

"What ...?" was all Roger could say, as he watched a stretcher being carried from the lobby of the small hotel. His face drained and his heart beat rapidly in his throat. Roger wanted to throw up as he watched the scene unfold.

She continued, "America's most recent addition to the top 10 most wanted list, Roger Macadam, struck savagely and for no apparent reason last night, executing a desk clerk, two FBI agents and two visitors to this small country hotel. The two agents, working on a tip-off, apparently surprised Macadam while he was booking in. Macadam apparently took revenge by killing the hotel visitors in cold blood.

"Although it's not entirely clear why the visitors were dragged seminaked from their bed and shot execution style, this reporter offers that Macadam, after being confronted by the agents, overpowered and shot them. He then executed the couple in the lobby of the hotel purely to make a statement. Once again we await ballistics results to find out if this was the same gun which was confirmed to have killed a desk clerk in Houston on Tuesday.

"This is Elaine Hodges for CNN, wondering when the authorities are going to reign in Madman Macadam."

"Madman Macadam? They'll see mad." Roger reached for the agent's phone and dialed Crane.

"Crane. What the hell did you do?" Roger started to feel nauseous.

"What did ..." Crane started to answer.

"You said you'd look after those people and more innocent people have died." Roger's voice was raised as anger took hold of him.

Crane reacted savagely. "Who the hell do you think you are talking to? A man and a woman killed two of my agents last night. Sounds a lot like the terrorists I'm chasing."

"Fuck you Crane. You think I would risk setting up an operation like this to only kill two of your agents?"

"You tell me Macadam."

"You stupid bureaucrat! How many agents were in your team yesterday?"

"You know there were eight!"

"Given the new circumstances, how many will you have in your team by this time tomorrow?"

Crane started to answer, then paused. He saw where Roger's thought process was going. Roger noted the pause and said, "So I would've gained nothing by killing two of your people. God! I could've killed a couple the other day, but didn't. I can't wipe out the entire police force can I?" He paused, but Crane, who was deep in thought, gave no answer.

"How'd you know it was a man and a woman?"

"My guys were outside and called it in."

"Why'd you only send two agents?"

"I sent them all, but pulled them off after an hour. I didn't think anything would happen. I thought you were talking crap."

"It was stupid and irresponsible. What time did you pull them off and what time did your agents call it in?"

"They called in 15 minutes after the others left."

"So you were being watched?"

"Looks like."

Roger was silent for a period while his brain processed the information. "I think they knew."

"Knew what?"

"Everything! Your guys followed them in and yet were both taken by surprise. They go and drag a couple of innocents from their beds to make a statement. Did anybody else in your unit know about the plan?"

"Nobody." He thought for a second. "They all knew something was going down, but that's all."

"They knew your guys would be there. The execution of your agents and the random couple was premeditated and done for a reason!"

"To stress a point." Crane made a flat and unemotional statement.

Roger was deep in thought. "More than that." He paused while he thought. "They did it to tell me who's in charge and prevent me from trying to trap them. We are dealing with somebody that is happy to kill innocent people simply to warn me. I think one of your guys is involved."

"What are you talking about? My guys are …"

"New to you Crane," Roger interjected. "You don't have to act the tight-knit team leader to me. You told me yourself, this team was thrown together to hunt me down. Do you even know who did the throwing?"

"DC!"

"Wow! I should be honored. I've been noticed at the Capitol!" Roger's sarcasm rang in Crane's ear. "So your people could be answering to anybody and keeping an eye on proceedings, right?"

"I suppose!" Crane was quiet and thoughtful. "So! Why are you so sure one of my guys is involved?"

"I am not that sure. In fact, for all I know, maybe you did the shooting."

"A marine will never execute his own team."

Roger was thinking aloud rather than communicating. "It feels too clinical to be a chance crossing of paths. They knew your guys were there. Hell, they might have been watching you the whole time you were there. They knew when your guys left and they were expecting your agents to follow them in. I'm going to find out who it was and I'll let you know."

"In the meantime …"

"I know. I'm a felon on the run."

-- o --- o0o --- o --

"Hi honey! How are you holding up?"

"Roger!" Anne was surprised to hear his voice. "Why are you …?"

"Don't panic, Annie. I'm fine."

"They're probably listening."

"They're definitely listening so let's not discuss sex, ok!"

Anne laughed. Her husband could always turn a dark situation into something better. Roger had decided to call her. He hadn't wanted to, for fear of inadvertently implicating her in something. It became too much for him. He wanted to speak to his wife.

"Is Katie around?"

"At school! You know Katie. She's not one to dwell on things she has no control over."

"She's ok then? No problems at college?"

"She hasn't said anything. Her friends have been supportive. Everyone who knows you, knows you're innocent."

"I'm glad."

"So! Did you call because of the news this morning?"

"You know me well. Those poor people."

"You didn't do it." It was an unequivocal statement of fact, not a question.

"I know, but I did have a hand in it. I arranged with Crane ..."

"Agent Crane. I've met him."

"I didn't doubt that. Anyway I arranged with him to use my credit card so he could flush out the killers. I think his team may have at least one bad apple."

"Do you trust him?"

"Not even as far as I can throw him."

"So why are you making deals with him?"

"It would be a great benefit to me to flush out the killers and he has the manpower to make it happen."

"True!"

"Anyway, I have ... Hmm! I can't tell you because people are listening." He almost mentioned the camcorder still wedged in the big old oak tree in Buffalo. Roger was more than a little intrigued to find out what was on the DVD. He hoped for answers, but could never risk getting close to the hotel at the moment.

"How's Atifah doing?"

"Atifah! She's full of crap." She looked up and smiled as she heard her name and realized he was talking about her. "She's ok. I think these circumstances ..." He trailed off. "Anyway! I'd better go. I have a lead in New York. We're heading there today."

"What? Are you really?"

"No! I'm saying so to keep the listeners guessing. Actually, it's DC, or maybe Vegas."

"You wish. Stay safe Roger."

"I'll do my best. You stay safe too. You know I can't live without you."

"I know! It's the effect I have on skinny middle-aged balding men." Anne tried to keep sounding upbeat, but the quiver in her voice gave her away. Mike was treating the two girls well, but she wanted things back to the way they were. They all did.

Roger reluctantly hung up the phone. He sat for a few seconds, his mind going back over the conversation and how her voice had cracked. He was missing her.

Roger had never meant to be on the run and even though he was running, in his mind he was always simply moving to somewhere else. It was at this point he made a conscious decision to solve this riddle and have their names cleared. He was going to fight back and there was nothing the FBI, Homeland Security, or anyone else could do. Roger had found his direction.

His mind sprang into action and started to process plans and scenarios. He had money and it was time to start using it to protect Atifah and himself.

Pretty soon they had left the hotel, without raising any alarms and were on their way back along Interstate 10 heading back toward Houston. Instead of bypassing the city as before, Roger directed Atifah to go straight into town. He was on home soil and felt good about it.

After a short search through a mildly dingy and semi-industrial area of Houston, he signaled her to slow down. "You see the small building over there?"

"The house?"

"You can drop me off up the road, then circle back. They can darken the windows of the car. It takes about an hour. I don't know why I didn't do this before. Take the car in there and have them darken the glass to the darkest legal limit. Then you won't have to drive the whole time."

"Ok! What are you going to do?" She looked around at the streets already filled with people going about their daily routines.

"Don't worry about me, I'm going to lie low and keep out of the firing line." Roger pointed to a four storey parking building.

"When you are finished go in there and pick me up. I'll be on the second floor watching out for you."

Atifah agreed and dropped Roger on the sidewalk. He quickly darted between two buildings and was soon out of sight and nestled, almost comfortably, between a couple of trash cans. Meanwhile, Atifah headed back down the street to the small house and glided into the driveway.

Inside, the building resembled nearly all small automotive businesses. Various shades of tinted glass adorned display stands around the small converted office and behind the high counter, a young unshaven man was thumbing his way through a book. The young man looked up and then came to immediate attention when he looked into Atifah's big green eyes. "Can I help you?" He cursed himself for not finding something a little more suave to say.

"Hi!" She was doing all the things she needed to do to hold his attention. "I'm so tired of this sun." She waved her hand in a large generally heavenward arc. "Even with the airconditioner running I am getting so hot. Can you do something to help keep the sun off me?"

The exact cue the young man was looking for. The chance to explain in depth to a stunning woman what he did every day was all he lived for. He smiled like he'd won the lottery. "Of course!" While Atifah looked on, he explained the differences between different types of window tinting and their adhesion methods, how the law had recently changed limiting the darkness of the tint. He even told her he could give her a certificate dated before the law change if she really wanted to go dark. He eventually came back to earth. "So! How dark do you want to go?"

She leaned toward him playfully. "How dark can I go?"

An hour later the job was finished and Atifah had driven back to the parking garage where she was to meet Roger. She was pulling into the open sided building, hidden from the world by a thin dark vinyl layer on her windows. The new vinyl was still soft, so she opened the door to take a ticket which had popped its head out of the narrow slot to her left. As she removed the ticket from the machine, it slipped between her fingers and fell to the ground blowing behind her in the gentle breeze. As she got out to chase the small piece of card, a large black Chevy pulled up behind her. The hairs rose on Atifah's neck. She knew this was an agent. She smiled at the driver as she leaned down toward the ticket. He didn't react to her, but impatiently shook his head back and forth in slow purposeful movements. He looked like he wanted to pass fast.

The ticket moved in the wind again and bounced a few times along the roadway, before stopping under the grille of the Chevy. She stood up looking apologetically at the driver. He ignored her. As she bent, she leaned on the hood of the Chevy, picking up the elusive piece of paper. Standing up she mouthed the word "Sorry!" to the driver and climbed back into her vehicle.

She needed to alert Roger and stall for time. She climbed back out of the car and feigned looking for something on the floor, while fumbling through her pockets. The agent didn't need much prompting. He sat on his horn.

She shouted to the driver. "Be patient! I've lost my key."

The agent opened his door. "C'mon lady! I'm in a rush." The young burly agent stuck his head out.

She shouted again. "Found it! In my pocket." She hoped Roger had been able to hear her shouts. She knew she couldn't risk the agent seeing Roger getting into the car, or their journey would be over.

-- o --- oOo --- o --

Roger felt the phone buzz in his pocket as he crouched between two cars. He had heard the shouting, but initially he hadn't been able to recognize Atifah's voice above the hum of the vehicles in the street.

As his phone rang he knew it was Atifah. His brain fired into full alert. He lifted the phone to his ear and he heard the hiss of the connection and the words, "Agents! Get out!"

Roger listened as the distinctive sound of the Chevrolet V8 roared up the ramp a floor below him. In only a couple of seconds they would be on his floor. He could never reach the stairwell before he was left stranded in full view, as the car rounded the top of the ramp. He darted for the steel railing and paused. As the vehicle started the ascent to the second floor, he climbed over the steel railing and scrambled down. Holding onto the steel, he swung and gripped a round steel pole on the floor below and slid to the railing.

Following the same process again, he was on the ground outside the building in a matter of seconds. In the distance he could hear the sounds of police sirens approaching. He headed off along the main road in the opposite direction to the sirens, walking fast, but not too fast to avoid attracting any attention to him. He pulled his phone from his pocket and re-dialed the phone in Atifah's hand.

She hadn't seen him leave the building and was heading up the ramp toward the second floor. "I'm out. Thanks."

"How did they know?"

"Not important! But how did you know?"

"Not sure! A gut feel."

"A good one! Park the car and take a walk for fifteen minutes or so. Be careful, this is not the best neighborhood. If you go out of the parking and turn left, there is a dingy looking diner about a hundred yards or so down the road. Stop there and have coffee. I'll contact you in a while."

"Ok!"

Roger pushed the phone back in his pocket. He resisted the urge to look behind him and kept walking. He heard the police vehicles approaching from behind and the screeching of tires as they turned into the parking garage. Hoping everybody would be more interested in the cops, he continued along the street.

He knew he was vulnerable and felt uneasy, as though people were watching him. He was easily recognizable. He'd had more recent airtime than anybody else in America, including the president. He kept his gaze down and walked.

-- o --- oOo --- o --

Atifah parked the car and took the steps down to ground level. She could hear the revving of the big engine above her as the agents sped from floor to floor. Soon after, she heard the police roar in with about as much stealth as the proverbial bull in the china shop. Looking back up the small road, she watched the agent's vehicle pull out from the parking and speed off, heading back toward downtown Houston. She strolled across the road and entered the small diner.

Ordering coffee, she sat and watched the parking lot with the blue flashing lights driving in circles, sure they'd find something, but Roger was already gone. The only thing she didn't know, was where.

She finished her first cup of coffee and then sat a while.

"Refill?" The waitress wasn't asking as much as stating a fact and to prove it she started pouring the coffee.

"Thank you." Atifah smiled and glanced back at the road.

"Stood up?" Again, it almost sounded like a statement of fact and not than a question.

"No! Just killing time. My husband is late."

"Husband?" was a question. "No ring?" was a question too.

"It's in the car." She was telling the truth. Atifah shrugged her shoulders, but the waitress wasn't buying it.

"Complicated huh?" She'd heard it all before. She had witnessed more daytime rendezvous than she cared to remember. "Never mind honey! When you're older you'll realize all men are dogs. Tell me! This *husband* of yours … is he somebody else's husband too?" Atifah's eyes leaked the truth but she smiled. "I knew it! Dump him honey, before you waste the best years of your life on this bum."

"You are right! It's complicated."

"It's really not. It's simple." She stood up straight, smug in the knowledge that she'd called it right. "This bum is meeting you during the day, in this obscure hole, then going home and creasing the sheets with his wife. Best of both worlds! And suckers like you give him the license to continue. What happens when he's finished with you?"

"It is complicated. I wasn't joking."

Atifah settled back sipping her second cup of coffee. She checked her wristwatch. Twenty-three minutes and still nothing. The ever-present waitress caught sight of her checking her watch and smiled a smile saying, 'I told you so'.

At one hour and forty-two minutes, Atifah was starting to feel concerned. The fourth cup of coffee was kicking in and she could feel the caffeine coursing through her veins. She wanted to run out the diner to find Roger, but then the phone rang! "Hello!" A pause and then, "Ok! I'm on my way." She stood up handing the waitress her cash.

"All right! So I may have it wrong this time, but sooner or later you will think back to this conversation."

Atifah smiled back. "I truly believe you are wrong…" She looked down at the waitress's name badge. "Dianne. I hope I can come back here one day and explain the whole story to you."

"I look forward to it," she said as she half waved her hand in a dismissive gesture.

Atifah left the diner, turning and heading for the parking. She noted a police car still parked on the second floor. They were still searching for clues left behind by Roger. She climbed up the steps to the first floor where she had left the car. She glanced around as she sat in the car and noticed a small CCTV camera attached to the wall in the corner. She turned and looked in another direction.

She paid and then left the building. She turned left, leaving the city in the direction Roger had taken.

-- o --- oOo --- o --

Roger kept walking a long way to where the roads and the spaces around them started opening up becoming less crowded. A no-man's-land between city and suburbia. Up ahead a police car was idling along the road, paying way too much attention to the few people walking by. He would definitely be spotted. He needed to get off the road. He turned into the first open gateway. The huge steel gates were hiding piles of deceased automobiles from the road. The scrapyard was large and would be a convenient place to lose himself for a while.

"Can I help you?" a quiet, accented voice came from behind him. There was no ignoring the voice. All he could do was to turn and face the person behind him. This was bound to happen eventually. Roger's mind spun as it processed masses of possible scenarios.

He needed to be as un-American as he could. "G'day mate." He used a broad Australian accent and pulled his mouth to the right, half closing his right eye. He hoped it did the trick.

The man in front of him was a short, thin Indian man, balding and almost completely grey. He held out a grubby hand. "Riyaz! Riyaz Patel."

"G'day Riyaz." Roger gave the man a savage handshake. If Riyaz recognized him, he hid it well. "I'm lookin' for a windshield wiper mechanism for a '98 E-Class."

"I don't think I have such a thing. We did break an E-Class last week, but a much later model and the front was wrecked anyway."

"Pity!" Still holding his accent. "It'll cost me five hundred bucks to go to the agent."

"Have you tried e-bay?"

"I haven't! A great idea mate." Roger sensed the cop car was driving slowly past the gate. He needed to move out of sight. "D'you have a shithouse. I'm bustin'."

"Sure! No problem. This way."

As he was going in the office door Roger heard the distinctive sound of tires running over the dirt and gravel behind

172

him. He hadn't turned to see the cops, so they didn't know he was aware of their presence. To his relief, as he entered into the tiny grubby stall, he saw a small window to his left. As soon as the door closed, he lifted the window and peered outside. It opened at the back of the building, not more than five yards from a tall concrete fence. In one smooth movement, he pulled himself through the window, allowing himself to slide slowly through and arresting his fall with his hands. Slowly, he allowed the window to close. As soon as he was out and after a quick glance around, he moved to his left to avoid being seen through the windows. A quick peek over the fence assured him that nobody would see his flight. Keeping as low as possible, he jumped and half rolled over the six foot fence and dropped quietly to the other side. He headed for the gate.

Once out of the gate, Roger made his way down the street for a block and then turned into a small ally. He started to run at a reasonable loping pace and pretty soon was putting a considerable distance between himself and the cops who by now would have realized their hunch had been correct.

As Roger exited the ally, a delivery bicycle was leaning up against the wall outside a dirty looking door to a business called Deft Deliveries. Not looking around, he took the cycle from its position and jumped on, swinging his leg over the old saddle. A quick fumble with the pedals and he was on his way.

He pedaled a few times, then dropped off the sidewalk onto the road and pedaled like his life depended on it. Soon this area would be crawling with police.

The roads were flat, so he was able to maintain a good pace for a while, only slowing into intersections to ensure he didn't round a corner and smash into the front of another police car.

He turned back onto the main road and set about covering as much distance as he could. The muscles in his legs were burning, but he kept going. Way behind him the wailing of sirens told him they knew he was no longer in the toilet.

-- o --- o0o --- o --

Roger kept his head down and cycled for several miles until he cycled right into the suburbs. He slowed his pace and the burning in his legs eased. He leaned the bicycle against a sign post and after a quick check along the deserted street, walked on. He felt a little guilty about leaving the old bike on the side of the road, but the situation didn't allow for anything more.

He dialed Atifah's number while turning into a smaller road. He gave her instructions which he estimated would have her passing him in about ten minutes, depending on how far he'd cycled. He then found a shady spot behind a large electrical installation and waited.

Thirteen minutes later, he watched as she drove past him and headed off up the road. He thought he'd let her drive on for a few minutes to check whether anybody had followed her. He was still unsure of how they had known his position and thought it better not to take chances.

After a minute or so, he dialed her again.

"Hi! See if you can find somewhere to park and wait for me."

She was puzzled. "What here?"

"Yes! Anywhere."

"Ok! Hold on." He heard the engine pitch change in the handset while Atifah parked the car. She came back on. "I'm parked."

"No problem! We'll wait a couple of minutes."

After a further few minutes, no black sedan had come into view nor any police cars. Roger decided it must be safe. "It's all clear! You can turn around and head back in the opposite direction."

"Ok!"

Pretty soon he saw the Ford coming slowly back down the road. As she approached, he stepped out from behind the electrical box and flagged her down. She smiled as she approached. He heard the doors unlock as she pulled up alongside him. "Going my way?" she asked as he opened the door to climb in.

As he sat beside her, he leaned over kissed her gently on her cheek. "Thank you," he said. He was grateful she'd had her wits about her.

"You're welcome!" she answered, pleased by his action.

"That was way too close. I don't know how I was spotted though."

"I do." She was proud of herself. "The parking lot had cameras all over. Somebody must have seen you and phoned the police."

"Damn! I need to be more careful." He paused in thought and then continued, "And a hell of a lot more observant," he said slowly, still thinking. "I wonder if they'll be able to guess my link to the car now?" he thought aloud.

"I don't think so. How would they know?"

"From the surveillance footage. They probably saw me answer my phone, then high tail it out."

"They didn't see me phone. I dialed from my lap. I didn't want to risk having the agent see me calling."

Roger tried to go through in his mind how the footage might look. Would they be able to see her mouth move? Would they be able to connect her movement and his escape? This could change the entire situation and their ability to stay hidden. What of the agents? How had they been so fast, given he was probably reported to the police? He wondered if Crane was yet aware of him being spotted. He decided to call.

"Crane!"

"Macadam! Are you coming in?" Crane joked.

"Not yet. Maybe you can answer me a question?" Roger paused. "How did your guys get to me so quickly after I was reported to the police?"

Crane also paused, a little confused. Not wanting to say too much he replied. "Intel."

"You had no idea did you?"

"None at all! Are you telling me we have another department after you as well?"

"It looks that way but it seems thay have a better intelligence department working for them. Is it a normal thing?"

"Two departments! Sure!" Crane was puzzled. His brief had come from high up the food chain and although it did happen, it was courtesy to inform the other department. He was starting to feel a little uneasy about the case. Why had the bureau gone to such cost to put this team together and then bypassed them with another team. There were a few strange happenings going on.

"Odd!" Roger hung up the phone and spoke to Atifah.

She waited for him to speak. "As I thought. Crane knew nothing about the agents. We have somebody else after us. Somebody other than Homeland Security." Roger grew concerned. He'd guessed there might be two teams after him. The callous and unnecessary killing of innocent people meant this second team was operating above the law and would not be working hand in hand with Crane. He needed to recover the camcorder and give a copy of the DVD to Crane.

"Let's head for Buffalo again. Let me drive for a while." Roger was also feeling a little uneasy about the car. He was sure by the end of the day, not only would they have a car description on TV, but more than likely an unclear image of 'the woman' too. They were running out of time and options and if it came down to a chase he wanted to be behind the wheel.

On the way back to the highway they stopped over at a mall he knew well. Inside there was a small one-man store selling theatrical supplies. He often passed by and looked at the vast array of wigs scattered throughout the shop and yet he'd never seen anybody buying anything. How the shop survived puzzled him. He handed Atifah the cash and told her to go and buy a couple of different styles of wigs for both of them and anything else she might see as useful.

Within a short while they were back on the road again headed for the rough little town of Buffalo.

A quick drive past the hotel confirmed the camcorder was still perched high in the branches and no stakeouts were evident. He didn't think they would bother staking out the hotel which he had allegedly hit the previous night. They still had a while before the sun set, so Roger proposed Atifah buy a decent meal and they could find a spot to eat.

While they sat silently chewing on their respective delicacies, Roger, who had been deep in silent thought, suddenly spoke out. "I have a feeling things are going to change."

"How d'you mean?"

"I think when they look at the footage on the surveillance video they will put two and two together and start looking for you too."

"I'm sorry, I ..." Atifah's shoulders sagged and her head dropped, but Roger cut in quickly.

"Sorry? It wasn't your fault. You saved us. I'm the one that wasn't keeping my guard up properly. I should be apologizing."

She chewed on her lip while she thought. "I don't think they could see me making the call. I kept the phone on my lap when I spoke."

"I don't think the connection will be glaring, but if they have good quality video with a short refresh rate then we may be in trouble. Maybe we'll be lucky though." Roger tried to downplay his fear a little, but he had no knowledge of the capabilities of the agents for dissecting and examining the footage. He knew he was high on the list of national priorities and he knew they couldn't keep up the running forever without being spotted. They'd had a good run. Roger had already decided to change tactics and start to gather information, in an attempt to clear their names. To achieve this, he knew, over the next few days he was going to have to come in contact with people. He continued. "Even if they don't work it out, we can't simply keep running. We'll eventually make another mistake and then we'll both end up in jail."

She didn't say anything but nodded. She knew exactly what he was saying. "We have to stop running and start thinking about getting our names cleared."

"I know!"

"The first step is getting the camcorder back so we can see what, or who, we caught and hopefully it will give us something we can use to start the ball rolling."

Within a short while, the Texan sun set and before the sky had fully darkened, Roger re-traced his footsteps back between the buildings from the small road. The light hadn't been repaired yet, so the whole area was still in darkness. Making sure nobody was around, he strolled to the tree putting himself out of sight behind it. The bright spotlight was on, lighting up the front of the hotel and making it difficult for anybody to see him from the other side of the road.

Quickly he scaled the tree and retrieved the camera. He cut off the duct tape which held the camera in place using a small pocket knife. He stuffed the device into the belt of his pants and scrambled down the tree. As he landed he thought he heard a car door close nearby. but could see nothing. Keeping low and to the shadows, he made his way back toward the waiting car. He looked back and saw an elderly couple entering the hotel, seemingly oblivious of the horror that had unfolded there last night.

Once back in the narrow road, he broke into a quiet trot and soon arrived at the car. Atifah was seated in the driver's seat with the engine running, as Roger had instructed. "Ok! Let's go."

"Where?"

"Mexico."

"Mexico?"

"I want the world to think we have crossed the border."

"How do I get to Mexico?"

"Head back toward Houston, Katy and San Antonio again." Roger was already fumbling with the camcorder and all its extensions. Soon the LED lights lit up. After a few attempts, he managed to light up the little screen as the DVD started recalling the events of the night before.

Finding the skip button, he sped through the long periods of time where nothing happened. After what seemed like an eternity and with Roger hoping the events would unfold before running out of media or battery, he saw two shapes quick-stepping into the foyer. He backed up then pressed play and the screen flickered. The couple, neatly dressed in black suits, finished walking up the few steps to the lobby and entered into the small hotel.

Once inside they approached the desk clerk. The usual conversation and smiling took place. The scene appeared to be any late night check-in. As he watched, Roger saw the clerk point to the back and the man disappeared off to the left. The woman stayed behind making what looked like small talk with the clerk. He smiled and gestured as he spoke.

Two agents appeared out of nowhere walking quickly up the steps toward the door. They appeared to pause briefly at the door, having expected to see the man and the woman but only finding the woman. They stepped forward toward the woman. She turned to them smiling, then in a flash, her partner appeared again from the street, his silenced gun held behind his back. The agents didn't even have chance to turn their heads. The agent to the left was shot in the back of the head and crumpled forward. The second agent turned toward his partner, unaware of what had happened and the bullet caught him in the left temple. He was on his way to the floor even before his partner had landed.

The clerk hadn't even had time to react and was still smiling when the woman turned. His head was thrown backward as the impact of the bullet hit him in the forehead. The young man slumped back into the high chair behind his counter and then fell out of sight. Roger watched as the woman moved to the door closely observing the street. She turned and rejoined the man who was already on his phone. He placed the phone in his pocket and spoke to the woman. The two of them disappeared off to the right of the visible area of the lobby. They returned after a while leading the two scared looking guests at gunpoint. The two were pushed roughly to kneel next to the bodies of the agents. They were simultaneously executed as they leaned forward. They fell on top of the agents and the two killers turned casually and walked out, leaving the bodies to be discovered later that night.

Roger realized he hadn't breathed for a while and let out a gasp. He'd never witnessed anything like it. The execution was cold, heartless and calculated. He hung his head in his hands as he thought of the smile on the desk clerk's face seconds before and how the smile must have turned to pure terror as he realized what was about to happen. What were they up against? What sort of person does it take to execute innocent people?

Atifah turned to him. "I take it the camera worked?" She spoke quietly, almost in a whisper.

Remorse came over Roger like a wave. "Yes!" was all he could manage.

Atifah knew not to speak any more and they drove on for a couple of hours in silence.

As they neared the turn off to Flatonia, Roger spoke again. "Hopefully we will have another good sleep tonight." She nodded in agreement.

They underwent the same routine as the previous evening, with Atifah collecting the key, much to the delight of her new-found friend. Roger slipped in through the side window again. Neither of them had eaten since lunch, so Roger phoned room service and ordered snacks. Once again the day seemed to hit them like a speeding train. Atifah showered first and performed her nightly prayer ritual, while Roger showered. When he walked out of the bathroom she had already finished. The two crashed again in the shared comfort of the large bed. Tonight there was no question of sleeping in the chair. They climbed into bed like an old married couple, stopping short of the goodnight kiss. Sleep would be no problem tonight.

SATURDAY, 11TH

"We have a problem, people." Crane spoke to the faces around the table. The remaining six agents were disgruntled at working this early on a Saturday morning.

"Yeah! We're at work on a Saturday." Derrick England was not one to hold back.

"And we're going to be here a long time if we don't start making headway," he threatened. "You guys are supposed to be the best of the best. You were sent from all over to bring this Macadam in. What do we have?" He looked around at the blank faces.

"We can't help it if he keeps moving. The guy is like a ghost. He doesn't show his face."

"Wrong! He did show his face. Yesterday. The local police and another department managed to find out he'd shown his face, but we missed it," he continued. "How is this possible?"

They all had 'what the hell can we do about it' looks on their faces.

"Kozlowski and Mills were executed and we were right there. We could've prevented it. What is happening?"

"Macadam is pure evil." Agent Wilson voiced her opinion.

"It's not Macadam." All of a sudden Crane had their attention.

"Why not? He's the one we're chasing, right?" Terri Wilson sat forward in her chair. He hadn't told them about his conversation with Roger. He opted to keep it quiet.

"He's the one we're chasing," Crane echoed her words.

"And besides, Mills called it in. A man and a woman entered the lobby."

"True, but he could've taken you two out in the mall. He used a false bomb to hold up a bank for God's sake. Would a killer with a gun do that?" He pointed at Johnson and Roberts. "And remember he sent us out there. He could've taken out the whole team if he'd wanted to."

"Maybe he couldn't."

"He could. This man is a chemical engineer. He not only knows how to blow something up, he also knows where to place the explosion to have the biggest impact." He paused. "Mills was a marine. He was caught unawares. No civilian could creep up on a marine on full alert? Remember, Mills wasn't on a stroll, he was in there expecting trouble."

"Maybe Macadam's had training," England added his two cents worth.

"Macadam weighed the same as Kozlowski's right leg. He's had about as much training as you've had sex." This brought a stifled laugh from the team and a disgruntled frown from Derrick England.

Not to be outdone, England continued, "He took down these two trained agents in a flash." He waved his arm in the general direction of the agents.

Caleb leaned forward and placed his elbows on the table. "Don't misunderstand what happened. Macadam read the situation perfectly. He had planned a way out before we even knew it was him."

"He knew exactly how to control the situation. Killing us didn't enter his mind. If it did, he'd be dead now," Roberts added to Roger's accolades.

"Your point?" England showed his disinterest.

"My point is," said Johnson, frustrated that England didn't get it, "he disarmed two trained agents. He did it with his brain, not his hands. Macadam is less of a fighter than you are England, but twice as clever."

"We'll see." England had a thing about being told when somebody could outsmart him.

Crane re-entered the conversation. "Wilson and Crosby. Head over to the parking where he was spotted. Johnson, you and Barnard go and visit the black an' whites. Find out who called the Feds and why we weren't notified. Fetch the videotape from whoever has it and let's see if we can get ahead of these people. You two," he addressed England and Roberts, "Put your heads together and get into Macadam's mind. I want this guy off the streets." They left the room mumbling to each other.

-- o --- oOo --- o --

After a quick but amazing buffet breakfast of cereal, yogurt and fruit juice, followed by fried 'everything' for Roger, which they ate in their room, he sent Atifah out to buy a low spec laptop computer and stationery. He needed to edit the video on the DVD. She also bought a pack of about 50 DVD's. They only needed a couple. He knew this editing would take a while and so suggested she spend time by the pool or relaxing somewhere. She might as well use her anonymity while she still had it.

He located the spot in the video where the shooting took place and using the Movie Maker software, managed to create a mini version of the video.

Having a bigger and clearer screen allowed Roger to concentrate on the content. He watched it several times over, scanning the picture for clues and jotting down notes as he watched. There wasn't a clear picture of the male killer's face, which would cause a problem in proving his innocence. The killer was bigger and heavier than he was and had more hair. A court would argue about wigs, perspective and padded jackets, if he was lucky enough to see the inside of a court. There was a good picture of the female, which he enlarged and studied closely. He could prove Atifah's innocence, but not his own. Also he could only prove her innocence in this killing, which wasn't enough. Even more unfortunate, she would have to break her cover to do this.

He created a couple of copies of the short version of the video, watching the killing over and over, wondering how people could get to the point where they could pull the trigger and watch an innocent person die. He realized then that getting caught was no longer an option. Handing himself in was also no longer an option.

There was a knock on the door. "Housekeeping!" A woman's voice rang out. The electronic lock beeped.

"Hold on!" Roger wanted to jump into the bed and cover himself up to the eyes. It wasn't right! "Can you come back in a while?"

"Sure honey! Don't be too long." The door clicked closed again.

Now he was trapped. She would be back and she would want to clean. He peered through the drapes. The roadway outside was by no means busy, but somebody climbing out of the window would be sure to attract attention. He closed the drapes again.

His sunshades sat in their case on the small desk next to his new laptop. He had an idea. He put on the glasses. By sitting in the low chair in the corner, placing his arms on the rests and joining his fingertips together in front of his face, he could obliterate almost all his features.

He jumped up and grabbed the new wig Atifah had purchased. He hadn't planned to use it yet and had to check it out to see if there were labels attached. Adjusting it in front of the mirror, he placed it on his head. "Not bad!" he said to himself. He sat back down assuming his face covering position.

The light! Blind people don't have the light on. He jumped up again and switched off the light and sat down again. As he sat, he noticed the computer still on. Again he sprang from the chair and closed the computer. In the now near darkness, he sat in his chair. Something else was bothering him. He wanted the light behind him as much as possible. Again he jumped up and adjusted the position of the chair in front of the window facing in. It wasn't ideal, but when she opened the drapes and he was sure she would, he wanted as much light behind him as possible.

There was a knock at the door. "Housekeeping! Can I come in?"

"Ok!"

The door opened. "Jeez! I can't see a thing in here." The light came on and Roger kept looking straight ahead.

"I know what you mean."

"Oh my God! I'm so sorry I ..."

"Don't worry! No permanent mental trauma caused." Still looking ahead and not daring to move his eyes from a small black dot on the wall. Roger knew while the internal light was on, there was a chance she would be able to see through the shades. "You can open the drapes if you want, you know, do our bit for the environment." He still had his fingertips together with his thumbs touching his chin and his index finger touching the end of his nose. His face was mostly obliterated from view.

"I'll do that," the woman said, not wanting to look at Roger as is usual when people share space with 'challenged' individuals.

He was a little uncomfortable as she leaned across him to open the drapes, but he knew he couldn't protest. As she shifted sideways between him and the bed, Roger feigned a shock as she knocked his foot. "Sorry! Am I in your way?" He knew damned well he was in her way and leaned forward placing his hands on the arm rests of the chair as if he was going to stand up.

"No! No problem. I can squeeze past." Roger relaxed back as the drape was flung open letting in a stream of brilliant sunshine. She sidled back past him again, this time taking care not to knock his foot. Moving to the other side of him, she flung open the other drape and Roger could feel the heat of the morning sun on his neck.

"So! How long have you ... at least, have you always ..." She trailed off. She had started a sentence she didn't want to finish.

"How long have I been blind?" he asked for her. "Not long at all. That's why I haven't learned sign language yet." He wanted to laugh at the puzzled look on her face. She wasn't sure if he was serious or not. He could see she was starting to look at his dark glasses. She realized she had been averting her gaze for no reason. He was thankful the sunlight was streaming in behind him.

"Do you see nothing at all, or can you see a bit? I know people that are legally blind but can still see a little." She waved her hand at Roger's face from the foot of the bed.

"No! Nothing! You could be waving your hand in my face right now and I wouldn't know." The woman snapped her waving hand back to her side and continued her journey to the light switch. The light clicked off but made no visible difference in the brilliant sun. "If you need me to move, shout."

"I will!" she said as she moved into the bathroom.

For a while Roger could hear the movements in the bathroom. He knew she could emerge at any time and therefore had to remain focused on the same spot. If he lost concentration and happened to glance up when she walked in, she would immediately know there was something wrong. He blinked a few times while the cleaner's gentle humming reverberated around the bathroom.

Eventually she emerged from the doorway. She looked straight at Roger who was still sitting in the same position. "You have a nice voice." Roger had been listening to the woman humming and singing. She had a clear and enjoyable tone to her voice with a natural smoothness. A quality enjoyed by only a few people. She enjoyed singing but didn't take compliments easily.

"No I don't."

"You do. Have you tried auditioning for American Idol?" Roger could see the woman was way too old for the competition, but he thought it would be a nice touch and might brighten her day.

It worked. "You're kidding right?"

"Not at all! I could listen to you sing anytime. Have you released any CD's?"

"No! Are you serious?" She was taken aback.

"Of course. I mean I'm no expert but I like it." Out of the corner of his vision, he could see the broad smile stretched across her face.

She set about making the bed and vacuuming the floor with a renewed gusto. She didn't say another word, nor hum another note, other than to say goodbye as she left with a spring in her step. She would never forget the blind guy who said she could sing, but more importantly, she would follow the news trail of a hateful terrorist, Roger Macadam, each night and never know she had shared the same room with him.

The door clicked closed and Roger stood up. "Mission accomplished!" he said as he sat back down at the desk and opened up the computer.

The light on the data card lit up and within moments Roger had the world at his fingertips. He had no clue where he should start, but at this point all he knew was Homeland Security were involved. What better place to start than with what you know!

-- o --- oOo --- o --

At lunch time, Atifah walked into the room, carrying a tray laden with small neatly cut sandwiches. There were various other snacks too. She bubbled with a renewed energy. She had spent the morning close to people and in full view. For a while she was no longer on the run and the experience went a long way towards repairing her body and mind from the stress of the previous few days. Roger, grateful for the break, thanked her for the lunch and ate like he hadn't eaten for a week.

While she'd been out, he had set about scouring the internet for clues about Homeland Security. He started with the act itself and then the reporting structure. As he read, he jotted down notes and after a while the small desk was covered in handwritten notes. He had gathered a fair amount of information, but nothing at all would help his cause. He hadn't expected to in such a short time. You can't enter 'Why am I being chased?' in the Google search box and expect results.

He looked over the notes again while eating and felt satisfied with his morning's work. He now knew what Homeland Security was all about. He'd always 'sort of' known, but now he had a better idea.

He turned away from the notes. "So! What were you doing all morning?"

"I had an incredible time." She paused and Roger noticed the contented look in her eyes. She was at ease. "I met a friendly guest from room 134 and we chatted about the differences between life here and in the UK". For obvious reasons, the Middle East hadn't entered the conversation. "We had a Coke on the sunbed by the pool and relaxed."

185

"I'm glad you enjoyed it. I think we might stay for the weekend. I'd like to start tracking down whoever's behind our little problem." He pointed to the notes. "I've made headway, but I have a long way to go."

"Fantastic." She looked happy. "Maybe I'll go with Vanessa for a long walk."

"Sure! Don't take any chances and keep your guard up. I have already slipped up once today."

"How so?"

"The cleaner came to clean the room and I wasn't ready."

"And?" She was expectant of an answer but he was taking too long.

"And … I pretended to be blind. I put on my shades, sat in the corner and pretended to be blind."

"Clever!"

"Not really! When we arrived here you told the desk clerk I had gone out to the drugstore. Pretty good for a blind guy."

The smile dropped from her face. "Don't worry about it too much. She is on day shift, the desk clerk is on nights. Hopefully they will never meet."

"What if they do?"

"Then the likelihood of them talking about me is pretty small. Like I said, don't worry, but don't let your guard down too much."

"I won't." The happiness was gone from her face

"Hey!" he said, looking into her serious and troubled face. "You looked much nicer when you were happy." She lifted her gaze toward him. "Don't worry about it. We're miles from anywhere. Go find your new friend and relax. I'm just saying be careful." Her countenance brightened at the thought of companionship and pretty soon she was gone again.

As soon as she left the room, Roger was back on the internet. He hadn't come up with anything concrete when approaching his search from the direction of the Department of Homeland Security, so this time he decided to search from where this started. Oman!

Given that he had been pulled into this from the outside, it made sense to start looking into the main players in this game. A quick search for Oman and oil revealed about five and a half million web pages of information he already knew. Adding a few choice keywords, he managed to narrow down his search and found an interesting and recent document outlining the possibility of potentially large oil reserves in the southern parts of Oman. Roger downloaded the document.

The document was published by the Center for Strategic and International Studies. Roger wasn't exactly sure who CSIS was, so before reading further, he navigated to the CSIS web site. CSIS, as it turns out, are a panel of experts and advisors. They publish recommendations to government, big business and whoever else is interested. Reading further he found they were a non-profit organization relying on donations from various sources.

Roger's immediate thought was to move on as they appeared to be clean of any potential to do any damage. However, reading on a little further, CSIS appeared to lack for nothing. They appeared to be propped up by wealthy backers. He decided to read the document anyway.

As suspected, the document outlined the potential for a massive oil reserve in the south of Oman, near Salalah. The apparent stock of oil would be located inland from Salalah. The document contained satellite images of the area, with what looked like drilling sites where drilling had already started. There were no references on the graphic, so confirmation of the position would be impossible, but it was in the desert.

Making notes as he read, Roger jotted down the author's name, Gavin Carter and navigated back to the website to see if he could locate anything about him. He soon discovered that Gavin had authored other documents as well. He appeared to be a Middle East expert, whose primary focus was one of a political nature. It struck Roger as being strange the author had strayed from his topic a little when reporting the oil find. All of a sudden CSIS seemed much more interesting to Roger.

After a couple of intense hours of research, Roger leaned back in his chair, stretching his arms above his head. He yawned, letting out a disgruntled groan. He had found no link between CSIS and anything to do with his situation. On the surface CSIS appeared clean in all respects. Gavin Carter, he'd found, was a Yale graduate. He had a PhD in politics and had written several papers on the Middle East, wherein he discussed security aspects and made suggestions regarding policies. He'd also given input to the Global Forecast document for 2010, spelling out his security reservations in the Middle East where Oman didn't even feature.

He also wrote a chapter in the 2013 forecast, where Oman featured much more prominently. Roger thought this strange, as historically Oman was a low profile state when compared to other states in the area like Syria, Iran or Iraq. Roger recalled wryly that when he was preparing to fly to Muscat for the first time, most of his friends didn't even known Oman existed, let alone know where it was.

Roger tried a few combined searches for words like oil, Oman, Gavin Carter and came up empty, save for the ubiquitous two million unrelated results. He needed to take a break. He stood and walked a few circles around the small room to stretch his legs. Walking to the window, Roger felt the urge to climb out and run up the street. He'd been cooped up too long. His muscles were starting to revolt. Turning, he did another couple of laps around the room, then dropped to the floor and started doing push-ups. He didn't bother counting, but stopped when he thought it must've been about fifty.

Turning onto his back and hooking his toes under the bed, he counted off one-hundred and twenty crunches and didn't stop until his abdominals were burning. He laid his head back onto the floor, aware of his heavier than normal breathing and stared at the white ceiling above his head. He'd spent nearly the whole day with Google as his buddy and was no further along the path than when he'd started.

Roger's little world erupted into confusion and panic when he heard the electronic lock on the door beep. Not knowing what to do he spun over onto his stomach and was about to stand up, but his his reactions had been way too slow. He was relieved when Atifah walked into the room and closed the door behind her.

"Hello! How was your day?" It was as if a ray of sun had shone through the window. She once again came bearing gifts of edibles from the weekend buffet and laid the trays on the bed.

"You are an absolute star." He was still on his stomach on the floor.

She stopped, looking down at him with a puzzled look. "What are you doing down there?"

"My exercises!" He looked embarrassed at being found out. "I haven't done too much moving around lately and my muscles are getting weak."

"Uh-Huh! Can you get up?" she asked, grinning at the prostrate form on the floor then changing the subject. "So! What did you find out?"

"Nothing! Absolute diddly-squat!" He climbed to his feet looking over at the platters she'd placed on the bed. "Looks good."

"Eat! You paid for it."

"Speaking of which we must take stock of how much cash we have left." He picked at the hot snacks. "And what did you do this afternoon?"

"We walked about five miles through the country and then crashed at the pool and relaxed."

"Sounds like fun."

"It was! It's only when I see you I start to stress again."

"Anne tells me the same thing." After shuffling the food around, Roger picked up one of the plates and started eating in earnest. He hadn't realized how hungry he was.

After eating in silence, he told Atifah he needed to get back to work and once again opened the laptop. Within a couple of minutes Roger was back in cyber space, intent on solving the riddle and discovering who was chasing him.

He sat staring at the Google results pages, moving his hand from the mouse to the keyboard and back as needed. Thoughts rushed through his head. Still any possible link or action evaded his thought process. Page after page of irrelevant blue links appeared in front of him. One link after another was tested and documents skimmed over, but he found nothing.

After what seemed like ages he lifted his head from the screen to find Atifah sleeping on the bed and the sky already darkening through the window. Soon, passersby would be able to see inside as the light outside decreased. He stood by the window for a while, watching the small town of Flatonia going about its quiet weekend life. The yearning for a quiet walk down the street flashed through his head again and as if wanting to crush the thought before it settled, Roger closed the drapes and turned his back on the world outside.

After about an hour of sitting silently in the darkness, listening only to the sound of Atifah's gentle breathing, his frustration got the better of him. He crept across to her and shook her shoulder gently. She stirred and opened her eyes.

"I need to go out." Roger's tone was flat. She started to pull herself up.

"No! It's ok! I may be a while. You can sleep. Leave the window unlatched and I'll let myself in." She sank back into her pillow without resistance.

Roger picked up his recorded disks and opened the window. The warm evening air caressed his face. He paused looking up and down the street. The sound of distant voices made him wait before climbing out the window. He lowered himself to the ground and turning, closed the window behind him. Keeping out of sight to the best of his abilities, Roger made for the car park. Soon he was headed for Houston again.

-- o --- oOo --- o --

Roger drove right into Houston. It felt like forever since he'd seen the city at night. Memories of better days flooded his mind as he saw the familiar signs of the day ending and the night starting.

He circled a few times in the traffic, lapping up the normality of life going on around him. He had been filled with an incredible sense of loneliness such as he hadn't felt before. This was a good remedy for the loneliness.

Rounding the corner at the intersection of Lamar and Travis, Roger saw what he was looking for. A trashcan was standing on the corner close to his door. Only a few people were on the corner. He slowed to a crawl, pressed the button and waited while the driver's side window slid down. As he passed he tossed the DVD into the trash, then put his foot down at the same time as allowing the window to slide back into place. He dialed Crane as he headed back out of town.

"Macadam?" Crane barked from the other end.

"The same!"

"I thought I wouldn't hear from you again."

"I told you. I'm going to prove I didn't do it."

"I'm listening."

"I'm waiting for you at the corner of Lamar and Main. Hurry before I change my mind." He hung up the phone.

Twenty-two minutes later his phone rang. "Where the fuck are you?" Crane was angry at being stood up and failed to notice the black sedan drive slowly past him. The two agents in the Ford didn't see him either as they were scanning the sidewalk for Macadam.

"Are you on foot?"

190

"No! I'm parked illegally."

"Get out and walk toward the corner of Travis and Lamar."

"You're in the city?" Crane was talking as he walked fast toward the intersection followed by Barnard and Crosby.

"I was," Roger lied.

"How far?"

"All the way to the corner."

After a pause, Crane spoke. "Ok! I'm here. Where are you?"

"Can you see the trashcan on the corner diagonally opposite the parking?"

"Wait!" A shuffling followed. "I can see it."

"Look inside. I threw a DVD in there."

"Hold on! I'll get it." He started talking as he made his way to the trashcan. "What's on the DVD?"

"It's not pleasant. I captured your people and the guests getting executed on candid camera."

"You did what?"

"I thought it would get me off the hook, but there's no distinct picture. There is a distinct image of one of the killers and I can assure you it's neither of us two. I want the woman taken off your suspect list."

"Slow down Charlie! I want to see what's on here first. Besides, I don't even know what the woman looks like."

"It'd be stupid of me to give you a video of somebody that even remotely resembled the girl wouldn't it?"

"Got it! Ok! I'll have a look and call you back. You're full of surprises Macadam."

Heading back toward Interstate 10, Roger clicked on the news on the radio. After a few adverts the news came on. He listened through the entire broadcast, but soon realized there was nothing new to report and he seemed to have lost favor with the news teams. He wasn't even mentioned. It appeared as if America's most wanted terrorist was old news already. He wasn't disappointed not to hear his name.

SUNDAY, 12TH

As he approached Flatonia, Roger got an uneasy sensation in the pit of his stomach. He checked his rearview mirrors and saw miles of lights behind, but none close enough to warrant this uneasiness. In front of him the offramp approached, but he saw no sign of anything suggesting a problem. To be safe he carried on past the turning. After a few miles he turned and came back, on the watch for somebody following. Nothing.

His mind worked at a furious rate, processing the events of the day and making sure he hadn't forgotten anything that might lead the agents to him. Nothing came to mind. He thought back to the parking episode of the previous day. As he approached the hotel, it dawned on him, maybe the agents had a fix on the Ford. If it had been spotted at the hotel, they could already have Atifah by now. He turned in the street and headed back toward the interstate. Before reaching the highway, he turned and drove about a mile, then located a spot where the vehicle would not attract too much interest. Locking up he set out to walk the couple of miles back to the hotel.

He approached the hotel with caution, keeping low and scanning the parking area. Over on the west side of the parking lot, a large black Chevrolet stood menacing in the darkness. He could vaguely see two silhouettes inside the vehicle. Roger cursed under his breath. He wondered why they were outside. Maybe they already had Atifah in the vehicle and were waiting for him.

Keeping to the shadows and out of the line of sight of the two agents, he made his way back to his room. He approached cautiously knowing they might be inside already. He could hear his heart pounding in his head as he crept under the window. The window hadn't been moved, but he could see nothing beyond the drapes. Gently he slid the window open making almost no sound, but knowing if somebody had been in there, he would already have been caught.

He listened to the sounds inside the room. After a couple of minutes of straining his ears, he was sure he could hear Atifah's breathing and nothing more. Looking around, he slid the window the rest of the way up and lifted himself into the black hole. He had no clue as to the whereabouts of the agents. He lowered himself to the floor and moved to the bed. After waiting next to the bed long enough for his eyes to adjust to the darkness, he stooped locating Atifah's head. He placed his right hand over her mouth at the same time his left hand held the back of her head so she couldn't free herself. She woke in a panic, but calmed as she heard Roger's voice whispering close to her ear.

"It's me! It's me! Don't panic!"

He felt her relax. He released his grip and whispered next to her ear in an almost inaudible tone. "I'm sorry." She cleared her throat as her heartbeat slowed a bit. He continued, "We need to go. Silently."

She answered with a hoarse "Ok!"

She took a second to process what happened and then she jumped into action. Without a word being spoken and in near silence the two dressed and packed. They were traveling light so even in the dark, in a short while, they were packed and standing by the window. Roger moved the drapes a fraction of an inch and peered outside with one eye. There was no movement. He guessed if the agents were here after them and he was sure they were, they would still be in the parking area waiting for him to come back.

He lowered himself to the ground, then helped Atifah out of the window. Going back along the same route he had taken to bypass the agents on the way in, they headed away from the hotel. Roger signaled to her showing her the location of the agent's car. Looking back from a distance, Atifah was saddened at leaving the hotel. This was the most stable and relaxing period she had spent in America.

Once at a safe distance she spoke, "How did you know. I'd have driven in without thinking."

"I don't know. Something was telling me to be careful."

"How did they know?"

"I don't even know they did. We couldn't take a chance. They looked like agents and it looked like they were staking the place out, but it could as easily have been the morning shift waiting to start work."

"I'm sure they were agents," she agreed with his assessment.

"I don't know how they located us, or why they didn't move in to arrest us. I thought they had you and they were waiting for me."

"And you still came to rescue me?"

He didn't speak, but she moved in close and kissed him on the cheek. "Thank you."

"I'm sure you'd do the same for me."

"Don't count on it," she laughed.

"The car is a couple of miles up the road."

"No problem. I love to walk." She shivered. Even though the night was warm, the change from bed to walking the street after three in the morning is more of an adjustment than even the most hardened person would manage.

After an almost silent but fast paced walk, the white Ford could be seen in the distance. Roger had been thinking while he walked. "Did you give the registration of the vehicle to the desk clerk?"

"I don't even know the registration of the car."

"Hmm! I'm trying to work out how they knew we were there."

"Were there cameras in the parking?"

"I don't think so. I did check, but even so, they would have been internal. Maybe somebody saw me and called it in, or maybe a cop drove past and called in the car."

"Do you think it was the car?"

"I think so. They must have been examining the surveillance footage from the Houston parking." The same thing had crossed his mind a few times. "Maybe they didn't have enough to swoop in and arrest. I think it was speculation, but they probably had eyes out there looking for the car. I think we're going to have to dump it. Especially when they realize we're not coming back."

"Why are we going to the car now?"

"They're not looking for it here and it's a common car. At the moment, they know it was reported outside the hotel and they can't pin it back to any resident. They probably have nothing else but the remote possibility the car will come back."

"Why are we running?"

"Because there were what looked like agents sitting outside the hotel and we're wanted for murder, terrorism, bank robbery and probably a few more felonies and misdemeanors by now."

"So you drag me out of bed at three in the morning and you don't even know if they were agents?"

Roger paused at the vehicle. Smiling and shaking his head he turned to her. "Shut up and get in the car. If you're lucky I won't kick you out somewhere on the highway."

Once they were on their way, Atifah asked, "Where are we going?"

"I've heard Acapulco is nice this time of year."

"Where's Acapulco?"

"Mexico." He saw her turn her head toward him. "I want the cops to think we're in Mexico. In the meantime you can sleep. We have a distance to cover. I'll wake you if I need you." She didn't need prompting again.

-- o --- oOo --- o --

Roger headed back to Interstate 10 making his way for San Antonio. When he turned off onto the I410 loop she was still sleeping soundly. Bypassing San Antonio, he got onto Interstate 35 and headed for Laredo. It was going to be a long day.

At about 8:30, Atifah surfaced and looked around.

"Ah! It lives. I thought about waking you for your prayers, but you were snoring so loud I thought you must be tired."

"Where are we?" Then after a short pause. "Thanks, but I wouldn't pray before performing the ritual ablution. Snoring?"

"I'm lying. You weren't snoring. We're somewhere between San Antonio and Laredo. I'll pull in at the next truck stop and buy breakfast and gas."

"Sure. No problem!" She paused a second while her mind shot back to being pulled out of bed in the middle of the night. "Do you think it will be safe?"

"How'd you mean?"

"Do you think they have my picture from the parking?"

"I can't say for sure, but even if they have, people will only start seeing it this morning." Roger thought about it for a second. "Besides, those cameras are not great. I can understand them getting the plates easily, but the chances of getting a clear shot of your face are pretty remote. It's dark in the car."

"I'd like to know what they have on us now. Feels like ages since I've seen the news." Her mind wandered back over the day of relaxation.

"True. I listened to the radio, but there was nothing early this morning. We're old news now."

"I wish." She shook her head, sorry to have woken up and come back to the world of despair. "We need to see CNN."

"Maybe they'll have the news on at the truck stop."

"Nice! Maybe I'll be able to watch myself while I buy breakfast."

"If those were agents outside the hotel, then they're on the lookout for the Ford. It means they will probably have a picture of you. All we can hope is for the picture to be unclear."

Roger eased off the highway at the next truck shop and parked, making sure he was out of sight of the pedestrian traffic from the small diner serving the truckers with their breakfast. He looked back and could see the reflection of the front door to the diner in a large convex mirror used by vehicles to determine whether the roadway was clear when rounding the building.

A row of trucks of various kinds lined the large dusty lot. He looked around, scanning the scene. "I think this looks safe. No sign of CCTV cameras on this side, only over there." He pointed toward the gas pumps. "They're far away."

He handed her the cash. "Buy yourself coffee and sit a while. See if you can see anything on the news."

"What if I'm on there?"

"Then pay for your goods and leave. I'll keep an eye on the entrance from here. If I see anything suspect, or if anybody follows you out, I will speed round and meet you out front."

She took a deep breath and started toward the diner. She rounded the corner and in a short while he watched her enter into the glass doors and disappear from sight. Roger eased back into the seat and watched the distorted image of the front door in the mirror.

Inside, Atifah looked around at the faces that looked up from their breakfast as she walked in. The majority turned their attention back to their meal.

The large lady smiled at the girl from behind the high counter. "Yes Honey! What can we do for you?"

Atifah scanned the boards behind the woman and eventually, running out of options, pointed to the specials board. "Two specials with coffee, one to eat here, one to go."

"Sure! Anything else for you? You want bacon with those?"

Atifah smiled at the woman. "No thanks, just the specials."

"It'll be about ten minutes, ok Love?"

"No problem! I'll take a seat over there." She walked across the room and sat down at a two-seater table facing in the direction of the TV. She waited for the news. She didn't have to wait long. Pretty soon she was watching as Elaine Hodges began tearing the two of them to pieces. In the backdrop behind Elaine, Atifah could see the face of Roger as large as life.

A short while into the report Elaine put her finger to her ear and adjusted the monitor. She paused while somebody was speaking to her. "This just in. Police are on the lookout for a white Ford Taurus like the one on your screen right now. The registration plate is visible on the bottom of your screen. They think the driver, a young woman, may have a connection to Macadam and his illegitimate marriage partner. If you see the vehicle do not try to apprehend the driver. Remember, these terrorists are dangerous. Call the police on Houston 5553232. I repeat, do not try to talk to the driver. Macadam is a cold-hearted killer who will not hesitate to bring harm to you and your family."

Atifah looked on in disbelief as they showed an image of the Ford in the parking. She could recognize herself behind the wheel. The image was dark and she knew nobody else would identify her features, but it was more than a little unnerving to see herself driving the car that half the country would now be on the lookout for. She muttered an Omani expletive as a large, rough looking truck driver approached her under the pretext of wanting the salt. He was shocked at the utterance, but soon regained his composure.

"Hi! Can I use your salt?"

"Sure!" She handed him the grubby container.

"You sound like you're having a bad day."

"Sorry! You heard did you? I'm normally careful who I swear in front of."

"No problem! I've been known to cuss a bit myself. The good news is that I have no idea wha you said." He grinned a big beaming grin from under his dark beard. She courteously acknowledged the trucker and turned her attention back to the television.

Not to be outdone by a flat screen he continued, "Anything I can help with?"

"No! Thank you. I'll be fine."

He turned, a little disappointed and returned to his table. His companions had a giggle at his inability to hold the girl's attention. Atifah didn't notice. She was intent on the screen.

She also didn't notice when he left his seat again and walked behind her to ask for more coffee from the counter. On his way back to his seat he tried again to strike up a conversation. "So! Where are you from?"

Atifah, again surprised at his proximity, turned to him. "Sorry! I didn't hear you."

"Where are you from? You swear in a foreign language but I can hear you're from England. Where in England?"

"Oh! London mainly. I studied in London." She wanted to tell him to go away, but under the circumstances she didn't want to attract undue attention. She humored the guy.

He started to tell her he'd been to Manchester a few years ago on business, but now he had his own truck and so didn't need to travel. His mouth moved, but his words blurred into a monotonous low hum as she strained to listen to what Elaine was saying. She heard Elaine signing off and knew she'd missed the report. Hiding her annoyance, she turned her attention to the trucker standing beside her. Smiling, she quickly came up to speed with the conversation and managed to hide the fact that she hadn't heard a word.

Pretty soon her meal arrived, carried by a hard-looking gothic waitress in a frilly pink uniform. Somehow there was something not quite right with the picture, but she thanked her and ate her meal in relative peace. All the while she was conscious of the attentions from the friendly trucker table to her left.

She got up from the table after she'd finished eating and with Roger's meal in her hand, made her way to the high counter to pay for the meals.

"Where're you headed?" The trucker was again standing beside her.

"Laredo."

"On business?"

"My husband and I are visiting." She threw in the husband bit to dissuade the trucker from further attempts at making contact.

"Husband?"

"Yes!" She flashed her wedding band at the trucker who was visibly disappointed. She paid her cash over. "Maybe we'll see you on the road." She made small talk.

"Maybe!" He smiled again. He'd lost but there was no animosity.

By now the truckers from his table had all finished and were paying their respective bills. She left the shop and the truckers followed. Not so much followed - but came out after her. From where he sat, Roger watched. He noted the glances, but he'd seen them all over since he'd been with Atifah. He could see there was no threat. Three of the truckers went in the opposite direction. The remaining two made their way for the trucks parked off to his right. He would be in view of them. Before they came into sight, Roger climbed through the front seats and crouched on the floor behind the driver's seat.

Atifah, approaching the car, saw Roger had gone. She knew to make for the driver's door. She didn't look behind her to see what was happening, but from between the seats, he watched as the drivers looked again at Atifah and then the face of one of the drivers changed. Almost imperceptibly, recognition came over the trucker's countenance. Roger watched as the trucker called to his friend and pointed and discussed. Something wasn't right. He'd recognized the car.

Atifah climbed into the car. He spoke from behind the seat. "I think those truckers have recognized the car."

She looked over at the two drivers. One of the truckers darted for his cab and started the truck, a large fuel tanker. "Go!" Roger almost shouted at Atifah. She fumbled as she tried to slot her key into the ignition.

Too late! As she pulled forward, the truck pulled forward at the same time, cutting off their exit. Roger looked around. The only other way out was through two heavy looking gates behind them. They were locked.

"Damn! That's annoying." Roger stated the obvious, while his mind started to race through the options. "Play innocent. Hit the horn."

Atifah gave two short blasts. There was no sign of movement from the truck. "Go and see if you can persuade him to move. Be nice and if he says anything, you know nothing about anything."

Without looking sideways, she climbed out of the car, paused while she collected her thoughts, then marched toward the cab of the truck. She banged on the door then climbed up and peered through the window.

"You've blocked my car." She shouted above the rattling of the cab as the huge engine turned over below it.

She noticed the nervous look in the driver's eyes as he turned to her, but he didn't register what she was saying. "You've parked across the road. I need to get out."

"I don't think so lady."

"What?" She feigned no knowledge.

"I saw your car. On the TV, inside. The police are on their way to question you."

"What are you talking about?"

"Your vehicle was on the TV. On the news! I saw it!"

"I think you were mistaken, I …"

"No mistakes. I remember numbers. I remember yours from the news."

Atifah realized she wasn't going anywhere and climbed down from the truck. Panic gripped the driver as he remembered she might be dangerous. He opened the door and sprang from the cab. "Wait!" He could not allow her to reach her car. He gripped her shoulders in a vice-like grip and threw her back toward the truck. She fell under the tanker's large trailer. She looked up and saw the burly trucker bearing down on her and scrambled away from under the huge tank. As she emerged the other side her bearded admirer grabbed her to stop her escape. The other driver had ducked under the trailer and raised his hand as if to calm her down. "Don't worry lady. It's only until the cops arrive."

When Roger saw what was going on, he looked around for something he could use as a weapon. Nothing was visible. Both of the truckers were bigger and far stronger than he was. He needed to avoid a confrontation. Without hesitation, Roger jumped through to the front seat and clasped the door trim with his fingertips. In one motion, he ripped the interior panel away from the door and aiming his foot, he kicked the door speaker off of its mounting with one kick. The twisted speaker would never be used again, but a quick and somewhat vicious twist and the speaker was in his hand. He ripped the wires out of the back.

Reaching behind him, he grabbed the bag containing his breakfast and shook the contents wildly onto the rear seat. By the time he exited the vehicle the truckers had already caught Atifah on the opposite side of the truck. He approached the truck as he wrapped the speaker in the bag. The two men started as Roger came up on their side of the truck. The color drained from the one driver's face as he recognized Roger. Roger appeared menacing, calm and in control.

He slapped the speaker against the side of the truck. The magnet stuck fast to the steel side panel. He felt like Clint Eastwood. "You have about two and a half minutes left to get everybody out of the diner. I suggest you move." For a second even Roger wanted to run and get the people out, he was so convincing. The drivers had never seen a real life terrorist and they stood, unable to move. "Two and a quarter minutes and people will die. Go!" It was enough. The bearded driver ran to the diner. The other one ran away.

"You ok?" He placed his arm around her shoulder.

"I'm fine." She was shaken.

"Get the car. I'll move the truck." She disappeared under the truck as he climbed into the cab. The engine was still running. As he edged the truck forward, people began pouring from the diner and running away from the truck. He shut off the engine and climbed back to the ground. By this time Atifah had pulled around next to the truck. He signaled for her to move over and he sat behind the wheel. "Let's go!"

Roger floored the gas and for the first time he felt the power of the V8 engine. This had been the right car for the job. He felt sad thinking the association was soon to be over. "We're going to have to dump the car pretty soon," he said as if chatting at a Sunday afternoon tea party.

"What can we do now?" Once again she over-simplified the situation with a single question, one which carried such a huge answer. She was worried. They had been seen together in public and her bearded friend had a good look at her, several times. For the first time, neither of them could walk around freely and the car in which they were speeding down the interstate, was marked.

"It was only a matter of time." Roger lightened the tone. "We did well to have lasted as long as we did." He looked at her anxious face. "We deserve a medal." She managed to crack an insecure half-smile, but it was soon gone again.

"Don't look so glum! We were on holiday before, now we're like Bonnie and Clyde." Again she attempted a half smile, but she wasn't fooling anybody.

"How are we going to travel?"

"We'll work something out." The same question was reverberating around Roger's own mind. They needed to exit the interstate at the next off-ramp, but beyond that he had no plans whatsoever.

"Where are we going?" Roger had signaled to take the glide-off. Atifah was no longer relaxed as she sat next to Roger. She was upright with her hands clasping her knees. She kept on looking around as they passed other vehicles, trying to see whether people were watching them.

"We need to be off the highway. In fact we need to try to go as far away from the interstate as possible before we dump the car."

"Then what?"

"Then we use plan-B."

"What's plan-B?"

"I have no idea but plan-A is no longer working for us." His attempt at humor didn't work. "Look! We'll keep away from the main roads and drive in the direction of the Mexican border. Maybe we'll be able to cross over, buy another vehicle and be back in a new, legal vehicle." He smiled to reassure her. "I'm going to do my best to keep us out of trouble. Ok?"

Atifah was shaken and worried. She was chewing on her bottom lip to try to control the quiver as she tried to hold back the tears. Roger was once again looking at the quiet, scared child he'd first met. She turned away from Roger and wept silently, only the occasional shudder of her shoulders gave away her crying.

"Listen!" There was no movement from the girl. "Atifah! Look this way!" She turned slowly and light glistened on the tears as they rolled down her cheeks. Her crying now exposed, she sobbed uncontrollably. Roger was saddened by the image. He'd become used to her as a partner and had pretty much forgotten she was not much more than a little girl. He held her hand as she cried. And cry she did.

He thought it better not to finish what he wanted to say, but left her to cry. Within thirty minutes she was all cried out and sleeping. Roger drove on, knowing he needed to protect this girl and in order to achieve this, he needed to dump this car.

-- o --- oOo --- o --

He listened to the news as he drove.

"In the news at this hour, the Omani government has temporarily staved off what looked to be an imminent strike by the international forces. The hundred-thousand strong force is mustered in various strategic places in the Middle East."

"Sultan Qaboos bin Sa'id, of Oman achieved the détente in the face of mounting international aggression, by inviting a United Nations envoy to inspect all the areas of concern. The Sultan has throughout, maintained a passive stance on the issue, stressing an open-door policy to the international community. Secretary of State, Hillary Clinton, will accompany the envoy and is expected to report back to the UN in about two weeks."

"In the meantime, Roger Macadam and his illegal bigamous wife are still on the run from authorities in South Texas. The pair was captured on CCTV at a filling station south of San Antonio where truck drivers tried to apprehend the terror suspects. Police have again issued a warning. This couple is armed and dangerous. Please do not try to apprehend them. If you spot the couple, call your local police or the national Macadam hotline on Houston 5553232."

-- o --- oOo --- o --

The road he was traveling was less busy than the highway, but not in as good a condition. The going was somewhat slower, but he might travel several miles before seeing another vehicle. He was also comforted by his thinking that there would be less chance of passing traffic cameras, or the occasional traffic cop. He did worry he would be visible from a helicopter. It was only a matter of time before they realized he was no longer on the highway but then, as he'd wanted, the car was simply another Taurus.

Along the way he made a left turn onto a road where he had no idea where it led. He knew this road was smaller than the previous and he felt in this case, smaller would be better. He could see the road stretched out before him, without any breaks and with nowhere to hide.

After another hour or so, he saw in the distance what looked like an old farm shed or small barn. There were no other buildings around. When he got close, he pulled off the road and drove the quarter mile or so through the desert dust to the old building. It was derelict and dirty, but would be big enough to hide the car until nightfall.

Atifah woke up as he stopped the vehicle in front of the old shed. "Where are we?"

"I can't say for sure. I thought it would be an idea to be off the road until it gets dark. I'm going to have a look around." He stepped out of the Ford and moved over to the large wooden doors hiding the dark interior. He tried the doors, but they looked like they had been padlocked for the past hundred years or so. This lock was not going to open. He strolled around the structure to where a broken window revealed the interior as being empty and big enough to house the car. Around back and facing away from the road, a broken stable door allowed him access to the shed.

Inside it was dusty but empty. His footsteps, which remained in the dust, showed nobody had set foot in the shed for years. The wood was old and hard but the structure looked strong; built in the old days. The wall planks where he'd walked in were laid horizontally. Two vertical beams about fifteen feet apart were anchored into the floor slab and ran up to the top of the wall where the wooden wall met the roof. They were probably used to anchor the wall planking onto. If he damaged those struts, the entire rear wall would probably fold and fall. It wasn't particularly dangerous, but it would leave the back open and the car visible.

Stepping outside, he signaled Atifah to bring the car around. He retreated back into the half-darkness and looked around for something sharp. Finding what he thought was a cut off corner of an old steel sheet, he scored down across the grain of the wall boards, right next to the vertical struts. After about an hour of continual scraping, his fingers were bleeding and sore. Roger estimated he had scored about a quarter of the way through the boards and lost about two pints of sweat in the process. He then measured the doorframe to the scored line, using his arms spread apart and went outside and measured the same distance. Using the line made by the rusty nails up the side of the building as a guide, Roger scored the outside of the wood in a similar place to inside. He didn't go as deep, but deep enough to break the surface of the planks. He hoped it would be enough.

Taking a breath for a second in the cool interior of the shed, he called to Atifah who had been sitting on the hood of the car and didn't show any signs of feeling the heat at all. "Please spin the car around," he said. Standing in the doorway, he used both arms to suggest the place where she should point the vehicle and the direction she should come from. As she edged closer, he wiggled his fingers signaling her to come and then held up his hands to say stop.

One last look at his markings to double check his thinking and Roger climbed into the driver's seat. "I think maybe you should wait over there, just in case." Atifah moved to the side.

Roger eased the car forward until he felt the bumper stop against the door post. He started to accelerate the car. It was no good as the wheels spun in the loose dirt. He tried another tack. This time reversing back a bit and hitting the door with the bumper. The door stood firm. Realizing he was raising a small dust cloud which was visible for miles out here on the flat plains, Roger backed up the car and closed all the windows. Taking a deep breath he put his foot down.

He knew he didn't want to overrun, otherwise he would drive straight through and out the chained doors at the front of the shed. The car trundled forward at an even pace. This would definitely do something. At the point of contact with the doorframe, Roger slammed his foot on the brake pedal. A deafening crack like a rifle shot sounded from next to him and after a brief moment, he was glad he'd closed the windows. The entire structure shuddered and sent a hail of debris and dust flying from every point on the building. Atifah stepped backward. She thought the building would fall, but it held.

Roger opened his eyes. After a couple of seconds of adjusting to the light, he peered through the gloomy dust cloud. The car had stopped only inches short of the front door. Covering his face with his shirt sleeve in a vain attempt to prevent him from breathing the dust, he climbed out of the vehicle and made his way through the cloud to the gaping hole at the back of the shed. It wasn't as perfect as he'd hoped, but the hardwood planks had broken pretty much along the score lines. With a bit of juggling, he was able to reconstruct the back wall well enough to look good from a distance. His ears were still ringing from the crack when he turned his proud smile to Atifah. "What do you think?"

"Not bad!"

"We'll wait a while for the dust to settle and then we can sit inside out of the heat."

After a short while Roger peered in through the now rickety doorway and stepped inside the structure. Once his eyes adjusted to the light, he could see the car, almost invisible, covered in a fine grey dust. He called to Atifah. "Come in." Then when she got closer. "Try not to disturb the dust on the car. It'll help in making it less visible."

They climbed into the vehicle. Although the cloud had almost settled, the air was still full of dust and they both covered their faces with their clothing when going inside.

The afternoon darkened into evening. Roger grabbed his keys. "Right! Shall we go?" He turned to her expecting an answer, but he felt her hand on his arm.

"Ssh!" was her answer. He froze as he saw what she'd been watching. Through the thick dust on the windscreen, he could see the glimmer of the lights from an approaching vehicle. There was nowhere to go. The terrain was flat and there was little vegetation for hundreds of yards in all directions. He slid the key into the ignition as the lights pulled up to the front door.

"Get down!" The two of them lay across the front seats together, neither made a sound. They listened as they heard the engine die and two doors open and then close. Then came the unmistakable sound of the police radio crackling into life but neither of the police walking around outside were talking on the radio.

They missed what the first speaker said. It sounded like a woman. The answer came. "Nah! This hasn't been opened for years." More muffled talking from the first cop followed by "I'll have a look!"

They could hear the crunching of shoes in the gravel and then the movement of the cop's flashlight as he peered through the window to their right. Roger's hand moved slowly to his keys in the ignition, careful not to touch them. He knew the element of surprise would only last a second. He couldn't drive forward because the cop car was parked in front of the door. The only way out was backward and by the time he'd completed the move, the cops would already be firing at them.

His mind raced. He would need to propel the car backward with the lights off into the unknown. He had seen earlier there was no obstruction for a long way, but what of ditches and loose dirt? He should have checked these things.

"There's a vehicle inside." Roger's fingers closed around the keys.

The woman's voice became audible as she walked around the opposite side. "What is it?"

"It looks like an old Ford, but this car hasn't moved for years. It's covered in dust."

"You think we should cut the chain?"

"Nah! You can hardly even see the color of this one. If this thing had driven a hundred today there would be no dust on it. Besides, that lock hasn't been opened in years." She joined her partner on the window side of the shed. "Have a look here. Nobody could see through the windshield."

"Guess so! Ok! Call it in. This one's clear. Only three more to look at and we can go home." Roger's hand relaxed on the keys. The flashlight seemed to do another quick scan of the car and then the shed turned dark. Again the two doors opened and closed. This was followed by the engine roaring into life and the sound of the tires rolling over the gravel and rocks. The sound disappeared into the night.

The two of them started to breathe again. Atifah gave a nervous giggle. "I thought we were done for."

"Me too! Why the hell didn't they go round back and look in the back door. They would have had a clear view of the plates from the door."

She laughed again. "Somebody is watching over us today."

"Damn! That was close." He gave a nervous but relieved laugh, while gasping back deep breaths realizing he must've been holding his breath throughout the whole episode. "I think we'll give it another hour and we can get out of here."

"How are we going to go?" She was a little puzzled. She'd thought they were leaving the car here.

"I think we can drive through the night and then look for a place to dump the car from about three onwards. You can sleep if you want, but you'll definitely wake up when I reverse out of here. We have a long night ahead."

-- o --- oOo --- o --

Roger took the opportunity to connect to the internet and carry out more research. Again he turned up nothing concrete. He knew he was missing something. He felt the link was there but was eluding him. Before long, frustrated and disgruntled, he closed the lid of the laptop and laid his head back. His mind was racing through the searches and documents he'd read. "What about 9-11?" He flicked open the laptop again and started punching the keys. "9-11 predicted" He said as he typed. To his astonishment, everybody from Nostradamus to the X-Men and of course the Bible had predicted 9-11. After paging through the first few pages of two million plus results, he came across information which interested him.

Roger didn't involve himself in politics, nor did he entertain vendors of conspiracy theories. However, having now been on the receiving end of a concocted story, he was much more open to what he'd always referred to as 'such garbage'. Article after article described how the American government had possessed knowledge of the attack. How the warnings had been ignored, squashed and covered up. A couple of weeks ago Roger would have dismissed all of this as drivel, but now he found himself transfixed on the contents of the pages. After a while he needed to pull himself out of the pages as the stories sucked him in. For the first time in his life Roger could understand the lure of a good conspiracy.

By the time he had pulled himself away from the search engine, an hour had passed and he had a new perspective. Black wasn't necessarily black and white wasn't necessarily white. They were merely various shades of grey. If there was any truth to these conspiracies, then the perpetrator of these crimes was the most powerful organization on the planet, the U.S government. His mind was buzzing with excitement and horror at the prospect of such atrocities being committed by the same people that the 9/11 dead had voted into power. His logic told him not to be ridiculous, but his questioning mind told him not to pass this off as a mere conspiracy. There were coincidences. Too many references.

Roger knew he had to move on. He packed up the computer. It took a moment for his eyes to adjust to the darkness before he could look around. A glimmer of light from the night outside caused a glow from the door at the back of the shed. He turned off the interior light, before opening the door and stepping out into the dark shed. Atifah stirred as he tried to open the door as quietly as possible. The air still hung heavy with dust, but nothing like it had been earlier.

Roger walked to the door and peered out. The air was cool but clean outside. In the distance he could see the lights on the main road, but they were few and far between. Nothing else moved around him. All other visible lights were way off in the distance. The sounds of the night were normal for this desert-like area and the only man-made sound was the distant movement of commuters on their way to their destinations.

He turned to go back inside. Even in the near blackness he could see the cracked wooden wall. How those cops had not been around the building astounded him. He made his way back to the car and climbed in. Atifah surfaced. "What time is it?"

Roger flicked the key and the dash powered into life. "Nine twenty-three and forty-two seconds."

"Are we going?"

"It's time."

"What if we are spotted?" Since her run in at the truck stop she was much more nervous than she had been. Atifah had enjoyed a degree of anonymity but now she joined Roger as being a recognizable fugitive.

"Vehicles on the road at the moment are on their way home after a long day at work. The last thing they will worry about is a dirty old Ford."

"And roadblocks?"

"They don't know which direction we took. We weren't followed and this is a huge area. If we are caught it will have to be the result of really bad luck on our part. As soon as we can, we'll dump the car."

"And then what? Are we going to walk?"

"I don't know yet but rest assured, as soon as I know, you'll know." She didn't answer, so he continued. "If you have any ideas or thoughts please speak your mind. Right now I am open to suggestions."

"We still have those hair pieces and theatre make-up."

"You're right! I'd forgotten about those. Hell! Maybe we'll catch a bus or a train." She laughed. "We must remember to take them out the trunk before we ditch the car."

Roger turned the key and the engine turned and fired into life. "Shall we?" He turned to her, now semi visible from the glow off the dash.

"Let's do it!"

Roger selected reverse gear and punched the gas. The already broken back wall almost exploded as the car came into contact with it. There was no loud crack this time and the building didn't even shudder as the car broke through, the only sound was that of the hard wooden planks as they bounced off the roof and doors of the Ford. The vehicle stopped a few yards from the building and after cleaning the windshield, Roger waved at the large gaping hole in the back wall. "Goodbye little cabin. It's been a blast."

"I'm not so sure about that," Atifah answered.

"This building hid us against all odds. I will always remember this little shed." He selected the correct gear and edged forward into the darkness. There seemed little reason to attract attention by putting his lights on, so he pulled slowly onto the dirt track and trundled his way back to the main road. He sat way back from the road and waited for a sufficiently large gap between cars before switching his lights on and pulling onto the road.

MONDAY, 13TH

Roger only had a general direction in mind, not a plan on how to get there, nor any idea of what to do when they arrived. He spent much of the night zigzagging through rural southern Texas.

At around four in the morning he decided it was time to be rid of the Ford. He knew they were not far from the border town of Laredo, but had no desire to drive into town. He wanted to find a hole to crawl into for the day.

The area seemed full of homesteads and small farms. There were also a bunch of small industrial areas dotted about, but he wanted something quieter. Eventually, he settled for an area of relatively dense vegetation alongside a small tributary to the Rio Grande. It was sufficiently far from any roads to be seen by passing motorists. The brush was thick enough to offer them shade from the heat of the day. It wasn't the best place they'd stayed at, but it beat the highway for the daylight hours.

Atifah woke when he started bouncing along the dirt road. She sat up and laughed.

"What are you laughing at?"

"I was going to ask where we are, but I can see we're nowhere."

"This will be a safe and cool place to stop for the day. At least, I hope so. We'll only be able to see properly when the sun comes up." She laughed again.

"What's the plan, Roger?" She sounded serious. "We can't keep running by night and sitting under the trees by day."

"I know. I was thinking about it while I was driving." He paused while gathering and processing his thoughts. "It's only a matter of time before we're caught the way we're going." Another thinking pause. "It's not going to be easy, but we need to be proactive and go after the people behind this."

"But who are they?"

"I don't have a clue, but we do have something they want."

"What?" She looked around the car, trying to think what they could possibly want.

"Us!"

Atifah stopped looking around. She sat in silence while the concept sunk in. "You want to use us as bait for killers?"

"I can't think of anything else. Believe me I have spent the last few hours trying to find an alternative but ..." He didn't finish the sentence.

"It will be dangerous," Atifah said.

"It will be."

"We could be killed."

"I could be," he corrected her.

"What? Are you going to toss me out on the side of the road?"

"Of course not I just ..."

"Then we're in this together." Roger thought about his passenger. In such a short time, the young girl had all but disappeared and left a woman matured by unrivalled circumstances. This was unfairness of the highest order. He wasn't going to argue, but he had a deep desire to protect her.

"I want you to give me your word you'll do things my way."

"I ..."

"I'm serious! I need your commitment. I don't mind discussing things, but if we can't decide then it's my way."

"I was going to say I give you my word but you don't need it. You have my obedience. Of course I will listen to you."

"Good! I'm glad. I will need help." He was taken aback by her acceptance, but his point was absolute and she knew he meant it.

Roger located a spot in the trees where he hoped he would be hidden. He switched off the engine and the lights and sat back, listening to the pre-dawn sounds all around. The silence of the night was broken by the gentle trickle of the nearby river and random noises from creatures waking for the day ahead and those turning in from a busy night. The sunlight started to lighten the sky in the east and tiredness flooded through Roger's head. He wanted to sleep.

"So what's the plan?" Atifah wasn't about to let him nod off.

"I don't know exactly, but back there we passed small farms. I thought we could arrange to have the government come and join us there so we can chat."

"Are you going to phone them?"

"Not sure yet! I don't think Crane and his little Crane-lets necessarily have anything to do with the killings."

"How do you know?"

"A feeling. Maybe one of them is involved." His eyes were heavy, but he fought the desire to sleep. He needed to look around in the daylight, to check whether it was safe for them. "We'll think of something! I want to try to attract the correct people."

"What if ..."

"It won't happen. This time I'll be sure it doesn't happen. We'll clear all the people out. I promise."

Before the sun broke above the horizon there was enough light for Roger to take a walk around and determine whether the Ford was visible from any direction. Even beyond the trees it didn't look like there was going to be much passing traffic. He settled in his seat. He pushed the seat back giving him ample foot room and then laid the back-rest down to near horizontal. "If you're hungry we have stuff in the trunk. I think it's going to be a long day."

Atifah laid her head back to try to sleep but gave up. She'd slept well through the night while Roger had been traversing the country in about five times the amount of time it would have taken on the highway.

-- o --- oOo --- o --

Once the day was in full swing Atifah decided to take a walk. She opened the door and climbed out, gently closing it again after her. He didn't even stir. She looked around. Roger had found the most desolate spot in America. There was nothing. The river was more of a small creek about twenty feet wide and no deeper than two to three feet. The water was gently flowing and clean. She, on the other hand, was grimy and dirty. She had a change of clothes in the car and the sparkling water was inviting. She bent down to test the water. It was far from warm, but she wouldn't freeze to death.

With a new spring in her step, she walked to the car and extracted the towel she'd 'borrowed' from the hotel and her new clothes. Back at the river she looked around, listening for any sound which might give away the presence of someone else in the vicinity. Checking back at the car to see if Roger was still sleeping, she slipped off her clothes down to her underwear. She stepped toward the water then paused. A naughty grin spread over her face and she removed the remaining two items. Crouching, as if it would help her from being seen, she slipped smoothly into the water. Pretty soon she crouched in the shallow water. The sense of freedom as the cool water swirled around her body made her feel refreshed.

Planting her feet on the riverbed to push against the gentle current, she dipped her head backward in the clear water. The muffled sounds of the flowing water relaxed her and she paused briefly before lifting her head out of the water. As she broke the surface of the water she heard something. Almost indiscernible and only for a split second. She was sure it was the sound of a man's voice. It may have been a cough, or maybe a minute slice of a conversation, she was unable to tell, but she knew it was a man's voice.

She froze! She couldn't climb out of the water for fear of being seen, but she couldn't stay in the water if men were approaching. She listened, but no further sounds came. What was cool and invigorating seconds previously, became cold and imprisoning. She listened. Still nothing. Had she been mistaken? After all, she'd heard this as she broke through the water with all the other noises and water in her ears. It seemed like she sat there in the cold harsh water for an eternity, but no more sounds came.

"Let's go. Quickly!" She spun around to see Roger crouched on the bank holding her towel for her while scanning the trees around. The distant sound of voices had awakened him from a deep sleep, a sleep which would have taken a bomb blast to wake him a few weeks ago. He was wide awake, his senses tingled and his heart pounded in his chest from the abrupt awakening. She climbed up the bank taking the towel and wrapping it around her. She picked up her clothes and ran for the car, following close on the heels of Roger. He was so intent on the voices that he hadn't even looked at Atifah. She was relieved.

At the vehicle Roger opened the door for her and she sat. He closed the door, not by slamming, but by closing it gently and then giving a firm nudge with the palm of his hands. The door closed almost silently. He circled around behind the car and sat down in the driver's seat.

"You heard them?" He still hadn't looked at her, but was scanning the surroundings for any sign.

"I thought I did but I wasn't sure."

Roger reached down and pressing the buttons, slid the four windows down. The noise of the small electric motors seemed deafening as the outside sounds rushed in through the opening windows. There it was again. They couldn't work out the words, but somebody shouted.

"I think it's kids." Roger was moving his head in small motions trying to pick up the sounds.

"I think so but they sound far away."

They sat in silence for a few minutes until they were convinced the sounds were moving away. Roger relaxed back into his seat.

"We can't go on like this much longer. We're living on our nerves. I haven't had a good night's sleep in ages."

"I'm sorry I ..." she started.

"Sorry? What for?"

She looked down at herself covered in a towel and dripping wet. Roger laughed. He had known she was in the river and had even passed her the towel. However, his mind had been so focused on the possibility of being detected that he hadn't even realized. Other, lesser important brain functions had carried out the action while he'd been on full alert.

"You're all wet!" he said astonished.

"I was in the water. What do you expect? You passed me the towel."

"Why?"

"I wanted to freshen up." She was laughing now too.

"Ok! I'll take a walk to let you take off your wet clothes." She didn't answer, but the 'little-girl' grin told him there were no wet clothes. He raised his eyebrows and climbed out of the vehicle and walked down to the water's edge.

Picking up a small pebble, Roger tossed it into the water deep in thought. They were a few miles from Laredo and the Mexican border. It was time to have the authorities think he'd crossed the border. It made sense to him for somebody in his position to escape persecution in this way. If the FBI, or whoever was chasing him, thought he was in Mexico or at least going to cross, it might divert attention to the border. He hoped it would allow him more freedom and reduce reaction time. He ambled back toward the car.

He hadn't noticed at first, but all of a sudden he realized he was listening to the sound of a helicopter in the distance. This was bad. The car was well hidden from passersby, but the canopy overhead was a little sparse. They needed to move away from the car and quickly. It would be one thing to have the car discovered, but a serious problem if they were spotted.

"Quickly! We need to move." He opened the door of the car. "Grab what you can. There's a helicopter coming."

Atifah was finishing buttoning herself up. "Where are they?"

"Still a way off, but we can't take a chance."

"Are they after us?"

"Not sure. It might be a rancher, but we can't afford to be caught in the car and if we move it we'll stick out like a sore thumb." He knew there was a chance the car wouldn't be spotted, but also knew they could drop a helicopter down in a very short time. They would be unlikely to escape from an armed agent on foot. The best thing they could do would be to hide. If the car was spotted then move on and close the Ford chapter for the last time.

"Quickly. Down to the river."

"The river?"

"Yes! If they spot the car they will probably come back with dogs. We'll go upstream a bit and then hide."

Roger helped her into the cool water and they turned upstream. Pushing against the current was difficult. They moved about a hundred yards, then in an open spot they climbed onto the bank and ran another fifty yards next to the river. In a series of steps they traversed the creek back and forth, in on one bank and out on the other. Sometimes both on separate banks, then another short run and then back in the water again. Sometimes, they would step out of the water, walk a few yards and then walk backward back into the creek. Then they would carry on with the body-aching walk upstream. Roger knew they couldn't outrun the cops on the ground. The cops had to believe they were long gone.

The helicopter sound was still around but wasn't getting closer. Roger was starting to believe it may have been a rancher checking his fences.

"Are you ok?" She was looking tired.

"I'm ok!" She put on a brave face.

"You look tired. Maybe you can stop over there." He pointed up ahead where the trees thickened. It would comfortably hide them against being seen by a helicopter. If they were cornered by ground forces they were dead but looking further ahead, it looked like the river left the trees for the open farmlands. They wouldn't escape being seen there.

"What do you mean I can stop?"

"You can lie low and keep out of sight in those trees. I'm going to find a spot to see whether they find the car."

"I don't like that idea at all."

"I'm only going a short way back so I can see if they spot the car."

"Are you going back to the car?"

"No! We parked it under trees so they won't see it from this side. If they come from the other side they will see it for sure. I need to see where the chopper is. Keep out of sight. I'll be back."

Once he located a secure spot for her, he dropped his bag under a log and ran back down the river. The going was much easier with the current.

Before long he spotted a large tree, one he could climb and look back toward the vehicle. He wouldn't be able to see the car, but he only needed to see the sky to the west of it.

After a climb which was more precarious than he had expected and continually checking in the direction of the helicopter noise, Roger managed to perch himself in a branch reasonably comfortably. Looking behind, he could see the chopper. It was too far to see detail, but the coloring allowed for the possibility that this was a police helicopter.

Roger watched as the pilot made his way slowly along the wooded tract. They were looking for something or somebody. He cursed under his breath. The chances were if he could see them they could probably see him. They were headed his way and would soon pass over where Atifah was positioned. If they kept the same course and speed, Roger estimated they would see the vehicle in the next two to three minutes. He consoled himself by believing they had to pass the position of the car and look back before they would see the vehicle.

For now, he'd seen enough. It was time for him to move. He climbed down through the branches. He'd always been able to climb trees well. He jumped the last fifteen feet or so. The impact he felt as his feet connected the soft moist ground made him realize he should have climbed a bit further. He wasn't as young as when he last climbed a tree. He started back toward Atifah through the water, keeping a careful eye on the light between the trees in the canopy above. He came upon an opening in the trees he'd already crossed twice. This time Roger hesitated. The helicopter was close and he didn't want to be caught in the middle.

As he looked up, the chopper could be seen between the leaves a short distance away. Roger shrank back and made for a small dark patch of vegetation. He hoped it would be thick enough to provide cover. He crouched and pushed his way into the damp leafy plants, trying his best to pull the leaves over him as he burrowed in. Looking up he saw the underside of the helicopter as it passed slowly overhead.

For a second he thought the chopper was going to stop overhead and he held his breath. Realizing how stupid it was, he cursed himself and started breathing normally as the noisy rotors started to thrash the vegetation around him. Both he and Atifah had escaped undetected. He knew the car would not be as lucky. When the tail rotor was no longer in sight, he pulled himself free of the plants and ran back through the clearing and back toward Atifah.

"Did you see them?" he asked as he approached her.

"Not much. A shadow, passing over there." She waved her hand along the flight path the chopper had taken off to her right.

"I'm sure they will see the car the way they're flying." Looking at his wristwatch, he continued. "It's still early, so we're not going to see darkness for a few hours yet. What do you want to do?"

"What do you mean?"

"Should we wait and see if they're going to find the car, or should we accept they will and move off on foot?"

"Where are we going?"

"I think we need to head back toward one of those small towns I told you about. I have an idea."

"We can't simply stroll along the road."

"Of course not! We'll need to stay off the roads. There's not much cover down here in this part of the country."

"Then maybe we should rest and travel at night."

"I thought so too, but I think we should try put more distance between us and the car. We should keep going as long as we can enjoy the cover of these trees."

She laughed. "I haven't been enjoying it at all."

"Let me help you carry."

"I'm ok at the moment." They picked up the bags and started back upstream, always mindful of the sound of the helicopter. About an hour or so later, distant sirens on the main road led Roger to guess the car had been found. Another hour after they ran out of cover and decided it was time for a rest. They both collapsed in the shade under the trees with a wooded canopy behind and the flat open black brush prairie beyond. Off to their right, they knew Interstate 35 was carrying its continual flow of traffic, but right here there was nothing.

Roger took out the phone to try to make a call, but there was no network coverage in their current position. "I'm going for a walk."

"What?"

He repeated, "I'm going to walk toward the interstate to see if I can pick up a signal."

"How far is it?"

"Hopefully not too far! We need to cover a distance this evening so get some rest and try to remain hidden – unlike earlier," he chuckled. She smiled, embarrassed.

"I'll keep my clothes on this time." She smiled at Roger who smiled back.

After getting her as comfortable as possible and pointing out the limited water supply, Roger placed two empty bottles in his shoulder bag and set off across the plain. There were no hills to talk of, but the gentle undulations of the near desert terrain allowed him to monitor progress toward the interstate. He checked the phone at the brow of each rise and eventually started to see the signs of an active connection to the network.

Two hundred yards later on one such rise he sat on the ground and dialed Anne's phone.

"Hi," she answered her phone in the usual way.

"Annie, honey. It is so good to hear your voice."

"Roger! You too." She knew better than to ask where he was.

"Everything ok?" He knew she wouldn't elaborate if it wasn't. She was a selfless person.

"Everything's fine. How are you two coping?"

"With the government? No problem! Without you? I'm not coping at all."

"I know! You just can't live without me can you?"

"I can't Annie." His voice cracked a little. He paused and swallowed to regain his composure.

"We saw you on the TV. The speaker was pure brilliance."

"Hah! One of the close calls. Have they shown any footage of the murder I was supposed to have committed in Buffalo?"

"Footage?"

"I set up a camcorder to try to catch the guys out. Crane was supposed to have his guys there, but he opted to only leave two of them. I filmed their whole execution on DVD. It was terrible. As cold as ice."

"Oh my God! No, I haven't seen anything like that." She wasn't sure whether she was more horrified at the thought of the execution, or by the 'matter-of-fact' way her husband was reporting it to her.

"Hmm! I gave it directly to Crane. Maybe I was wrong about him." Roger was thoughtful. "We're crossing the river into Mexico tonight. We've had too many close calls and we're getting tired." He paused again. He hated lying to her.

"Roger! Are you ok?"

"I'm fine Honey. We need to find somewhere we can book into a motel and sleep for twenty hours straight without having to keep guard and worry about the Feds knocking on our door."

"But Mexico?"

"Only for a few days. Until we get our strength back."

"You look after yourself Mr Macadam. I want you back."

"You too honey. I'm missing you."

"Me too."

Roger reluctantly hung up. The battery was showing a low signal and he cursed himself for not charging the phone while he was driving. Slowly he stood and turning, he headed back toward Atifah.

Back in the trees again, he located the girl who had fallen into a deep sleep. She was propped up against the base of a tree. A small spider was making its way across her shoulder. Roger took a twig and flicked the spider to the ground where he stepped on it with the full weight of his body. Anger and frustration coursed through his veins and he ground the already long dead spider into the dirt. He grunted and sat down scowling. Roger sat next to Atifah and thinking she might fall over sideways, he leaned up against her.

Roger wanted his life back. He drifted off to sleep with anger and frustration spinning around his head.

-- o --- oOo --- o --

"We need a car," Roger said with a deep sigh. They had awoken when the sun was deep on the horizon. Roger was feeling good. He'd slept heavily and woke with a hungover sensation in his head. Atifah had stirred as she woke and the slight movement had woken him. They woke up leaning on each other. She'd had her head on his shoulder, but there were no more uncomfortable feelings.

She was still seated and was repacking her bag. "I second that!" She paused as if expecting a response. "How?"

"I think I will have to steal one."

"Steal one?"

"I don't think there is any other way. We need to make our way toward people if we want to set a trap for these killers. Not right into Houston, but somewhere we can invite these people on our terms. They're ruthless and we don't want there to be any mistakes."

Even Atifah's high morals were slipping. "Let's go shopping. Are we looking for anything in particular?"

"Any car to carry us back to Flatonia."

"You're going back there again?"

"Why not? By now the agents will have realized we're not coming back. They sure as hell won't expect us to return."

"And then what?"

"I'll be thinking about it on the way there. I don't have all the answers yet, but I am forming a plan."

"And the actual theft. Do you know how?"

Roger answered, "I've never tried. I know the theory, but I have no idea how to steal a car. This will be something I can scratch off my bucket list."

They set off in silence across the open land in the general direction of the main road. They both felt a little vulnerable as they left the cover of the trees, but neither said a word. They both knew they would be covering a great distance on foot this evening.

As they approached the main road they changed direction and started walking parallel to it. As much as a lift would have been welcome, they couldn't allow the chance of somebody recognizing them. They wanted the Feds to think they were in Mexico and so they remained out of sight of the highway, at least fifty yards off into the desert.

By the time they started their walk parallel to the highway it was already dark. The two of them were tired. The opportunity they needed to solve the vehicle problem arose unexpectedly.

As they were walking over the rough dark ground alongside the fence of what looked like a small farmstead, a car inside the fence started its engine. They both ducked into the short brush so they wouldn't be spotted. They listened as a family got into the car and the vehicle reversed over a gravel driveway. Roger squinted his eyes to try to see what was going on. He could hear the sound of squabbling kids and then the lady shouted to her husband who had since climbed out of the car for some reason. "Jack. You've left the truck out. You said you'd put it away."

Roger looked at Atifah and raised his eyebrows. She didn't see his expression in the dim moonlight but she could picture it. She reached over and gently grabbed his arm as confirmation she'd heard. The good news didn't end there.

The man replied. "No problem. We'll be back in the morning." Turning his attention to his son who was already opening the gate to the property, he shouted, "Be sure to shut the gate properly. We don't want the animals wandering out."

So Roger would need to ascertain the nature of the animals. He didn't want to stroll in and find he was talking about a killer Rottweiler. On the other hand, they had a truck at their disposal for the night. From where he lay nestled in the brush, Roger could see the truck. It looked like an old F250, but it presumably worked and would be better than walking.

As the family pulled away across the gravel road, the two stood up and walked around the corner of the fence to the gate. A few lights had been left on in the house, so he would need to scout around to check nobody else was home. Then there was the issue of the suspected Rottweiler. His eyes scanned the shadows for any sign of a dog. He hadn't noticed any dogs while they were getting in the car and most dogs, even lazy ones, would have followed the family out.

Roger examined the latch. There was no lock so it was easily opened. He rattled the gate. Still no sign of a dog. "Wait here!" he half whispered. The gate creaked and rattled as he opened it. He was on full alert while he proceeded inside, slowly at first, but a little more boldly as time passed. He first walked over to the truck and peered inside. He could see the keys were not in the ignition. He needed to check for other people in the house. Moving quietly across the yard like a cat burglar, he approached the building. His ears were still straining for the sound of movement anywhere around him.

All of a sudden pandemonium broke out. There was a loud commotion of squawking and honking. Huge wings were flapping all around Roger as six large geese threw themselves wildly in all directions, one of them striking at Roger and clamping onto his thigh. He thought he'd been attacked by not one but several killer dogs. He kicked at the birds but never came close to connecting. They ran around him almost as startled as he'd been. He'd found the animals.

He managed to escape from them and ran back toward the truck. After a few indignant sqwarks the birds settled again and all Roger could hear was the stifled laughing coming from the gate.

"What?" Roger hoarsely whispered to Atifah.

"That was …" She was still laughing, "the funniest thing I have seen in a long time. Did you do the moonwalk in the eighties?"

"Ha! Ha!" Roger replied. At least the question as to whether anybody else was in the house had been answered, unless the person was completely deaf.

Giving the birds a wide berth he climbed the few steps to the doorway and tried the door. It was locked. By now Atifah had walked inside the gate and moved cautiously past the birds. "What are you doing?"

"I need to find the keys."

"So it's breaking and entering?"

Roger smiled. "Added to murder, treason, terrorism and now grand theft auto, I don't see breaking and entering as a major problem."

She joined him on the steps. The top part of the door had nine cottage panes and the bottom half was solid wood panels. He turned to her –. "Be careful, I'm going to break this pane." The glass shattered the night as it fell inside the door. This gave rise to more indignant squawking from the birds. "Put the glass somewhere while I look around for the keys. Be careful."

The door led onto a small dark passage which backed onto an old looking kitchen. Roger looked around. He could see they were not wealthy people. The kitchen was clean and well lit, but it lacked the conveniences found in suburbia kitchens. The gas stove was old and a bit rusted but clean. The old electric refrigerator hummed in the corner.

Locating the key hooks on the wall, Roger found the keys with the Ford logo and dropped them into his pocket. He could hear Atifah was still sweeping the glass. He climbed the stairs to the bedrooms and looked around. Identifying the main bedroom, he opened the closet and soon found what he was looking for. In a box on the top shelf he found a six shot revolver. He knew nothing about guns, but he could see this was clean, well-oiled and was accompanied by a pack of thirty shiny brass shells. He packed everything back in the box, tucked it under his arm and went down the stairs to find Atifah finishing up.

Closing and locking the door behind them, they left. They remembered to keep their distance from the geese and were pretty soon through the gate and making their way toward the interstate. They settled for the long and less comfortable drive ahead.

-- o --- oOo --- o --

The hotel was quiet. From the parking area they could see the high front desk and above, the top of the desk clerk's head as she sat passing the night away reading a book. It was Atifah's friend from the weekend.

Atifah checked the camcorder to see it had charged sufficiently on the journey. The green light was on.

"What are we going to do?" They had hardly spoken all the way here.

"I have an idea, but I don't want to risk these people's lives. We need to get them to safety."

"I doubt they're going to get up and leave in the middle of the night."

"'Course not! We need to take them out of here at gun point."

"We don't have a gun."

"We do!"

"We do?" She spun her head toward him. In the darkness he could feel the anger blaze in her eyes. He hadn't told her and she was angry. "What are you talking about?"

"I found it in the main bedroom."

"Why didn't you tell me?"

"You probably would have talked me into leaving it behind."

"I would have."

223

"I know and you'd have been right. I would have listened to you, because I didn't want to bring it but we're up against ruthless, terrible people. We need it."

"Do you even know how to shoot?"

"I think so. Just point and click. I've done it in Counterstrike."

"Counter … this isn't a game Roger!"

"I'm joking. I think I'll be ok."

"Ha!" She emphasized a false laugh. "You make me angry Roger. Now we really are armed and dangerous. You should have told me, I don't believe in using guns."

"Neither do I. That's why I chose not to tell you. I agree with you on this. I have never owned a gun and never will."

She stared forward, angry at being deceived. Then, making a conscious effort to be calm she asked, "Ok! So what now?"

"Now we go in and scare these poor people shitless."

-- o --- o0o --- o --

"Hi. Can I help … oh my God!" The young girl's jaw fell open and her face drained white. She knew the face of Madman Macadam.

"Don't panic. We're not here to hurt you." The young girl was frozen with her fingers tightly clamped on the edges of her book. Roger hadn't displayed the gun yet. He hadn't needed to. "Are you ok?" Roger prompted. She sat frozen. She knew from the news she was about to die.

"Michelle! It's me," Atifah spoke gently, standing to the left of Roger. It took effort for the girl to slowly shift her gaze. Her jaw hung open and fear was in her eyes.

"You!" she said looking at Atifah.

"Yes! You remember. We were here at the weekend." Her gentle tone relaxed the girl.

"But I …"

"If we'd wanted to harm you we could've done so already." Her eyes flashed back to Roger. He was once again using his engineer's diplomacy technique and the tone of his voice caused her already tight hands to bunch into white-knuckled fists.

Atifah saw the reaction and stepped in.

"Roger! Wait over there while I talk to Michelle."

"Listen to me." She leaned over toward Michelle, still gentle enough for the girl to relax again. "You've seen the news but it's wrong. Roger didn't kill those people." She wasn't buying it. She had seen it on the news and they had warned her in the staff meeting. Michelle knew she was going to die. "Roger will not hurt you. We're here to stop you getting hurt."

She stiffened as Roger approached again. He spoke in a softer tone, "We think you and your guests may be in danger. When we left here in the early hours of Sunday morning there were people parked outside in the parking bays to the west. These are the same people that have been setting me up and killing innocent people." Michelle didn't respond.

Atifah tried again, "We need to get the guests out or they may be in danger. Can you help us move them out without spooking them too much?"

Michelle started to realize she was still alive. All the words spoken to her over the last few seconds had queued in her ears and simultaneously flooded her brain.

The expression on her face changed from dread to confusion. "What?"

"Michelle!" Roger helped clear the confusion. "We need your help. How many guests do you have at the hotel?"

Her hands were shaking as she started tapping her keyboard. "There's a couple in four, a single woman in five. There's an old man in seven and another couple in nine."

"And staff?"

"There are two of us on nights at the moment. Peter is sleeping at the moment in twenty-one."

"You're a star Michelle. Now! Where can we stash them so they'll be safe and warm? Remember, we don't want to startle them too much."

"I … I don't know. I mean … how safe?" She was still stammering, but she was beginning to function again.

"Can we move them to another hotel?" Roger was thinking aloud.

"I don't have the authority to do that."

"Here's an idea. You go and wake them up. Ask your other staff members to help you and take them all to your place …"

"My place?"

225

"You take them out the back way and put them all in the hotel bus. I saw it outside. You can tell them you think you saw me in the parking lot and you've phoned the police and they're on their way, but you want to ensure your guests are safe. You'll be a hero."

"I don't know about my place. My mom's sleeping."

"Take them on a joyride then."

Atifah cut in, "Listen! Michelle! We only have a few options here. These people are ruthless killers and we believe they're on their way here. We need to make these people disappear or all of your lives are in danger."

"Can't we call the cops?"

Roger was getting impatient. "These people work for our government. Who knows who else is involved? Besides, we have it on DVD how they took out trained FBI agents. Do you think your local sheriff will be able to stop them? They will all end up dead."

"Ok!"

A pause, then Atifah asked, "Ok? What?"

"Ok! I'll take them to my place."

"That's my girl." Roger was relieved. "Go and round them up. Tell them you recognized me from the TV when I booked in and you want to take them all to safety. They'll probably want to call the police, but maybe tell them you left your wallet on the desk and it has your address in it. You don't want us to come after you."

The girl paled and froze again. As he spoke, she realized her wallet was on the desk. She glanced sideways. Roger caught sight of her fear.

"We're not going to hurt you. Take your wallet. We are the good guys here."

She relaxed again. Roger pointed to the wallet. "Go ... take it. We're not coming after you."

She grabbed her wallet and tucked it into the side pocket of her hotel-issue grey pants. She turned, walking toward the rooms, but at the door she turned back. "Are you guys ..."

"We're leaving as soon as everybody else is out and safe. We'll hide behind this desk until you get everybody to safety."

As soon as they heard the mini-bus pull away, Roger sat behind the desk and examined the foyer layout from the chair. He placed the handgun on the desk in front of him out of sight from the rest of the room. Then he walked around the desk and looked from all directions to see if the weapon was visible from anywhere.

Meanwhile Atifah positioned the camcorder amongst the magazines in the corner and made sure the angle was correct to allow for filming as much of the foyer as possible.

Roger sat again and spun around on the chair looking all around him and measuring distances from the chair. He located a pen and placed it on the desk to his right. He practised turning from the desk at his right and knocking the pen onto the floor. Then he would crouch, pick up the pen with his left hand and then come up from the floor, right to where a guest would be standing. As he did so, he slipped his right hand around the handle of the cold, metal gun. He practised this move over and over, until his movement was slick and felt natural.

Roger took out his bank card and held it between his fingertips. He was processing vast amounts of possibilities in his mind as he went through the plan in his head one last time. Satisfied, he said to Atifah, "Ok! This is it." He knew this was literally a 'do or die' situation. "Take your phone and hide on the other side of the parking in the trees. Call my phone when you see a car pull in or somebody approach. You can talk me through the approach. Ok?"

"Ok! I think."

"You'll be fine. If anything goes wrong you'll need to run. Go on foot until you are far enough away to find someone to give you a lift. The old truck won't outrun their cars. You'll need to contact Mike and tell him to take you to my lawyer."

"You're not talking sense Roger. Nothing will go wrong."

"Go now!" he urged her. "Remember what I said."

Atifah started the camcorder. "You'll probably forget." She disappeared out of the door.

Roger settled down at the desk. He fired up the computer and booked himself in as Mr Smith, then, after a few tries he managed to work out how to pay using his credit card. Taking a deep breath he swiped the card. He quickly received the message that his card wasn't valid, but the message was already at the bank. He knew at least two government departments had seen the transaction.

He sat back and thought through the plan one more time. He looked down at the gun, ominous and dark. He picked it up and felt the coolness in his hand. He wondered whether he was going to be able to pull the trigger if needed. He decided to switch off the safety and as he pushed the small lever, the barrel fell forward displaying six empty chambers. "Oh shit!" He sprang up from the chair and ran out of the door to the truck. In the dark he fumbled around, until his fingers closed around the small, heavy box of ammunition. He picked it up and ran back to the foyer. Sitting down again and breathing heavily, he loaded small, deadly cartridges into the weapon. It felt like he'd no sooner finished loading the gun, when he heard the sound of an approaching helicopter. This was it. He put on the hotel issue jacket hanging over the back of his chair, then in one quick movement loaded the weapon and placed it on the desk in front of him.

The helicopter dropped down a few hundred meters from the hotel and then lifted again and disappeared into the night. His phone buzzed.

"It's her."

"What?"

"It's her. The woman from the DVD and her partner. They're approaching the steps now."

"Ok!" He hung up. He spun to the book he'd opened on the desk to his right. As they came through the door and approached the desk Roger lifted his head slowly as if finishing the last few words of the page then turned, knocking his pen under the desk. "Damn! Sorry!" Then in one slick, practised movement he stooped, picked up the pen in his left hand and raised his head at the same time, closing his hand around the handle of the handgun.

The agent was stunned. "Macadam? What an unexpected surprise. Here we were thinking we would be taking out another innocent." Out of the corner of his eye, Roger saw the female agent to his right draw her weapon.

"Unless she places her weapon on the floor and kicks it across to me, your nuts are scrambled eggs."

"Let's not be hasty now. Macadam …"

Roger raised the level of his voice to display the urgency, but spoke slowly. "I want to see her lowering her piece and sliding it to me with her foot." The two men's eyes were unblinking, waiting for the slightest flinch from the other. The agent knew Roger was serious. He nodded to his partner. Reluctantly she lowered her gun slowly to the floor and slid it across the tiles to Roger's feet. "And her backup."

"This isn't the movies. She …"

"Her backup! Now!" Roger kept his cold unblinking stare focused on the agent in front of him. "Or your baby-making days are over."

228

"We both know you aren't going to shoot …"

A shot rang out deafening Roger and stopping the agent in mid-sentence. Roger knew he had to remain in control. He was dealing with people that wouldn't hesitate to execute him in an instant. He had video footage to prove it.

The agent's face changed from a condescending smile to terror, as the bullet tore through the flesh of his inner thigh, inches from his under-carriage and exited his leg lodging itself into a wooden panel behind him.

Roger spoke before giving the agent time to react. "Don't move! Next time I won't miss." He paused while the agent regained his composure. "Don't misinterpret this situation. I have seen what you are capable of and the only reason you are still sporting your genitals is because I want information and I will not hesitate to kill both of you if you make one wrong move. Am I understood?"

The agent spoke through his teeth, clenched in pain. "You've made a big mistake."

"Her backup weapon! Now! Slowly!" Roger hadn't removed his stare from the agent's eyes.

The female agent reached behind her back removing her weapon, then crouching, she sent it across the floor to Roger.

"Now lady, turn around and lie down on your stomach with your hands behind your head. Slowly." He hadn't looked at the woman once, but he could see the motion out the corner of his eye. He waited while she slowly lay down. "Now your turn! Hold it by the handle and put it here." He pointed with his left hand to where the weapon should be placed on the counter, slightly below Roger's head height. He didn't need to be prompted for the others, as the agent placed two more guns on the counter.

"Now step back."

Making the agent lie down would mean he would go out of sight from where Roger sat, so he stood and moved around the desk. "Right. Turn around nice and slow and lie down on your stomach. Hands behind your head." The agent complied.

"Good! Now we're all cozy, start talking. Who do you work for and why are you after me. I want the truth."

"I cannot tell you who I work for and I'm after you because I follow orders."

"Let's get something straight. That was the last non-committal answer I will accept. I want to know who gave you the order to kill innocent people." Roger was calm and cold. "Was it Crane?"

"Crane's an idiot, put in place for the media. The people I represent are not idiots by any stretch."

"So! Who are they?"

"If I tell you I'll be dead by morning."

"If you don't tell me you'll die anyway."

"You won't kill me Macadam. I know you too well. You don't have it in you."

In the distance, the sound of approaching sirens could be heard.

"You'd better run Macadam, they're on their way here and then you will be shot by these trigger-happy Texans."

"I don't need to run. I have the culprits."

"What do you think it will achieve? It's the word of a wanted man against the word of an FBI agent. These people are clever. Very clever. They have already pictured this scenario and they already have a plan in place to counter anything you might think of."

"Did they think of that?" Roger pointed to the small camcorder on the shelf.

"You have us on video?"

"For the second time."

"A huge mistake Macadam. Go! Run now! Give me the tape. You don't want to mess with these people."

"It's done! The cops are on their way." Roger took a copy of the old DVD out of his pocket and placed it on the counter. He picked up the five guns from the agents, then hooking his fingers through the trigger guards, he started to head for the door. He stopped. Turning he walked back. He raised the gun and took aim at the calf muscle of the woman. She let out a stifled scream as the bullet tore hotly through her flesh. She writhed and twisted grasping at her leg.

"You're being stupid Macadam. These people won't be found out. They would sooner start a world war than be found out."

Roger leveled the gun and blew a small neat hole in the calf muscle of the male agent. With trained control, the agent shuddered as he resisted the urge to claw at his leg and let out a controlled gasp of air as he fought back the pain. "You've given me something to go on with." Roger was cold. "You'd better stop the bleeding."

"Macadam! This is a mistake!" The agent spoke through clenched teeth.

Roger stepped around the two, keeping enough distance to avoid any chance of a lunge. Keeping his eyes on them at all times, he moved to the corner and picked up the camcorder.

After collecting the agents' guns he ran out across the parking to the truck. Atifah ran out of the trees as he approached. Keeping the lights off, they sped out of the parking in the opposite direction of the approaching sirens.

"Did you get anything?"

He passed her the camcorder. "Not a lot, but I think a starting point. He kept on saying these people were clever. Unfortunately the local cops came too quickly."

Atifah fiddled with the camcorder. She pushed a few buttons then gasped as she watched. "You shot him?"

Guessing she was talking about the first shot, through the counter, Roger said. "I needed to keep control. He didn't believe I would use the gun. I had to prove to him I would."

"You shot him in the leg." She was in disbelief.

"Lucky for him he was tall." She didn't catch the meaning, but Roger laughed to himself. "It was the flesh. It will heal. I shot them both again before I left too. We couldn't afford to risk them coming after us. They are stronger and more callous than either of us."

"You shot the woman in the leg."

"We have them on DVD executing innocent people. Don't feel too sorry for them."

"How can you shoot somebody in the leg?"

"How can you shoot somebody in the head? Listen! I left a copy of the old DVD there for the police to find, so those two should get what they deserve." Roger had become serious again and a little irritated. "I've been feeling pretty bad about the people that died thanks to me, so don't judge me because I wanted to stop those two getting away. They're murderers."

She noted the anger in Roger's voice and backed off. They drove in silence for several miles before he spoke again.

"Do we still have all the theatrical stuff?"

"It's in my bag."

"Good. I think we must find somewhere to have a meal. I feel like I haven't eaten for days."

"You haven't. Not properly anyway."

"Let's see what you bought."

She dug in her bag and pulled out the same wig which Roger had used in the hotel to avoid being detected by the housekeeping staff. He looked and switched on the inside cab light and examined the wig. It was a scraggy grey wig which was more grey than white. Hair you would look at and say: "Good head of hair for an old guy." He pulled the wig into place. "How do I look?"

"Not my type of old guy, but it works with the greying stubble there. You've got that old hardened criminal look like Clint Eastwood in Unforgiven."

"Damn! The last thing I want to look like is a criminal."

"You don't look like you though."

"I don't?"

"Not at all!"

"Then criminal it is." He flashed a smile at her which looked out of place in the new face. "Now! What about you?"

"I have this long black wig. Now they have me branded as a short-haired blond, it's time to be long and black again." She pulled the hair-piece over her head and was transformed in an instant back to her old self again.

"Great! We'll wait until the sun comes up and then go find a place to have breakfast."

"Where are we going now?" She looked at the dark road stretching out ahead of them.

"I don't know. I think back toward Houston."

They were on a main road, but he was looking for the first opportunity to return to the interstate. The going was slower on the main road, but there was less traffic. At a couple of instances along the route he came close to and even ran alongside the interstate, but it seemed to take ages before he was able to join the flow of trucks and cars all headed for destinations unknown.

Roger knew it would soon be morning and the owner of the truck would be home. If their disguises worked they would eat in Katy and catch a bus into the city, leaving the truck where it could be picked up later.

Roger had no direction. He didn't know what the next step was, but he knew what he wanted to achieve. He knew he needed more information to solve this riddle, but reflecting on the happenings of the night, he realized this was big and he felt he was in over his head. As was his style, he would never let anybody know his anxieties, but would work through them and keep a smile on his face.

He felt the clue he needed lay in the killer's words, but he was stumped as to what the clue was. He replayed the events of the night over and over in his head, but nothing emerged.

TUESDAY, 14ᵀᴴ

As the sun started to burn into the back of Roger's eyes they turned off toward a truck stop. He parked some distance from the diner to ensure they would not be seen getting dressed into their theatre outfits.

They pulled their wigs into place having a light-hearted laugh at each other as they did, not at all like they were on the run from the entire country.

"Wait!" Roger looked at Atifah. "I have an idea."

To the rear of the truck stop, chickens pecked and scratched idly around a large fenced area. Tiny chicks followed their mothers around mimicking the scratching and pecking. He climbed out of the truck and made his way to the rear of the diner. After checking for people, he disappeared into the hen house and emerged seconds later and made his way back to the truck.

Roger sat next to the girl, holding a small brown egg. He cracked the egg on the edge of the door, breaking the shell into two and separated the yellow from the clear. He threw the half containing the yellow onto the dirt outside the truck.

He dipped his fingertip into the egg and leaned toward the girl. She backed off with a puzzled look on her face. "Don't tell me you never did this as a child?"

"Did what? Smeared egg on my face?"

"Trust me!" He leaned forward again.

He laughed at the pained expression on her face as he gently smeared the wet sticky fluid onto her flawless skin. Roger was amazed at how soft her skin was and he found himself thinking about the possibility of an allergic reaction. He quickly put it out of his mind.

"Wasn't so bad was it?" He threw the balance of the egg out of the open door to join the other half. "It will become tight as it dries. Don't worry about it." She sat in silence while the egg dried, but she still hadn't lost the pained expression. After a few minutes, Roger flipped the sun visor down, in front of her. He was relieved to find the cosmetic mirror in place. "Have a look," he said proudly. She peered into the small mirror. Her mouth dropped open as she looked at the old face looking back at her.

"I'm old. I look like my mother." She smiled a stiff smile.

"You'll have to change into something a little less … eh … attractive though. Maybe my old dirty shirt!" He pulled his khaki

234

shirt out of the bag and handed it to her. He saw the expression on her face change. "I know! It's all I have but I only wore it a few days."

She pulled the shirt over her own and let it hang over her denims. She screwed up her wrinkled nose as she caught a whiff of the stale shirt and felt like crying as she looked down at herself. "At least you don't look like *you* now!"

"I know! I look like my mother."

"Don't worry! It's only so we can try to have a decent breakfast. Now we look like we could be husband and wife." She laughed, shedding the scowl from her face. Roger smiled back.

He pulled the truck up to the diner. They walked to the doorway. Roger peered inside. It was all quiet. One other person sat on the opposite side of the room. He lifted his head and glanced at the couple as they came through the door. On the opposite side of the shop were empty stalls with padded red vinyl seats. He knew he'd been on the road a long time because the seats looked inviting and comfortable. High above the area, a television was playing softly to itself.

Roger walked up to the greasy looking man behind the counter. "Can we get a breakfast?"

"'Course you can." The man's entire countenance brightened as he spoke. He somehow didn't seem so greasy when he smiled.

"Great! Can you whip us up something incredible?"

"Absolutely!"

"No meat for my lady though. Hash browns, fries, fritters, everything your doctor would frown at."

"No problem. Give us ten minutes. Take a seat in the meantime."

The two made for a table on the side of the room, opposite to where the other patron was seated reading his newspaper.

"Doesn't it feel good to be around people again?" Roger whispered to Atifah as they sat.

"I'm not sure I can count this as people. It's more like person."

"It's still good to be out." Roger was talking in a low voice so as not to be heard, but not whispering so as to attract attention.

After a short while their breakfasts arrived piled high on their plates. A meal for royalty. They both started eating at the same time, then simultaneously looked at each other. Neither spoke but they both knew what the other was thinking. "Damn! This tastes great."

They chatted between themselves while they tucked into their food.

"Are we going back to Houston again?" Atifah was puzzled at the lack of direction.

"I think so! There are more resources there." He paused as he pushed a piece of crisped bacon in his mouth. She looked on in disgust.

She looked at her plate as she spoke. "Then what?" she paused, expecting a reply. "What are we going to ..." She lifted her eyes as she spoke then stopped dead as she saw the look on Roger's face. Something was wrong. He was focused on the television. He'd stopped chewing.

Without turning around, Roger almost shouted, "Please turn up the volume!"

Afraid to look, Atifah turned slowly toward the television. She didn't immediately recognize what was going on, but as the reporter's voice became louder her jaw dropped in disbelief.

"No!" A single word from Roger laced with pain and venom sent a chill down Atifah's spine.

"… appears he entered the house of his long-time best friend in the early hours of this morning where he callously executed his family and his friend."

Roger heard no more. For the time being he didn't hear that his wife had been found naked in bed with Mike. He watched through tunnel vision as he saw a black body bag on a stretcher being loaded into a coroner's van.

"Nooo!" The word resounded around the diner, a brew of pain and anger. He watched in stunned disbelief. "No! No!" He couldn't get any other word out. "No!" Roger rummaged for the keys to the truck. He started for the door, oblivious of anything else but the need to get home and find out if there had been a mistake. "No!" he muttered as he walked through the doorway.

"Sir, I …" The greasy man thought Roger was trying to escape without paying. Atifah threw notes on the counter which more than paid for the breakfasts. In the same moment Roger turned and glared at the man with such hatred that his eyes looked dark and sinister. He reached up to the wig on his head and slid it off down the side of his head. The counter-hand was stunned to see

236

the wig come off, but he was obviously not an avid news watcher. He didn't recognize Roger. The same could not be said for the other early morning patron, who looked like he was trying to disappear under the table.

Roger's eyes blazed with hatred. Atifah caught up to him and pushed him firmly so he would start walking. After offering a little resistance Roger turned and walked to the truck. Anger was burning his lungs as he breathed. It burned his eyes as he blinked and it burned his skin as he moved.

Atifah saw, as he fumbled with the keys, that he was in no condition to drive. She snatched the keys from his hand.

"GIVE THEM TO ME!!!" Roger spoke with such force that she stepped backward.

She resisted the urge to comply with every fiber in her body. She stared into his eyes, matching the ferocity of his glare as best she could. She spoke slowly, but with force. "I'll drive!"

Roger knew she wasn't going to back down. For an instant he wanted to punch the girl in the face and take the keys, then knock her to the ground and kick the life out of her, but the instant passed and his anger momentarily subsided. He glanced aside and knew he'd lost. He climbed into the passenger seat and Atifah got in behind the wheel.

"Where to?" she spoke with conviction and power, but there was no need. Roger slumped forward and wept like a baby.

-- o --- oOo --- o --

After what felt like hours of driving with Roger slumped forward, he sat up. Shocked at the sudden movement, she turned to look at him.

"Pull over!"

"What?"

"Pull over here."

Atifah pulled onto the pavement. As other vehicles sped past, the wind from the trucks rocked the vehicle.

Roger looked straight ahead of him as he spoke, "You need to contact the Sultan and tell him to get you out." He was emotionless and empty.

"What?" He didn't answer but started fumbling on the floor around his feet.

"You don't even know if it's true yet."

He lifted his head robotically from what he was doing. "I do and so do you." His voice, like his movement, was mechanical and flat. She started to understand what Roger was doing when he picked up the handguns, putting them in his belt and socks.

She grabbed his arm as panic seized her. "Don't leave me on my own Roger!" It was an impassioned plea, shaking Roger from his trance.

"You don't want to go where I'm going. It's not your fight."

"The hell it's not."

"It was neither of our fight but it's become mine and mine alone."

She floored the gas pedal knocking Roger back into his seat. "STOP THIS TRUCK!" Roger shouted.

"I'm not letting you leave me here. We're in this together."

Anger coursed through Roger's veins. Slowly he cocked the revolver in his hand and leveled it at her temple. "Stop the truck." His voice possessed a terrifying coldness, causing her to lift her foot from the gas. She turned to Roger catching his glare and then, facing forward, she leaned to her right placing her temple against the barrel of the gun.

She spoke in her slow confident voice. "Without you I am probably dead anyway so shoot. If you don't, I am coming with you."

Deep down in a lost part of Roger's conscience, he felt admiration for this brave girl. "It has become dangerous and I don't know whether I can protect you."

"I didn't sign up for your protection. Besides, you need me."

He knew she was correct. Slowly he lowered the gun. "I'm sorry. I didn't mean that."

Emotion took hold of the girl. She pulled the vehicle off the road for the second time. It was her turn to slump forward onto the wheel and cry. After a short while she sat back with tears streaming down her face. "I'm sorry. I'm so sorry."

"I know you are. Me too!" Roger was cold and without emotion.

"Roger!" He looked up at her. "I don't want to have to wonder if you are going to be there every time I open my eyes. I want to know we are in this together. I want your word."

He looked at his feet. "I don't know if I …"

"Roger!" He looked back at her. "I want to see your eyes. There is nobody else I would rather have alongside me. Nobody!" He started to look down again, so she leaned forward grabbing his chin and pulling so he was again looking into her eyes. "I ask nothing more than your promise that you will look after me as best you can, and we'll stay together through this."

Once again he tried to look away and once again she pulled him back. "Promise me Roger."

Hesitating, he answered. "Ok! I promise."

She let his chin go. "Thank you!"

"That's enough for you? My promise! I'm a thief, a killer and I may end up a murderer. I could still leave you the next time you are sleeping."

"I know you better than you think I do."

She pulled the truck away from the roadside and was soon driving towards Houston.

-- o --- oOo --- o --

They were silent for the hour and a half journey back to Houston. On the outskirts of Houston, they swapped seats and Roger took over the driving for the four hour trip to Dallas. He knew by now the vehicle would have been called in stolen. He knew he had to dump it soon.

They had both put on their wigs and for the main part had driven in complete silence.

"There it is," Roger pointed out the tall building on Main Street. He then circled the building until he saw the ramp to the underground parking. Driving a short distance further, he managed to find a parking overlooking the exit.

"What is it?" They hadn't spoken much on the journey. When Roger spoke he sounded upbeat, but there was something missing in his voice. A change had come over him. He was hurting.

"The CNN Dallas bureau is inside."

"What are we doing here?"

"Waiting!"

"For?"

"Elaine Hodges."

"Are you going to speak to her?"

"After a fashion."

"You're not going to hurt her?"

He turned to the girl and with a deadpan face said, "She didn't do it. I'm not going to hurt her."

"Then what are you going to do?"

"I want to speak to her."

She wanted to ask more, but she could sense he was becoming frustrated at her questions.

They waited only a short amount of time and were shocked to see Elaine drive into the building. So unexpected was her arrival, that Roger nearly missed it. He had expected to see her leave, not arrive. She had probably been covering the story at his house and must have been traveling almost alongside the pair the entire way to Dallas.

"Now we wait until she goes home," Roger said, wanting to break the silence for Atifah's sake. He'd have been satisfied to never speak again.

The long journey should have allowed him to think things through, but every time he would start thinking his mind would replay the image of the body bag being loaded into the coroner's van. His entire thought process would cloud like a drop of milk in clear water. He found himself wondering who was in the body bag. It hurt in a way he'd never imagined possible. Tears would well up in his eyes. The hurt would be followed by such an intense hatred for the perpetrators of this crime that he felt his head would explode. After the hatred passed he would relax again and his mind clear only to start the process over again.

After a couple of hours, Elaine's car once again pulled up the ramp from the parking below the building.

"We're on!" Atifah didn't respond. He started the truck and pulled into the traffic, keeping a reasonable distance from Elaine. At one point he thought he'd lost her, but he managed to catch her further along the road. Once they were out of the city, he worried he would be spotted, but keeping two to three vehicles back it seemed she was oblivious of any tail.

Eventually she turned into a driveway of a modest house. As her vehicle stopped, Atifah looked back to see a small child run into the yard to greet his mother.

"She has a child." Roger was unsure whether it was a statement of fact or a warning from her.

"I told you I won't hurt her. I'm going to question her. Nothing more."

She seemed satisfied with the answer and didn't speak any more. Roger turned the corner and drove on another hundred yards or so, then stopped. They climbed out of the vehicle and strolled back in the direction of the house. They walked past on the opposite side of the road but saw no movement. On the way back past the house, the front door opened and a small plump Latino woman came out. Roger did not look back but they heard the voices clearly.

"Say bye to Maria. Byebye Maria!"

"Byebye! Stephen!" The woman's melodious voice floated back.

Roger looked at Atifah and smiled. It was a cold, menacing smile. Not the kind she was used to seeing. They walked back to the truck.

Roger drove on a little way, looking for a place where he could park the truck without attracting unnecessary attention. This he did in the shadows of a low-hanging tree. A quick walk around satisfied him that the truck, while visible, was not easily detected. He decided this would be a good enough place to spend the night.

As the light faded, the two settled down for the long night ahead. Atifah lay across the seat and slept with her head on Roger's leg. Roger sat and rested his head back, but did not close his eyes. The news clip kept playing repeatedly in his head.

WEDNESDAY, 15TH

Long before the sun's first rays hit Roger's open eyes he lifted his head. His neck was stiff but he felt no pain. He was numb from the long night of watching a black body bag being carried to the van over and over again. Long before midnight, he'd given up trying to sleep and sat in numbness, staring at the roof of the truck. The darkness had made it all the more difficult, as the images started to play themselves in his open eyes as well. Eventually he let the numbness engulf him. It felt better there.

As much as his heart wanted to suggest the possibility of a mistake, his mind knew the truth. Logically there was no other explanation. He no longer had the urge to listen to the news. He no longer cared whether he lived or died. The only thing in his head was the numbness.

Atifah moved and it brought him back to the world of pain. Here was his other source of conflict. He'd promised to take care of the girl. He looked down at her in the near darkness as she slept across the seat of the truck. For the first time since they'd met he looked on the girl as an object. He didn't want to take care of her. He didn't want anything to do with her. He wanted to push her out of the truck, drive off, and forget he'd even been to Oman, but it wasn't in his nature not to follow through on his word. As for the girl, he felt nothing toward her now. No anger, no love, no hate. She was an extension of his numbness, a task that had to be completed. His world had emptied in a single news report.

He tapped her shoulder. "We need to get going before it gets light."

"Where are we going?"

"We're going to visit the reporter."

Atifah sat up in the truck and stretched her stiff neck. "What are you going to ask her?"

"I'm not! I'm going to send America a message." He was cold and heartless. She knew she wouldn't be able to stop him. On the floor in front of her, her foot knocked one of the weapons Roger had taken from the agents. She leaned forward and picked up the small handgun. It fitted snugly into her hand. Atifah made like she was moving the guns aside and then sat back with the gun still in her hand. She wasn't sure why she felt the need to carry it, but she knew he was not himself

Roger started the truck and headed back to Elaine's house. He pulled the vehicle up her short driveway, parked and looked up at the house. It lay in complete darkness. He didn't know who was inside the house other than Elaine and her child. He scanned the area for CCTV or a sign that the house was protected by something more than the front door. He saw nothing out of the ordinary.

After checking the truck's interior light to make sure it wouldn't light up, Roger opened the door and stepped into the fresh morning air. "Wait here!" he whispered to Atifah. He let the truck door swing closed, but stopped it short of closing to avoid making any noise. Atifah watched as he strolled around the house, testing the windows. He disappeared around the side of the house.

Locating an open window to what looked like a downstairs guest bathroom, he lifted himself through, feeling around for items and moving them. It didn't take long before he was standing inside the little bathroom.

He opened the door which led into a modest hallway at the base of the stairs. He guessed the stairs led to the bedrooms. Roger moved quickly and quietly up the stairs, keeping to the edge of each step to avoid creaking as much as possible. He looked around. There were four doorways facing him. Two open and two closed. One open door led to a bathroom, the other to a draped dark room. He decided to check in there first.

Creeping and keeping to the edge of the floor boards where they should be more solidly fixed, Roger entered the small room. A desk occupied one wall with all the usual 'home office' equipment dotted around the room. Exiting slowly Roger made his way to door number three. It was closed but not latched. He pushed the door. Inside, he heard the distinct sound of a child stir who was talking to himself in a language only understood by a sleeping child. For an instant Roger smiled as he remembered how Katie used to talk to herself in her sleep. He'd forgotten how he and Anne would stand at her bedroom door, laughing a quiet, stifled laugh for fear of waking the small child. A black cloud came over him and the smile fell from his face, leaving only anger behind.

Door number four was the jackpot door. The door was closed fully so there was no quiet way of opening it. Without the slightest thought to what might lie beyond, Roger opened the door and walked in. Looking around in the half-light he found the light switch and switched it on. He had the element of surprise. Elaine and her husband surfaced slowly under the circumstances and both raised themselves onto their elbows.

"Good morning Elaine!" Roger was flat and emotionless. "I'd like to have a little chat."

Terror filled her eyes as she realized what was going on. She glanced at the gun in Roger's hand.

"What do you want?" Her husband was shaken awake much faster than he'd have liked.

Chris Hodges looked younger than Elaine, even though he was a little older. His thick blond hair, even throughout the rest of the day, looked much like it did at the moment, shaggy and unkempt, like he hadn't brushed it, but it gave him a youthful appearance that at times had caused the gossip mongers to conclude he was Elaine's toy-boy. In fact, Chris was an established business man in his own right. Their modest three bedroom home was a choice they had made years earlier and belied their wealth.

Roger could see his mind was ticking over and guessed he'd gone into protection mode, the point when a husband and father is at his most deadly and self-destructive. Chris shifted onto his other arm and Roger guessed from his movements that he may have a weapon in the drawer next to his bed. He needed to remove any risk. "Before you decide to do anything rash, make sure you know, nobody is going to be hurt unless you try something stupid. Do you understand?"

"Ok!" Looking down the barrel of a hand gun, Chris found it difficult to believe that nobody would be hurt.

Roger spoke slowly and with purpose. "Good! Now understand this. Regardless of what your lady has said about me to the public, at this point I haven't killed anybody. Do you understand me?"

Roger noted the change in his voice. He was starting to calm down, at least at the subconscious level. "Yes."

"Good! Now listen to me." Still slow and emotionless. "All I live for was taken from me last night. If you do something stupid, I will kill your family in front of your eyes so you have to watch. Do you understand?"

"I won't let you do it." Atifah had missed most of the conversation, but heard how Roger would kill this man's family. She had the handgun leveled at Roger. The heads of the two in bed spun to look at Atifah, confusion on their faces. Roger didn't turn his head but remained fixed on Elaine's husband. He noticed the anger and self-destruction come back into the man's eyes. Roger remained calm keeping his gun trained on the husband to keep him in his place.

"Atifah! I have been telling these kind people that nobody will get hurt. Now suppose I'd got a fright and shot them when you came in?" The air was thick with anticipation.

"I'm not going to let you shoot anybody." She was insistent. "Put the gun down."

"I was about to. Now! Before anybody gets excited and a gun goes off, please put your gun down so I can do the same." He could see Elaine imploring Atifah to pull the trigger and he watched the almost imperceptible disappointment on her face when Atifah lowered the gun. He continued, "Did you understand everything I said?"

The man hesitated but was beaten. "Yes!"

Roger walked to the small drawer and opened it. Inside a chunky revolver lay in waiting for an event such as this. "You shouldn't leave these lying around you know. It's only a matter of time before your kid gets hold of it." He picked up the handgun. He clicked it open and emptied the cartridges onto the floor and then joined Atifah at the end of the bed.

"What's your name?"

"Chris."

"Chris! I'm going to lower my gun because I don't want to shoot anybody, but it will still be in my hand and if I see you move too quickly or try anything stupid. I will shoot. Do you understand me?"

"Yes!" Chris knew there was nothing he could do now.

"Are you two married?"

The question shocked Chris and Elaine. It was not what they were expecting. They nodded in unison glancing at each other.

"How long?"

"Over eight years." He was still confused.

"Then, no matter how good or bad you might think your marriage is, you both know the companionship and closeness that comes with marriage. Am I right?"

They sat in silence.

"If I gave you this gun right now, would you be able to shoot your wife and kid?"

"No! Of course not." He glanced again at his wife.

"Then why would you believe that somebody who has been married for way longer, could pull the trigger and kill the two most important people in his life." Roger was blank and expressionless. His eyes had glazed over, but a tell-tale tear trickled down his cheek.

He was shocked back into the present. He shook his head and wiped his cheek, but his eyes remained vacant. "Elaine, call your camera man. No tricks. Tell him to come out here because you have an exclusive. Tell him nothing more." He thought for a second, then added,. "If I hear a police siren, even in the distance, I will shoot your kid. Do you understand?"

Elaine came to life. He wanted to tell his story and the exclusive was hers. "Yes! I'll need to get dressed."

"You can use this phone." Roger tossed the agent's phone onto the bed.

"I'll need the number from my cell." She didn't want to reach for her phone without telling the gunman.

He nodded toward her phone.

She slowly reached for the phone. Picking it up, she quickly dialed a number from memory. She looked at Roger. "I'll still need to get dressed." Her naked shoulders told him why. She heard the voice of her camera man "Don! We've got a story." She paused. ... "A big one! Can you get here in 15 minutes? ... At home ... Ok!" She hung up.

Meanwhile, Roger's mind was racing through the possible outcomes of his leaving the room so she could get dressed. He didn't like it. "It's going to be difficult. You may have noticed, my partner in crime here doesn't have a stomach for violence regardless of how you've painted her." He rubbed his forehead which was starting to throb. "Ok! I'm going to step outside. Outside your kid's room." He emphasized it. "Atifah! Call me if anyone tries anything stupid."

There were no events to talk of. Elaine and her husband dressed and were on their best behavior. Within a few minutes, Elaine's cameraman was banging on the door. By this time, under Roger's careful eye, they'd hung a plain sheet on the wall in the dining room. Roger made sure there would be no clue as to their whereabouts. He didn't want the police to pitch up halfway through his broadcast.

Don walked in. He was a tall man of medium build, but was strong from years of lugging his camera equipment around. He was about thirty-five years of age and by her own admission, was a major contributor to Elaine's success. His camera work bordered on genius and he was afraid of nothing. The two of them had seen plenty of reporting action together, prior to her settling down and having her son, Stephen.

"Macadam?" Don hadn't expected to see Roger here and was more than a little shocked.

To his amazement, Elaine now relaxed, introduced the two like they were at a dinner party. "Don! This is Roger Macadam. Roger … Don Adams." The two men were uncomfortable and didn't know what to do.

Roger nodded his head "Don! Did you tell anybody where you were going?"

"Nobody. I live alone." It wasn't strictly true, but he hadn't told his girlfriend where he was going. She was still sleeping. Under the circumstances, Don thought it best not to let on he had anybody at home.

Turning to Elaine he said, "Don't you need to call in to establish the link or something?"

"No! We'll film it and edit before airing."

"Doesn't work for me. If you do that it will never air."

"Why?"

"Because it's the way things are going down at the moment. These people have great power and a long reach."

"But it will air, I promise you. I'll …"

"It won't. We go live or not at all."

"It will take a while longer and we'll need to run a cable to the van."

"Ok. Make it happen." Turning to Don he gave directions. "I want you to set up over here, but be sure to only get the sheet in the background. I don't want to see any carpet, drapes, or walls, in the picture. The rest of you I want seated behind the camera so I can see what you are doing."

Don started setting up, while Roger monitored a call between Elaine and CNN and pretty soon they were ready to go live. Roger turned Elaine's TV so he could see it behind the camera. He switched on and turned down the volume to avoid feedback. He wanted to make sure the shot was live.

He was aware of the CNN announcer announcing a breaking story as Don leaned over the camera and counted Elaine down with his fingers in the air. "We're on in 3 … 2 … …"

"Good morning viewers. This is Elaine Hodges reporting from somewhere in Dallas. For the last couple of weeks we have been following the trail of one Roger Macadam and the trail of death following him across Texas." She chose her words carefully. Although she somehow knew her life wasn't in danger, she didn't know Roger and didn't want to say anything she might regret.

"For the first time, live and exclusive to CNN, we have Roger Macadam with us." The camera zoomed out and panned across showing the two of them. Roger didn't want to include Atifah in this. "Roger! What is it you want to tell America?"

Roger replied slowly and somewhat nervously. "The truth."

The camera zoomed in on Roger and he turned to the camera, still looking emotionless and blank. "Good morning." He got straight down to business. "A couple of weeks ago I was on business in Oman." He hesitated. "To cut a long story short, without me knowing I was married by Islamic custom to a young girl that I brought back to America. I later found out this marriage had been performed in order to facilitate the girl's escape out of the country in secret without her being spotted. I knew nothing of this at the time."

Roger faded and Elaine needed to liven things up. "You were initially wanted for bigamy."

"That's right!" He was still blank. "It's true we were married, but I wanted to explain the situation to the authorities. Unfortunately I was never given the chance." He hesitated again, gathering his thoughts. "Suddenly I was being chased by Homeland Security, saying I had something to do with the 9/11 attack."

"Are you saying you didn't?"

"I was in New York on business on that terrible day. I have never been involved in any form of terrorist activities."

For the first time viewers saw a flash of emotion in Roger's face. "I don't even break the speed limit, or park in a no parking zone." Soon the expression was gone and the vacant look returned.

Elaine was about to speak, but Roger started again. "People started dying around me. I want to say to the families of those people, if I am in any way responsible then I am so, so sorry. I give you my word I did not pull the trigger on any of those individuals. To this day I have never killed anybody, accidently, or otherwise." He lost focus and his face blanked again.

Once again as the length of the silence grew, Elaine grew anxious and was about to speak, but Roger started again. "Last night these people crossed the line." He swallowed hard, but forced back the emotion while Elaine sat silently urging him to let it out. "Last night these people murdered my family." Anger and hatred crashed around inside his head, but he maintained outward composure. Don saw the tear drop from Roger's chin and adjusted his camera position to expose the streams down his cheeks.

"I'm here to ask your help America. I want to appeal to everybody to help me get the break I need to find out who is behind this. You can help me in this way. Wherever I go I am spotted and people phone the police or the national hotline. I would have done the same thing two weeks ago, so there's no hard feelings, but if a handful of Americans have heard and believed me then I ask you, wherever you are from Alaska to Florida, New York to Hawaii, I ask you to phone in and report seeing me. Wherever you are. It will help me if you can phone in and say you think you saw me in your parking garages, malls, city centers, anywhere. I cannot do this on my own."

Roger was great, the camera worked perfectly. It nearly brought a tear to Elaine's eye. The threat to her family was long forgotten. "Do you want to say anything else?"

Roger stumbled when he spoke and the reality of the situation sent him back into his vacant and protected world. "Sorry! What was that?"

"Do you have any messages for anybody?"

"Yes! Again, to the families of those who lost their lives, my condolences. I have handed over the murderers and the proof of their committing the murders to the police in Flatonia and I will hand a copy to Elaine. I hope the justice system works on these individuals." His face hardened. "And one more message to two people. To the one that gave the order and the one that pulled the trigger. You can stop looking for me now, because now I'm coming after you."

Being the brilliant and award winning cameraman that he was, Don cut the feed to leave the viewers hanging. He didn't let Elaine sign off. He knew they wouldn't be ready for them to end in the studio. There would be a dramatic pause before the studio took over. "We lost the feed," he lied. "But we got everything."

Elaine was shell shocked. She had seen the tears. With all her years of journalism, she knew when somebody was lying. She had learned to tell the truth from the hoax. For most of the take, she had focused on the feed, the news and the hype, but now she saw the man. This man hadn't even seen the inside of a courtroom and yet she had aided in him being guilty, convicted and awaiting execution. She was shaken back to reality when Roger stood up.

She acted quickly. "You need to take us out of here."

Roger wasn't sure what she meant. "What?"

"We need to finish the feed without you. From somewhere so you have time to get away. You need to take us somewhere so we can finish the report with a recognizable background. The authorities are probably on their way here to question me." She started making toward the door. Roger was taken by surprise.

"Wait!"

"We don't have time to wait." She looked at the gun in his hand pointing at the floor. "You're no more a killer than I am. You won't shoot me. I'm getting my kid. Don! Pack up your gear. We're moving to a new location. Bring the sheets."

Chris wasn't as sure. "Honey! I think we should ..." He was stopped short as Roger placed the weapon in the palm of his hand.

"She's right. I've never killed anybody and they are probably on their way."

Elaine turned her back on the two of them. "Chris! We need to move. We'll discuss it later."

Suddenly everybody was in motion. In a short while the gear was packed up and they were ready to go. They left the house in the crisp morning air. Chris held Stephen in his arms. He had long since handed the gun back to Roger.

"Let's get out of town back down the I45." Elaine took control of the situation. "We can pull off before Ferris. There's a golf course there. It should be deserted at this time of the day." She and Chris jumped in the back of the truck. Don followed in the van.

Roger climbed into the cab, then had second thoughts about it. He jumped out. "You drive," he said to Elaine. "You know where you're going." Roger helped her down from the truck. "Keep your kid with you. It's warmer than the back of the truck."

Roger climbed into the back of the truck and turned to Chris. "I'm sorry about ... back there ... well sorry about everything."

Chris waved his hand. He didn't need to say anything.

Roger continued, "Elaine's right. She needs to go on air saying I held you all at gun point. You must call a friend, or the local police, to pick you up, so people can see you're alive after I leave. Or else you might end up like the hotel staff or …" he trailed off as he didn't have to say the words, 'my family'.

-- o --- oOo --- o --

"We're going to establish the link. You two had best be going." Elaine was speaking to Roger and Atifah.

"Thanks Elaine." Roger was awkward. He wanted to hug her, but it didn't feel right. Instead he reached out to shake her hand and squeezed it gently, before placing two DVDs into her hand. "I have a few copies of the first disk but the second one I have only one copy. Don't let them get in the wrong hands, but please don't publish them yet. I don't want to send the bad guys into hiding. I want to flush them out."

"What's on here?"

"You'll see."

Roger waved and said his thanks and pulled away leaving the four figures standing in the small amount of light generated by Don's battery powered camera lights.

"Now what?" Atifah was pleased Roger had brightened since meeting Elaine. He'd seen she believed him and having an ally seemed to help.

"Crane and his team." She stiffened at the thought.

"A bit risky don't you think?"

"Not if we're careful. We also need to return this truck. We'll get Crane to do that too."

"How are we going to move around?"

"I'm hoping we can go and pick up the SUV. The heat is probably off it by now. They know we were in the Ford, so hopefully they're no longer looking for the SUV. We will probably have to get new plates though."

"By get, you mean steal."

"Not steal, swap. I'll replace them. I'd like to try to get plates from the same type of vehicle. At least if they run the plates from a distance it will come up with the right type of vehicle."

She smiled as she saw Roger coming back to life. "We could have done with that idea about two weeks ago."

"I know!" He wasn't smiling, but for the time being he was thinking about things other than the news clip.

They needed to fill the truck and so stopped over in Corsicana, a short distance from the interstate. Roger decided he

251

was too easily recognizable and so had Atifah drop him near two small abandoned warehouses, some fifty yards from the road along an overgrown concrete driveway. It looked like the building might have been previously used for storage of grain. Empty cloth bags lay strewn around. Roger sat in the shaded interior while Atifah drove into town to fill up. He managed to maintain a degree of alertness while he waited, but there was not enough stimulation to prevent the news clip starting up in his head again.

Hatred and anger clouded his mind again with a concoction of numbing sadness and invigorating rage. In the twenty or so minutes while Atifah was gone, his heart rate changed several times from a pounding in his chest such as he had never felt and then back to normal. Through the tunnel of blurred vision and tears, he saw the truck turn into the driveway and quickly he pulled himself together.

Atifah pulled up in front of the doorway as Roger walked out. She climbed out of the truck and held out a slab of chocolate. He shook his head and turned away from her. She saw the damp streaks down his cheeks and decided she could not afford to leave him alone for too long.

Suddenly a bullet ricocheted off the rough door frame behind him. He listened, unperturbed as it thudded and echoed into the interior of the warehouse. Roger looked up and saw four men trying to keep low in the long grass at the entrance to the driveway. He made out the voice of one of them who said, "I told you it was him."

Roger watched as one of them took aim with a small handgun. He heard the crack of the pistol and whine as the bullet passed to his left, followed by the smack of the lead shell slamming into the plastered wall at the back of the warehouse.

He looked at Atifah. She was bewildered and hadn't yet grasped what was happening. He had promised to take care of the girl! "Move!" he shouted. "Through there!" He pointed to the gap between the two buildings because he didn't want to be trapped inside. She took off keeping her head low. She screamed as the next bullet slammed into the wooden panel above her head. Roger didn't hear her. He stood facing the attack oblivious of danger, conscious only of the hate. He took note of the red shirt of the man doing the shooting. None of the others were shooting. He could see they only had one gun between them. He watched as the young man raised himself up and took aim at him.

He took off after Atifah slowly as another bullet struck the wood behind him. As he rounded the corner he stopped and looked back. All four were up and moving. The man in the red shirt was reloading on the run. Unconcious thoughts were thrust in and out of focus in Roger's head. Questions, answers, calculations. They would cover the fifty yards in a couple of seconds. The delay in loading would hold the red shirt back but he would pass the fat guy, who was overweight and slow. The red shirt would reach the corner in second place. Roger looked around at Atifah who was heading for a broken down house behind the warehouses. It was one of those old wood and iron houses. It would offer no protection from bullets at close range.

His mind raced, his senses heightened and tingling. He was aware of every sound and without seeing, could hear two of the men were still in the grass, while the first two were already on the paved driveway. He was sure they wouldn't sprint blindly round the corner. They would check they weren't going to be shot at first, but they would be in a hurry to not let Roger get away. He glanced around and at first picked up a short plank of wood, but discarded it for a longer piece of old galvanized steel water-pipe. He could hear footsteps approaching. He heard the lead runner slow as he approached the corner. He heard the sound of the breathing and the pace slowing of the second runner. Roger walked toward the corner at an almost leisurely pace, his senses aware of every visible thing, every sound and smell. He was aware of the different layers of chipped and peeled paint beneath his fingers on the pipe in his hands, but more than anything else, he was aware of the taste of bitter hatred like bile in his mouth. He could see the scene unfolding around the corner. He listened as the third runner approached and began to slow. Now was the time.

Roger raised the pipe above his head and stepped around the corner. The two in front were unaware of Roger as they looked back, ushering the two slower runners in. The fat guy was the first to realize what was happening. A shot rang out as the pipe smashed the wrist of the shooter. The bullet shot into the ground. Before the young man had grasped what was happening, Roger had leaped at the falling weapon, clutching at it as it bounced dangerously on the hard ground. Fumbling the small but lethal object into the palm of his hand, he stood and aimed the weapon at the two against the wall. The other two, unable to change trajectory, arrived fractions of a second later. The fat guy fell to his knees, red faced and breathing heavily. Three of them raised their hands in surrender, the fourth, the 'red shirt', fell as he attempted to support his hand which hung broken and limp from somewhere above where his wrist used to be. He hadn't yet started to feel the pain.

Roger stared blankly along the barrel of the gun which was aimed at the head of the young man in the red shirt. His eyes again blazed with anger, bringing fear to the hearts of the four people in front of him. Rage coursed through his veins and pounded in his temples. For what seemed like an eternity, he didn't say a word. His mind not thinking, but an instinct-like emotion wanting to pull back on the trigger and watch them die. His finger started to squeeze.

It'd happened so fast. The four young men were still in a state of confused bewilderment. Fear started to creep in and the blood drained from their faces. Roger was unblinking and focused.

A gentle voice brought him back from the brink. "Roger! Don't do it." Atifah had turned and seen Roger going back to the corner. Fearing for his life and not thinking through the outcome, she turned and came after him. This was not the scene she had expected to find.

The look in his eyes was not the look of a sane man. She spoke in a consoling tone. "Roger! They're young boys. Don't hurt them."

He surfaced slowly through the clouds in his mind and saw the terrified faces of four youngsters in front of him. The eldest, the red shirt, was no more than twenty-two. The animal subsided and reason took control.

Roger looked from one scared, shaken face to the next then spoke without emotion. "What were you thinking?"

The crouching figure of the red shirt had started to feel the pain and was unable to answer. The front runner stammered but could get nothing intelligible out. The fat guy, the youngest of the bunch by a couple of years, stayed on his knees, his bottom lip quivering. The fourth kid, also young, looked down at his hands.

"Do you know who I am?"

The front runner answered. "Roger Macadam!"

"Correct! Do you know what I am?" Roger was still expressionless.

The boys remained silent, not wanting to answer.

"Speak to me guys. Why did you shoot at me?"

"They say you are a terrorist." Still acting as spokesman for the group, the front runner spoke almost apologizing.

"They say I am a murderer and a terrorist." He paused. "Do you think you would stand a chance against a murderer and a terrorist? You can't even catch a stupid engineer."

He hung his head. "I guess not."

"You can thank this lady for saving your lives." They looked around, not knowing whether they were supposed to say anything. "Well?"

They all muttered their thanks to Atifah.

"Do you have transport?"

Again, they were silent, not understanding the purpose of the question. Did Madman Macadam want to steal their car too?

"Do you have a vehicle?" Roger was still using the same tone in his voice. Having to repeat himself was irritating, but the numbness stopped him from raising his voice.

Red shirt was in pain but when he realized his friends were not stepping up, he managed to gasp out a few words. "Walked … here!"

"You!" Roger waved his weapon at the fastest of the four. "In the front. Direct us to the nearest medical centre. Atifah! You drive. You two can help your friend into the truck."

As the boy was about to climb into the cab, Roger grasped his shoulder, stopping him in his tracks. "Don't be stupid now. I will be watching. If you try anything foolish you'll get a bullet between the shoulder blades."

The young man knew he was sincere. He'd seen the look in Roger's eyes.

Atifah backed out of the driveway and headed, at the instruction of the young man next to her, to a small regional hospital. She pulled up at the entrance. Roger sprang off the back of the truck and gave instructions to the two boys who helped their friend out of the truck. The guy in the front sat still, not wanting to pre-empt Roger in any way. To his relief, Roger signaled him out of the truck. He walked around to the driver's side. "I'll drive," he said to Atifah. She slid across to the opposite side of the long bench-like seat. Without even looking back at the four friends, Roger pulled away fast leaving a flurry of dust in the early morning sunlight. Within a couple of minutes he was back on the highway heading south.

-- o --- oOo --- o --

Within a short time but without a single word being spoken, they turned in toward Madisonville again. Before reaching the town Roger turned off to where the SUV was parked under the trees to check it was still there.

After a quick scout around they put on their disguises and headed for town. They pulled into the same mall parking where Roger had been spotted by the policeman. Looking around, Roger soon spotted an SUV the same as his. The color was different and he hoped the authorities would allow for the possibility of a re-spray. He scouted the area for CCTV cameras but saw none.

Within a few seconds he had changed the truck plates with those of the SUV and sauntered back to the truck. It was still early and there were only a few people around, so he was able to return to the truck and mount the plates before climbing back in next to Atifah.

"Do you want to buy something to eat while we're here?" Roger dug in his pocket for cash.

"Sure! What do you want?"

"Nah! Not hungry."

"But we haven't eaten for ages."

"Maybe! I don't feel like eating. Get yourself something."

Atifah started to climb out of the truck, paused and then climbed back in.

"What's wrong?" Roger was puzzled.

"I'll wait!" She guessed Roger wouldn't be persuaded to eat so she decided to force the issue.

"You haven't eaten either."

"It's ok! Let's go get your car."

Roger started the truck, then switched it off again. He forced a smile. "Clever girl! I'll have a muffin and coffee."

She smiled at Roger and bounced out of the truck like she'd won the lottery.

Left alone to his own thoughts, the cloud settled over Roger again. Tired of seeing the news clip playing in his head, he started counting the cars as they passed by on the main road. He hadn't slept for hours, but there was no sleep in him. He started to feel a little shaky, enough to know deep down Atifah was right. He needed to eat and he needed to sleep. He also thought about how she had been happy to sacrifice her breakfast in the hopes that he would come to his senses. He made a mental note to try to override the feelings of nothingness he'd felt for her earlier, no matter what happened.

She arrived back at the truck and handed Roger his coffee and two of the biggest muffins he'd ever seen. He shook his head as he took them. "I said a muffin. This would feed a small African village."

She smiled. "We do what we have to. Let's hit the road."

He placed the muffins on the seat between them and started the truck.

Back at the SUV, Roger swapped over the plates again, then reversed the SUV out from its hiding place. The vehicle lurched as the wheels mounted small rocks under the tires. At one point the roof of the SUV made contact with a low lying branch, something he would have panicked about a few weeks ago, but now he simply powered his way out.

After a while he was parked next to the truck. Opening the doors, they transferred all their belongings and the mounting pile of federal issue hardware and cell phones into the SUV.

"We need to find a remote location with good all-round visibility." Roger was onto the next plan.

"What about the shed we were in? You could see for miles around there."

"True! I was thinking of something a little more bullet-proof and less dusty, just in case."

Atifah was still trying to occupy Roger's thoughts. She guessed he hadn't slept for many hours and knew her ability to sleep while he was driving would not be forthcoming over the next few hours. She would need to remain alert in order to keep him alert. "Let's drive away from the highway and look for a place where we can set up and get ready."

-- o --- oOo --- o --

The Texan terrain was flat. For miles in all directions, fields of various colors from green through yellow and brown, lay strewn across the landscape like a large checker board. Any of the few buildings they passed on their route offered good visibility, but the majority were wooden sheds and wouldn't satisfy their need for protection.

Roger headed out westward from Madisonville and spent a couple of hours zigzagging back and forth across the landscape, not knowing what he was looking for, but knowing he would know it when he saw it.

Doing in four hours what could have taken two, Roger turned south when he reached the town of Temple. The terrain had become too lined with trees for good visibility. His gut-feel told him he needed to travel further south. They passed through several small towns on the way as they headed down the 190. Roger noticed he was traveling next to a railway for a long time. At times it would disappear from sight, but for the most part it ran adjacent to the road. The track entered the various towns, running alongside the road and exited again next to the road on which they travelled. He found himself wondering how often the trains ran on this line and where they were headed. Without notice, he pulled over and spun the SUV round, heading back into the small dusty town of Milano.

Atifah, taken by surprise, questioned the action. "What's wrong?"

"Nothing! I want to find out when the trains come by here." She didn't understand the reason, but the answer seemed to satisfy her. She asked nothing more.

Following the rail, he found what appeared to be a loading yard. It looked like the line was used to move livestock from this yard. He pulled up into the yard, parking behind a Union Pacific sign board.

"See if you can find somebody and ask them what times the trains come through here."

"What trains?"

"Any! Can be freight or passenger."

Atifah, without any argument or questions, climbed out of the vehicle and walked towards the loading platform area. She returned a short while later. "There are several trains coming through at various times of the day. They're mostly freight. They apparently have a timetable of sorts but don't always stick to it."

"Excellent."

"Are you thinking of catching a train?"

"No! Nothing like that. I'm trying to think of a way to let Crane know where I am without thinking he's walking into a trap."

Atifah had a worried look in her eye. She was fearful of the cold brutality of the agents. "Are you a match for your government? They might send in a swat team."

Roger sat deep in thought. "Crane's people are not doing the killing."

"You already said one of Crane's people is probably involved." She looked at the two large muffins on the seat between the two of them. "You're not eating or sleeping. How can you be ready for trained killers?"

Roger didn't turn his head. He was still deep in thought, thinking about the way he could use the train. "I'll be ready," he said coldly.

He turned back onto the main road aiming south along Highway 36, passing through Caldwell. After that, the line seemed to move away from the road for a few miles and Roger was on the verge of turning back, when the sight of a distant piggyback train marked the convergence as they approached Somerville.

Somerville lake stretched out to their right and in the distance Roger could see the tiny specks on the water which he knew were boats. As he approach the lake, he could see both sailing and motor boats. Roger started to concoct a plan. "Ok! This is the area. We're looking for a building we can inhabit for a while."

"What type?"

"I don't know exactly, but one far away from other buildings and one that won't be used for a while."

"A brick building?"

"As close to the water as we can find."

They turned off after the center of Somerville and started looking closer to the water. Somewhere after the dam wall, Atifah had spotted a small flat roofed, double storey building which looked like it might have been used as a workshop in its heyday. They turned off the road and approached the building along an overgrown and somewhat fragmented concrete driveway. The building was closer to habitation than Roger would have liked, but the distant drone of a small boat told him it would do. The rail was in line of sight less than a thousand yards away and all other buildings were hidden from view by trees, most of which were a good four to five hundred yards from their building.

They stopped at the workshop in front of a large double doorway. Roger peered inside the workshop through one of the dirty windows, all of which were still intact. Inside, the overhead gantry and rusted chain block confirmed this was probably an old auto or boat workshop. The block would have been used to lift engines out to work on them. Old engine parts strewn around told Roger this place hadn't been used in a while.

"It's perfect," he said to Atifah. "Well spotted."

Locating a heavy rock and small, old style, galvanized water pipe, Roger soon had the old rusted lock lying on the floor and the SUV parked inside the building. It would be dark soon and they wouldn't be able to use light for fear of being seen. It was going to be a long night.

They still hadn't eaten and the two large muffins lay between them on the seat. "Do you want one of these?"

"No. They're yours and you need them."

Anger flashed through Roger's mind but he subdued it. He reached and took one of the muffins and started to eat. He placed the second on her lap. She smiled but had seen the anger ignite in his eyes. Once again, she moved her foot in contact with the weapons on the floor in front of her. It was as if it gave her a measure of comfort to know they were there. She ate the muffin in about a third of the time it took for Roger to eat half of his. He placed the remaining half back on the seat between them. They were both thirsty and shared half a bottle of warm soda.

Roger reached for the money and counted the remaining cash. There was still plenty. He would consider the best use for the cash in the morning.

"It'll be dark soon. I want to take a walk toward the water when it's dark, so I'm going to look around a bit to get my bearings. Are you coming?" Roger was trying to be civil, but it wasn't coming across well.

Atifah wasn't taking his abruptness personally. "Sure. Why not?" She knew it was essential to keep the man busy.

"I want to find landmarks while we can still see."

He swung open the large wooden door. The glare from the fading day struck their eyes causing them to squint. The dirty windows prevented much of the light entering the building. Atifah enjoyed the last rays of sun on her face, but knew it would be dark in a short while. Roger had no idea how dark it would be and paced out the distance from the door of the SUV, to the point of entry to the building.

Outside Roger continued looking around in silence, pacing out distances. He noted the distance from a random post in the field to a low wire fence. The fence would need to be navigated in the darkness. Beyond the fence were trees and beyond that lay what looked like an up-market low density suburb. He assumed the water lay beyond the suburb. Off to their right hand side a canal was visible with the rail tracks passing over the canal some eight hundred to a thousand yards from where he now stood. As if on cue, a train which wasn't currently in view, could be heard clattering across the low iron bridge.

The two of them followed the fence to see what lay between them and the canal and then back in the opposite direction. In the thickening gloom, they headed back to the workshop. By the time they reached the building the inside had reached the level of darkness Roger had assumed it would. He held her sleeve and led her back to the vehicle. She felt her way back to the passenger side door. They climbed into the vehicle in silence.

Atifah wanted to say something to break the silence, but the right words wouldn't come, so instead she sat, not talking. Sometime later, Roger told her he was going to take a walk to the water's edge. They left together, feeling their way in the darkness.

Outside the night was dark, but the glow of lights from the direction of Somerville and the abundance of stars offered relief. The lights from the houses between the workshop and the water glowed and shimmered between the trees. They headed in the direction of the houses without speaking.

They easily found the fence in the dark and climbing between the wire strands, they made their way up between the low sparse trees and were soon standing on the edge of a small road, listening to the muffled sounds of life all around. Somewhere in the distance somebody was playing music. Not loud enough to disturb the neighbors but loud enough to hear from the street. Memories of a distant life flashed through Roger's mind. It felt more like a primeval emotion than a memory. He was comforted by the houses around him.

"I think it's that way." He pointed up a side road. Distinct sounds of sailing ropes and tackle could be heard tapping against the aluminum masts in the gentle evening breeze.

They made their way along the road keeping their eyes open, but their sharpened senses told them there was nothing to be concerned about. Somewhere off to their right the sounds of laughter and more music could be heard, leading them to guess there might be a public bar or a house party going on. Making their way through the empty streets, both of them unconsciously mapping the route back, they came upon the entrance to a small marina area. Two rows of small to mid-size lake boats were moored along both sides of a wooden jetty. Roger noted the position of the access points to the various boats and the exit area. It could be used for a good escape route if needed.

They walked in silence along the jetty. A few of the boats had the glimmer of internal lights on board and were occupied. Others were in darkness awaiting their weekend occupants. In the half-light of the street lights some thirty yards behind, Roger found what he was looking for. Tied up against the jetty between two unoccupied single mast sailing boats was a twin-engine, 'fun-and-fishing' boat which was in complete darkness with the sign on the bow – 'For Sale'.

The boat looked to be about twenty feet long and fairly broad across the beam. The hull was split into two, though not enough to call it a catamaran and two large outboard motors were mounted on the transom at the rear. Roger climbed aboard the craft, lowered himself onto the wooden deck and went straight for the skipper's seat. A single black key protruded from the ignition switch, nestled between some dials on a wooden dashboard. A quick turn of the key and a glance around the dials told him there was fuel in the tanks and the starter battery was charged.

"As I thought. Nobody would try to sell a boat without fuel in the tank would they?"

"Are you going to buy this?" Atifah had followed Roger onto the boat and had picked up on his earlier counting of the cash.

"No." He switched off the power and removed the key placing it in his pocket. If he needed to escape in a hurry, he needed to know where the key was, not merely assume he knew. "We're not going to buy it. It's just in case we need to get away in a rush. Ok! Let's head back."

They climbed off the boat and walked back along the road. They both knew exactly where they were going.

-- o --- o0o --- o --

They hadn't spoken on the journey back to the workshop. The silence was starting to take its toll on Atifah. She was not exactly chatty by nature, but still enjoyed a conversation now and then. Roger had cut himself off. His distant behavior seemed to be worsening as tiredness and anger took hold. He frequently had to force back angry outbursts. He was sorry he'd promised to take care of the girl and he started to resent her presence. On occasion she had tried to make conversation, but the short, abrupt answers made her uncomfortable. They reached the workshop and felt their way in the darkness, climbing into their respective leather seats. Without saying a word, she eased the seat back and went to sleep. Roger sat upright with his hands on the wheel and didn't move until the sun began lighting up the workshop.

THURSDAY, 16TH

He wasn't aware of the time, but as the inside of the building started to light up, Roger eased his way out of the vehicle. He decided to start looking around. The workshop was dusty and unused but was still littered with engine parts. Under a tarpaulin in the corner, half an engine lay broken and dirty but recognizable by the transverse cylinders as an old VW Beetle engine. He smiled as he thought of the old Beetle he'd been given by his father when he started university. He'd often thought he should have kept it and given it to … The cloud moved back over Roger and he stopped smiling.

Roger crouched and pulled the engine out to where he could see it. The inside of the engine was exposed where the casing had been smashed and the cams and gears were visible, rusted by the passage of time. There was no place for the fan or heater box, so Roger guessed this to be an old 1200cc from the 1960s.

"Perfect," he muttered to himself. The plan developed in his head. For what he was thinking, he doubted absolute precision would be needed but he added, "You never know when there's an expert in the audience."

He stood and looked around. The ceiling above him was lower than over the main workshop area. He climbed the steps which led to a mezzanine level.

On the mezzanine the wooden floor boards creaked as he walked. It was the remains of an old office with a broken desk and filing cabinet. He walked to the edge and leaned on the handrail. An image skipped through his mind of the workshop manager leaning in this same spot keeping an eye on his mechanics as they stripped and fixed the engines on the floor below.

The workshop was a reasonable size, he guessed about four thousand square foot. The steel structure of the roof trusses were visible and in good shape. There didn't appear to be leaks in the roof and overall, they had a pretty good hide out. He opened one of the dusty windows. The view stretched back to the road. Turning around from this elevated position he could see through the window at the back, right across to the trees where they had navigated their way in the dark last night.

The view was blocked on both sides, something he would need to address, but the flat ground all around allowed good visibility for up to three hundred yards once outside the structure.

Roger walked outside and around the workshop. The only structure visible and the only direction he could be seen from, was what looked like the top third of a grain silo back toward the railway lines, about five hundred yards away. This was the perfect spot to meet Crane. He would start to prepare for the meeting today.

Aware of a movement from inside the building, he turned as Atifah came out through the side door.

"Good morning." He saw she was not looking the clean and bright image he was used to. Life on the road was taking its toll on her and lack of cleaning was leaving her looking grubby and unkempt.

"Morning," she answered still half asleep. "Did you sleep?"

"Like a baby," Roger lied. The drawn, unshaven face and black rings under his eyes told the full story.

"You still haven't eaten half of your muffin."

"You can have it."

"Roger." He looked at her. "I don't want it."

Thinking before he spoke, he said "Listen. I haven't felt much like eating lately. I think it comes from not sleeping. I'm sure things will improve."

"When?"

"Soon!"

She tried a different tack. "I need you Roger. I cannot do this on my own." He looked away from her. "Please look after yourself so you can look after me."

He saw right through it. Roger became incensed at the thought that she was appealing to his decency, which was seriously impaired at the moment. He could have easily climbed in the car and driven off without her. He cursed himself again for promising to watch out for her. Roger was closing in on forty-eight hours without sleep. The last thing in his mind was taking care of this little girl. What he wanted was to find two people and watch as the life force left their bodies. His thoughts drifted and he felt comforted as the thought floated through his mind.

"I'm going to get something. You need to eat. I need to eat." She pulled the wig onto her head and tried to straighten the long black strands with her fingers. By now it was looking a bit tangled.

Roger ignored her, showing his indifference, hoping she wouldn't come back. Atifah climbed into the car and started the engine. Anger flashed through Roger again as he realized she expected him to open the main door for her. He thought about leaving her to open up, but he pushed the thought down. Better to keep the peace. He opened the door and she reversed out. She smiled and waved to him. He waved back.

"Fuck you, bitch!" he shouted out loud as she pulled away, shocking himself with the volume and ferocity of his words. There had been no reason for the outburst. Atifah hadn't heard in the interior of the vehicle and so was unaware of the flash of anger that had briefly surfaced in Roger.

As she pulled onto the roadway, the anger and the question about the source of it faded. Roger turned to continue his search, already oblivious of the thoughts that had incensed him seconds earlier.

He located two topless forty-four gallon steel drums. They had been used to catch rainwater in former years, but now were half full of dirty and stagnant water. He tilted the drums and one by one, rolled them on their edges into the workshop.

In a small storeroom at the back he found two large welding-gas bottles. He opened the valves allowing the bottles to hiss before becoming silent as the pressure inside equalized with the air outside. He would have liked a couple more bottles this size, but he'd noticed fire extinguishers in red wooden cabinets along the wharf and on the jetty. He hadn't seen the actual bottles, but from the size of the cabinets he was sure he would get another four bottles from there. He laid the cylinders down and rolled them into the workshop with his feet.

A rusted chain block hung from the gantry up near the roof trusses. He pulled on the chain but the pulley wouldn't turn. Tugging the chain, he managed to maneuver the gantry crane along the steel tracks to the mezzanine railing. He double stepped up the steps and standing on the railing, he was able to lift the heavy chain block off the steel hook. He let it fall to the cement floor twenty feet below.

The loud crash of the impact with the accompanying puff of dust reverberated through the building. Back down the steps, Roger picked up the heavy block. With the block in his left hand he tugged on the chain. It moved a little. Working the chain back and forth, the pulley inside soon started to turn with grating sounds at first but more freely as the rust freed from the pulley inside.

"Sure don't make them like they used to," Roger said to nobody at all.

He dropped the block to the floor and continued his search which turned up nothing else useful.

Not wanting to allow his mind to wander back to seeing body bags being loaded into the van, Roger uncovered the engine and pulled it to the middle of the floor. There was too much casing around it. Using the smaller of the gas bottles, he smashed the engine casing until only a small portion was left attached to the cylinders. He left the cylinders in the middle of the floor and scooped the broken casing into a pile using the palms of his hands.

He ripped two infra-red motion sensors from the corners of the workshop. They had once been attached to a working burglar alarm, but now only the sensors remained. He mounted them so that they were pointed toward the door. More than this would be needed, but it was a good start.

He heard the sound of a car approaching on the broken concrete road. He sprang up the stairs like a gazelle and crossed the small office space to the window. It was Atifah returning. He descended the steps again and opened the door to allow the vehicle inside quickly.

She climbed out of the vehicle with the food. "Hi, how are things going?"

Roger grunted a half-hearted greeting in return.

"It went well, thanks for asking," she replied to the unasked question. Roger ignored her.

"I'll need you to go back into town this afternoon."

"Sure! No problem."

If truth be told, she had enjoyed being away from Roger for a while. She felt for him but she realized she was witnessing a self-destruct sequence in action. She wanted to be with him to keep him on track, but she still enjoyed the time away. "What do you want?"

"A few things. I'll make a list." Roger leaned into the vehicle and pulled out a piece of paper and a pen. He started narrating as he wrote.

Looking around the roof as he summed up in his head, he said. "Fifty ... no, one hundred yards of twin core cable. The ordinary thin one for bedside lamps." He went on. "A wheel grinder, the cheapest you can find. Oh! And a metal file. The roughest you can find. Then, find a vet or pet shop and buy five remote control dog shocking collars. Make sure they work up to five hundred yards."

"Who are you going to shock?"

"Me!"

"You?"

"To ensure I don't get caught napping."

"I don't think there's much chance."

He ignored the sarcasm. "Find the ones that vibrate as well as shock. Also, I will need tools. Hold on!" Roger went over to his SUV and opened the rear door. Rummaging around he managed to locate the plastic tool envelope which he opened and spread out.

He wrote and spoke together. "Get a small screwdriver." He drew on the paper and pointed. "About that size."

"What type, flat or cross?"

"One of each." Then with a last glance around the tools. "I think I have everything else I need here."

"Then I need some elastic bands. I'm not sure what size, so buy a bag of various sizes. Bigger and thicker rather than those little ones." Roger did a few quick calculations, then said, "Get twelve reels of dental floss. Fifty yard reels. I think it's the standard size." He paused, thinking. "And lastly, buy a five gallon plastic bottle and fill it with gas."

Atifah no longer bothered asking questions, nor did she even wonder what he was doing. She had other worries. "Can we eat first?" She had noticed the shaking fingers and drawn look on Roger's face. He hadn't been eating or drinking. She handed him a bottle of water. Roger looked puzzled at the water but took it anyway. As he took his first sip he realized how much he needed the water and started gulping the water down.

"If you drink it too fast it won't stay down."

He stopped drinking and said sharply, "I haven't just crossed the Sahara. I'm thirsty."

"I know! That's why I bought the water." She felt a little indignant at his lack of gratitude.

He hesitated a long while then said, "Thanks! I needed that." He drank down the balance of the bottle and threw the empty bottle into the corner of the workshop.

"Let's see! A small roll of fencing wire, the strong type and half a dozen six inch roof nails, the thicker the better. I need four, but you may need to buy more." Roger thought for a while longer, then added. "Some silicone rubber sealant. You know the stuff to go around the bath. That's about it I think." He looked back through his list and said. "Oh! And get me five rolls of duct tape. You always need duct tape. And get me two packs of razor blades, the flat double edged old fashioned ones if you can still get them."

"What's all this for?" She didn't want an answer. She wanted to ensure he wasn't doing anything stupid.

Roger looked back over his list. "Nails, floss, silicone rubber and dog collars are our intruder alarm and pretty much everything else is to scare the intruders when they get in."

Atifah held out his food to him, refusing to eat her own until he sat and ate his. To Roger, everything tasted like sawdust. He forced a few mouthfuls down and then pushed it aside. Atifah was happy he'd taken something in.

"Alright, then I'm going back to town," she said, hoping for a smile. She was missing the old Roger's company. She only saw brief flashes of his former self at times. For the most part, Roger was distant, engrossed in his own world and became annoyed when interrupted. She understood the reason, but she didn't like it.

-- o --- oOo --- o --

She arrived back to find Roger was not around. She opened the door and went inside worried he'd disappeared. As she entered, the movement of a chain hanging from the roof above caught her attention. The top of the chain was out of sight, up beyond the low lying roof above her. Her heart leapt as she heard the loud grunt of a man in pain and Roger's feet swung precariously into her field of vision.

"ROGER! NO!" She ran under the swinging feet, rocking high out of her reach. Panic gripped her. She looked around. Seeing the staircase, she bounded up two steps at a time.

Roger's arms were stretched high above his head grasping the small hook as he spun slowly and could look at her. "I slipped."

"You slipped! I thought you'd hanged yourself. I thought you were dead."

"Can you help me down?"

She was confused for a second. "Yes! How?"

"You'll have to go back down the steps and pull the chain to lower me down."

"I should leave you up there you fool." She was starting to see the humor of the man dangling in mid-air. "You gave me a fright!"

"This is a tiny hook and my fingers are starting to hurt."

"Sure!" She returned to the lower level, but not as fast as she'd gone up.

She discovered which side needed to be pulled to start the slow downward movement. When his feet were about six feet from the ground, he dropped the rest of the way. He moaned as he shook his hurting hands.

She ran to him and thrust her arms around him, hugging him closely to her. "Please don't scare me like that again."

"Why would I hang myself? I sent you into town to buy stuff I need." Roger was uncomfortable with her hanging on him. Not uncomfortable in the sexually charged way like before, but uncomfortable in that he didn't want her hanging on him. He pried her arms from his shoulders pushing her away a little too dismissively. She felt it.

"I'm sorry!" She lowered her head. Such subservience used to signal respect to Roger, now it appeared as weakness and enraged him.

"No problem!" He looked around. "Did you get everything?"

"Yes!" She was still looking down. He felt the rage welling up inside of him, but he pushed the monster back out of sight.

"Good! Let's have a look."

He went through all the items, nodding approval at each step.

"Great! Let's get started."

"The angle grinder needs electricity."

"I know! I'll see if we can manage without it. If not then you're going to have to find somebody with electricity to do a bit of cutting." Roger spoke as he started laying out the articles on the floor in an organized and systematic way.

Roger began by rigging a harness for the huge gas bottles out of the fencing wire and hooked them up to the crane. Using the chain, he raised them up to the roof. Then, climbing onto the top of the steel gantry and with an effort, Roger lifted the gas bottles and anchored them in the steel rafters. Back on terra firma, he looked up, satisfied. "We'll get the fire extinguishers tonight." Once again, he hadn't included Atifah in any of his thoughts. She had no idea why he wanted a fire extinguisher, nor why he'd wired the gas bottles into the roof. She felt no inclination to ask.

"Please do me a long and boring favor?"

"Sure! What do you want?" she answered.

"From the office window up the stairs you can look both ways along the rail track. Call me if you see a train coming."

"No problem!" She disappeared up the stairs, relieved to be away from him again.

Roger retrieved one of the agents' cell phones from the car and switched it on. To his relief, the signal was strong. It was something he hadn't thought of. He followed her up the stairs and left the handset next to her. In the distance, a horn sounded signaling to workers it was lunch time. Roger looked at his watch which read 12:30 exactly. "Perfect!" he said to her. She gave a reluctant grin.

For the next few hours, Atifah kept watch over the desolate line, while Roger ran a network of cables back and forth across the roof girders from various locations back to the mezzanine. At one point he was suspended from the steel structure when Atifah called to Roger to tell him a train was visible.

"Call Elaine! Her number is in the phone. I'm coming to you." Roger started making his way to her along the gantry, making use of the roof trusses for propulsion. By the time he'd climbed down, Atifah had already connected to the reporter and was waiting for him.

"Ok Elaine! Here's Roger." She handed him the handset.

"Hi Elaine. I wanted to know what's going on. I haven't seen a television to find out what the status is. Am I a free man yet?"

Elaine was hesitant. She knew that by now her phone would probably be tapped. "The official word hasn't changed."

In the distance, the box cars clattered over the joins in the tracks reverberating through the iron bridge. "But you've developed a huge fan base. Our phone rang off the hook with hundreds of people who are worried about you. We've started up a web site for you. You can visit it at www.macadam_is_innocent.com if you want. There are hundreds of people on your side."

"That's great." His words said one thing, his tone another. "I'm sure they will be watching for me to comment there. It is heartening to know people believe me."

"That's not all. After you aired, the FBI phones were inundated with calls. You were spotted in forty-six states. You've become a celebrity."

"Great to know. Anyway, I'd better go." The train was gone and there was little point in continuing the conversation. He had no interest in his celebrity status

-- o --- oOo --- o --

As Roger had predicted, the FBI headquarters flew into pandemonium and excitement the moment the call had been cleaned and amplified. Derrick England pointed out that the pitch of the noise from the train had changed. He thought it was probably because the train was going over water. Crane had to admit it wasn't bad for a geek. The hum of what sounded like a far off outboard motor later in the recording and the distant sound of what was probably ropes and tackle tapping on aluminum masts in a gentle breeze backed up his thoughts.

"I want a list of all the train bridges in Texas and the surrounding states going over, or near a body of water big enough to take small craft and sailing boats." Crane bellowed at the faces around the table.

"Open bridges," England added without lifting his head from the screen he was looking at.

"Why?" Crane was a little angered at being corrected.

Agent England was enjoying being able to display his brilliance to the row of dumbass sub-humans sitting all around. Derrick, like most techies, had an inherent intolerance for stupidity. "Because ..." He paused for effect and to think the words 'you dumb fuck', but he didn't say them – "the open bridge allows all the sound to escape and reach the recipient quicker, sharpening the pitch on the leading edge of the sound and decaying to a lower pitch while the slower waves catch up. See." England pointed to a graph of the sound wave on his screen. "Whereas a closed bridge will muffle higher frequencies keeping the pitch more even in the attack and delay." It was a bit theoretical, but he knew the morons staring blankly at him would never know the difference.

It was enough for Crane. "Open bridges ... and for each line I want a list of trains passing at this time. Go. Start calling now."

-- o --- oOo --- o --

By the late afternoon Roger had successfully tested his theory on the switching of the dog collars. He wrapped a thick rubber band around the collar remote and held it away from the

272

button using the steel nail. He then packed silicone rubber between the rubber band and the button. Once the sealant had dried, the collar was activated by slipping the nail out and the collar started buzzing every time. He was pleased with himself as the dog collar vibrated across the old steel work bench. Now he needed to test the range.

Atifah held the collar in the office area, while Roger walked the visible perimeter and tested the range at each corner. She had to listen for the buzz, then press the button on the remote in her hand, buzzing the collar around Roger's neck to report the success.

Making a small guide with a loop of wire and mounting a blade under it with duct tape, he found the weight of the nail was sufficient to cut the floss as it fell down dragging the nylon filaments onto the sharp edge. He smiled as things started to come together. When she asked, he explained that should they set off the signal, it would be better if the string didn't remain connected to the nail, as it would be a little suspect if they were to pull the floss and find a six inch nail attached to the end.

Next he completed the wiring of the roof and ran wires to the infra-red motion detectors. The place was looking like the inside of an old telephone exchange. It was impressive even though nothing would ever work. He only needed to lead somebody to think it would work.

As the sun dipped below the horizon in the early evening, the two of them took a trip in the SUV to the opposite side of the lake. Navigating using an image from Google maps, Roger found a route to a secluded point which was public enough to leave the vehicle without attracting undue attention. He hoped he would be able to see it from the water at night. He had searched the agent's mobile for a GPS, but without luck. He would need to navigate the old way.

Roger looked up and down the water's edge memorizing the position of various light sources along the bank. He would need to navigate across the water in the dark and locate this position. In the distance, the yellow glow of Somerville reflected off the low lying cloud, lighting up the water a little which helped his planning. The opposite direction was oily and black. Roger knew he would be navigating toward the black. Not a welcoming thought, but standing on the point at the water's edge looking back at the land, he could visualize himself approaching and the image of the various lights to his left and to his right was planted in his brain.

Without any fanfare they climbed back into their vehicle and headed back. Roger switched off his lights as he left the road to avoid drawing attention and found his way back to the workshop in the near darkness.

No sooner were they inside when Roger said he was going back to the jetty. Atifah wasn't sure whether he'd mentioned it in passing, or whether she was supposed to go with him.

"Sure! Let's go." Taking the initiative she moved towards the door.

Roger was a little shocked, but followed into the darkness. Once they were outside he said, "You don't have to come with me. You can stay."

"It's no problem. You're pushing yourself beyond human limits. You'll need me there to pick you up when you can no longer get up on your own."

"I'm fine!" Roger replied to the girl striding through the long sparse grass in the darkness ahead of him.

"You might be at the moment, but how long do you think you can keep this up?"

His reply, delayed in coming and quiet as if he wasn't sure he wanted her to hear, sent a cold chill through her. "Only to the end."

She stopped and turned toward Roger – "You'd better not be planning to leave me any time soon."

Roger caught up with her quicker than expected and nearly bumped into her in the dark before retreating a step. "Don't worry! I'll see to it you survive this. I gave my word didn't I?"

"I don't like the way you are talking Roger."

Anger he'd suppressed so well in front of her started its journey from within. "Let's move!" He was blunt and she heard the change in his voice. They didn't talk again until they reached the jetty.

Looking around at the sleeping boats, Roger said, "It's all clear." The party was going on again somewhere in the distance. Roger assumed it must be a pub servicing the locals and boat owners. It sounded more subdued than last time. "You go that way and I'll go over there. In those red slatted boxes are fire extinguishers."

"Ok!"

"If you can fetch those two," he said, pointing to the two boxes to their left. "Then I'll get the others."

She set off without saying a word. They met back in the same spot a couple of minutes later. She noticed the one remaining extinguisher was the one closest to the boats. She hoped it meant he wasn't quite dead inside yet. They left in silence the way they'd arrived.

Atifah woke early the following morning, long before the light had started creeping into the workshop. She could see nothing in the thick darkness surrounding her.

"Roger?"

"What?"

"I thought you had gone."

"What's with your fear of me leaving. I said I would see you through this." Another night of anger and no sleep was telling on his patience. "Didn't we have this conversation last night?"

"I meant gone, as in out of the car, not gone for good. I wanted to know if you were here. I never know."

He grunted a reply. Then after a long pause he said in a more placid tone. "Look! I can't sleep! Every time I close my eyes I see the body bag and I know it contained somebody in my family."

"You cannot survive with no food and no sleep. You really can't."

"I know. You're right." He was being genuine. He'd noticed the shaking of his hands and the dizziness. He knew he had to be in better form when the showdown came about. He'd spent hours thinking about it through the night. "I will eat something today."

"Good! I'm worried about you." She reached across the gap between them and placed her hand on his leg in an attempt to reassure him she was there for him. Roger had been slumped in his seat and her hand was much higher up his leg than she'd planned. Roger tensed and she withdrew her hand quickly. "I'm sorry! I didn't mean ..." she trailed off.

"I think it would be better if we kept our hands to ourselves."

It was a cold encounter. A far cry from the clumsy and awkward moments of a few days ago. Roger was a different person, hardened and resolute. There was no more play in Roger Macadam.

-- o --- o0o --- o --

They didn't speak again until the sun started showing through the doors and windows. They sat in the darkness, Atifah worrying about Roger, Roger worrying about nothing. The numbness engulfed him.

"I have work to do." Roger opened the door and climbed out.

Once again she didn't know what was expected of her, but she followed him into the half-darkness of the workshop. He picked up the dog training collar remotes, the dental floss, fencing wire and nails. He had already removed the bright red LED lights that lit up every time a button was pressed and constructed his floss guide and cutters. They ventured off across the long grass to the corner of the plot, where Roger anchored one end of the floss to the base of a small shrub. Then backing up in a straight line, holding the floss a few inches above the ground and allowing it to run through the top of the grass, Roger worked his way across the gaps in the fence, joining the depleted floss to the new one as the old one ran out. It wasn't necessary to run the nylon thread right to the end of the property, because there were only a few places where somebody could come through the fence. He anchored the remote to a fence pole using the thick fencing wire and ran the thread through a cutter unit on an adjacent pole. He placed the nail under the rubber band and taking up as much slack as he dared, he tied the dental floss to the flat end of the nail.

Roger knew the slightest tug on the dental floss would loosen the nail from its position and start the collar vibrating. He repeated this for the remaining three sides of the property. It wasn't foolproof, but he hoped it would be enough. All the while Atifah trailed behind, mildly impressed with his genius, but not enjoying the overall process. Roger worked in silence, denying her existence.

She watched as Roger staggered, fighting back the dizziness and rubbing his eyes. With the lack of food, water and sleep, Roger's mind was starting to play tricks on him. He would see movement in the grass when there was none. He had black dots floating in front of his eyes all the time.

"I'm going to string up those bottles we picked up last night. Will you take a drive into town?"

"Of course."

"See if you can find a drug store and buy me chocolate bars for breakfast. Get whatever you want for yourself."

Atifah had other ideas. She knew enough to know the relief felt by eating chocolate would be short term. "Sure," she replied anyway.

As soon as she had disappeared, Roger headed for the roof, binding the extinguishers in place above the workshop. He had finished wiring the still full bottles in place when Atifah arrived back with breakfast. The moment she stepped out of the vehicle, he knew chocolate bars were not on the menu.

"What did you buy?"

"A bit of this and a bit of that," she replied grinning at Roger.

"I only wanted sugar."

"I have your chocolate but first you need real food." She turned her back on Roger as she reached for the boxes of food.

"Isn't it a bit early for Chinese?"

"No! It's a bit late for last night's Chinese. Chinese is always good. Eat!" It seemed she was taking no nonsense. Roger knew he had to eat even if it meant forcing it down. "Sit in the car I'll serve you." She fussed around Roger handing him the food utensils and the bottled water. He needed them. She gave him no chance to stop eating.

To Roger, the tasteless food was almost gagging him, but eat he did. Once he finished the carton of Chow Mein, he knocked back an entire bottle of water she'd already opened for him. The food tasted like plastic and even the water tasted of chemicals. He wrote it off to not having eaten for a few days and having no urge to eat at all. He immediately tried to stand to get back to work.

"Sit for a while!" she demanded.

"No time! I need to set something up."

"You can do it once you have rested for a while. You haven't stopped in days. You've lost weight, you look haggard and you need a rest."

The room spun as he stood up and he thought better of it. He sat back in the vehicle, which normally stopped the room spinning. This time it kept going.

He sat back and rested his head for what seemed like hours, but was only about thirty minutes. Each time he tried to move the room would spin faster. For a while he thought maybe the food was coming back up. Maybe he'd eaten too much. He laid his head back against the headrest. Atifah was at his side in the open door. He started as the back of the seat began to move backwards. She was laying his chair back using the button on the door panel. Through the swirling mass of light and sound he heard her saying, "Relax. Lie back and sleep." He fought it thrashing his hands back and forth, trying to push the girl away and stand up, but all Atifah saw were a

278

few twitches of his fingers. She smiled as he sank into a deep and undisturbed sleep.

Turning, Atifah took the box of pills from her pocket. She re-read the dosage instructions on the side of the box. Then smiling, she closed the door of the vehicle leaving Roger sleeping.

"What can I do for the day?" She kept smiling. She was happy to see him sleeping.

-- o --- oOo --- o --

Roger opened his eyes as the sun was beginning to dip onto the western horizon. Puzzled to find himself alone in the vehicle, he had no idea of time or date but he was refreshed. He held up his hands and could see the tremor had subsided.

He stretched out his arms, amazed he'd slept without dreaming. He opened the door of the SUV and climbed out. Atifah called from the mezzanine office when she heard the door close. "Roger! I'm up here." She didn't know what to expect from him, but knew this was neither the time nor the place to mention sleeping pills.

He found her warming herself in the last rays of the day seated in a makeshift chair by the large dirty window. The window was dirty enough to cloud the vision, but clear enough to allow the late afternoon sun to warm the entire area.

"What day is it?" Roger didn't know. "I feel like I've been sleeping for days."

"It's still Friday but you have slept the entire day. I was beginning to wonder if you would wake up at all." The grey slate-like look in his eye had given way to a spark she hadn't seen for days.

"Shall we go and get something to eat?" He was hungry again and barely remembered the Chinese food from earlier the same day.

"Already bought something." She pointed to the bags on the crooked filing cabinet.

"What? How? ..." He'd woken up in the car. "How did you ..."

"I took a walk into town." She saw the shock in his face. "... Don't worry! I wasn't followed and I stepped over your traps."

"What if you were recognized? You might have been caught."

"But I wasn't so we're ok." It was pleasant to hear him caring again. "I bought healthy food so eat up. We'll strengthen you up again for your showdown."

Roger tucked into the various items, knowing he had to eat. The food was going down much easier than it had for the last few days. After eating, he leaned back, his stomach full and thanked her for the meal.

"I enjoyed the walk." She was relishing hearing him talk again. "Ok! What's next?"

"When it gets dark, we're going back to the lake so I can make a call from the public phone."

"And then?"

"And then we wait for Crane's lot to arrest me."

"What if somebody else pitches up? There are agents out there that probably have a personal vendetta against you."

"Maybe! But I'm phoning Crane's mobile, which can't be traced, from a different phone."

-- o --- o0o --- o --

"Crane?"

"Yep!"

"You know you've declared war!"

"Macadam?"

"Who else?"

"It wasn't my team."

"You have no idea who it was."

"I know it wasn't mine."

Roger was watching his watch. He knew caller ID was already displaying the number on Crane's handset. The need for tracing calls was almost obsolete these days, but he wanted to give Crane the impression of having the upper hand. He'd already dialed one of the cell phones in his armory to check the call was identifiable. It was.

"I don't care. I have armed myself and I'm coming after you and your team. The game's all changed now."

"Changed how?"

"Come on Crane. Don't act stupid. From now on I'm no longer running away."

"Where are you?" Crane feigned lack of knowledge, but the screen on his phone showed the number. He'd already written the number down and handed it to Agent England who was already hard at work on his keyboard.

"I'm a lot closer than you'd think. Best keep your eyes open Crane and tell your team to keep their eyes open too. I don't intend to take prisoners. Anyway. Better be going or I'll have black cars pulling up at my front door." He hung up in thirty-eight seconds.

"It's a pay phone in Somerville." England had located the number.

"Somerville?"

"On the lake. It's on the craft dock."

Crane stood and barked orders at the team. "We move out in fifteen minutes. I want a chopper and full SWAT kit for everybody. Night vision, the works. I want maps and satellite images of the whole area. See if there's a railway bridge nearby. We're looking for somewhere Macadam could hide without being seen by neighbors. If we have to break down every door in Somerville, I want Macadam tonight."

"How are we …"

"I don't care. Make it happen. I want the entire team on the ground and I want your comm. links encrypted. Nobody knows you're there. We can't afford another Buffalo."

In little more than an hour, Crane's team lifted off from the roof of the FBI building headed for Somerville.

-- o --- o0o --- o --

Roger knew he had a little time to kill. Before going back to the workshop, the two of them went towards the already high level of noise emanating from a small building, which although rough, was home to the holidaymakers in the evenings. It wasn't the biggest club around, but the patrons seemed to be enjoying themselves. One of the patrons would not end the night as happy as they sounded at that moment.

Roger located a few automobiles parked around the corner of the building in the darkness. He tried a few doors until one opened. Jumping in quickly, he killed the inside light, then popping the hood and the trunk, he located a small pouch of tools and set to work loosening the screws around the new halogen headlamps. In a short time, they made their way back to the workshop. He was carrying the battery and Atifah was carrying the headlamps.

Back at 'home', Roger wired the lamps facing the large door testing them then working in the dark, he ran wires up to the mezzanine where he joined them to a small switch which he'd removed from his own SUV. In one last test, the flick of a switch lit up the entire door area in a brilliance that shocked the eyes. He killed the light instantly.

"You remember where we drove to yesterday?" Roger spoke while adjusting the wiring.

"The other side. Yes!" She was still not privy to his plan.

"I need you to go and wait for me there."

"How are you going to get there?" she asked confused. Roger took the boat key from his pocket and shook it. She remembered the boat for sale.

In the distance the sound of a helicopter alerted Roger to the possible approach of the agents.

"It could be them. Quicker than I expected. You'd better go."

"Be careful!"

He ignored her. "If I'm not there by sunrise then you'll need to contact the Sultan and tell him to get you out."

"Roger, I ..."

"Go! Be sure to park far away from the point and try to keep the car out of sight. Crane doesn't know where we are so they may be over there looking. I'm hoping they will put the clues together and start this side where the public phone is."

As soon as she had pulled onto the road, Roger walked the perimeter of the grassland and armed all his traps. Roger was convinced they would try to take him at night. He guessed between 2:30 am and 4:00 am, when people are in their deepest sleep. The same reason why criminals tend to hit in the same period.

He had already marked a large circle on the floor of the workshop, about 20 feet across, and placed the two drums outside the circle. He poured the gasoline onto the water, then closed the door, shutting out the only bit of available light and jamming it closed with a folded piece of paper. He would hear the paper drop, but the agents wouldn't think something so quiet would be a signal. They would believe it was there to keep the door closed.

He made his way up the steps and positioned himself against the wall. He tested the location of everything, then placed the four collars around his neck. Now all he had to do was wait in the darkness.

SATURDAY, 18TH

As he suspected, the collar connected to the trip wire on the western fence buzzed at 3:07 on his watch. He hadn't needed it as he was wide awake. Working at a frenetic pace, he removed the batteries from the collars. He couldn't risk something setting them off while he was hiding.

He knew the agents were only guessing his whereabouts, so they probably wouldn't attack every building with guns blazing. At this point they had no idea he was inside.

A short while later he heard the folded paper drop to the floor as the door opened. It was showdown time. No flashlights flashed around the room so the agents were using night vision. They were quiet, but the movements could still be heard. There was a slight crunching as the shoes trod down on the dusty cement surface. Roger's senses were buzzing they were so alive. He was seated low down and would not be seen until somebody hit the steps. He wouldn't wait that long.

He hit the switch and the stolen halogen beams blinded the agents as their night vision goggles reacted to the light.

"Good morning gentlemen!" Roger remained hidden from the shocked agents below. "Before anybody decides to take a wild shot at me, I would like you all to look at what I have in my hand."

Roger held the last remaining remote in his right hand, his thumb firmly placed on one of the four buttons. He stood slowly and found himself looking down the barrels of five automatic weapons. The eyes of the agents were still adjusting to the light.

"I will say this only once. If my thumb lifts from the button we all die. If you look up into the roof area you will see six canisters, two large and four small."

The agents remained fixed on Roger.

"Other than this remote I have no weapon on my person. I do have a weapon up here with me. It is positioned six feet away on the floor. Now! Look up and look at the canisters above your heads."

The agents looked up.

"I want you all to understand something. I have toyed with the idea of ending my life several times in the last couple of days. I urge you not to test me. You WILL lose." He hesitated. "Are we clear?"

There was silence from below as the agents started to take in the enormity of the situation.

"Firstly, before we get down to business." He pointed to the agent closest to the door. "I want you to go outside and call all your friends in. You have one minute to be back here with your buddies or these agents die."

The agent hesitated. He slowly raised his hands, then carefully removed his helmet. Roger recognized the face of Caleb Johnson. "There's nobody else," Caleb said slowly.

"Agent?"

"Johnson."

Roger looked at his watch feigning frustration. "Agent Johnson. You have about fifty-five seconds left."

"Macadam. There's nobody else. This is the team." He paused then seeing Roger still looking at his watch, said, "I give you my word. There's no one outside."

Roger dropped his arm. "A bit understaffed aren't we, for picking up an international terrorist."

The agents said nothing, but shifted uneasily.

"Ok! Starting with you …" Roger pointed at the agent furthest into the room. "I want you to take your weapons, your helmet and communication devices and drop them in one of the barrels of gasoline at the back, then go and stand in the circle I've drawn on the floor. Including your cell phones, everything."

One by one the agents moved to the barrel and threw their automatics and electrical devices into the gasoline and then moved into the drawn circle. As Agent Wilson took off her helmet her long, dark hair fell to her shoulders. Roger smiled. "I apologize. I should have said lady and gentlemen." Roger was comforted by the presence of the girl. He was sure there was still enough chivalry left for the male members of the team to want to protect her.

As the last agent was about to move, Roger stopped him. "You can keep your little radio thing with you. Everything else … in the drum." The agent obediently dropped everything into the container keeping the headset and the attached battery pack in his hand. "Good. Take the radio and place it on the floor in front of you, then join your friends in the circle." The agent obliged. "Right! Everybody spread out. There's plenty of space. Stay inside the circle."

By making them spread out, he was reducing the risk of somebody trying to stop him, should he have to go down there with them.

"Good! Now we can talk." Roger looked at the agents. "Who's missing?"

The agents were silent. Five of them were calm, but one was fidgeting and he made Roger a little nervous. "You!" Roger pointed the remote at the fidgeting Derek England. "Who's missing."

England had never been in a situation like this. He had never seen combat of any kind. The only reason he joined this party was because he thought six to one were good odds. He stammered, "I ... I ... don't know what you mean."

"I was told there were nine of you. Two were killed. There should be a minimum of seven agents, but I only count six."

"Agent Crane stayed behind." Caleb Johnson stepped forward.

"Thank you agent Johnson."

"All right! Lady and gentlemen." Roger moved to the railing. "I have been searching for clues as to why I have been persecuted and found none. The only link I have with the killers of my family is somebody in this group who led his ... or her own people to their death. One of you let the killers know of my whereabouts." Out of the corner of his vision Roger saw England shifting uneasily.

"Your partner over there is fidgeting and making me nervous. Everybody down on your stomach! Hands behind your heads!" There was a quick shuffling as they all dropped down on their faces. Roger was happy they were taking him seriously. "You! Skinny boy." He was talking to England. "Stand up." England stood. "Remove your clothes."

Derrick looked around for support from his partners but received none. "C'mon! We haven't got all day. You can leave your underwear on ... Ok! Hands up and turn around ... shirt back on and the rest in the drum ... wristwatch as well."

He watched as Derrick walked delicately and threw his clothing into the drum. "You can push it all down with the rod next to the drum." England's vulnerability level shot through the roof and his nervousness caused his body to shake uncontrollably. Roger felt happier he wouldn't try anything stupid and he knew there were no hidden weapons. "Ok! You can sit."

Addressing the rest he said, "I think I will be much more relaxed if you all do the same. We'll start with the lady. The rest of you keep your eyes to yourselves." Agent Wilson stood with an angry scowl on her face. "I apologize, but I think it's in your own best interest." She obliged grudgingly. She lifted her hands, spun around then self-consciously picked up her shirt. "You can put your pants back on too. Lose the belt and empty the pockets."

She walked to the drum and emptied her clothes and boots inside. As she was walking back into the circle, Roger stopped her. "Clout the skinny bastard alongside the head for me. He was checking you out while you were undressing."

England's eyes opened wide with shock. Wilson wanted to vent a little and she didn't hold back. England had always given her the creeps. This clout was long overdue. She lashed out with a ferocity that would have scared any of the agents in the circle, but it left Derrick England weeping in the fetal position on the cold hard concrete. Roger could see in her face she'd forgiven him for the embarrassment of stripping down.

The same procedure was followed for the remaining agents without further interruptions. Roger continued in the way a school teacher would address an assembly of students. "Now I have you all vulnerable, I feel much more relaxed." He grinned, but his humor was met only with dark scowls from the agents seated below.

"You probably saw my recent television appearance where I spelled out my intentions. I believe none of you were involved with the deaths of my family and you need to understand I have no intention to do you any harm. I only intend to watch two people die before I take my own life. Having said that, if it looks like I'm getting nowhere then I have no further leads. So as they say, the buck stops here. If you choose not to cooperate with me I will not hesitate to end it for all of us."

"As I have already mentioned, one of your group is my only link to the killers of my family." The agents all glanced uneasily around at each other. "I would like the person to tell me what I need to know."

Roger stood silently and waited.

Agent Crosby, sensing nobody else was going to say anything spoke up, "How do you know it was one of us?"

"Only the people in this room and Agent Crane were party to the information and that's why I arranged for you to arrive at the hotel before the killers. So! Somebody in your circle led the killers to the hotel and let them know you were staking the place out. The killers only moved in after your team left. I'd have thought you'd have worked it out by now."

Crosby continued, "What if it wasn't one of us? Suppose it was Crane?"

"That would be very unfortunate. I've spoken to Crane. He was clueless." Roger waited again in silence.

It was Wilson's turn. "These agents are trained not to give secrets away. You can't keep us here all day."

"I know! Only until sunrise."

Nobody wanted to ask what happens at sunrise.

"Who of you know what that is?" Roger pointed to the scraps of engine on the floor. Nobody answered. "It's an old VW engine." He paused. "The casing is made of a magnesium alloy. Who remembers from high school chemistry what happens when you burn magnesium?" Still no answers. "Let me tell you. It burns white hot. So hot, that when one of these engines caught fire on the highway, the fire department wouldn't even bother trying to put the fire out. They would simply let it burn."

There was a little uneasy shifting from the agents. "I'm not altogether sure if it will work, but I have rigged those bottles with a poor man's napalm which will explode and shower the entire building with a mixture of napalm and chunks of the engine."

"If it does work, then when they find the burned out building in the morning they won't even find a trace of a body in here. We'll all have disappeared and the steel melted. You'll all be a mystery." He paused again for effect. "You might feature in a mystery series in a few years: The vanishing FBI agents."

"Who of you have kids?" Roger changed the subject. Again nobody answered, but he saw Agents Wilson and Johnson shift uneasily. "Ok! Tough crowd. Well you know which of you have kids. If nobody has spoken by the time the sun rises those kids will lose one of their parents." He sat down and relaxed.

The silence and his calmness were unnerving the agents. Derrick England couldn't take it anymore. "You'll die too."

"I have nothing to live for except watching the life drain from the killers of my family. If I am unable to find them … well then I have nothing to live for, period."

England started to panic. He stood up. "You can't kill us if we don't know." He started moving toward the door. Roger stood and let him go. As he neared the door, Roger pointed to Agent Crosby, then looking at his watch said. "You have two minutes to bring him back. I don't care if he's alive or dead, but he is back inside in two minutes or everybody else dies." Crosby hesitated and looked at the agents. "Time's a wasting."

Agent Crosby sprinted for the door. The rough ground outside prevented England from making a fast getaway without his shoes and he was soon overtaken by the real agent. A short scuffle ensued and Crosby dragged the computer expert back inside and dumped him back in the fetal position on the cement floor.

"Twenty-seven seconds! Well done!"

Roger leaned on the handrail and the hatred returned to his eyes. He spoke with purpose, "The next time somebody tries to leave, they won't reach the door." He sat back down. England sobbed as he lay on the floor muttering to himself.

Once again silence reigned in the workshop and the agents began to feel uneasy. The silence stretched on and on. Although they were still an hour or so from sunrise, the waiting and not being able to see the time was playing tricks on the agent's minds. England was the first to crack again. Sitting up, he turned on his colleagues. "What's wrong with you? Can't you take him out or something? You're supposed to be the experts. I trusted you idiots to keep me safe."

The agents all turned and glared at England. Roger spoke from the top. "Shut up, you little shit! You should be thanking them for keeping you alive. If it was only you and I, I'd have pulled the plug on us long ago."

England lost it. He stood angrily. "You fuck off! You fucking terrorist!" He was pointing at Roger. "We don't negotiate with terrorists in America. You want to screw a Muslim, go to fucking Saudi." He paused for a second, about to sit back down, then added, "No wonder your wife was fucking your best friend."

Roger stood slowly. All expression fell from his face. His eyes were like dark holes in his skull. Anger coursed through his being. Shifting the remote to his left hand, he walked robotically down the steps and past the group who watched him with trepidation. Next to the drum, Roger picked up the steel rod used by the agents to submerge their belongings. He walked to the skinny kid and blankly, without thought or compassion raised the rod above his head. England raised his arms instinctively, but Roger hadn't thought of hitting his head. The rod came down fast making a low pitched noise as it parted the air and crashed into the kid's kneecap.

The pain was the worst he'd ever felt. He gasped for air as the pain shocked his body. His hands grabbed at his knee as the rod came down again cracking and breaking the bones in his left shoulder. He fell over onto his side squealing as the air escaped from his lungs through his pain-constricted throat.

Roger looked down at the writhing form and still showed no compassion. The only thing keeping him from bringing the rod down again on the skull of the kid, was his need for answers. "Too bad your last hours will be in pain." He spoke flatly, monotonously, but in perfect control. He turned and headed back up the steps.

Without a word being spoken, Roger sat back down and waited for the agents to speak. The only sound was the sobbing of Derrick England as he lay unable to move. The slightest shudder sent a searing pain through his body. It was better to remain still.

"I've changed my mind," Roger stood speaking slowly. "I'm not waiting around here until daybreak." He looked at his watch. "You have two minutes to tell me which of you is the one. It starts now …"

Worried glances shot from one agent to the next. Even Derrick raised himself up onto his good arm, his other arm hung limply onto his legs.

"C'mon Macadam. Let's not do anything rash," Agent Crosby urged him to reconsider. "If you die then it's all in vain."

"I told you I have no need for life anymore and your good friend over there has reminded me how worthless life can be." Roger continued to look at his watch. There was no count down. Only the chilling knowledge of a coming shower of burning gasoline gel, which would instantly scald the flesh from their throats as they tried to gasp for air.

Out of the corner of his eye, Roger saw somebody starting to move as if they were about to stand. Without looking at the agents he spoke, "If you stand you'll be denying the others the opportunity of making peace with their maker."

Roger was starting to worry he'd been wrong. He was sure by now the person would have started talking. His mind started running through the options to back out without alerting them to the fact that the steel bottles were empty, but once again Derrick England couldn't take the pressure.

"STOP! Stop! It was me." He would have run, but he couldn't stand. "It was me. I gave them the information." England swung his broken body around so he could face Roger, grimacing as he did so. "I didn't know they were going to kill anybody. I didn't!" He glanced around at the agents imploring them for forgiveness, but their faces told him it wouldn't be coming anytime soon.

"You have my attention." Roger lowered his arm and looked vacantly at the agent.

"I was put in the team to supply information as I received it."

Roger waited, knowing this might be a stall for time. "I want the names and locations of the killer of my family and of the one giving the order."

"I don't know. Honestly I don't." Roger believed him. "All I can tell you is I gave the information to a businessman in Dallas."

"Go on!"

"The guy's name is Frank Baker. He's a securities dealer and sits on the boards of several companies. He owns about half of the companies in America."

"What information did you feed him?"

"Anything and everything. He wanted to know what we knew about you."

"And what was in it for you?" Roger looked on with a dead expression. Internally, he was excited to have a lead and he sat again getting himself comfortable. He wanted to know what this guy knew.

"Money and power. I'm a Bonesman. I help them. They help me."

"What's a Bonesman?" Roger had heard the term, but had no idea what it was.

"At Yale, there's a ..."

"Yale?" The name of the university had surfaced a few times in his searching and now the killer agent's comment about how clever his superiors were, started to have meaning.

"College! I was invited to be a member of the Skull and Bones secret society ..."

Roger smiled. "I can see we're wasting our time here." He raised his watch arm again.

"Wait!" Panic entered England's voice. "It's true. Let me finish." He painfully shifted his position. "I was made a member because my father was a member. Serious players have been Bonesmen. Both Bush presidents were Bonesmen and plenty more. Industry's richest and most powerful people are Bonesmen."

"I look at you and I don't see rich and powerful."

"This is my first job. I didn't even apply for it."

"If this is such a secret society, why are you so happy to start chatting about it?"

"What they do is secret. Every idiot's heard of the society. I'm not going to tell you about what goes on there, I've given a pledge."

"Ok! So you're a member of the Skull and Bones Society."

"Yeah! Frank Baker organized me this job a while back, so when he called and said he wanted me on this task team so that I could feed back information to him, of course I agreed."

"What did he want the information for?"

"I don't know! I didn't ask questions."

"I still don't understand what's in it for you."

"At this point nothing, but the society owns nearly everything worth having. In a few years I could be head of the FBI if I want!"

"How do you contact this Frank Baker?"

"Through email, but he's a big time businessman, an old guy. He's worth millions." England looked around smugly, happy to be able to drop the names of the wealthy, if not famous. "You'll never get close to him. He has a huge ranch. It's guarded."

"Is he being protected by the likes of you?"

"He's protected by money."

"We'll see about that." Roger picked up his laptop and descended the steps to hand it to England. "Fire up your email."

"He won't answer his email now!"

"I didn't mention his. I want to see yours."

England shifted and pulled himself up painfully with his good arm. "I won't be able to access it without the VPN."

Roger placed his foot onto agent England's outstretched leg and twisted on his crushed knee cap. England screeched and threw himself backward, writhing in agony. Between gasps and sobs, he looked up at Roger. "Why the fuck d'you do that?"

Roger looked on without remorse. "You're the expert. You have five minutes to pull up your email on this screen, or I'm going to give you so much pain you will wish you would die."

England once again pulled himself up. This time he took the laptop and switched it on. Using his good arm, he typed slowly on the keyboard. Roger again glanced at his watch. He needed to speed things up. It would start getting light soon and Atifah would leave in his transport.

He grabbed the crane and ran it to a point above England. Then wrapping some of the excess wire into a loop, he hooked it onto the hook of the crane. He started pulling on the chain until the wire was at the height of England's neck. He squealed in panic. "What are you doing?"

"You're going too slowly."

"You said five minutes."

"I don't think you're going to manage it and I'm a man of my word."

"Ok! Ok! I'm in. Here's my mail."

He finished tapping on the keyboard a few more times and then handed back the laptop to Roger.

"I want to pay Mr Baker a visit. Where do I find him?"

England looked down. "I don't know."

Roger moved his foot which England misread and panicked. "I don't know," he repeated in a voice raised in volume and pitch. He gave himself away. Roger didn't believe him. He knew exactly where Frank Baker was.

"Pain is the best truth serum. Did you know that?" England's eyes widened. Roger moved in slipping the wire loop over his head. Then with his right hand, Roger spun the chain and the wire tightened around England's neck.

Roger felt neither pity nor remorse for the young man as the veins swelled on his neck. A stifled gasp was cut short. The wire stopped short of cutting through the man's skin, but the bulging eyes, racked with fear, told the story. England knew he was about to die. He clawed at the wire around his neck and his face reddened. The other agents protested, but Roger glared at them with a dead stare all the while holding the button depressed on the remote. Agent Wilson turned her head away.

He spun the chain back and England slumped over sideways supporting himself on his good arm and gasping for air.

"Now! I am going to ask you one last time." Roger knelt down and with his nose inches from England's, he stared his dead, emotionless stare into the younger man's fearful eyes. "I want to know his address."

England gasped and coughed. "I told you, I don't know it, but I've been there. I can give you directions," he stammered between gasps. Roger scribbled as the agent spoke. When he was finished, Roger removed the wire from around England's neck.

"Wasn't that easy?"

There was no reply.

Roger returned to the office mezzanine and positioned himself so that he could see the agents below while he opened a few of the emails from Frank Baker. Satisfied that England had been telling the truth, he copied the emails to his desktop along with the corresponding mails from the sent items folder. He then spent a few minutes looking through a few other emails to check if there was anything else useful, but he found nothing. Roger scribbled information onto a piece of paper as he read.

He closed the laptop and faked a call to somebody on the cell phone asking to be picked up on the road in three minutes. Then went back down the steps. He spoke to the agents in general. "I sure hope none of our national secrets are in this guy's hands. I thought you agents were supposed to carry poison capsules in case things get unbearable. This guy folded like a piece of paper."

Agent Johnson looked at England in disgust and mumbled. "He's not an agent."

He handed the radio and headpiece to agent Wilson. "I'm going out and leaving you now. I want you to inform your accomplices out there that I'm going out and it is in your interest for me not to be hassled in any way."

She looked up at Roger and said, "There's nobody out there."

"Hmm! And who piloted the chopper?"

"An assigned pilot. He's waiting at the helicopter and armed. Crane made us use the comms gear encrypted. Nobody knew we were here." She looked around at England. "Now I know why."

"Maybe the skinny guy's friends are outside and that would be unfortunate for you. We've seen they will have no concern for your lives."

"I didn't tell them I was coming," he spluttered, still battling to breath with the pain in his throat.

"Lucky! Or we'd probably all be dead by now." Roger had no reason to disbelieve them. It was their lives at stake. He hung the headgear on the crane hook and slid it down out of their reach.

Roger picked up the camcorder he'd left running when the agents had arrived and switched it off. At the doorway he turned. "Agents!" he called, "I've armed the alarm. You can see two of the sensors there … and there." He pointed. "There are two more that you can't see from your location. If you remain in the circle you will be fine. These headlights will drain the battery in about four hours, by which time the power shouldn't be enough to trigger the alarm. For your own sakes, ensure the lamps are dead. If you see the little red light turn on in one of those sensors, it'll be the last thing you see. It's been a blast, or luckily not!" Roger turned and left closing the door behind him.

He realized time was running out. He walked, quietly at first and then picked up the pace a little. He headed for the small craft jetty where he could see the agents' helicopter sitting in silence in the car park area close to the jetty. He could make out the pilot seated inside. Everything was quiet, even the bar. Roger untied the chosen boat and pushed it back from the wooden structure as he climbed aboard. He hadn't tried the engine, but he knew the risks. He put the key into the ignition and turned it.

The noise cut through the silence like an explosion. The engine turned over a few times and then spluttered into life. Roger engaged the reverse gear to continue the movement he'd started with the push and spun the wheel as he cleared the adjacent craft. As he came about into position, he spun the wheel in the opposite direction and engaged the forward gear. He eased the craft forward, until he was clear of the last boat, then opened up the throttle. The boat was by no means a speedboat, but it cut its way through the oily black water. The opposite bank looked different from this angle. His eyes scanned back and forth along the bank for a recognizable pattern.

He was starting to think he wouldn't recognize the lights. He looked back toward the town and remembering the view from last time, he realized he needed to be further to his left hand side. He sped up and veered left, parallel to where he believed the bank would run. After a minute or so the light patterns fell into a recognizable formation and the same moment he saw a flashlight being waved directly ahead and only a short distance away. He shut off the throttle which slowed the craft down, but it was too late to avoid the inevitable. Roger grabbed the woodwork to avoid being thrown as the boat came to a sudden halt on the sandy lake shore. The impact was not as bad as he'd expected, but the boat was beached and wouldn't be going anywhere soon.

"I thought I was going on alone," Atifah's voice sounded from a short distance away. She had spent the night on the exact sandy point Roger had stood examining the lights. She had full faith Roger would arrive at that precise point and didn't think for a second by waving her flashlight she'd averted, what could've been, a nasty accident.

Roger shook the surprise from his mind. "Thanks!" he said to her.

"For what?"

"For signaling your location to me. I might not have seen you otherwise."

Surprised at the comment, she moved toward the boat in the darkness. "The car's up there," she said pointing.

"Great! Let's go."

They began walking. "Where to?"

"Dallas."

-- o --- oOo --- o --

Back at the car, Roger plugged the laptop into the cigarette lighter and fired it up. "Are you ok to drive?"

"Sure! If I get tired I'll let you know."

"Head back into town. I'm checking now for the quickest route. When you hit the main road, aim north. I wish I could fly a helicopter." The last part he said quietly, but she heard.

"I can."

"What?"

"I can fly. The Sultan ensured I learned to fly while I was at school in London. I was sixteen when I started lessons. There are even a few female commercial pilots in Oman now."

"Are you serious?"

"Yes! I'm not the best pilot, but I've done sixty odd hours since I passed my licence."

"Incredible! Ok! So we're going back to the small craft harbor." He smiled a rare smile.

As they were approaching the chopper Roger said, "There's an armed guard inside. We need to flush him out."

"Ok!" She was apprehensive, but trusting.

"There is no better lure than a damsel in distress. I'm going to chase you along the wharf. When we are positioned between the chopper and that floodlight, I'm going to catch you. Scream a bit or something. I'll knock you down and then pretend to whack you around a bit. Ok?"

This instruction didn't help her feel any better, but she understood what was required. "Yes. I can do that."

"He'll either come up behind me and point a gun at me and tell me to stop, or he'll drag me off. Either way he won't be looking at you. You need to point the gun at him and keep it trained on his body at all times. I'll talk to him. Go!"

She ran along the wharf whimpering which Roger thought was a nice touch. As planned, he caught up to her right on time. He jumped in the air and brought his fist down stopping as it touched between her shoulder blades. Taking the cue, she stumbled forward and rolled on the cement wharf side. Roger was on her in an instant, yelling obscenities at the girl as she rolled back and forth covering her head with her arms. As Roger was thinking they should receive an Oscar for this, the pilot ran up behind them and stood and shouted.

"Stop!"

Roger stopped.

"Get up! Slowly!"

Roger winked and smiled at Atifah as if to say, "What did I tell you?" Doing as he was told, Roger raised his hands, placing them behind his head and stood slowly giving her time to slip the weapon from her belt.

"Right! Turn around. Let's keep it slow!"

Roger turned and smiled at the pilot. "You have a gun aimed at your chest. Place your gun on the floor and we'll let you live."

The pilot, a young man in his late twenties looked puzzled. Roger nodded his head in Atifah's direction and the look of puzzlement faded into one of despair as he realized he'd been caught out. He stooped to put the gun down. "Don't try anything stupid or you'll be dead before the sun rises." The pilot hesitated, then continued to lay the gun on its side. "Good lad! Now! On your face. Hands behind your back." The pilot complied.

Roger took the reel of duct tape from his pocket and taped the pilots hand together. Next he spun him over and placed a piece of tape across his mouth. Roger helped him to his feet and took him to the darkness behind the helicopter between two sheds. There, Roger bound him to a pole. "This stuff is strong and sticky. If you wriggle it'll tighten on you, you understand?" The pilot nodded. "Now! In about two hours this place will be thriving and somebody will find you. Don't waste your time before the sun comes up. There's nobody for miles understand?" The pilot nodded a second time.

The two turned and headed for the chopper. They opened the light weight doors and climbed inside. Roger looked on as the girl scanned the mass of switches and dials in front of her. "Can you do it?"

"Let's see. Cyclic and collective … fuel master … battery." She flicked the switch and the panel came to life. She continued doing her checks. "Fuel … transmission …tail rotor … clutch." She looked up at Roger and beamed a big smile. "I think I can do this."

"You're a star."

She continued the process in silence, opening the throttle, switching on the fuel boost and then finally she smiled and depressed the starter button. The engine turned over a few times and then fired into life. She depressed the fuel cut off and brought the revs up.

Atifah switched on the radio and placed her headset over her ears. Roger grabbed her shoulder as he saw what she was doing. She looked round at him. Through the noise, Roger put his finger to his lips, telling her to remain quiet. She reached over and cupped his headphones over his ears.

Her voice came clearly through his headset. "It's only internal so we can talk."

"Good." He spoke in a clear voice and a little too loudly.

"You don't have to shout." Then she continued, "Let's lift this baby off the ground."

She mouthed her way through a series of checks. Roger had no clue what she was doing. The rotor moved a little above them, then stopped. Roger was about to ask what was wrong when they started moving again. The helicopter shuddered as the revs increased. She did her final checks, speaking the words as she carried out each task as if trying to extract the checks from a recently memorized list before an exam. "Mags ... clutch ... boost ... transponder ... position beacon."

Finally she looked up again, smiled and then opened the throttle. The machine shuddered and moved. Roger felt the movement as the aircraft lurched and lifted from the cement. As their altitude increased, the sun came over the horizon and Atifah, at Roger's instruction, turned the craft and headed north-east toward Dallas.

He told her to keep low over the trees and desert scrub. She was avoiding all buildings, preferring to bank left and right than going over objects. She sped across the terrain like a Vietnam war veteran. To say Roger was impressed was an understatement.

They made wide arcs around settlements and flew low along waterways and rail tracks, all the while listening on the radio for any sign things were not going their way. After a short flight, they crossed Interstate 45, then headed to the east of Dallas, avoiding the built up areas between Dallas and Fort Worth. Roger knew there were military bases somewhere there, so decided to stick to the ranch lands to the east.

Roger looked around the cabin of the small helicopter. "Let's see what we have here." He loosened his harness-like seatbelt and climbed through to the economy class section behind. The agents had left nothing visible, but as he opened a small locker under the seats he found four bulletproof vests. He pulled two out. In doing so, he dragged out a black webbing belt with five small black grenades attached. Roger had played enough computer games and seen enough television to know vaguely how they worked, but he had no idea of their power, or whether they were stun grenades or the real thing. "These may be useful," he said to himself. There was no way Atifah would hear him above the noise and with her headphones on.

Moving back to his seat, he handed Atifah her jacket which he helped her into, while she was maneuvering the craft between the treetops. Roger put his own jacket on and clipped the belt around his waist. He practised unclipping and re-attaching the grenades a few times without looking. Then he picked up the bag from the floor, opened it and took out two of the pistols. After loading them, he placed one in his belt and the other he held on his lap for Atifah to use.

He tapped his knee nervously while the landscape moved below him.

Keeping Dallas in view in their left window, but distant enough to avoid builtup areas and especially avoiding small air fields and military bases, they circled around in what was a huge arc, until the center of Dallas lay due south. Then keeping low, they dipped in toward Dallas.

The distinctive shape of Lewisville Lake lay ahead. Roger was looking for landmarks leading him to a 'huge mansion', by England's reckoning. He wasn't wrong. In an area of smallish suburban ranches north of Lewisville Lake, England's words, 'You won't miss it', came to mind.

"Over there!"

As the helicopter approached, the mansion grew into a monster of architectural splendor. The green, rough surrounds gave way to manicured gardens and a paved network of immaculate pathways and sculptured lawns. Roger guessed this house would be priced in the tens of millions range.

Roger was expecting to see armed guards dotted all around with snipers on the rooftop, but there was nothing of the kind in view. A large, circular, flat lawn in front of the house was the perfect landing spot for a helicopter and before Roger could mention it, Atifah was already swooping down to the area. She knew a helicopter was always going to ruin the element of surprise, but a quick landing would at least allow them a moment while the 'enemy' scrambled.

She flew in low and landed on the circular lawn as fast as she could, making the landing a lot more bone jarring than she'd have hoped. They disembarked from the chopper as she cut the engine and made their way quickly for the front door, while the blades started to slow down.

Roger reached the unlocked door first and burst through at the same moment as a young teenage girl was approaching to find out what the noise outside was. Roger grabbed the girl without warning. In her surprise she didn't even have time to shout out, as Roger spun her around and clasped his left hand over her mouth. At the same moment a security guard rounded the archway leading away from the massive, elaborate entrance hall into an equally elaborate lounge area. The guard leveled his pistol at Roger and shouted something which Roger didn't understand, but the expression on the guards face turned from surprise to horror as Roger turned and he could see the fear-filled eyes of the girl and Roger's weapon pressed against her temple.

"Put it down!"

The guard was stunned. He knew who Roger was. Roger had been all over the news for the last couple of weeks, but he was the last person he'd have expected to see here. His training and logic were at odds with one another and he hesitated.

"Don't test me!" The shadows had returned to Roger's eyes and the guard could feel them penetrating deep into his thoughts. His expression was cold and lifeless. He was a step closer to finding out more information. The guard had followed his story and he knew he could kill this girl in a moment with no remorse. He stooped forward placing his weapon on the floor.

"Good choice! Now fire up your radio and tell anybody listening everything's fine. Tell them they should go back to whatever they were doing. The next guard I see aiming a gun at me, you and the girl die. You understand?"

The guard nodded and reached cautiously for the radio clipped to his belt. Roger added, "Tell them it's Colonel TS Crane from the FBI and I've come to ask Mr Baker a few questions. Got it?" Again the guard nodded. "Be authentic."

Atifah was uncomfortable watching the stress in the young girl's eyes while Roger's hand was clamped across her mouth. Such fear she had never witnessed. She knew the girl was their only way of staying alive and held back from intervening.

Then standing like a statue in the entrance, the guard delivered the message to his control room. The large white letters 'FBI' emblazoned on the side of the helicopter helped corroborate his story. After a short while of waiting, no further interruptions were forthcoming. Roger guessed the story had been accepted.

"Ok! Shall we go and see the boss?" He looked into the frightened eyes of the girl. "Where can we find your daddy?" Realizing Roger was not about to release his grip, she pointed up the elaborately curved staircase. They moved cautiously up the wide marble stairway with the guard in front of them. Roger and the girl followed a few steps behind and Atifah behind him. As they rounded the corner onto a wide and ornately decorated landing, a man in a nightrobe came from the opposite direction almost bumping into the guard. He stopped dead as he assessed the situation.

"Mr Macadam!" he half asked, half stated. He was calm and made no effort to do anything, other than stand and talk. His calmness unnerved Roger a little. "I've been expecting you."

"Why? I didn't receive an invitation."

"You're not a stupid man Mr … can I call you Roger?" Roger didn't answer. "I knew you'd reach me eventually. I knew you'd come looking for answers. I don't have them all, but I may be able to answer a few. Follow me!" He turned his back and led the group into an oversized elaborate bedroom with the largest bed Roger had ever seen, positioned centrally along the opposite wall. Roger pushed record on the camcorder in his pocket and placed it unobtrusively on a shelf next to the door.

The 'old guy', as agent England had put it, was a thickset man in his mid-forties. He had an enviable head of dark hair and a round face. He was probably six-two and still as yet unshaven.

"Would you like coffee Roger?" Roger was taken aback by the matter-of-fact way this man was handling the situation. Again Roger remained silent, having difficulty assessing him. "Can I pour for your beautiful wife too?" He cracked a wide grin.

Anger welled up inside Roger and the corner of his mouth twitched. "Oh come now Roger! You have maintained such incredible control up to now. Don't let me down now."

Roger realized this man was playing the same game he had been playing all along and was enjoying it as much as Roger himself had enjoyed it. "Why don't you let the girl go? She's done nothing to you and we both know you aren't going to hurt her." He turned his back on Roger and started pouring coffee from a silver coffee pot on a decorative silver tray.

"How do you know?"

"You've done an excellent job of hurting nobody up to this point. You're not a killer Roger and neither am I. We're the same, you and I."

"I doubt it."

"Really? I've followed your progress with great admiration. I've known your every move because I know what I would do. You don't kill. Let the girl go. Samantha will be very happy to get her daughter back unhurt."

"Samantha?"

"The help."

"This is your maid's daughter?" Roger smiled a knowing smile. "You have photos of you and your wife holding your maid's daughter to the left of the staircase."

"Observant. Very observant." He cracked another wide grin. "Don't hold it against me for trying. She is my daughter after all." He turned holding two cups of coffee. He held one out to Roger.

Roger smiled a wry smile and then pushing the girl down a little too violently, he said to her, "Sit and don't move." With his arm free he took the cup from the burly man standing in his nightgown.

Instead of drinking the cup he leant down and handed it to the girl. "Here drink!"

Baker reacted immediately. "No! Don't drink that." For the first time he became flustered and lost control a little.

Roger looked at him and smiled. "Drink!" he said in a commanding tone. "You saw your daddy pour it. It must be fine."

"Beth! Don't drink it honey. The cup is dirty." Baker fought to regain his composure. He wanted to spring across the room and snatch the cup from the child, but the gun in Roger's hand caused a dilemma for him.

The girl's tear-filled eyes darted between the people in the room, bewildered with what was going on. Roger took the cup from her, stood over her and looked straight into the eyes of the businessman. "Do you think she might drink it if I tell her I will shoot her daddy? Let's stop playing games shall we?"

The momentum of the situation swung in Roger's favor and for the moment Baker was on the back foot. To make matters worse a blond thirty-year-old, also clad in a gown, walked into the room. Recognizable from the photograph he'd seen, Roger knew this to be the lady of the house. She was the splitting image of the young girl. She let out a gasp, then headed for the child, apparently oblivious of the gun in Roger's hand.

Roger was taken by surprise and was not ready for a charge. He might have been knocked over, were it not for Atifah seeing what was happening. She intercepted the woman about six feet from Roger and threw her roughly to the ground. She let out a gasping squeal as the air was forced from her lungs.

Roger glanced at Atifah and assumed command again. "Mrs Baker I presume." She didn't answer. She was still seated on the floor recovering from the impact. Roger looked up at Atifah, thankful for her intervention. "Can you take the girl into the bathroom and console her. I have something to say to these people which is not for young ears." Atifah leant down and took the girl, pulling her to her feet. "Check her for a phone and if there's a window in there, don't leave her alone." He watched as the door closed.

"Please don't hurt her." The woman had her breath back.

"Sit!" Roger pointed at the bed. "You!" He pointed at the guard. "Down on your stomach and hands behind your head." He paused while the guard lay down. "If I see you so much as twitch, you'll die."

Roger turned his attention to the couple on the bed. "Firstly, do not presume to know me. I am not the person I was a few days ago." He was addressing Frank, but was speaking to both of them. "Secondly, you know what I am here for. If I don't get it, I am going to kill the guard, then blow out your knees and elbows, both of you, and you're going to have to sit there in unbearable pain and watch while I rape and slowly kill your daughter."

Roger had won. Fear and worry clouded the eyes of Frank Baker. His calm cockiness was gone and was replaced with terror. His wife, sensing his fear, broke down and started to cry.

"I told you I don't have all the answers you want."

"I only want two things. The man who gave the order to kill my family and the man who pulled the trigger."

"It's not as simple as..."

"The names ..."

"I don't know."

Roger hesitated a long time, as if giving Baker the opportunity to recant his words. "It's a pity. She's a cute kid."

"C'mon Macadam! You're not the type of person to hurt a child." He was pleading.

"A week ago I wasn't. Today, anything's possible." Roger grabbed the woman's ankle and dragged her roughly across the bed. Her gown slipped up revealing a long and shapely leg. She let out a stifled cry of pain as Roger placed the muzzle of the gun hard against her kneecap.

"Stop!" Roger looked up at Baker. "For God's sake man. You can't do that." He looked into Roger's dark expressionless eyes and knew in an instant he was wrong. Roger could and would do it. "Stop! I'll tell you what I know. Don't hurt my family."

Expression returned to Roger's eyes. He let go of the woman's ankle. She shuffled back toward her husband and let out another quiet gasp, this time partly fear, partly relief.

Roger leant back against the opposite wall. "Begin …"

"Firstly, I don't know who gave the order. I mean it. We only know what we need to know."

"Who are we?"

"We? We're just pawns in the game. Some voluntary, some not. Like you, an involuntary pawn."

"Is this the Skull and Bone's society?"

"Ha! Yes and the Bilderberg group. The Illuminati, the KKK, the Nazis. Yes that's us."

"What?"

"We support all these groups. They're our decoys. Our public face."

"Decoys?"

"While the world focuses on these groups, they are oblivious of what is happening under their noses."

"What is happening?"

"You wouldn't believe me if I told you."

Roger was getting tired of the questions. "Try me!"

"We are …"

"Who the hell is 'we'?"

"We don't have a name. All members are handpicked by existing members to create an exclusive international club of the wealthiest people in the world."

"The world?"

"Of course! Money knows no boundaries."

"So who are these members?"

"The wealthiest of the wealthy. Oil barons, heads of state, industrialists. People from every nation. We recruit anybody who will be of benefit to recruit."

"For what reason?"

"Money, power. Whatever we want."

"Power?"

"I'm sure you've heard mention of a new world order. It's been bandied around since the sixties. I think most presidents since Kennedy have mentioned the new world order."

"You own the presidency?"

"Of course. Money owns everything. Occasionally a president starts to show a conscience for the lies he spins and then we remove him."

"Kennedy?"

"And others?"

"Obama?"

"He has no conscience. We decide who gets into power and we decide when he leaves."

"So why me?"

Baker laughed again. "Don't flatter yourself Macadam! It wasn't you, it was just the convenient situation you gave us. When you flew to Nairobi, there were more than fifty people on the same flight, all headed there on errands for us. In fact, twelve people with you on the plane to Africa also shared your visits to Oklahoma and New York as well. We have thirteen people that we could pin the bombings on if we needed to. We have their names, addresses, contact numbers, birthdays, their entire life history and their bank balances. We know every time one of those thirteen individuals leaves the States, where they go and who they go with. We always have a backup plan. You simply presented us with a usable opportunity to merge two projects, coming home married to that young girl in there. How'd your wife take it by the way?"

Anger flared through Roger's being. He had to fight to keep control. "Let's go back to my original question. Who gave the order?"

"I'm in no position to lie to you. I don't know."

"And the triggerman?"

"He's one of ours. An FBI agent. He's ruthless and you won't stand a chance against him. Let it go for your own good."

"Let it go? I want to see him on his knees begging me to end his life."

"Not going to happen. There is not a crueler person in this country. He's highly trained and I have seen him control pain with my own eyes. You won't be able to hurt him, but he will hurt you."

"Everyone has a weakness."

"Not this man."

"Call him here."

"No! You want him? You get away from my family to meet him. I'd sooner die right now at your hands, than risk bringing him here. I mean it. You want him, you go elsewhere. He doesn't simply

305

kill. He kills slowly and painfully and if he thought he was being trapped, he'd kill everyone in the house, just in case." Roger thought about using the girl as a threat, but decided against it. He suspected Baker was telling the truth, or at least some degree of the truth and he hadn't yet reached the point where he would place the family in danger. It would make him as bad as the people he was chasing.

"Ok! How do we do it?"

"What?"

"I want to meet him."

"For what? Do you think you can appeal to his sense of decency, or get him to confess so you can feel better? You don't know what you are dealing with. I'm not going to do it."

Atifah opened the door to the bathroom and walked out. The girl was seated on the floor behind her. She saw the man first and reacted. She jumped, pushing Roger as the large central pane of glass shattered. Roger stumbled forward losing his balance and catching the movement of the man out of the corner of his eye as he fell. Deep in his being something was awakened and pulsed into life. He turned his head and saw a suited man making his way toward the window from the veranda outside. He could see the man's gun was aimed at him and he knew the man had already squeezed the trigger.

Autonomous reaction took over Roger's being and without thinking, he followed through the motion of his fall and rolled. Before he even knew he'd done it, he stood, simultaneously firing six rounds at the centre of the man's chest. It wasn't elegant like in the movies, but it was quick and did the job. One bullet hit the man in the stomach, one in his hip. One grazed the man's shoulder and lodged itself in the wall behind him and two found their way into his left arm. All of these shots would have seriously angered the man, had the first shot not entered his brain through his left eye. The man looked at Roger in shock, then his right eye rolled back and he fell backward onto the veranda outside. In an instant, Roger had summed up what was happening in the entire room. Baker and his wife were still reacting to the breaking glass, the little girl was busy covering her ears and Atifah was already on her way to the floor, relaxed and unmoving.

He bent down and turned her over. She grunted as the pain shot like lightening through her chest. She couldn't breathe and grabbed, clawing at the front of Roger's clothes, as she tried to suck air into her lungs. Roger, seeing the panic in her eyes, knew she'd been hit.

"Calm down!" He looked around for blood but found none. "Relax. You'll be ok." He had no idea whether she would or not and his voice gave away his fears. He ran his hand up her side and his finger found the hole in the bulletproof vest. He opened the vest and checked her side and breathed a sigh of relief when he saw the inside of the vest was intact. "You're ok! You're ok!" he consoled her. "It didn't go through."

Her grip on his shirt collar eased as the meaning of his words sank in. She started to breathe short shallow breaths as she started to relax.

"I thought I'd lost you there." A movement caught his attention and the gun reacted. "DOWN!" Roger screamed at the guard. He'd only raised his head to see if everything was ok, but with Roger's senses heightened and his heart pumping at a rate he'd never experienced, it had looked like he was getting up. His head went back down again.

"I take it back Roger." Baker looked at the gaping hole where his window used to be. "He did have a weakness."

Roger's heart had slowed down, but still pumped like never before. His muscles twitched and his eyes darted around the room. He felt like he'd downed a quart of espresso. He looked down at Atifah again, then stooped to help her as she struggled to sit.

The spring in Roger started to unwind a bit and he started to comprehend what was happening. "He was the one?"

"Yes! FBI agent Mallory. He was on our payroll."

"How'd he know I was here?"

"I called him."

"What?"

"You were getting too close, so I had him move into the guest house. I called him when the helicopter landed."

"You knew I had the helicopter?"

Baker smiled a knowing smile. "No, but I have never had a helicopter land in my garden unannounced before. I knew it was you."

"You seem proud of what you ..."

"It's as you called it, it's a fact. I have no feelings on the matter. No pride, no disgust, no feelings. If I feel that I am something more than my neighbor then so be it. It's not illegal to be a 'me chauvinist' is it?"

Roger smiled a disbelieving half smile and looked resignedly at the man lying on the veranda. "So I've shot the key to finding the person that gave the order to kill my family."

"I'm afraid so."

"Then we're going back to plan A."

"What do you mean?"

"It's simple! I need you to point me to your senior." Roger paused. "I will find the person I'm looking for."

"You're wasting your time Roger. Be satisfied at getting the guy that killed your family. I didn't expect you to do that. Go home and start over."

"Have you forgotten? I'm a wanted criminal. There is no home for me. Besides, I'm only going on your word that he was the one. The word of somebody who openly admits to dealing … in what? I don't even know."

"I'm a businessman. Nothing more." Roger noticed a bead of sweat run down the man's cheek from his temple area. He looked into his eyes and knew he was lying. The uncertainty was gone and he knew the way forward.

"I said plan A! Who's going first?"

Stress returned to the faces of the two on the bed. Roger had played the bluff game a few times now and he was getting good. He moved toward the woman again who screamed a stifled scream and backed away from him as he approached.

"Macadam! For God's sake man. Stop! I can make this go away."

"Not if you don't give the orders."

"I didn't say I don't give orders, I said I didn't give the order to eliminate your family." He was starting to sweat badly now. He realized he had already said too much. He hadn't expected Roger to come out of the meeting with Mallory alive.

Roger stood, poised in thought as if contemplating his next move then shrugged. "Not good enough." He restarted his advance. Once again he grabbed at the ankle of the woman. She squealed and kicked savagely at Roger but missed. Roger stood up. "Up 'til now I hadn't killed anybody. Now I am a murderer. Don't fuck with me woman!" Roger lunged at the woman, grabbing her leg and dragging her across the bed until she slipped off the edge and fell hard onto the carpeted floor. She grunted as the air was once again expelled from her lungs by the fall. Again he placed the muzzle of the pistol against her knee.

"Stop!" Baker was reaching desperation. Roger looked up at him expectantly. He sat silently, deep in thought.

Roger prompted, "You have the power to stop this happening, but happen it will unless you give me what I want."

Baker looked at the young girl seated on the floor of the bathroom as she cowered, covering her head with her hands. She was terrified. Frank Baker wanted it to stop. He wanted Roger to go away. The look on the gunman's face told him it wasn't going to happen.

"Put the gun down. I'll tell you what I know."

Roger backed off and once again the frightened woman scrambled onto the bed and back to her husband.

"We are looking for a reason to take Oman without creating too much hatred for the American government."

Atifah stepped forward. "Why? What is so valuable in Oman? Oil? Gas? We don't have big reserves."

Baker smiled an almost sad smile. "No honey! We're not interested in your oil. Our group is invested in the arms game. Every time somebody goes to war we make money. When America goes to war we make a pile of money." He adjusted his position on the bed. "We don't even want Oman. It's a stepping stone. We want war against Saudi. There's nothing better than going to war against a desert. Do you realize how many bombs have to be dropped on a desert to create an impact?"

Roger interjected, "War kills innocent people."

"People die every day. Some naturally of festering and painful disease. Others have their insides splattered all over the road. The lucky ones end up in frail care, pissing in their beds and not knowing who they are. We're not doing anything which won't happen anyway."

"That's how you justify it? They're going to die anyway?" Roger felt the anger surfacing again. "Your wife and daughter are going to die one day. Why'd you get so stressed when I wanted to shoot them?"

Baker looked down at his hands folded in his lap. Roger pushed, "How long has this been going on? What scale are we talking about?"

Baker smiled a resigned smile. "Vietnam! Maybe even before, but definitely Vietnam." Roger looked on in horror as the story unfolded. "I have heard it goes back to before Jesus was born. I have no knowledge of the start, but it's old."

"So your group financed the bombs and guns used to attack North Vietnam?"

"My group financed both sides. The longer the war was fought, the more money we made." He paused. "And the scale is bigger than you can imagine."

"Hold on! You financed weapons fired on American soldiers."

"Like I said, we're all pawns in the game. Besides, have you got insurance, savings in the bank?" Roger didn't answer. "They invest in the same companies, so don't get all high and mighty. We're all guilty of profiting from war."

He continued, "Why only make half the profits? Look at the DRC. There's huge potential there. Multiple groups are killing each other. If people are so stupid that they can't sit down and talk … it's not my problem."

"What are you talking about, 'not your problem'? You are financing death and destruction. You are financing terrorism. How can you say it's not your problem?"

"Don't be naive Roger! They will fight anyway. Somebody will sell them guns and if they can't get guns they'll use sticks. Why shouldn't I make some profit?"

Roger was dumbfounded.

"Look at South Africa. They were at war with themselves since the sixties. Now, the same terrorists the government of the day fought are running the country. How many young kids were taken from school and conscripted, only to die fighting for a cause they had no interest in. For what? Don't judge me for wanting to make a bit of money from the brainless bastards running these banana republics."

"Do you even hear yourself? How do you justify supplying America's enemies with weapons?"

"Think about it Roger. America is the most powerful country in the world. The only enemies America has are the ones we manufacture." He saw the disbelief on Roger's face. "I told you our group is not American, it's international. We're working toward a new world order, not a new American order. We're taking over the world in a way that will leave people begging us to take it over when we're ready."

"How can you possibly have so much clout?"

"Did you vote for Obama?"

"I don't vote."

"Wise! The Bush-Obama follow on was an experiment. Hell! If we can put a black man in the White House we can do anything. I think two terms will be sufficient though."

"Obama is one of you?"

"Make a list of all Obama's pre-election promises and tick off those he has implemented. He's a goddamn politician. He'll go where the money is. He'll say what he gets paid to say and he'll do what he gets paid to do. If by some strange twist he grows a conscience, he has family he'll need to protect. It doesn't take much of a 'close-call' to get his attention."

Roger's head swam as he took all this in. The enormity of the situation was beyond comprehension. Baker was smug as he saw the horror in Roger's eyes, but then started to worry a little as he saw the disbelief leave and the greyness return.

"I'm going to die aren't I?" Roger spoke.

"What are you talking about?"

"You wouldn't be telling me all this if I was going to walk out and tell the world."

"Nobody's going to believe you. This has been going on for decades. Don't you think we have the ability to cover it all up by now?"

"What if I go to the papers or CNN?"

"You might find a local rag willing to run the story, but nobody would believe it. This is too big to break the story in a local hick town rag. If you're thinking about your girlfriend at CNN, she's already headed for the unemployment line. We own everything. Besides, even if you managed to find somebody interested with the balls to run it, it'll be your word against mine."

Roger realized there was no turning back. He was into something big and he was in deeper than he had imagined. He knew the camcorder was running and there might never be another opportunity to get this story out.

"Ok! So humor me. What was my input into 9/11?"

"At this point it's all conjecture."

"What are the assumptions then?"

"You and your good wife over there are part of a wealthy family in Oman. Records have been discovered to prove you paid for the pilots training."

"But I didn't. How can you prove that?"

"They're transactions. A good database man can work miracles."

"But I didn't do it."

"You did. Your balance hasn't changed, but when you go to your account history you'll find debits and credits between your account, an Omani bank account and a flight training school. I told you. We own everything."

"I'm getting tired of this." Roger was starting to feel the need for personal revenge seemed to pale by comparison to the size of this story. If what Baker was saying was true, this was going to be a battle simply to stay alive. He didn't want Baker to see his fears creeping in. "I want the name and location of your senior. I want the person that killed my family."

"It won't do any good ..."

"Stop!" Roger looked Baker in the eyes without blinking for a long while. Baker started to fidget. Roger spoke slowly and with purpose. "If the next words to come out of your mouth are not a name and directions, then all of you die here slowly and painfully. You'll go last."

-- o --- o0o --- o --

"Take her to the chopper." Roger had what he wanted and now he pointed for Atifah to take the young girl.

"What are you doing?" Baker started to stand.

"Back on the bed." Roger pointed the gun at the Bakers. "You think I'm an idiot. If I think a single soul is suspicious of my arrival your kid takes a dive."

"Didn't you hear me? I can make it go away. You don't need to do this. Leave my kid, take me along."

Roger made his way toward the shelf where the camcorder was still running. "I would've given my life for my kid in an instant. I wasn't given the choice." He stopped for a second and turned to Frank Baker. "An evil man once said we're all just pawns in the game. Some voluntary, some not."

"She's a kid Macadam."

"And it's in your power to keep her alive." He reached for the camcorder.

"What the hell …?"

"No longer your word against mine now, is it?"

"Don't do this Macadam. There's nowhere for you to run and nowhere you can hide. My organization is big, powerful and around every corner. You'll never escape them."

"I'm sure it's in your power to have the chopper blown out of the air. You are going to have to make difficult choices. Daughter … Organization." Roger made the action of balancing in the air.

-- o --- oOo --- o --

It was a short distance to Lee Miller's mansion by air, even with the looping detour. Situated south of Dallas on a large ranch, outside of Corsicana, the house equaled Baker's house in grandeur, but seemed smaller. Once again keeping low and bypassing as many buildings as possible, they flew in toward the front of the house intending to set down on the expansive front lawn.

Roger felt uneasy as they approached. Something was wrong. Something didn't feel right. "Wait! Circle round the building."

Atifah opened the throttle a moment before setting down and lifted up again. They circled the lonesome building, fifty feet from the ground. Roger checked the roof and the grounds around, but saw no sign of anybody. Maybe that was it? There was nobody around. Whatever the cause, Roger was uneasy and the hairs on his neck stood up.

There were gardens to the left and right of the house and outbuildings to the rear. They could only set down on the front lawn. He signaled to Atifah. "Ok! Set down in front, but keep your eyes open. Go in slow."

Once again, she circled to the front of the house and started the slow descent. The helicopter was no more than ten feet from the ground when Roger saw what had bothered him. A window in the upper floor was open. Every other window in the building was closed. As they had circled overhead, Roger had seen the air conditioner units nestled on the flat portion of the roof out of view from the front of the house. There was no reason to have a window open. He reacted!

"Back up! Back up!" Atifah heard the panic in his voice, but didn't understand the command. She looked at Roger for clarity. He pointed upward. "Go back up!" Once again she opened the throttle and the craft lifted back into the air.

"Sorry! I wasn't sure whether you wanted me to go backward or back up in the air."

"No problem! Circle around a bit. I think Mr Baker phoned ahead."

Roger climbed into the back with the girl. "Your daddy doesn't like you too much does he?" She didn't answer. Without headphones on to muffle the noise of the engine, she didn't hear a word he said.

Roger took two grenades and using his duct tape, strapped them to either side of the girl's neck. She didn't protest, but once again burst into tears. He felt no compassion for the girl. He thought only of the task at hand.

Next, he took off the two laces from his worn sneakers and bound the loose sneakers to his feet using more duct tape. He shook the shoulder of the sobbing, unstable child and motioned her to sit again.

Atifah spoke to him, "What are you up to Roger? What do you want me to do?"

He scanned the flat prairie around. "Set down again, but have the front pointing in the direction of the lake over there." He pointed.

"Ok!" She started toward the grass again.

"When you've set down climb through the back. Don't get out your side door."

"No problem!"

As they descended, Roger tried to catch a glimpse inside the open window but he saw nothing.

Once they were down, Atifah killed the motor and climbed through to the rear. "Roger! What have you done?" She reached for the girl.

"Leave her!" The command was clear and decisive. She backed off immediately. "There's a marksman in the upstairs window. We step out of this helicopter and we're both dead." He handed her the dirty string. "Tie this around your right wrist." He was busy tying the other cord around his own left wrist. "I hope Baker wants his daughter back."

Once they were finished Roger tied the other end of the string to the thin wire loop on the small pin holding the handle of

314

the grenade in place. Atifah could not contain herself. She withdrew her hand. "Look at her Roger! She is terrified."

"We don't have a choice."

"We can fly away right now. Frank Baker said he could end this."

"Think! If Baker could end this then he's the decision maker. If he's not the decision maker then he can't end this. He's buying time. Do you understand?"

Atifah continued unabated. "We can take her back home. So what if he's the decision maker? We go back to our old life and …"

"You still have an old life. Mine's gone."

She stopped in her tracks. "I'm sorry! I wasn't thinking."

Roger knelt in front of Atifah and looked her in the eyes. For the first time since he heard of the death of his family, Atifah saw warmth in Roger's eyes. "I promised you I would do my best to pull you through this unhurt." He paused. "I always do my best to deliver on my promises." He smiled a comforting smile. "Besides, you saved my life back there. I owe you my life."

She smiled a little and looked him in the eyes. "Don't worry. I'll be collecting."

"In the meantime we have limited options. I think there is a marksman in the upper floor window waiting to take us out. We can't both hide behind this little girl and I'm sure the marksman will have instructions not to hit the girl." He turned his attention to the girl. "Honey, listen to me! Do you know what I have taped to your neck?"

She shook her head slowly from side to side between sobs. "Good! We're going to hold your shoulders like this." The girl shuddered and let out a small stifled whimper as Roger grabbed her t-shirt. "We're not going to hurt you! We only need you to help us get inside. Understand?" The girl was in shock and didn't answer. "While our hands are on your shoulder you'll be safe." There was still no answer from the terrified child.

Roger continued to tie Atifah's string to the grenade. "Hold onto her shirt and do not let go for any reason." Atifah nodded. "If she trips we need to hold her up or we're all dead."

Roger attached his own lace to the pin on the other side and grasped the girls shirt. He adjusted the strings to ensure any onlookers could see them. "Ok! Let's do this."

They stepped out of the chopper on the side facing away from the building and then circled around the aircraft bringing Roger into view first. He knew there was a risk, as the girl would only come into view fractionally later, but he was sure the marksmen would wait until he could take them both out. No shot rang out. Roger was relieved. They made their way to the elaborate front door positioned at the center of the house. Roger tried the door. It was locked.

"Get behind me." The two girls moved round in an arc putting Roger between them and the door. Roger raised his pistol, aimed it at the lock where the slide entered the wall and fired. The little girl shuddered and let out another squeal as the gun fired, lifting her hands to cover her head. Roger kicked the door a few times and it eventually swung open.

"Let's go."

Roger entered first, ready to take the first bullet as if it might have made a difference. If he was shot all three of them would have died anyway. Similar to Baker's mansion, this house had two curved staircases leading from the lobby up to the first floor landing. Making assumptions about the upstairs window, he made for the stairs. When they reached about halfway up the stairs, a voice rang out from somewhere up on the floor above. "Mr Macadam! I am unarmed and I am coming out into view."

Roger stopped and all three of them froze. Not knowing whether to answer or not, Roger aimed the pistol at the top of the steps and waited. A balding man came slowly around the corner with his hands held high in the air.

"Mr Macadam! My name is Hilton. I am Mr Miller's butler. He asked me to show you to his room." He started to turn.

"Wait!" Hilton stopped in mid-step. If Hilton was more than a butler, he didn't want to give the man time to prepare himself around the corner. "Wait there until we reach the landing." Hilton didn't move, not even looking around at the intruders. The three of them made their way up the steps. Once they were two steps behind the 'alleged' butler, he was told to continue.

Roger didn't have any preconceived ideas about Lee Miller, but nothing would have prepared him for what he saw. Miller was seated in the corner of an elaborate white bedroom with the thickest white pile carpet he'd had ever seen. The smell of tobacco smoke hung thick in the air and Miller hissed as he drew on the oxygen mask in his right hand. He leaned heavily onto his right elbow on the arm of the wheelchair.

"Come in Mr Macadam!" he grunted in a deep, hoarse, smoker's voice.

Roger started the camcorder recording and then eased into the room with the two girls in tow.

Lee Miller was about seventy-years-old, but appeared much older. The fifty-five years of smoking had taken its toll on his voice, his lungs and his skin. Roger thought him to be at least eighty-five.

"My God man!" he croaked as he looked at the grenades mounted below the ears of the young teenager. "Take those off her. She's a kid." The excitement caused Miller to enter into a bout of wet, chest heaving and breathless coughing, which was ended by wiping his mouth on the whitest handkerchief Roger had ever seen. The white brilliance of the linen in the room was offset by the dirty image of this old man sitting in his wheelchair. Roger waited for him to regain composure.

"You have a marksman in the building. She remains armed." Roger was blunt and to the point.

"Hilton! Escort the gunmen from the building. I'm not going to be responsible for this girl's death." Hilton left the room. Miller addressed Roger, "I had two gunmen in the building. You'll be able to see when they cross the lawn below this window. Once they're gone, please release this girl. She's traumatized." He spoke through the mask in between sucking the oxygen into his damaged lungs.

"That's Baker's girl isn't it?"

"Correct." Roger watched as the two gunmen crossed the lawn toward a large black Chevy. "How do I know there's nobody else in the building?" He turned toward Miller.

"You don't, do you." He drew on the oxygen again. "You said there was one. I told you there were two. Sit behind her in the corner if you feel better. Take those things off her neck."

Roger could see Miller was concerned for the child, so he complied, pulling the tape gently from her skin.

"Do you mind if I smoke?"

Roger looked at Atifah in disbelief. "I'd prefer you didn't."

"All right!" he hesitated, a little disappointed. "So! What is it you want to know Mr Macadam?"

"I want to know the name and location of the person that gave the order to execute my family - and I want you to confirm the name of the person that pulled the trigger."

"What do you feel you will gain by knowing?"

"I'll decide at the time."

"What if I told you I gave the order? How would it help you?"

Roger was perplexed. "Did you give the order?"

Miller smiled. "Mr Macadam! I understand Frank Baker gave you an unofficial and unexpected rundown of our organization." Roger remained silent. "You must realize this organization is powerful. It transcends manmade boundaries. It's cross cultural, cross language, cross border, cross everything. It is the only truly international organization of its kind. It means wherever you go, you will not be able to escape. Why don't you go back home and live out the rest of your days in peace? What has happened is unfortunate, but you cannot win." Miller pulled again on the oxygen.

"Unfortunate?" Roger spoke slowly and with disgust. "My family is dead. They died at the hands of somebody who could pull innocent people from their beds and execute them."

"Executions happen all the time. Saddam was executed a short while back and everybody was happy."

"He was sentenced to death for killing other people. He was a bad guy."

"By whose reckoning?"

"What are you on about?"

"Suppose I told you I gave the order and Hilton, over there, pulled the trigger. What would you say?"

Roger was stumbling, but he pulled himself together. "I'd kill you both."

"That's what I thought." He paused again. "Baker gave me to you as a gift. I'm expendable because I don't have much longer anyway. I am able to tell you, the trigger man was a heartless person working for the FBI. Went by the name of Mallory."

"He's dead."

"I know! Baker told me. He didn't expect you to survive the encounter and hence he gave you more information than he should have. Don't draw conclusions too quickly Macadam. Listen to what I'm saying." Miller paused to catch his breath. "This organization doesn't have leaders or a hierarchy as such. It has a lot of individuals with a single purpose. We meet in conventions, chapters, work groups and committees like any good organization and leaders are picked arbitrarily for each gathering."

"What is the purpose?" Roger was intent on learning as much as possible.

"Money of course! Obscene amounts of money." He stopped again and hissed as he drew on the mask.

Roger was getting impatient with the stopping. "So who killed my family?"

"I've told you already. You weren't listening."

"You're talking in riddles and I don't have time for this."

"Macadam! Listen to me. This is as far as you are going. I'm not going to lead you onward to anybody else. Baker gave me to you because I'm expendable." He paused again then repeated himself. "You will go no further in this organization."

Roger was taking it in too slowly. He paused for a long while then said, "Go on! This organization of yours …?"

"Ok! We don't need leadership, because we are all focused on a joint goal. We know what we want and we don't care who has to be hurt … or who dies … to achieve our goals. As long as we don't step on each other of course!"

"Why are you telling me this?"

Lee Miller smiled. "About thirty-five years ago, I'd had enough. I'd made more money than I had ever planned and I had everything to live for. I was thirty-five-years-old and I ruled the world. I was living in this same mansion and had everything going for me. I spoke to people within the organization and said I wanted out. It was over … a few days later, I arrived home from a trip to Washington and my wife and daughter were both dead. Raped and shot execution style."

"I'm sorry. I know how it feels."

"No you don't! You have somebody else to hunt down, I only had myself to blame."

"What do you mean?"

"I wasn't new to the organization. In fact, I'd been to Washington to lure possible presidential candidates into the fold. I was doing the bidding of this organization and I was doing it with enjoyment. I knew what I was dealing with. I was naive enough to think I could resign … like it was a nine-to-five job." Miller laughed which set off a bout of raspy coughing.

Roger waited until he stopped. "Why would such an organization exist?"

"I have a theory. I don't know you'll like it, but it's the only logical answer I can find. Believe me, I've asked myself this question every day for thirty-five years." He paused again while he drew bottled air into his lungs. "Remember, as farfetched as this might sound, it's conjecture. I have no proof, only speculation.

"The same day I discovered the bodies of my family, two government agents, not too different from your Agent Mallory, came into my house. They gave me a video and said only two words before they left, 'Be warned!' Then they left. After I'd watched the video, I knew I was a partner for life. I knew these people could do what they want."

"What was on the video?"

"Me! Raping and murdering my own wife and child."

"Did you …"

"Of course not! They manufactured the video with look-alikes or make-up or something. Remember it was the mid-eighties. Only Hollywood could have the technology to pull something like that together. Even I couldn't see the difference. To this day, I don't know if I was watching my family getting murdered or a mock-up." Miller became emotional and paused to breathe again and pull himself together. "It was real and after they were shot, they landed exactly as the police photographed them. It would have stood up in court. I was trapped. Either I carried out the bidding of the group, or I faced an execution of my own. I still don't know if I made the right choice."

"There must be direction coming from somewhere. Who decided your family should die?"

"Don't you get it?" Miller was starting to sound a little frustrated and tired. "Nobody in the organization knows where the direction comes from. One day it will come from known sources, other times from somebody new."

"How do you know the instructions are legitimate and from legitimate members."

"You know!"

"What?"

"You know! You simply know."

"What kind of people would join a group like this?"

"Ambitious and money hungry people." His eyes saddened as he said the words. "You know! I saw a documentary a couple of years ago where they were discussing smokers. A nightclub owner was being interviewed and he said something that stayed with me. He said smokers are festive people."

"So!"

"I realized he was wrong. Smokers aren't festive, but they are a certain type of person."

"Again! Why are you telling me this? I don't smoke."

"I know! It takes a special type of person to be able to suck on fumes, knowing they will kill you. You have to have a dimmed view of the future."

"Where are you going with this?" Roger's voice raised a bit, showing his frustration.

"Don't you see? If you don't value your future, you don't care about it. If you don't care about it you'll be willing to live for current pleasures at the expense of your future. If that's the case, you'll spend more money now and ignore future needs and hence appear more festive." Miller paused again. He was talking too much. "It's a type of person. Like this organization. It's made up of a certain type of people. That's why we're of one mind."

Miller took a long draw on the oxygen mask and then dropped it in his lap. He leaned uncomfortably to his right and opened a small drawer on a brilliant white writer's desk next to him. He reached into the drawer and withdrew a small, brilliantly shiny hand gun. Roger saw this and whipped his arm out leveling his own weapon at the man's head.

"Relax Mr Macadam. If I were going to kill you, I'd have only sent one marksman away. There's only one bullet in here and it's reserved for me. This is long overdue."

He saw the perplexed look on Roger's face and continued, "I have emphysema and my lungs are riddled with cancer, which has spread to every major organ. None of it is as bad as the cancer I have profited from for the last few decades."

Roger relaxed when he realized what he was talking about. "So help me take them down."

"Take them down?" He placed the gun in his lap and the oxygen mask back over his face. "I thought you were intelligent, but you don't hear what I am saying do you? This organization has eyes everywhere. You can't escape them. The eyes are those of kings and business leaders. Or they might belong to a clerk in the bank. They're all greedy self-serving individuals wanting to benefit from the organization, but they're all hooked in so the organization can benefit from them when it needs. There are no memos, no letters and no emails. All instructions are by word of mouth. There is no paper trail. All transactions are carried out from some individual's bank account because they know the money will come back again. It's the perfect cover. No proof."

"There must be something we can do."

"There is! Go back to Frank Baker. Give him your video and let him end it for you."

"What can he do?"

"He can make it all go away. He can get the word out and they'll find evidence to prove you didn't do anything wrong. It'll be in the news for two days and by next week you're yesterday's news."

"Why can't you do it?"

"I told you already. Frank Baker gave me to you because I'm expendable. If you survived the marksmen, then I was to confess everything to you so you could end my life for me. Within an hour, word would go out and you would be hunted down and killed. We could end this whole episode free of mess and it would all be forgotten in a week."

Roger sat back, his brow creased with worry. "Why are you telling me this? Why have you told me ... all this?" He looked over at the two girls. The worry etched on their faces and the innocence fast disappearing from their eyes. "Why have they been involved?"

"Macadam. Listen to me. There is nothing left for me, but I have given you the information you need to live. Why? I don't know. Maybe I'm trying a last ditch effort to score points with my maker."

"You think your maker will forgive you?"

"No. Not at all, but it's my last hope." He paused again to let the aching subside. "I told you I had a theory as to why this organization exists. It's a theory, nothing more. You can treat it with as big a pinch of salt as you desire."

"A few years ago I was in Johannesburg South Africa. A grubby little street kid came up to my car begging for money. He was thin and drawn and in his hand he had a plastic bottle containing a little glue. I dismissed him and chased him away from my car. As I looked back, I saw him sucking on the bottle. I didn't think of him again until a month later." Miller's chest rattled as he drew on the oxygen. "I was in Rio and sure enough another kid, could have been the same one for all I knew, came up to my car with the same plastic bottle in the same hand." He paused again as Roger looked on wondering where this theory was going.

"It's a worldwide problem. So?"

"I know! Don't you see? We all accept it's a worldwide issue and we close our minds to anything else. Why is it a worldwide problem?"

"What do you mean?"

"You have two destitute kids separated by a few thousand miles of ocean. They've never met. The people they know have never met. They've probably never been to school, probably can't even read. And yet they both know how to suck on glue to destroy their brain cells. Who would benefit enough to teach this to kids. Glue manufacturers, store owners, drug pushers?

"None of them Mr Macadam. Nobody would benefit enough to sell glue to street kids. Drug pushers won't get the markup they would from drugs. Storeowners might turn a blind eye to the odd scruffy kid, but he won't chance getting caught pushing and the industrialist would sell millions of tubes of glue. The amount these kids buy wouldn't affect their bottom line."

"So what's your theory?"

"It's demonic!"

"You kept me hanging on for angels and demons?"

"I told you it's a theory, but think about it. You yourself asked why this organization would exist. Not only exist but persist. It hooks in world leaders, business leaders, entertainment leaders, news leaders, church leaders and basically anybody willing to do the bidding of its leader."

"It's leader? You're talking about the bad guy? Satan! Come on Miller. Give me a little credit."

"… or one of his lackeys. If you can come up with another suggestion, let me in on it. Did you go to Sunday school?"

"No! I never had the pleasure." Roger was getting tired of the mumbo jumbo.

"Me too, but for the last thirty years I have searched for the answer and one way or another I ended up with the Bible in my hand." A strange calm came over Miller and for a while the rattling in his chest was almost inaudible. "Sure, I used to go to church before, but it was a Sunday excursion for image and for the perception of stability. All the members go to church, synagogue, mosque, or temple, whatever. It was only when I started reading, really reading, I found a whole different story to what they teach at the pulpit."

"Everybody knows that."

"Are you sure? Do you *really* know that?"

Roger paused and waited for the old man.

"Here's a quick biblical knowledge test for you."

"I said I didn't go to Sunday school."

"I know, but this should be easy for you. How many wise men visited the baby Jesus as he lay in the stable?"

"Are you for real?"

"How many?"

"Three! The three kings! Everyone knows that. Where are you going with this?"

Miller smiled. "If you remember nothing else from our meeting, remember this because this is what started me thinking. No wise men visited Jesus while he was in the stable. An unnumbered group of men visited Jesus when he was living in a house. Go away and read it. They are referred to as magi. To the best of our knowledge they were Zoroastrian priests from Media or Persia. Our churches, our schools, our media, even our Christmas cards give us the picture of three kings carrying gifts. Hell! We've even given them names, but the fact is that we have no clue how many there were."

Roger was deep in thought.

Miller continued, "And we don't know when this took place, but we do know, based on the information provided by the magi, that Herod slaughtered all infants up to the age of two."

"Why are you telling me this?" Rogers voice was less certain as he thought through what Miller was saying.

"Everything is not the way it seems. Our leaders have fed us lies, lots of lies, for reasons beyond my knowledge. Maybe you can work it out. Look around you. Almost every person making it big in Hollywood, music, in business, in politics, hell, even in religion, all have one thing in common. They teach that what's wrong is good and what's right, biblically right, is bad.

"Almost everybody earning more than five or ten bar per annum are members of my organization. Last year, for the first time in history we had every position on the Forbes 100 list." He made a thoughtful pause. "Doesn't it sound strange to you? The organization is getting stronger."

Roger guessed this was the mind of a dying man, meandering through the alleyways of his guilt. Miller saw it in Roger's eyes. "I know what you are thinking. I'm not telling you this to sell you a religion. I'm not going to thrust a Bible in your hand. I'm telling you this because I believe there is only one way out for you. I told you the organization is powerful. There must be a force feeding it, directing it. It knows things. If you don't do what I say both of you will be dead within days. The organization knows where you are and it will come and get you."

Roger was not fazed by the news. He had been on the run for long enough to feel confident. "I'll take my chances."

"Then you will be dead. Take this from an insider, up 'til now you have been more valuable to the organization by being on the run. Now you're threatening the status quo. What you do with this information is up to you, but unless you listen and take my advice, you will both be dead. I told you this organization's eyes are everywhere. They're probably closing in as we speak."

Roger thought about the trapped agents and how long the battery would last. He started to see the old man's point. Whether he was making sense or not, the enemies could well be closing in.

"You're right! We may be running out of time. What do I do?"

"I told you. Go back to Baker and make a deal with him. Give him his daughter and your disk. Stop your threat on the organization and you'll be free."

"You mean make a deal with the devil?"

The old man grinned. "Now you're getting it."

"So you're not going to tell me who gave the order to kill my family?"

"I told you Macadam! The one that can make it go away."

"Frank Baker?"

"Who else can make it go away, but the one that put it there in the first place? He gave me to you as a gift so you could shoot me and they could close in and take you out … permanently."

Roger thought for a second, his mind spinning with the dilemma of making a deal with the person ordering the death of his family. Should he take out Baker when he sees him again, or exchange Bakers life for his and Atifah's? The dormant anger started to resurface.

"You're telling me this to save your own skin." As he spoke the words, Roger realized how illogical his words were. This man was sitting with a pistol in his lap waiting to take his own life.

"No Macadam. I'm telling you this to save yours. No other reason."

Roger couldn't think straight. His mouth corners twitched with anger. He motioned to Atifah – "Strap the grenades back on the girl." The little girl's eyes widened in terror. "We're not going to walk back into a trap at Baker's place."

"Is it necess …"

"Yes it's necessary. If we live, the girl will live." Roger felt no empathy for the child and had no feelings for the possibility of the girl dying. He turned back to Lee Miller. "What are you going to do?"

"You know what I'm going to do. This has been a long time coming and I think maybe I waited for this day."

"How do I know they won't come after me after I've handed over the disk?"

"Individually, the members of this organization are all upstanding citizens like you and me. They are led by a mysterious unchanging mindset, maybe demonic possession, I'm not sure. If you conclude a deal with Baker and he gets the word out, you'll be free by next week."

"There's a lot I don't understand."

"There's a lot you'll never understand. Remember what I said, if you choose any path but the one I've given you, you'll both be dead within days." The old man could see the thoughts going around in Roger's mind. "You're making the right decision."

"I haven't made any decision yet."

Lee Miller just smiled.

Roger turned to lead the two girls out of the room. At the doorway he stopped and turned back to Miller. "So why Oman?"

"Oman was to be a stepping stone into Saudi."

"I know, but why?"

"PRS. Problem, reaction, solution. It's all so simple yet alarmingly profitable. We create a problem, there's a reaction and we provide a solution, just like 9/11 allowed us to take Afghanistan and Iraq.

"It seemed logical at first to go for Iran but on later reflection, Iran has too many borders. We started the war machine in the direction of Iran, but soon realized it was more profitable to go into Saudi. With Iraq to the north and the little state of Jordan sandwiched between Iraq and Israel, we could easily hold the northern border. In the south, Yemen would fold once Oman was taken. We would control all access to Saudi. Saudi is huge and aggressive. It would take years of war to strangle them."

"Strangle them?"

"Cut off their ..."

"I know what strangle means, I'm asking why."

"It's slower, takes more troops and generates more money."

"All this is about money?"

"Everything is about money. Money and power. The organization owns more than ninety-seven percent of the total world wealth. We wheel and deal in people's lives every day. It's a sick world we live in."

"You mean the controllers of the world are sick."

"The Bible says it in the first book of John. The whole world lies in the power of the evil one." He dropped his head as he choked up. "I can't support the evil one anymore. I have ensured my staff will benefit from my death and the balance will go to various charities around the US."

Miller, for the first time was looking relaxed. "I don't suppose it will be any comfort to you Mr Macadam, but even though I had nothing to do with your case, I am truly sorry for the way things have turned out." A tear ran down his cheek and his eyes clouded over. He lifted his hand and waved to Roger, telling him to get going.

Roger turned again and without looking back, headed down the elaborate staircase. As they crossed the lawn toward the chopper, he heard the crack of a pistol shot from the upstairs window. He didn't look back. He felt no pity, no remorse, nothing at all. Anger was building inside of him.

-- o --- oOo --- o --

"Slow down the approach. We need to talk." Roger looked around at the small girl strapped in the seat in the back area. He spoke like he was about to discuss the state of their marriage, or tell her he'd had an affair. Atifah eased back on the stick and the level of the helicopter adjusted accordingly. They had finished the long, low flight around Dallas back toward Baker's lakeside property and were now approaching from the opposite side. The lake was picturesque behind the mansion in the distance, but neither of them noticed.

Atifah didn't answer so Roger continued, "You heard what Lee Miller had to say about this organization and what could happen." He didn't give her an opportunity to answer. "I'm undecided about how I'll react when I look into Baker's eyes knowing what I now know. Do you understand?"

"Of course!"

"If what Miller said is true, then it might not be in your best interests to be with me when I take the girl inside." He paused while she took in what he was saying. "It might be better for you to take the chopper south and try to cross over the Mexico border. If you can, you may be able to get a message to the Sultan to pick you up. You can start over."

She didn't hesitate with her thoughts. "Roger! I will tell you something. It may not go down well with you at this time, but it needs to be said."

"Go on!"

"I made you promise you'd protect me the best you could and I appreciate the way you have looked after me. You may never come to see me as anything but a young girl thrown into your life at a bad time. I understand. But I see you as my husband. If the truth be known I have come to like you deeply. Maybe even love you."

The tremor in her voice unnerved Roger a little. He kept his eyes forward and she immediately sensed his discomfort. "I'm sorry if I am shocking you when you are about to go into battle, but you need to know this so it makes sense when I say this. You protected me without question. You trusted me and stuck by me without knowing a thing about me. Now I will stick by you whatever happens. We live together, or we die together."

Roger's head was reeling from her words. Initially he could say nothing. For what seemed like a long while, they flew in silence. Then after a while, Roger spoke again, "Before you make such a sacrifice, think seriously. You do realize, even if we survive this, there is no chance of a relationship between us. It's not on the cards … at all."

"Of course."

"Then why?"

"I told you. I can't help my feelings."

"It doesn't make any sense."

"They're feelings. They never make sense."

"You're sure?"

"Absolutely! No doubts at all. We live together or we die together." Roger shook his head in disbelief. He knew any decision to take out Frank Baker had been dealt an additional complication.

"Ok! Let's go. Circle round and approach over the …" His words were cut short. Something he'd seen out of the corner of his eye caused the hairs to rise on his neck. He spun his head around and caught the glint of the sun reflecting off the shiny black roof of a large automobile parked between the trees about five hundred yards off to their left. His eyes focused as a puff of white smoke exploded next to the vehicle. Before Roger realized what was happening, the Soviet made RPG-7 shell had already covered half the distance to the helicopter. There was no time to sound a warning. He reacted without thought and without calculation. Roger thrust out his foot knocking the joystick out of Atifah's hand.

At an altitude of a couple of hundred feet this would have scared Atifah and caused her to worry about being able to recover. Hovering slowly at only twenty feet above the ground, there was no time to be concerned. The aircraft pitched violently to the right and twisted with neck jarring g-force, then slipped sideways off its table of downward moving air. The grenade had been destined for their space, but caught the spinning blades of the rear rotor and exploded, lacerating the rear of the fuselage. Inside they weren't even aware. It was already too late for the loss of their tail rotor to affect their flight path as the spinning overhead blade sliced through the small branches of the trees they had planned to fly around.

The blade ploughed up the ground below them, shattering and shooting metallic pieces in all directions, as the craft pitched on its side inbetween two trees. They were in no position to wonder what might have happened had they struck one of the trees.

The lightweight fuselage cracked with bone jarring ferocity, as it landed on its right hand side a couple of yards from where they'd been when Roger first saw the puff of smoke.

Roger was dazed. He hadn't expected the landing to be as hard as it was. "Are you ok?" The dust swirled around inside the cockpit as the helicopter lay still and silent on its side, the way it had landed. The whirlwind of the previous two seconds was gone. Roger was still strapped in his seat and dangled precariously above Atifah.

329

She started to move, stunned at what happened. "What … I didn't …?"

"No time. We have to move." Roger looked around at the young girl who hung limply in her seat, the two grenades looking like huge black swellings on the side of her neck. For the first time Roger felt pity for the kid. He pushed the button on his seat belt and fell roughly onto Atifah. She grunted from the impact. "Come on! We need to move. There are agents moving in."

The word 'agent' had undergone a degree of programming in her brain of recent times and she shook herself into motion. Roger climbed to the rear and helped the stirring child out of her seat.

Roger climbed out first looking back in the direction of the agents. He could see the two black suited figures running at near full speed down the gentle slope stretching up to the left of the house. Ahead of them a German shepherd was bouding towards the helicopter. It would be on them in a few seconds.

Roger braced himself and lifted both girls through the open door. "Quickly! To the trees." Atifah half dragged, half led the small girl into the trees. "Go!" Roger prompted from behind.

The little girl stumbled and Atifah looked like she was going to stop. "Don't worry! I have her." He scooped up the little girl and ran with her in his arms. Hearing a bark from the dog, Roger guessed it was getting close. "Up the tree!" The effort caused his words to wheeze a little. Atifah obeyed without questioning. As he reached the tree a short distance behind her, she turned and grasped at the girl as she was lifted onto the low branches of the old oak. He didn't stop to see how their climb panned out. In one motion Roger spun around, pulled the pistol from his belt, and loaded the weapon as the large short-haired German shepherd burst into view only thirty feet away.

Unsure of how dogs were trained, in one of those fleeting, spontaneous thoughts, he opted to keep the gun out of sight. The dog was on him in a flash and leapt from only a few feet away. Roger raised his left arm in defence and simultaneously whipped his right arm round in front of him. As the huge jaws clamped onto his left arm, he shot the pistol upward into the soft fleshy part under the dog's throat. He watched it close its eyes as the bullet exited through the top of its head.

It had been an instant, but had felt like forever. Then the follow-through came. The impact of the eighty-five pound dog at full speed was staggering. He was bowled over like a pin in a bowling alley and the two bodies crashed into the trunk of the old oak with a force Atifah felt in the low branches. Dazed again, he struggled to his feet. Blood was already dripping from the wound in his arm. He staggered like a drunk. "Let's go." The trees swirled around him as he battled to regain his thoughts.

The two girls were already on the ground, the smaller of the two looking at the corpse of the once fierce dog. "That way!" Roger was starting to think again. He was aware of the sounds of crashing undergrowth and two men running through it from somewhere behind. "Go! Go!" He urged the girls on.

In less than fifty yards, he knew running was useless. They would be caught in no time. "Go! Don't look back," he told Atifah. "And make some noise as you go."

Once again she didn't question. She trusted Roger's actions and didn't look back, but dragged the young teenager as fast as she could go through the wooded area. Roger stopped and positioned himself off the open path, below the foliage and behind a tree trunk. He knew he would only have one chance. In front of him the gentle sounds of the girls trying their hardest to escape, behind the thunderous crashing of the two agents as they quickly closed the gap. Roger held his breath and waited the long seconds as the crashing approached.

In an instant they thundered past, intent only on closing the gap between themselves and the people in front. Roger had to time it perfectly. Too early and they would have seen him as he stood, too late and they would be thundering into the trees beyond.

He stood and took a rapid aim, squarely between the closest agent's shoulder blades and fired two shots in quick succession. The agent had noticed the movement at the last moment and started to turn. The first bullet entered his skull just behind his left ear. The second one shot into the trees three feet above the agent's head.

The second agent had already started the pre-programmed drop and roll sequence and as his head was disappearing into the undergrowth, Roger fired two more shots at where he'd estimated the agent to be. He heard one of the shots smash into the base of the tree beyond him.

He knew he couldn't remain standing. If the agent was still alive, Roger had less than a second to live. He too dropped and rolled to remove himself from where he'd last been seen. He came to rest behind the base of a small tree and listened for movement.

He heard none. His ears strained for any sound. In the distance, a few birds started chirping again, after the crack from the pistol had shocked them into silence. Roger strained his ears for what seemed like forever and then he heard it. Off to his right, a twig cracked, muffled under foot. Not so much a twig as a thick stalk. He made his move, keeping low, as quietly as possible toward the sound.

"That's far enough." The barrel of a handgun was shoved roughly into the side of his head. Roger's heart skipped and then sank. He knew there was no escaping this. He'd failed.

"Impressive. How'd you do that?"

"We studied the ways of the Sioux people. Walking on the side of your feet. You know ..."

"You were incredible. I didn't hear a thing ... I'm sorry about your partner."

"I only met him today. Don't concern yourself. He knew the rules as do I." The man's voice was calming and Roger felt at peace with the situation.

"I suppose it won't do any good to ask you to spare the girl."

"Not at all, but I will give you my word it will be quick and painless."

"Thanks! She is innocent in all this."

"I know! We're all just pawns in the game. Some voluntary ..."

"Yeah! And some not." Roger smiled at the inevitability of the situation. He closed his eyes and three shots smashed the serenity into oblivion. The agent fell forward landing heavily on top of Roger and knocking him over sideways.

Roger pushed the body off and saw the outline of Atifah standing a short distance away. She was troubled at having shot the man and stood vacant, hurt by the image of the dead body in front of her. Her pistol was still pointing where the standing agent had once been.

Roger stood and looked in her direction. He was looking down the barrel of her weapon. "It's ok! You can put it down." He moved out of the line of fire and edged toward her. He reached carefully and took the gun out of her hand. She still stared at the body of the man she'd killed. Tears welled up in her eyes as he placed his arm around her shoulder and pulled her toward his chest. He pulled her in close and whispered in her ear. "You had to. He was about to pull the trigger. It's twice now. You were right. I do need you."

He held her for a few long seconds, then eased out of her grip. "Come! We have to go. Where's the girl?"

As he said it the girl stepped out from behind a tree. They walked in silence to where the helicopter had gone down. Roger signaled the girls to remain behind while he had a look around. To his amazement, nobody was sprinting down the hill toward the fallen chopper and nobody had come to find out what the shooting was all about. Roger could only assume they were sufficient distance away to render the sound negligible inside the house.

After picking up his laptop and camcorder, he returned to the girls and knelt down in front of the smaller of the two. "You've been very brave." For once he was seeing the girl as a little girl. She was no longer crying, but seemed to have resigned herself to what was happening. Addressing Atifah he said, "How did you get her to stay put behind the tree?"

Atifah was still in shock from taking the man's life. "I told her the truth - the man was going to kill us all."

"Good girl!" Looking back at the smaller girl he continued, "I'm afraid I need to strap you up again ok?" She nodded her head in numb acceptance of the proceedings. Roger and Atifah tied themselves on to her.

"You're bleeding." Atifah saw the sticky blood which had run down onto Roger's fingertips and now being smeared all over the small girl's clothes as he tied himself on.

"I'll be ok. The dog got closer than I planned." They started toward the house at the top of a gentle slope almost a thousand yards away.

They felt naked and vulnerable as they approached. The large black sedans parked in the front of the building meant the troops were inside. Roger was focused, but still undecided about what to do. He wanted to look into the eyes of his wife's killer as he died, but there was more at stake. Atifah had saved his life twice now and if Lee Miller was to be believed, her life was in the balance and dependent on his decision.

He added, "Don't forget. Tight grip on her shoulder." The little girl made no indication she'd heard them talking. She kept her eyes forward and walked.

They walked toward the front of the house. Roger held the silver-grey handgun in his right hand. With the bulbous grenades and the attached white laces in full view, they moved forward. As they approached, they caught sight of the agents in the windows overlooking the entrance. Roger released his left hand from the girl and lifted it up showing the connected string to the onlookers. They had already seen it.

As they entered the door, agents came into view in the huge elaborate entrance to the building. One unarmed agent came forward and spoke in a voice Roger recognized.

"Macadam. That's far enough." Roger stopped. "We meet at last."

"Hello Crane." Roger kept a dead-pan face.

"I assume you're here to return Mr Baker's daughter to him."

"I am. Where is he?"

"He's upstairs. Pretty much where you left him I believe."

"Is he ... ?"

"Dead?" Roger felt the little girl stiffen then relax. "No! Crying like a baby on his bed. He wants his little girl back."

"Good! So do I! Maybe we can swap."

Crane lowered his gaze with an apologetic look in his eyes. "Hurting the girl won't help."

"I have no intention of hurting the girl."

"You've had a good track record of using ... shall we say ... safe devices. Why should I believe those grenades are live?"

"Because I've had neither the tools nor the time to take them apart."

"Ok! So how does this work." A couple of Crane's agents had edged forward.

"Simple!" Roger replied. "Me and these two girls are going to take a walk up the stairs." He waved the pistol around as he spoke. "Any of your guys I find in my way will be shot, so I want them all to back off. NOW!" Roger swung the pistol around the room causing all the close agents to back off. "I have been forced to kill today already and I don't want to kill any more."

"Who died?" Crane looked anxious.

"A couple of your guys met the helicopter with what looked like a rocket powered grenade, not to mention the one that smashed into the bedroom upstairs."

"Daddy!" The little girl saw her father appear at the top of the stairs.

"Beth!" The color drained from Baker's face as he saw the grenades strapped to the sides of her neck. "Macadam, what have you done to my girl." Without stopping for breath he signaled to his wife. "Claire. She's ok."

The girl tensed as if she wanted to run, but both her captors assumed it might happen and firmed their grip. Roger spoke to Frank Baker as he clung to the railing. "Go back to your room and wait. We'll be up to talk to you."

Claire Baker rounded the corner and in the same non-thinking manner she'd displayed earlier, she began to bolt down the stairs. Roger, sensing the danger, signaled to Crane. "Stop her or she dies." Roger leveled the gun at the approaching woman.

Agent Crane intercepted the woman at the bottom of the staircase. She struggled to free herself, but Crane was powerful. He lifted her off her feet and spoke close to her ear. "Look!" The woman stopped fighting when she realized she wasn't going anywhere. "If you carry on your daughter's head will be blown off." The mother gave a pained whimper as she saw what was going on. She sagged in Crane's arms, then turned her attention to Roger.

"How? … Why? … You bastard! What have you done to her?" Mrs Baker bordered on screaming at Roger. "She's hurt!"

Roger, realizing she was looking at the blood oozing down the girls chest, spoke without emotion. "Relax. She's fine and if you behave she'll stay fine. Move back upstairs with your husband. Both of you! Back to your bedroom! We need to talk."

He continued, "Crane! I'd like you to join us. Have two of your guys hand over their flak jackets to the Bakers." Crane signaled to Crosby and Wilson and without a word being spoken, the two of them handed their weapons to the nearest agent, removed their jackets and handed them to Crane.

"All of you back off out of here." Roger waved the gun around as he spoke. "You can lower your weapons. The only time there is danger is if I, or this lady, gets shot. Put your weapons down." The agents hesitantly backed off on Crane's signal. Crane started to make his way up the stairs ahead of the three on Roger's command.

Inside the bedroom, it was like déjà vu. Baker sat in the same position as before, with his wife huddled next to him sobbing. She looked at Roger with hatred as they entered the room.

"Can I at least hug her?" Claire Baker spat venom as she addressed Roger.

He was about to answer, when Crane cut in, "I don't think it'll be a good idea. Here put these on." He threw the flak jackets onto the bed beside the couple.

"What for?" Baker asked.

Roger answered coldly. "If your little girl's head vaporizes, I want to be sure you live to have the vision spin round in your head for the rest of your life." Roger signaled to Atifah to sit and simultaneously pushed the young girl to the floor. The three of them sat with their backs to the wall.

"What do you want? Why did you come back?" Baker was quietly questioning, a worried look etched onto his face.

"I'm not decided yet. A short while before Miller blew his brains out he told me everything." Baker became uncomfortable and shifted uneasily on the bed. "Up until a few minutes ago I was coming here to kill you." Roger was matter-of-fact as he spoke. "I wanted you to watch as your family died in front of you. I wanted to see you hurt." Baker glanced around at his wife, his daughter and then back to Roger.

"Now I'm undecided." Roger took out his phone from his pocket and dialed a number. After a short pause he spoke, "Hi Elaine. Roger." There was a pause. "I have a bit more to your story. I'm at the house of one Frank Baker. I think you should bring your camera man … the address?" Roger looked at Frank who'd gone pale. He shook his head slowly, realizing what Roger was doing.

Roger covered the phone with the palm of his hand. "You are making my decision very easy for me. Maybe you should be keeping my options open." He stroked the head of the girl next to him. Frank dictated his street address which Roger repeated to Elaine, then hung up.

Baker started to sweat. "Ok! Ok!" he said, resigning himself to the fact that this was going to happen. "Take my family out of here. I'll tell you what you want to know."

"Tell him what?" Crane became interested in the proceedings.

Roger didn't want interruptions. "Quiet! You're here to observe." Looking back to Baker he continued, "No! They stay."

"They're innocent in this."

Roger saw the confused shock on Claire Baker's face. "So was my family. Maybe it's time they found out what you are. You don't need to tell me anything, I already know. You need to tell them."

"Roger! Please! There's no need for this. If the organization suspects my talking, you know what will happen. They'll close ranks. Not one person in this house will be allowed to live."

"What?" Crane couldn't help himself.

Roger didn't want to lose momentum because of him. "I said keep quiet."

Baker continued pleading his case. "They'll never air the segment. They own CNN." Roger dragged the girl up and Atifah rose too. He walked to the bed, picked up the remote and turned on the television. After flicking through the channels he stopped on CNN. "We'll watch from here to ensure they do. If they cut the feed, then you'll prove your worth to the organization by telling them to continue, or you'll watch your kid die."

"They don't care about me or my kid, only the organization."

"What organization?" Crane asked again.

"They don't have a name, but they pretty much own the world. Now keep quiet or I'm going to kick you out of here."

"Roger, you don't understand. The organization won't be hurt. They'll simply cover up the story. Nothing will come of it except we'll be dead, as well as Hodges. Take this from an insider, up 'til now you have been more valuable to the organization by being on the run. If you do this you will be threatening the status quo."

Roger stopped in mid-thought and a puzzled frown came over his face. "What did you say?"

"I said you're threatening the status quo."

"I know!" Miller had used the exact phrase. "Did Miller call you?"

"I spoke to him to let him know you were coming. I haven't spoken since."

Roger brushed past the coincidence and came back to the current situation. "You mean you spoke to him to set up the snipers."

"I'm not answering until my family is away from here. Let them go, I'll answer everything."

Roger became angered as he thought of this man having another man's family executed, yet didn't want to risk harming his own. "I've told you, I'm not here for answers. Miller told me everything. I'm here for retribution."

"But my family ..."

"Stays with us and if necessary, dies with us." Claire covered her mouth with her hand trying to stifle back the urge to cry out. Frank's daughter was either all cried out, or was hardening to the situation. The sobbing had stopped and she sat cross-legged on the floor. Roger continued, "So! Why don't you explain to your family what you are?"

"Macadam, I ..." Baker paused finding it difficult to say the words.

"Go on Frank. Tell them about the two guys that tried to take us out with a small rocket. Does your wife know we ..." He looked over at Atifah. "... that is, Atifah has saved your little girl's life from your organization, not ten minutes ago."

The color drained from Baker's face. "What are you talking about? What guys?"

"I don't know! Two guys in expensive looking suits. One of them had a killer dog. They're all dead now." Roger was losing control. He could feel it. "I have become a killer thanks to you."

"Macadam, I ..."

"What's up Frank? Afraid they'll find out what you are?"

"No! ... I ... I want them to leave."

"They're not going anywhere Frank. They're with us to the end. So! Let's start with how you set me up and had my family shot." Baker hung his head and sat in silence. A disbelieving look came over Claire's face.

"Is this why you have grenades on my daughter's neck Mr Macadam? You want a confession out of my husband to save your own skin. Frank is an upstanding citizen who works hard for his money. He's not going to lie to save your ass."

"I know Mrs Baker and he goes to church every Sunday and gives to the community. So did Lee Miller up until a short while ago. Now he is dead because the guilt of working for this organization caught up with him. Not so Frank?"

Frank still sat with his chin on his chest. "Come on Frank! Tell her who's behind 9/11 and the Vietnam war and the loss of life in the DRC. Tell her who gave the executive order to have my family butchered, like Lee Miller's family was butchered years ago."

"My husband doesn't have anything to do with those things." She was a lot less positive this time as she spoke. Somewhere deep inside she was realizing Frank wasn't arguing. "Tell them Frank."

Baker looked up, firstly at his daughter and then at his wife. He was about to speak when Roger stopped him. He wasn't sure whether it was the depth of the sadness in Baker's eyes, the bravery of his daughter, or maybe the doubt starting to creep unmistakably into the eyes of his wife, but all of a sudden Roger no longer felt the need to win. He'd already won. He didn't forgive the billionaire by any measure, but all of a sudden the world seemed brighter. Although he hadn't uttered the words, Frank Baker's guilt was public and his punishment started now. Claire might hang around for the money and lifestyle, but Frank had lost her in that moment. Beth for her part would remember this moment and question the situation forever. She could see the guilt in her father's eyes, even if she didn't acknowledge it straight away.

"Last time we spoke you said you could make this go away. How so?"

"Wait a minute …" Crane spoke up. "Nothing's going away unless I say so."

Roger turned to agent Crane – "No offence Crane, but this is huge. Much bigger than you can imagine. My story is a small portion."

"There's nothing small about murdering your family … and all the others."

"He didn't do it," Baker spoke hesitantly.

"Then who did?"

"Somebody else. I will release the evidence exonerating Mr Macadam within days." He turned to Roger, "You know what I'll need from you."

"Sorry! It'll be my get out of jail free card."

"You know the organization won't allow it to be circulating. Too much risk."

"Only you and I know about it. I want it to keep you in check, not the organization."

"They have eyes everywhere. They'll find it."

"Nobody knows about it."

"There are people in this house right now Macadam. You can never know …" He left the sentence unsaid.

"Ok Baker. Here are my demands. You release the evidence and you pull out of Oman. There is nothing of interest to you there. You feel the need to hop into Saudi, then you do it from your existing bases. Oman is out of bounds."

Frank Baker shook his head from side to side. "What makes you think I can overturn such a decision?"

"A video. Make it happen, or it goes public."

"What's in Oman for you Macadam? You've only been there a couple of times. It's only a desert."

"And the twin towers were only buildings. How the hell can you stand there and judge who lives or dies and in the same breath pretend to care about your family. They are people's families too."

"But not mine."

"You are a callous, unthinking person and you deserve to die a painful death."

"I probably will one day …"

"I'm not talking about one day, I'm talking about NOW!" The anger boiled over again as Roger aimed the gun at Baker's head and moved forward. Too late he felt the tug on his wrist. Too late he heard the click of the pin popping from the grenade on the girl's neck.

"Roger! …" Atifah realized what happened.

Crane reacted with the speed you'd expect from a marine. "Everybody down!" He lunged at the girl, hooking his fingers under the tape and twisting roughly. The girl gagged when the grenade briefly closed the air flow to her lungs as it was twisted out from below the duct tape. The black bauble clung to the tape precariously for a moment, then Crane clutched it in his hand and threw it through the broken window.

The black bomb struck the round stainless steel railing on Baker's elaborate veranda and for a moment seemed like it would bounce back, but instead bounced upward and dropping down, struck the bar again and bounced outward. No sooner was it over the wall, when the grenade exploded sending shards of glass from the edge of the aluminum frame back into the bedroom.

Atifah grasped hard on the shoulder of the girl, pulling her into her body, protecting her from the glass shower. The girl was equally instinctive in the way she grasped Atifah. She started to sob again, but remained clinging onto her captor.

The blast was muted by the concrete wall, so only the small dusty shards were moved. Everybody sat in silent shock at what had happened. Crane spoke first. "Baker! I've just saved your daughter's life" Turning to Roger, "and yours. I think I deserve an explanation."

Frank cleared his throat, "Agent Crane! I will never be able to repay you for what you have done, but what I am about to tell you, I do so for your own good. By Monday morning, evidence will surface exonerating Mr Macadam of guilt for all the deeds which you are hunting him for."

"I want to know …"

Baker raised his right hand cutting the agent off in mid-sentence. "Let me finish. I will give you evidence incriminating somebody else involved. You can then go and arrest this individual and bring him in. Mr Macadam and his lady will be able to rebuild their lives as best they can and you will have your man."

"But what has this to do with 9/11?" He turned to Roger. "Macadam? You are wanted for some scary shit."

"I told you. It had nothing to do with me. This was a case of …" He turned to Baker who finished his sentence for him.

"A set up." He turned back to Crane. "I know there are questions, but the less you ask the better. I promise everything will become clearer on Monday."

"If I don't have answers to all my questions by ten Monday morning, I'm coming back for you Baker." Crane was trying to sound tough, but he was perplexed by the situation. He moved toward Roger, but again Baker stopped him.

"What are you doing?"

"I'm taking him in."

"Out of the question! If you so much as enter his name in a report, he'll be dead by nightfall. Mr Macadam needs to be hidden from the world until the information is released. There are still people out there wanting him dead."

"I can keep him safe in lockup. Nobody will find him there."

"Sorry Mr Crane. It can't be allowed. Right now there are power hungry youngsters dotted throughout your organization who will turn him over in a second. No! Mr Macadam must disappear where nobody can find him. There are eyes everywhere."

"But if he's innocent ..."

"Innocence has nothing to do with it Mr Crane. His innocence didn't stop you going after him did it?"

"I have men downstairs who saw him walk in."

"They were mistaken. Mr Macadam was never here. They need to know their lives depend on them not seeing Roger here."

"Why should their lives depend on ...?"

Again Baker stopped him talking. He walked to the large elaborate dresser and pulled out a single leaf of crisp white paper and started reading. "Agent Tom S Crane, ex-marine. Trustworthy but hard headed. Fifty-five years old and divorced. There's a list here of services you have given your country. Agent Derrick England. A techie and IT specialist, transferred from Austin." Baker looked up at Crane. "He was recommended for this position by somebody within the organization. I thought he had huge potential. I watched him come through one of the feeder organizations." He started reading again. "Agent Johnny Mills, also from Austin, also an ex-marine, wounded in Afghanistan. He was killed in action a few days ago. Agent Terri Wilson ... Do you want me to go on?"

"Why? What is this about?"

"Things are not always what they seem. That is all I will tell you. There is one ... and only one option if we are all to walk away alive. You give me the chance to sort this out and we all live. If you don't then Roger's chat to Lee Miller will cost us all." He continued, "If there's uncertainty the organization will clean up. If we give them certainty and a solution, then life goes on."

"What about the bodies. Bodies don't disappear."

"I'll bring a cleanup team in here and by Monday they'd have never been here."

"Cleanup ... What the hell are you talking about? These are people. They have families. They ..."

Baker dismissed the rants of the ex-marine as if he was losing patience with the man. "Crane! Take control. Everything I say to you will only add more questions. I cannot tell you everything and you don't want to know everything We've cleaned up many times. You need to go down to your men and explain the last time they saw Roger Macadam was in the abandoned workshop in Somerville and that's all they can ever tell anybody. Understand?"

Agent Crane wasn't satisfied. "Or else what?"

"Look at it this way. Those men trying to take out Macadam down the hill … nothing to do with me! People in the organization are a little hasty and like things resolved. They don't like loose ends."

"And …" Crane wasn't getting it.

"At the moment in this house there are more than ten loose ends. By tonight when you're all tucked up in your beds next to your spouses, that number about doubles and by tomorrow when you and your partners arrive at work and start talking … who knows?" Baker walked lazily back to his bed and sat down next to his wife who'd opted to keep quiet. She was lost and didn't even know who this man was. "I am offering the organization a quicker, cleaner cleanup. No mess! No fuss! If we don't do it this way, all our families will be in danger by the time you reach home today. Wives, husbands, children. Do you want that for your people?"

It was a lot to take in and Crane sat back against the wall. Roger was, for a change, no longer numb. After the last few days, anything was possible and for the first time in a while he was seeing light at the end of the tunnel.

"What happens if my guys talk? We have no control over them when they leave here."

"Tell them the truth. Macadam has been found not guilty. This will be confirmed on the news on Monday."

"What if one of them speaks out?"

"They know nothing. Tell them to keep their traps shut until Monday. Besides, the organization doesn't concern itself with individuals and their conspiracy theories. A little folklore helps to give the organization cover. The Freemasons, the Bilderberg Group, the Skull and Bones Society, the John Birch Society, the Illuminati, they're all secretive organizations. They raise eyebrows and create suspicion, but we use them as feeder organizations and attention deflectors. People that do well in those organizations will do well in ours." Baker stood again and crossed to his dresser. He opened the cabinet and took out a decanter of whiskey and a few glasses.

He offered the drink around the room to blank stares. It was still quite early in the morning. "What? It's been a rough day already!" He poured himself a large double and replaced the decanter back into the cabinet. He continued, "We love this. While people are focused on these red herrings, the organization sits back and laughs. Every once in a while a few members meet at an expensive hotel. We rent out the whole hotel, arm it and then release a bit of information to the press. The next thing you know, we've been linked back to Hitler's army and we have a bunch of hotheads standing outside shouting obscenities at us while we have lunch, discuss our families and watch sport." Baker took a large slug of his whiskey. "No! The organization will be concerned if they suspect Miller has spilled the beans to Macadam, but they won't be interested if one of your troops talks about Roger."

A bewildered silence hung over the room. Twice Crane looked as if he would ask something, but stopped and shook his head.

Baker broke the silence. "Then it's settled. I'll put things in motion immediately. Crane, you can take your men out of here. Monday morning I will have information about the real perpetrator delivered to your office."

Roger spoke up, "You're not going to stand up and say you did this. Who's going to take the rap for this?"

"I'll get a volunteer."

Crane's jaw dropped, aghast. "Come on Baker! You'll never find somebody to take the rap for murder."

"Of course you can Crane. People do amazing things for their beliefs. People are willing to die for their god or their country. Think about it. In both world wars you had Christian killing Christian, when the basis of their belief is peace on Earth and goodwill to their fellow men. The German church incensed the German soldiers to kill the British and the British clerics stood and blessed the troops and prompted them to go and kill Germans. Millions died. Millions!"

He finished his drink. "Do you think the pilots that flew into the World Trade Center wanted to die? Do you think the kamikaze pilots in the Japanese attack on the US Fleet in the pacific wanted to die?" he paused. "Do you think Lee Harvey Oswald wanted to take the rap for Kennedy's death and do you think Ruby wanted to die for the death of Oswald?" He paused again. "We're all just pawns in the game. Some voluntary, some not. You and your men would be willing to die right now for your country, wouldn't you?"

After a short stunned silence, Frank Baker continued with his instructions, "I think you should leave now. Roger will have to go shortly and your men might be tempted to take him in." Crane was too dumbfounded to argue. He left the room and could be heard barking a few instructions as he descended the stairs. Baker stepped out onto the veranda and watched as Crane and his team climbed into their vehicles and drove off.

He turned to Roger and threw him a bunch of keys. "Here! These are the keys to my Jag. It's in the parking out back. Take it and disappear for a few days. I'll arrange for a presidential apology. Please take that thing off my daughter's neck and let her go."

Roger hesitated. "For God's sake man listen to me. Your choice of action is saving my family. You could walk out of here and bring our lives to an end."

Roger was reluctant. He knew the last piece of string would keep Atifah alive.

"I suppose my word is not worth much right now, but I assure you it will cause far more questions to be raised if you die than if you live. Do you think Crane and his team would happily let things settle, if you were not around to be pardoned on Monday? He's already asking himself questions. We have a logical story which requires nobody else to be hurt."

Roger looked at Atifah who nodded and started to untie her wrist. Roger knelt and as gently as possible, removed the tape from the girl's neck. As soon as she was free she stood up and ran to her mother who looked up at Atifah. "You bitch. I hope you die." Atifah dropped her eyes.

"Honey! I …"

She turned on her husband viciously, in a shrill half shout. "Don't you honey me! You put our lives in danger. I will never forgive you for this." She took her daughter out of the room.

"Don't worry about her. She'll come around. She can't live without her Jimmy Choo's."

Baker turned to Roger. "I need the disk. I can't chance it getting out."

"I hid it in the desert on the way up here," he lied. "The disk stays with me." Roger was adamant. "A week from now you might have a change of heart. This is my leverage. It stays with me. It may not bring down your organization, but it will bring you and your family down. I'm hoping it will be enough."

"What will you do with it?" Baker stopped as a vehicle pulled up outside. "Damn! I'd forgotten about the reporters. Stay here! I'll get rid of them." Frank left the room.

Roger and Atifah looked at each other and smiled. "Come with me." He helped her to her feet. His face changed as a thought passed across his mind. "Wait!" he said.

He crossed to the dresser and searched through the drawers until he found a writing pad and a gold pen. Roger scribbled on the paper.

*Commit this password to memory and destroy the paper. I will explain when
I send you the video.
Th15 15 th3 p@55w0rd 2 0p3n th3 v1d30
(This is the password 2 open the video)*

Roger folded the paper into a small ball and placed it in the palm of his hand. He then led Atifah out of the room. They traced Baker's steps down the stairs and out of the door as Frank was busy telling the reporters he hadn't seen Roger at all and it must have been a hoax.

"Elaine! Steve!"

"Roger! Are you ok?"

"I'm fine." He leaned forward and kissed Elaine on the cheek, at the same time grasping her right hand in his. Roger tried to deflect any suspicion away from his hand by apologizing and brushing her hair back with his other hand. Elaine felt the paper in her hand and took it. Nobody would ever have seen the exchange, even if they were looking for it.

"How're Chris and the little one?"

"They're well thanks. How are you holding up?"

Baker butted in, "Macadam! I said wait upstairs."

"These are my friends. I think I'd like them to break the story on Monday."

Elaine didn't miss a beat. "What story?"

Baker ignored her. He was irritated at being caught out, lying to the reporters. "Fine!" He turned to Roger. "The less people see you the better. Especially reporters."

"They're fine Baker. Don't panic. You worry me far more than they do." Turning to the reporters. "Elaine! Steve! I'm sorry to have wasted your time. It looks like a false alarm."

She wasn't in the habit of letting a story go this easily. "What story?"

"Evidence has surfaced proving us innocent."

"That's great news. So you can stop running now?"

"It looks that way."

"I'm so glad."

Baker cut in – "On Monday you will be receiving evidence at the same time as the FBI receives it. I trust you will air it."

"You can count on us."

Then, announcing in general, Roger dangled the keys from his finger. "People! I can't exactly say it's been fun, but Atifah and I have a date with a Jag. I'll let you know where to pick it up from ... when I'm finished with it."

"Where are you going to go?"

"Baker! I'll think of something."

From Baker's house, Roger and Atifah headed south for the small hotel in Flatonia where they parked a little way off from the entrance. They were once again chatting easily. The encounter with Baker had brought Roger back from the abyss of the past few days. Atifah cleaned up his arm while they sat in the automobile. The wound had been worse than he'd thought and he continued to lose blood which had dripped from his elbow onto the cream carpet and leather seat of the Jaguar. He'd laughed at her comment when she said, "He'll have to bring in a clean-up team." She tore Roger's right sleeve off, as well as one of her own, to use as a bandage.

Later they watched as Michelle, the night desk clerk, came on duty and decided to wait until they were sure they would not be seen by anybody before entering the hotel.

SUNDAY, 19TH

By the time Roger had decided it was safe to move, tiredness had kicked in and the two were sitting in virtual silence. They made their way for the front door.

Michelle was more than a little surprised and somewhat apprehensive to see them, looking around behind them as if expecting them to be followed. The nervousness soon gave way to her bubbly nature after a brief explanation of the situation. She knew, after seeing the news reports, these two had saved the lives of her and her guests. She had no reason to fear the couple and booked them into a room for the rest of the weekend.

Roger and Atifah both enjoyed a short sleep. They awoke to the sound of knocking on the door when the sun was already in the sky, but it had been a real quality sleep. One they hadn't felt for a while. There were no dreams, no sounds, just deep satisfying sleep.

Roger moved to the door.

"Hello," he shouted through the door.

"It's me. It's Michelle."

Roger opened the door and she walked in carrying a tray laden with breakfast. "Compliments of the management." Roger panicked as she spoke the words then relaxed as she continued. "They don't know it yet."

Roger looked at the food and for the first time in days, felt the emptiness in his stomach. "Wow! This looks incredible," he said to the Michelle.

"You look like you need it. It looks like you've lost a few pounds since I last saw you." She reached into her pocket and pulled out a pack of disposable razors. "I think you'll need these too."

Puzzled by her words, Roger looked in the bathroom mirror after she'd left and hardly recognized the shaggy, skinny man. His face was drawn and thin and he had dark black rings under his eyes. He lifted his shirt and looked at his bony rib cage. He tried to think back to the point where this transformation had occurred, but realized there was no specific point in time. Roger called out to Atifah who still lay with her eyes closed. "I'm going to clean up a bit."

"Ok!" she answered without opening her eyes.

Roger looked around the door at the girl lying with her hand covering her eyes. He hadn't noticed previously, but she too had lost weight. Her face looked drawn and thin from lack of sleep and lack of food. Even when they'd had food, it was always small amounts and never more than once a day since they were last here at the hotel. It seemed like months ago. Roger felt, for reasons he didn't understand, proud of the girl.

"Hey!" he called her.

She lifted her head "Yes?"

"Eat breakfast before it gets cold."

"Oh! Sure!" She struggled to sit up, but would have preferred to remain sleeping.

After a shower and shave, Roger walked to the TV and switched to CNN. He was disappointed not to hear of his exoneration, but knew it was only due to happen the following day.

Roger helped himself to breakfast and sat on the bed to eat. He reached for the remote, when an image of Lee Miller appeared on the screen, albeit in much better shape than when they had last seen him.

"In local news this morning, Lee Miller, tobacco and oil mogul, died yesterday after a long battle with cancer." The words resonated in Roger's ears. "The billionaire who held the 28th spot on the Forbes American top 100 at a net worth of close to ten billion dollars, was discovered this morning by his long-time butler. He passed away peacefully in his sleep." Roger and Atifah looked at each other, puzzled. "After his family was murdered in the mid-seventies, Miller became a virtual recluse, concentrating his efforts on his business ventures. Miller's spokesperson has confirmed that with no heirs it's believed Miller left his wealth to an unnamed long term business associate, who is also on the Forbes list."

"The bastards! They're keeping his money in the organization."

Atifah was beyond caring. She shrugged her shoulders and continued with her breakfast. "There's nothing we can do."

"Why are these people allowed to get away with this?" Frustration was in Roger's voice.

"Don't let your frustration take hold. It will destroy you."

Roger realized the girl was talking sense and they had a long day to kill in each other's company. He didn't want to drag her down with negativity, when this should be the most positive period for her since he involuntarily dragged her from her home. He was reaching with the remote to switch off, when behind the news anchor a map of Oman flashed onto the screen. Roger scrambled to turn up the volume.

"In international news this hour, the Omani government has satisfied a UN envoy that there are no Al Qaeda training bases in its desert as previously thought. The State Department blamed incorrect intelligence for the error. When asked about the possibility of starting yet another war based on incorrect intelligence, Secretary Clinton had this to say."

Clinton appeared in front of a media conference. "… With our new administration, America has moved into a new era in international relations. We have learned not to rush in blindly based only on intelligence reports. It would be stupid not to look into these things." Her smile showed her dig at the previous administration.

Roger was intent on the screen. "Can you believe these lies?"

Then to answer an almost inaudible question from the floor, Clinton smiled and answered diplomatically, "We're here telling you aren't we? We didn't go to war."

Roger, concentrating on the news, was taken by surprise when Atifah threw her arms around his neck and kissed his cheek. "You saved my country. Thank you."

Roger's heart was still racing from the shock. Smiling, he turned to her. "We've had a rough couple of weeks. Please be careful when sneaking up on me."

"Ok!" She smiled back.

"I think it will be safe for you to return home now."

"I hope so. The Sultan and the Omani people owe you a great deal." Then she reached and kissed him again on his cheek. "I owe you a great deal."

Roger felt uncomfortable and reached once again for the remote.

He leaned forward and switched off the television.

-- o --- o0o --- o --

Michelle had left instructions to have their meals sent to their room and for housekeeping not to disturb them. The two slept the day away in the complimentary bathrobes, only waking to pick up their tray from outside the door. It felt good to be clean and comfortable again. Although Roger slept better than he had for a long time, he kept waking as somebody walked passed his room, or

350

banged a window three rooms away. He knew it was going to take time before he would sleep right through.

When Michelle came on duty that evening, she brought in new clothes for them to wear and she took the bloodied and smelly clothes away in a black trash bag. "You won't want these again will you?" She asked out of politeness, but knew they were going in the trash anyway.

"No! You can throw them out." Atifah smiled a broad relaxed smile. She was at her most relaxed since her wedding in Muscat.

When Michelle left, Atifah turned to Roger. "What happens now?"

"What do you mean?"

"You know what I mean. What happens with us?"

Roger was uncomfortable and tried to sound consoling. "I told you there is no us." He saw the hurt in her eyes. "You are a young beautiful woman. You need to push on with your life. Go and meet a young, good looking Arab prince and marry and have babies."

"What if I don't want that?" She looked down at her hands in her lap.

"Atifah!" She looked up at him. "I was boring when I was your age. Now I'm even worse. It would be no life for somebody like you. I'm not always on the run from clandestine organizations." She laughed a shallow laugh.

"Besides, I have to make arrangements for my family. I'm not going to be good company for a few months. Maybe a few years. I think we need to face reality here. We've had a rough time, but six weeks ago you wouldn't have looked at me. Think about it. I'm an old man compared to you. You want to have children. I've already had mine." He paused for a second, then continued, "Besides, I haven't even had chance to mourn for my family. I'm full of hatred and anger and I'm still not even sure I will be able to let it all go. I loved my family more than anything else in the world. I'm not ready to try to replace them."

She was silent for a long while then said "No!"

"What?"

"I'm sorry for arguing! I'm a grown woman and I know what I want. I'm not letting go as easily as …"

"But I …"

351

"It's my turn to talk." She had a cocky way about her and placed her finger on his lips. "You owe me. I saved your life … twice." She knew he'd saved hers too, but this wasn't the time to quibble over technicalities.

"We kept each other alive and you know it's true."

"What do you expect …?"

She cut him off again. "I expect nothing from you Roger. I may be younger than you, but I'm not naive. I would never presume to try to replace somebody who shared your life for so long. Never! But whatever happens to us from here, you will always be my first husband even if I'm not your wife." He looked like he wanted to speak but she stopped him again. "Roger please, hear me out."

"I'm not asking you for intimacy. I'm not even asking you for a marriage. You can end it right now by simply announcing you divorce me three times and if you do it, then so be it. You will carry on your life here and I will fly back to Oman." She took his hands in hers. "I'm asking you please don't do that. Not yet. I'm asking you to give us time to see what happens. Nothing more!"

"How do you expect it to work out?"

"I don't know. I only know I don't want to end this yet. Not without a bit more time to see if there is anything there. If you need a few months on your own to sort things out I'll willingly fly back to Muscat and wait. I only ask that if you decide to end it then you do it face to face. Please give me that."

They sat in silence while Roger thought through what she had said.

"I have a job here. My life is here." He knew his life was no longer here. In fact there was nothing left in his life here, only things. He felt the cloud closing in again and didn't want to speak anymore. "I know we've slept all day but it's late …" He left the sentence unfinished. "We'll talk tomorrow." He hoped they wouldn't.

MONDAY, 20TH

Roger hadn't expected to sleep, but he did. He was woken by Michelle knocking on the door. For the second day in a row, the sun was already in the sky when he woke.

"Mr Macadam." Roger froze as she called out his name. What the hell was she thinking? He sprang and opened the door, dragging Michelle roughly through the doorway.

"What are you trying to do?" he half whispered. "You want …?"

"No! It's on TV."

"What?"

"You're on TV. The story is on all the channels." She was exaggerating, but Roger realized what she was talking about and jumped for the remote. Fumbling and dropping the remote, it seemed to take forever for the picture to display and the sound followed shortly afterward.

"… only this morning. We cross live to our reporter on the scene at FBI headquarters in Houston, Elaine Hodges. Elaine, tell us what the atmosphere is like there?"

"Thanks Cheryl. It's electric. There is an amazing buzz about the bureau, but at the same time a sadness for what this man has endured. An FBI spokesperson called a press conference this morning. The press naturally assumed Macadam had been caught, but we were informed he had been exonerated on all charges. A complete turnaround on his previous status. As you can imagine the impact of this episode on this man's life has been devastating. We can only assume what might be going through his mind right now."

"Elaine. Has Macadam been informed of the details?"

"As far as we know, Macadam is still on the run. This reporter hopes he's watching at the moment."

"So you didn't get to see the man?"

"Not yet. I'll be waiting here in case he comes in today. Cheryl."

"Thanks Elaine. If you've just joined us, Kevin Scott Wesley was taken into police custody this morning for carrying an illegal firearm. When checking the serial number on the firearm, it was found to be none other than the weapon used to carry out the murders attributed to Roger Macadam. Following Wesley's full confession, the FBI has issued a notice to the effect that Roger and Atifah Macadam are no longer suspects in any crimes."

"Wesley, a well-known and key member of the American Nazis, has been trailed by the FBI for a few months but his link to these brutal killings was never suspected. He is said to have confessed to the killings, saying Macadam will get what's coming to him because of his relationship with the enemy."

The image crossed to a clip of a thin tattooed man being led forcibly away by two burly men in black suits with the tell-tale Police shades. Wesley looked back at the camera and screamed with a crazed look in his eye. "When I get out I'll come after you Macadam. You <beep> Moslem <beep>." The news station had censored his language, but his lips were easy to read.

"According to FBI sources, President Obama is expected to be making an apology to Macadam on behalf of the nation within the next few days."

Roger switched off the television. He was unable to watch the charade any more. He had expected the news to be more liberating, but a sickening feeling churned in the pit of his stomach. He knew Wesley had been lied to in order to coerce him to take the fall for a series of organized hits on innocent lives. This was done by what looks to be the most powerful organization in the world. "How the hell do they get away with this? Where are the members of the organization while this man rots in jail, or worse? Can I sit back and watch this man be executed when I know he didn't do it?"

Atifah was excited about freedom, but the angry look on Roger's face kept her excitement suppressed. "I don't know Roger, but these people are powerful. I don't think we would have lasted much longer."

It took a while for her words to reach Roger. His emotions rejected them. "Of course! You are right. We were fast running out of options."

"Besides, he doesn't look like a nice man at all. Maybe he was a member of the organization."

"No! He doesn't look the type. He's not super rich. This guy was one of the organization's 'fall guys'."

"You are happy it's over?" she asked tentatively and then to be sure she did not come across as unfeeling in Roger's grief, she added, "At least happy to be free again and not on the run?"

"Of course I am. More relieved than happy."

"What should we do now?"

For the first time Michelle spoke up. "Right now you can come down to breakfast in the dining room. There are people that would like to thank you for saving their lives." She left the room after getting confirmation from Roger that they would be down for breakfast after getting dressed.

Atifah took Roger's hand and made him sit on the edge of the bed. "Have you given any more thought to what we spoke about last night?"

Roger hadn't. Right now he had things to do and funerals to arrange, but looking forward he knew he didn't want to sit back and watch the sham as it unfolded. He didn't want to have to go back to his empty house. He didn't want to drive the streets he'd driven so often with Anne at his side. Roger made a hurried decision.

He took her other hand in his. "Listen to me!" Her eyes dropped as if she knew bad news was coming. "I need a week to sort things out here. Then I will fly with you to Muscat. You can show me your beautiful country for a couple of weeks." She lifted her eyes and met his. Roger continued, "I'm sure the Sultan can put us up for a while." She started to smile. "I'm not making promises and I don't want to mislead you in any way. There's still no 'us', ok?" Her smile widened and she nodded. He tried in vain to pull her down from the high she was on. "We'll take one day at a time, but right now I don't want to sit here and watch this whole thing unfold and you never know if a trigger-happy fool hasn't seen the news so I want to leave at least for a couple of weeks."

Atifah could hardly contain her excitement. She jumped forward and flung her arms around his neck. He tried to calm her down and pried her arms off him. "You understand what I said? I'm not promising you anything, but we can take a couple of weeks to think it through properly."

"Yes! Yes! It's more than I could have asked for."

ABOUT THE AUTHOR

David Norton is a part time "techie" and a full time computer nerd who loves, more than anything else, to spend time with his family.

He has shared thirty years with an incredible lady and between them raised three incredible, self-sufficient adults. He has two mean dogs and there's an even meaner cat in the house. David's wife, Karen, claims to own the cat, but who owns whom is anybody's guess.

For more about the author, go to
http://www.deal-with-the-devil.com/about